WK 37

CW00504363

SHAPES OF BRIGHTNESS

Yvonne Oram

The idea for this story came from my mother, Muriel Oram. I knew she always wanted to record, in some way, events from the lives of her own mother and grandmother, but she died before that hope could become a reality. Going through her things I found two sheets of paper on which she had started to write Polly's story. I decided to continue with it and this novel is the result. I think Mum would be pleased, even though it probably bears little resemblance to what she had in mind. So, I dedicate this book to her, and to my sister Dee, and to all the splendid women of my extended family.

1906

Just as the train began to move out of Brighton station the carriage door burst open and two young men scrambled inside. Kate and Edith frowned at each other. They'd been looking forward to enjoying the journey alone, so they could talk together in peace. After Kate got out at Hassocks they wouldn't see each other for some time. The newcomers, quite unaware of the hostility their presence had aroused, were lying back against the seats, gasping for breath and laughing as though enjoying a joke.

Kate thought for a moment that they were brothers, as they both had fair hair and blue eyes, but she quickly realised her mistake. Their clothes gave them away. The bigger of the two - bigger in the sense of being more muscular, with broader shoulders - wore trousers and jacket that were obviously his Sunday best. He was very good looking but clearly a working man, unused to wearing such good clothes every day.

The other was perfectly at home in what he wore. Kate looked at the hands of this slighter, more delicately-featured young man and saw they weren't those of a manual worker. Hurriedly she lowered her gaze, aware that her curiosity was verging on bad manners.

'Please excuse our noisy entrance.'

She had known he would speak first and she watched him straighten his tie and then lean forward a little, pushing his hair back off his forehead. His voice was soft and she smiled as she nodded, her earlier annoyance forgotten. But it was Edith who spoke out first, as Kate knew she would.

'You only just caught the train.'

'Well, Joe and I were having such a splendid time in Brighton that we left it until the last minute before getting up to the station.'

Kate glanced across at the other young man - Joe. He had regained his breath and was comfortably relaxed but his face still had a healthy ruddiness. So, he worked outdoors she thought and wondered what these two were doing in each other's company.

'Too busy looking at the sea - wishing we could swim,' Joe beamed and in the warmth of his glowing smile they introduced themselves. Miss Katherine Summers; Miss Edith Summers; Mr Matthew Hersey; Mr Joseph Weaver.

'You're sisters?' Mr Hersey asked.

Edith nodded but Kate said firmly, 'I'm Edith's adopted sister.'

'And you've been visiting Brighton too?' Mr Hersey was determined to keep up the conversation, yet there was nothing offensive in his manner.

1

Kate saw that he simply wanted to be friendly.

Edith knew it too; that was why she was smiling. 'No, Mr Hersey, I live there. My father has a business - a shop.'

There was a disparaging note in her voice which amused Kate. The 'shop' was a large, lucrative store in the fashionable shopping area of town but Edith was going through a phase of despising her father's wealth.

'My sister's going to Hassocks,' Edith went on. 'I'm travelling with her and then on to London.'

Kate felt uncomfortable. This was another of Edith's new fads - calling her 'sister' and although Kate was touched she knew how much it annoyed Edith's father.

'Oh, really?' Mr Hersey turned to Kate. 'Do you have friends in Hassocks, Miss Summers?'

Kate could see Edith tensing up again in a defensive way and decided to give this inquisitive young man the truth. She knew Joe Weaver was looking at her with interest and for some reason wanted him to know and understand her situation. 'No, Mr Hersey. I'm going into service for a gentleman who lives near there: Sir James Gale.'

Joe Weaver gave a kind of hiccup and Kate realised he was struggling with laughter. Mr Hersey's smile and easy manner were quenched. His sensitive face registered pained embarrassment and he spread his hands helplessly.

'Ladies, this is a perfectly extraordinary situation. I am Sir James's nephew and I live with him at the Hall. Joe here is my lifelong friend - and one of our gamekeepers!'

Joe suddenly exploded with laughter and Kate found she couldn't hold her own sense of the ridiculous in check. For a moment Mr Hersey stared at them and then he too dissolved into laughter. Edith joined in, uncertain at first and then with less restraint as the comedy of the situation became fully apparent. When it seemed that Joe might expire from such hilarity Matthew struggled to loosen his friend's collar. Somehow this only made them laugh all the more.

The train pulled up at a halt and a soberly-dressed couple paced purposefully towards the carriage. The man grasped the door handle but then took in the scene of apparent abandon inside and with a startled look turned to hurry his companion away. She pushed past him to see what was going on and her face reddened. They heard uttered, in horrified tones: 'Young people! I don't know what the world's coming to!' And it was enough to set the four of them off again until the train pulled away at last. By the time they were moving through the gentle landscape of the South Downs they were themselves again and on friendly terms.

'This is just up your street, Matty,' said Joe, fastening his collar and glancing at the two women. 'He's a great believer in abolishing all class barriers.'

'Really?' Edith cast a mischievous look at Kate. 'Then you and my sister have a great deal in common, Mr Hersey - she supports the Labour Party. That's the only thing we disagree on. I'm more interested in the Liberals.'

Matthew's eyes lit up. 'Well then, we all share many aims.'

Kate watched, amused, as the two began to debate the aims Matthew had in mind. She could hear the idealism in every statement he made and wasn't surprised that Edith was looking increasingly impressed. She was an idealist too and a great follower of causes which challenged the status quo. Though it seemed that few retained their challenge, or Edith's interest, for long.

Joe leaned forward and asked: 'Do you think we'll build the New Jerusalem here, Miss Kate?'

She liked this form of address. It got round the awkwardness of them being fellow employees. She nodded.

'Yes, I do. But I know change won't happen quickly. We've a long struggle ahead.'

'Very long,' Joe agreed. 'My old Grandad fought for the Charter and they never did get the twelve points, now did they? Mind you, he fought for a lot else besides, not quite so high-minded.'

Again that warm smile. Kate smiled back at him. She liked his glowing good looks and the occasional teasing glimmer in his eyes and decided it would be very bad luck if he turned out to be married. But there were more important things to find out at the moment. She lowered her voice. 'Can you tell me something about the Hall, and Sir James?'

'But after university... Well, I'm not sure,' Matthew was saying. 'My parents are dead, you see, and left me with very little by way of funds. I shall have to earn my living in the sweat of my brow!'

It seemed entirely appropriate to Edith that this good-looking, fine-minded young man should not have to face the burden of a life of ease and luxury. She had quickly recognised that his political views were different from those expressed by Kate - much more exciting - and she felt admiration for the movement he described so eloquently, quoting from Shelley and looking not unlike a poet himself.

'There's so much to do,' she said eagerly.

'I know. James is rather stuffy, even though he's not much older than me, and he's trying to steer me towards the law or something frightful like that. Little does he know...'

3

They shared a superior smile at the expense of Sir James. Then Matthew relented a little. 'Mind you, he's a good fellow at heart. And he has his problems too: most of his cash was gambled away by his father. James is currently wooing a young woman whose father is some millionaire factory owner up north.'

Edith pursed her lips. Joe, overhearing said: 'Makes good sense you know, Matty,' and smiled across Edith's cool glance.

'You're wrong, Joe,' Matthew sighed. 'Firstly my Uncle should have nothing to do with a family whose money comes from what's little better than slave labour and, secondly, the sooner my lot stop lording it up at the Hall - '

'The sooner I'll be out of a job,' laughed Joe. 'Miss Kate, too.'

There was a pause, which threatened to grow uncomfortable. Then Kate put in gently, 'We'll soon be at Hassocks, I think.'

Their talk grew more general and after a while Joe helped Kate get her luggage ready. She had learned much about day-to-day life at the Hall; how everything was being run with the minimum of staff but that Sir James was hoping to improve matters as soon as marriage boosted his finances.

'And from what I hear it's not just the money he's interested in,' Joe had confided. 'She seems a nice, sensible young lady. She likes the Hall at any rate and wants to do it up smartly. Sir James will be able to improve the estate as well, and that'll give me more to do, thank goodness. He can make things more comfortable for his tenants, too. Some of the cottages are in a bad way.'

The train was slowing. Matthew looked thoughtfully at Edith.

'Are you really going on to London by yourself?'

She was surprised. 'Of course. An old friend of my mother is meeting me at Victoria. There's nothing to worry about.'

He shook his head and as the train pulled into the station he said firmly, 'Joe, I shall chaperone Miss Summers for the remainder of her journey: you must be responsible for escorting Miss Katherine to the Hall.' His tone was serious but the sparkle in his eyes gave him away.

Kate smiled. 'I've been told someone from the Hall will be waiting for me at the station.'

'Well, if it's old Dowser with his cart he'll be the worse for wear as usual, so you'll need Joe as a guide,' Matthew responded. 'Joe, I'll come back by the next train.'

Whatever his views on equality, thought Kate, he was still used to giving orders and getting his own way. Master Matthew had far to go. But Edith was smiling now, clearly content with the arrangement and Kate didn't object on her own account. She had found out that Joe Weaver was unmarried and at present had lodgings on the estate with the head gamekeeper and his family.

The train stopped and the four of them rose. Kate and Edith hugged each other briefly.

'Good luck, darling,' whispered Edith, 'and mind you're not swept off your feet by the golden-haired gamekeeper.'

'It might be quite nice. Will you keep the impecunious nephew at a distance?'

Laughing, they separated.

'This has been fun, hasn't it?' Matthew enthused as he and Joe handed Kate and her luggage down from the carriage. 'I hope we can all stay friends.'

Edith waved from the window for a while and then sat down, patting the dust from her jacket.

'So, you tell me you've just left a High School in Brighton and are visiting a family friend in Kensington, yet your adopted sister is going off to work as a cook for my Uncle. It seems very strange.' There was an edge to Matthew's voice that made Edith glance at him guiltily.

'You think I want it to be like this? It's all my father's doing.'

'I'm sorry - I've been rude. It's really none of my business.'

Edith fiddled with a button on her glove, then burst out: 'It's awful! I couldn't love Kate more if she was my real sister, but Father just won't accept it. She has to call him Uncle and my Mother Aunt. She's been with us since she was five, but I've always had the best - my schooling - oh, everything! Poor Kate had to go into service when she was fourteen. You can imagine the tension it all causes.'

Preparing to launch more fully into her story, Edith unpinned her hat and laid it on the seat beside her. Curls of honey-coloured hair fell forward around her face and she saw that Matthew, gazing at her with gratifying admiration, had missed some of what she was saying.

Out in the station yard it was obvious that Dowser had not arrived.

'He's not very reliable but it's old age, not the drink,' said Joe. He lifted the heaviest of Kate's bags and she took the other. 'Can you manage that?' he asked. 'It's a tidy step.'

'I don't mind.'

As they walked away from the station Joe remarked that she was very young to be coming to the Hall as cook.

'I've been lucky,' Kate explained. 'I was working for Lady Lanham when her cook was taken ill suddenly. I was the only one in the kitchen who could take over and I produced a dinner for sixteen guests that same night. When her Ladyship heard that cook wouldn't be coming back she gave me the post.'

She couldn't help the pride in her voice and wasn't surprised to see

5

him smile.

'That would be in London?' he asked. 'What did you think of the place?'

She talked enthusiastically about some of the sights she'd seen - the famous buildings and the parks, the river and all the great stores which supplied the wealthy.

'And the theatres!' she breathed, her face full of excitement. 'I love going to the theatre.'

They walked on for a while before he said, 'But there's a lot of poverty too - in London, I mean.'

She looked at him sharply. 'It's horrifying,' she said. 'Many people there live and work in disgusting conditions. I've seen some of it for myself!'

'Is that why you support the Labour Party?'

'One of the reasons.'

She talked now about political meetings she had attended and how she'd educated herself by reading as many books and pamphlets as she could lay hands on. He admitted, shyly, to doing the same.

'The reading, that is. Mostly things that Matty passes on to me.'

They paused at the next farm gate to take a rest and leaned on it together, looking into the field beyond.

'I'm surprised,' said Joe, thoughtfully, 'that you didn't want to stay on in London. You might find it dull here.'

Kate shook her head. 'I was very young when I went to live with Aunt Polly - Mrs Summers that is. I can't remember much of my life before that but I know I was looked after by some people near Pyecombe. I've always wanted to come back and live in Sussex.'

'Who wouldn't,' said Joe approvingly. He pointed to a hill which rose, smooth-topped in the distance. 'That's Wolstonbury. It's a fine view from up there.'

'I'd love to see that.'

'Then I'll take you some day.'

She liked his directness. Though she'd never walked out with a young man it wasn't for lack of interest. Indeed, at her last post the butler himself had lost his heart to her - a man twice her age. So far, though, she'd not been tempted. Walking out with someone meant that you must soon be thinking of marriage and she had no wish to give up her single state yet awhile. None of the young men who had so far caught her eye turned out to be worth that. So, although she warmed to Joe, she knew she must be cautious.

'Do you like music, Miss Kate?' ·

She thought for a moment. 'Some music - I do love ballads when they're well sung. Do you sing?'

'Passably. For a truly fine voice you'd have to go to my brother, Arthur.'

The sun was warm on her back and she listened, comfortably relaxed, while he told her about his brother, three years his senior, who was the local blacksmith.

'He was apprenticed to our uncle and took over the business when he died. He's doing well for himself.'

She glanced at him. 'And is he married, your brother?'

Joe shook his head. 'Reckons he's happy enough as he is, though there's plenty of local girls would like to change his mind for him.'

'Ah, but is it his fine singing voice they sigh for or his fine blacksmith's business?'

They laughed together in a friendly way. Kate felt perfectly happy out here in the sunshine, talking to him, and in no hurry to get to the Hall and begin her duties. She wondered idly how often she'd see him in the future; as under-gamekeeper he might have little business at the house.

'How long have you known Mr Hersey?' she asked.

'Call him Matthew,' said Joe. 'Outside the Hall anyway - he'll expect it.'

He turned round, leaning his back against the gate so that he could more easily look into her face. 'I've known him since we were nippers. My Dad was head keeper when Sir James's father was alive, so we lived on the estate. Matty's not much younger than Sir James and he was packed off here for the holidays. They reckoned the lads would play together but they didn't have much in common. So Matty used to come round the woods with me and Dad instead.'

She asked tentatively about Joe's father.

'Dead these six years. Diphtheria.'

Kate shuddered in spite of the heat. 'And your mother?'

'She lives with Art now. Keeps house for him, though she's always on at him to get married. I've two sisters as well: one married and the youngest still at home.'

'And you and Mr - Matthew - are really close friends? I mean, he can come calling on you easily enough but he can hardly take you home for tea, can he?'

Again they laughed comfortably. 'No, it can't be like that yet,' Joe agreed. 'One day, maybe. In the meantime we know a lot about each other and we see eye to eye on most things and get along well. So when we're together the rest doesn't matter much.'

He straightened up and lifted the bag again.

'Mind you, it doesn't seem half as strange as you being in service

7

while the other Miss Summers is gallivanting off to London.'

'I know, I know,' Kate muttered. 'I'll tell you about that as we go along.'

She took off her hat, then picked up the other bag and paced beside him. She knew he was staring at her hair, piled in thick, dark, shiny coils on her head. She hoped that he was wondering what it might look like spread loose over her shoulders. As they walked and talked she felt content.

1909-1911

She stood by the fence, looking out across the fields towards Wolstonbury, longing to be up there, climbing to the top. Not only for the view from the summit but for the exhilaration of the climb itself. She found herself opening the garden gate, then realised what she was doing and drew back, guiltily. As if there was any time to go rambling now, with Aunt Polly and Edith due on the hour. There was the bread and butter to be got ready and she must change her clothes and wash William's face. But it was hard to turn away.

Her husband came out of the front door and down the short garden path, carrying their baby son in the crook of his arm, rather as he would carry his gun. The two dogs ran at his heels and William watched them, fascinated. Then he beamed in his mother's direction and waved his arms. She reached out for him.

'What time is it, Joe?' she asked, anxiously.

'Not yet two, by the kitchen clock. The train won't be at Hassocks yet.' He smiled at her. 'And Ben Bartley doesn't hurry himself driving the trap. Plenty of time before they get here.'

He put an arm round her shoulders and drew her against him. For a moment she rested her face against his neck and William stared up at them with an air of surprise. Kate laughed and drew Joe's attention to the boy's expression and he released her and bent to stroke the chubby hands. Kate looked over their heads at the hill in the distance.

'Flo's doing the bread and butter for you,' said Joe. Kate sighed and he added sharply, 'Don't look so put out! We can manage without your precious thin slices for once. Anyway, if she's going into service she'll have to learn to do these things properly.'

Kate rather liked the way he jumped to the defence of his younger sister. Flo had been sent over by Joe's mother that morning with strict instructions to help Kate prepare for her visitors. The girl had done very little except play with William but now that the baby was no longer sleeping so much during the day, that was help in itself. Kate liked Flo. She was plain though, like all the Weaver females, with wispy light brown hair and washed-out blue eyes. It was a pity that the two men of the family should get all the good looks. She glanced at Joe, smiling. 'I'll go and get ready. I hope you're going to put your best shirt on.'

He didn't bother to reply. He always made a fuss if he had to dress up, except on the rare occasions when Aunt Polly came. Now he smoothed his thick, handsome moustache, grown only recently, and Kate smiled again.

'She'll like it, I'm sure. And I'm getting used to it now.'

'I thought you said it tickles your face when I kiss you.'

'Yes, but that's nice when you're kissing me elsewhere.'

His face reddened, as she'd known it would - he could still be prudish on occasions. But when she went to kiss his cheek he turned his face quickly so that their mouths met and she felt a sudden excitement and had to pull away.

'Honestly, Joe! They'll be here soon.'

He grinned. 'Later, then.'

As they turned back to the house Joe said: 'I wonder what fancy get-up young Edie will be wearing today?' And now it was Kate's turn to be defensive about family.

'She always looks smart whatever she wears; she's so small and neat.'

He looked at his wife, tall as he was, slim and straight.

'Too small,' he said. 'She takes after her father for that.'

'Not in any other way, though,' said Kate warmly, knowing Joe was never quite at ease with Edith.

'I know that,' he said. Then he glanced at Kate's troubled face and, shrugging, murmured, 'She's all right.'

He took William from her and sat on the bench outside the kitchen door, bouncing the boy on his knee. Up in their bedroom Kate changed quickly, barely glancing in the mirror. She knew she cut an elegant figure - the cream silk blouse, inset with lace on the bodice, went perfectly with the plain, dark brown skirt she'd made. She and Joe were doing well since he'd taken over as head gamekeeper, soon after their marriage, but it was only now that she felt comfortable spending more on herself. She always managed their money as carefully as she'd handled the below-stairs finances at the Hall and they were soon out of the cramped estate cottage allocated to Joe and renting this larger house, not far from the village. They spoiled William, of course, but they were still able to save and things looked well for the future.

So why, she wondered, was she standing by the bedroom window, her hairpins in her hand, looking at Wolstonbury and wishing she was walking up there? Something was bothering her but... But then Joe came in, looking for his best shirt.

Kate hurried down into the kitchen, her hair still loose on her shoulders.

'Flo, be a dear and help me with this, will you?'

Flo, who was holding a sleepy William, gazed enviously at her sister-in-law's thick, dark locks.

'It's a pity to put it up.' But she handed over the baby and took the brush and hairpins.

Kate sat in one of the straight backed chairs with William on her lap and as Flo brushed vigorously and then got busy with the pins she gradually felt herself relax. The lightly buttered slices of bread, laid out with the rest of the food in the parlour next door, were thin enough after all. The house was spotless and William, in a new, embroidered bib, looked delightful. Some of her unrest left her.

'You're very good at dressing hair, Flo,' she said. 'You'll make a splendid lady's maid one day.'

Flo blushed with pleasure. Her dearest wish was a swift rise from the lowly post of kitchen maid, which she would take up at the Hall in a few weeks.

'It's nice that you and Joe are both working for Sir James,' said Kate, idly. 'And I expect you're glad you don't have to move very far from your mother. You'll be able to visit her easily on your day off.'

'Oh yes,' muttered Flo. Kate smiled to herself, guessing that the girl was less than enchanted with that aspect of her new job. The poor thing had spent all her sixteen years in the same part of Sussex, under her mother's wing, the only travelling being a rare visit to Brighton. She always listened enviously to Kate's reminiscences about being in service in London.

'You'll find things lively enough at the Hall,' Kate went on, reassuringly. 'Lady Janette's a good mistress to work for and she likes a young staff about her.'

Flo finished with the hairpins, then murmured, 'Can I mind William while you look after your guests?'

Kate was surprised but realised quickly that Flo was shy.

'That's kind of you, dear, but I want you to see Aunt Polly and Edith. You've not met Aunty since our wedding and she was specially pleased to hear you've got this good post.'

'Oh...' Flo still seemed awkward. Then she said abruptly, 'But Joe says your Aunt's very smart, and I know how lovely your cousin looks - ' but Kate broke in with a laugh, assuring her that Joe had been teasing.

'It's too bad of him if he's made you think they're high and mighty people.'

'Oh no, he didn't say that. But I know your Uncle has that big shop in Brighton. I've seen it.'

'Which makes him a shopkeeper,' said Kate cheerfully, thinking how much Arnold Summers would hate the term. 'Just like Mrs Halfpenny at the shop in the village. Nothing special about that.'

William gurgled gently in the circle of his mother's arm and Flo laughed to see him. She suddenly looked quite pretty and Kate leaned forward to kiss her cheek.

'I last saw Miss Edith two years ago,' said Flo. 'I remember thinking that she doesn't look at all like you!'

Kate tried to speak quickly before the girl realised her mistake but already Flo was scarlet with embarrassment and stammering out an apology.

'Flo, don't worry. Sometimes I forget myself that they're not really related to me. Edie and I have always been like sisters.'

But that wasn't completely true. Sometimes, when she was alone with Edith and Aunt Polly they were happy and comfortable enough for it to feel as though they were really mother and daughters. Such times were rare, though. From her childhood the presence and the behaviour of Mr Summers had always held the three of them in check. She particularly remembered the time he had stopped her playing with Edith's dolls. 'Leave them - you've got your own toys.'

Flo glanced at her sister-in law. 'Do you remember your real mother?' she asked hesitantly.

Kate shook off her sudden dark mood. 'Goodness no! When Joe and I got engaged I went to see the couple who looked after me before Aunty and Uncle took me in, but they couldn't tell me very much. Apparently a friend of theirs had asked them to care for me. They're getting on a bit and I think I confused them with too many questions.'

Flo's eyes grew round with excitement.

'What if you're the orphan of a noble house?'

Kate groaned. 'Honestly, Flo, what rubbish have you been reading?' But when the girl bridled she added, less critically, 'Well, when I was a little girl I used to pretend like that, but not any more. I think I'd prefer not to know the truth now. It could be rather shocking.'

Seeing Flo's blush Kate turned away to hide her own smile. Really, it was wrong to tease the girl in this way but she did have some silly ideas!

Joe came clattering downstairs, pulling on his jacket. 'There's a motor car coming along the track. I saw it from the bedroom window!'

Flo squeaked in surprise. Kate was annoyed. 'Who can that be? It's not from the Hall, surely?'

Joe shook his head. Sir James always rode round the estate on horseback, like his father before him. It was more likely someone visiting the Hall who had lost their way.

'Let's go and take a look. Bring William - he's not seen a motor car before.'

Kate remarked tartly that the child was hardly old enough to appreciate such a rare sight but she followed her husband and Flo and stood with them at the gate peering down the rough track. Joe's dogs, excited by the noise, added their own to it.

'It's Aunt Polly!' crowed Joe.

'Oh, don't be silly,' snapped Kate. 'They're coming by trap from the station.'

'It is, I tell you. Someone must have collected them. Look!'

And now she could see Polly, sitting beside the driver in the open vehicle, being bumped and bounced about, her long face grim with anxiety. Behind her was Edith, enchanting in a small brimmed hat with feathers about the crown, waving and smiling delightedly. Kate glanced at Flo and saw that the girl's mouth had dropped open in awe. And after all she'd said about them not being wealthy or grand!

But she felt that Flo was rather more impressed by that hat than the noise and glitter of the car, which had Joe's eyes sparkling with pleasure. He flung open the gate as the car pulled up with a jerk.

'Well, Aunt Polly: what's all this?'

Now they had stopped Polly's face relaxed into an easy smile.

'Oh, I'm so glad we've arrived. I never thought we'd get here in one piece.' Then she turned hastily to the young man sitting at the wheel, stiff and rather dusty, in a long driving coat. 'Not that your driving was anything but perfect, Sam. It's just that I don't really like this machine.'

The young man flushed a little and almost smiled. Edith leaned forward.

'It's Father's latest acquisition, Kate. Isn't it a joke? We've driven here from Brighton, feeling like royalty the way people stared.'

She moved to open the rear door of the vehicle and at once the chauffeur leapt from his seat and rushed round to release his passengers and hand them down. The dogs yapped excitedly and Joe bellowed at them.

Kate hugged her Aunt, who immediately took her own, plain, hat off and William into her arms. Kate turned to kiss Edith and saw further enchantments. The young woman wore a dark brown suit, the long jacket embroidered on the lapels, with matching embroidery down one side of her skirt.

'Edie, you look lovely,' said Kate, trying to keep the envy out of her voice. Flo all but curtseyed when Edith greeted her. Polly drew the chauffeur forward, introducing him as Mr Sam Bundy, a junior assistant from Mr Summers' store.

'But he understands these machines wonderfully, so Arnold has asked him to drive us about sometimes.'

'It's a pleasure, Mrs Summers,' said Sam. Kate heard the Cockney twang to his voice and warmed to his friendly, gap-toothed smile. Flo had torn her gaze away from Edith and was now looking at the chauffeur as if he

13

too had stepped from the pages of some exciting novel. Kate sighed.

'Is this darling really six months old?' Polly was asking. 'He's growing so fast, Kate.' She hugged the baby close to her. Kate looked anxiously into her Aunt's face. Was it her imagination or were there more worry lines about the woman's eyes? She knew Polly had a difficult time of it with Arnold Summers, who could be short-tempered and belligerent. He doted on his daughter, though, and Edith's presence was usually some measure of protection for her mother.

The young woman came up and slipped an arm through Kate's.

'We've had such excitement the past few weeks,' she murmured. 'The last of Father's relatives was good enough to die and leave him some money.'

'Edith!' hissed Polly, horrified.

Edith was unrepentant. 'Mother, don't be a hypocrite. You know Father's relations were all quite awful.' Her eyes sparkled mischievously at Kate. 'It was the frightful Aunt who came to stay one Christmas and insisted on having a pot of tea to herself every meal. We put a piece of soap in it - do you remember?'

Kate was laughing. It had been worth going to bed without supper, just to see the Aunt's face. Of course Uncle Arnold had later repented and said Edith could go down to the kitchen for some hot milk, but the dispensation didn't extend to Kate and so Edith had refused.

Edith was chattering on. 'So Father's putting some of the money into the shop, expanding the business, he says, and he's spending the rest on smartening up the Summers family. Hence the car!'

Kate became aware of Polly's disquiet. A woman of good but simple taste, her Aunt was obviously uncomfortable at having to be part of such display. Probably her lack of enthusiasm had earned her husband's displeasure.

'Well, that's enough about us,' said Polly. 'I'd love a cup of tea!'

The three women strolled towards the house. Flo still hovered near her brother who was deep in conversation with Sam Bundy about the car. Out of the corner of her eye Kate saw the girl give a shrug and turn away.

******

'You've got a lovely view.' Edith leaned on the bedroom window sill, looking out over the garden. 'That's Wolstonbury, isn't it?'

Kate didn't bother to answer but waited for what Edith wanted to say. She had insisted on Kate showing her round upstairs before tea, while Aunt Polly played with William, and Flo bustled importantly in the kitchen. Obviously Edith had something on her mind.

'I was in London last week,' she said, 'staying with Clara.'

Kate nodded. Clara Riseborough was an old friend of Polly's and they exchanged visits every year.

'Mother stayed at home this time. Father wanted her to go with me and choose some new materials for curtains and things but she refused. She hates us having this money, you know. Father was very cross.'

Kate sat on the bed, absently smoothing the carefully embroidered coverlet, a wedding present from Joe's mother.

'Perhaps you shouldn't have gone, Edie,' she murmured.

'That would have made things twice as bad for Mother.' Edith moved away from the window to the washstand, bending slightly to see her reflection in the mirror. 'In any case I shan't always be at home.'

There was a new vitality about her, Kate thought - a bubbling excitement that did more for her looks than all her angel colouring and fashionable clothes. Had she fallen in love?

'You know, when he told us about the money I had half a mind to ask Father where the awful Aunt was when his mother was bringing him up all on her own and struggling to keep him at school,' Edith murmured with a wicked smile. 'I didn't, of course, but I was sorely tempted. Remember all the times we've had to listen to his "When I was a young lad"' stories? I swear the amount of sewing his "poor widowed mother"' had to take in to make ends meet got larger every time.'

Kate smiled. 'I've always felt that his father's family didn't approve of his mother.'

'I'm sure of it! They must have been shrivelled by the thought of welcoming an illiterate female into their midst.' And Edith puffed out her chest and gave a passable imitation of her father at his most pompous. '"Couldn't write more than her name, my mother, but goodness could that woman work...".'

Their laughter died quickly.

Kate said: 'He always speaks of her with admiration but never with any affection. It's as though she wasn't a real woman at all.'

'I know. And it's obvious that Mother thoroughly disliked her own parents from what little she ever says about them,' said Edith. 'Perhaps it's a good thing they're all dead.'

'You're very callous,' murmured Kate reprovingly and Edith shrugged. Then she stretched and sat down on the bed next to Kate.

'London was marvellous,' she exclaimed with sudden eagerness.

Perhaps she was right and Edith was in love. Maybe that was why she spoke of not always being at home. 'Did you meet Matty?' Kate asked carefully. What luck if it was Matthew. He had loved Edith for so long but although she was fond of him her feelings seemed to go no deeper. But maybe she'd just needed time.

15

'Oh yes, we always meet when I'm there,' replied Edith, absently. 'He's still set on being a teacher, you know. Such a waste.'

Before Kate could respond Edith laughed. 'Oh, don't look like that! I know you and Joe think Matty's doing the right thing. I just happen to believe he should never have changed his mind about going into politics.'

'What, even in the Labour Party?'

'He wouldn't have stayed with them for long. He'd have been such an asset to the Liberals.'

So it wasn't Matthew who had captured the young woman's heart if, indeed, she had lost it.

'You know Clara's a member of the suffrage movement?' said Edith. 'Well she took me to a meeting of the WSPU. That's the Women's Social and Political - '

'Yes, I know,' said Kate sharply, 'the Pankhursts' organisation. We're not completely cut off from the outside world here, Edie.'

Edith blushed and apologised but her enthusiasm soon reasserted itself. 'Kate, I wish you could have been there. I actually met Mrs Pankhurst and her daughters.'

Kate caught the glint of fanaticism in Edith's eyes. 'So you're taking up cudgels for the vote now?'

Edith clasped her hands together, smiling excitedly. 'Of course, I know a lot about it already... but I'd never really thought of what will happen when we do get the vote, Kate.'

'When we do? But Asquith is totally opposed to it.'

Edith dismissed the Prime Minister with a contemptuous gesture.

'It's a bitter struggle, but we'll win it. So many women are dedicated to the cause. Christabel says - '

'Miss Pankhurst?'

Edith's eyes shone. 'She's a marvellous woman. So intelligent! So full of energy and plans.'

She went on talking about the eldest Miss Pankhurst, but Kate wasn't listening properly. So it was infatuation that had caught up with Edith in London. Well, an interest in women's suffrage was no bad thing and the Pankhurst women were admirable creatures... Kate looked down at her fingers, still fiddling with the coverlet. She envied Edith her enthusiasm and vitality and her new sense of purpose.

She interrupted, 'Are you going to join the WSPU?'

Edith shook her head. 'Father would never allow it. If he even knew I'd met the Pankhursts he'd be furious: he thinks they're awful women. But just being with Christabel has shown me there's more to life for a woman of twenty than waiting around at home until I get married.' She gave Kate a triumphant look. 'I've decided to go to university.'

Kate stared. Of course there was no reason why it shouldn't happen. Edith had been educated at one of the best Brighton high schools and had turned out to be as clever as she was pretty. But "waiting around at home" until she married was exactly what Arnold Summers had planned for his daughter and it seemed unlikely that he would brook any interference with that scheme.

'Oh, he'll make a fuss, of course, but I can bring him round,' said Edith, untroubled. 'You know what a beastly snob he is, Kate. No matter how much he expands the store he'll always have the mind of a small shopkeeper. I'll make him see what a feather in his cap it will be to have a daughter at Girton.'

'It'll be splendid for you, if you can do that.' Kate stood up, glancing towards the window and the view over the fields. Edith also rose.

'I just wish you could have stayed at school, Kate, then you'd have done the same. You're really much cleverer than I am.'

'Me at a university? How silly.' Kate forced a laugh. 'To cook the meals, perhaps. I could have done that all right.'

'But it's unfair,' said Edith heatedly. 'If I adopted a child I'd never dream of giving it fewer advantages than my own. I know Mother feels awful about the way Father's treated you.'

'Well, she mustn't.' Kate was annoyed now. 'I was adopted to be a companion for you, that was always made clear. And your father found me an excellent place when I started work and I did very well. Don't forget I was made cook housekeeper at the Hall when I was only twenty-one. And now I'm married with a good husband and a lovely child and I'm very happy. Aunt Polly has no cause at all to be upset...'

She turned away, pretending to adjust the curtains, her eyes full of angry tears which she couldn't begin to account for. Edith came over and put an arm around her shoulders, unaware of the tears.

'Of course - and I'm glad you're happy,' she said. 'And I feel guilty about not visiting you for such an age - I don't want us to lose touch. Remember how often I used to come over just after you were married? It was lovely to get away from Brighton.'

And away from Mr Summers, Kate thought. She too had enjoyed those visits. Joe was busy working around the estate and she and Edith had spent hours together without anxiety or guilt. And when Mr Summers had been prepared to release his wife as well as his daughter, so that Aunt Polly could join Edith on a brief visit, their pleasure had been complete.

'It's changed since William was born,' said Kate, thoughtfully.

'Well, of course. You've so much to do looking after that young

17

hero!'

The hero was in the kitchen, enthroned on Polly's lap while Flo paid court to him. Kate suggested that it was time for their darling to take his nap and Flo hurried him away upstairs.

'She's a nice little thing, Joe's sister, but very shy,' Polly murmured to Kate. 'When I told her that I was in service myself before I married I thought her eyes were going to pop out of her head.'

Edith put an arm about her mother's waist. 'That's because you're such a sophisticated lady!'

'Has Edith told you about her latest fad?' asked Polly.

'Going to university? Yes: I think it's a fine idea, Aunty. Don't you approve?'

'Yes, I do though I don't believe she realises how difficult the entrance examinations can be. But I can't see Arnold agreeing to the idea.'

Edith frowned. 'I'll convince him.' She drew away from her mother. 'And it's not a fad. I can't bear the idea of staying in Brighton much longer. It's so dull! The only visitors we have are Father's boring business acquaintances or your Liberal Association ladies, Mother.'

'I'm sorry you find their company so tedious, my dear,' said Polly, flushing.

'Oh, I didn't mean to upset you,' Edith smiled winningly and gave her mother a hug. 'Yes, of course I like your friends. It's just that they're not - '

'They're not militant Suffragettes,' put in Polly with an edge to her voice.

Edith pouted. 'Oh, Mother, I've explained - '

'I'm sure the Pankhursts are excellent people, Edith, but I can't agree with their methods. Violence and law-breaking only turn the public against the cause. I think women like Mrs Garrett Fawcett have the right approach to gaining the vote.'

'But that meek and mild attitude has got women nowhere, Mother.'

Flo came back into the room to find a lively argument in progress about the rights and wrongs of militant tactics. She gave up trying to follow it after a while and went to put the kettle on the range to boil. Then Joe and Sam Bundy appeared and she could see Sam thought it strange the women didn't stop talking or that Joe didn't break into their gossip. Her brother simply stood listening and watching them with an appreciative smile.

They were very good-looking women, Flo had to admit. At first she'd thought the mousey-haired Mrs Summers quite plain, but that was only because she was so serious most of the time. When she talked about something with interest, as she was doing now, her face seemed to lighten and the rather sallow skin began to glow. Miss Edith was lovely, of course, in spite

18

of her lack of inches; and Kate completed the picture with her delicate skin and lively dark eyes. Flo thought, not without a touch of pride, that the three of them together looked as good as any society beauties who got their pictures in the magazines.

At last Joe moved forward.

'Why are the Suffragettes only after votes for women? Don't they know that a lot of men in this country still haven't got the vote yet?' he said, winking at Sam.

The three women, led by a furious Edith, turned on Joe. He seemed undismayed, but Sam drew back as though overpowered. He looked towards Flo and she saw a measure of relief in the smile he gave her. He picked up the big china teapot and took it across to her.

'Do you live here, Miss Weaver?'

Flo blushed. She explained quietly that she lived with her mother and elder brother - at least until she moved into the Hall. She dropped the knitted kettle holder and when Sam handed it back to her their fingers bumped together. Flo blushed some more and looked away, to find her sister-in-law's quizzical gaze upon her.

'Time for tea,' said Kate, firmly.

******

She buttoned her blouse and stared down at William, asleep in her arms with a satisfied look on his face. Kate thought, with a mixture of amusement and a strange annoyance, that he looked very like his father. She laid the child gently on the bed and crossed to the washstand, pouring water from the heavy, rose-patterned jug into the matching china bowl. She rinsed her hands then splashed a little water on to her face. Taking a towel from the holder at the side of the stand and patting her face dry she went to the window and gazed out.

Tea had been a lively meal with lots of talk and argument about politics and the state of the country. Polly and Edith were enthusiastic about Lloyd George's new budget.

'I hear he's calling it the People's Budget,' Kate had laughed. 'Will he be crying revolution next?'

'Now, don't you mock,' said Polly. 'Just think what he's achieved already; especially pensions for the old folk.'

'Yes and those same old folk made to feel he's God's gift to human-kind,' said Joe. 'I hope you Liberals won't forget it's the presence of Labour in the House that's guaranteed your reforms.'

During the discussion that followed Kate noticed that Flo, who had been listening with a bored expression on her face, was now chatting with Sam Bundy in a low tone and looking a good deal more perky. Feeling a reluctant responsibility for the girl, Kate tried to overhear what the young man was saying, while keeping up her end of the debate but found the task impossible. Then William began to howl and that was the end of tea and talk as far as she was concerned.

She glanced over her shoulder at the child. He was a good baby but had seemed more demanding lately. She loved him but wished he would grow up quickly.

The light on the downs had changed, softened in the late afternoon. There was a suggestion of cloud beyond the distant trees, which gave the day a new uncertainty. She thought it might rain tonight and wondered if, when everyone was gone, she might persuade Joe to look after William while she went for a walk.

She suddenly covered her face with the towel, blotting out the view. Walking wouldn't be enough, she knew it, not even if she was to climb right to the top of Wolstonbury. She opened her mouth and screamed silently into the folds of the towel, her breath hot and damp in the cloth.

'Kate!' Flo and Polly were below the window, strolling on the grass. Kate waved back to them patting again at her face and then drying her hands elaborately on the towel. Behind her William hiccupped and stirred.

******

'What a lovely day it's been, Flo.'

In the garden Polly had taken off her long-waisted, buttoned jacket to reveal a white blouse, plain but well cut. Flo decided that Kate had learned her simple elegance from her Aunt but she preferred Edith's more dashing style.

Polly was saying how much she loved the country. 'But I suppose you're longing to get away from it,' she added thoughtfully. 'Hoping to work in London as soon as you can?'

Flo gave her a wary glance. They were very direct, Mrs Summers and her daughters - that must be where Kate got it from. Somehow you couldn't avoid giving a straight answer.

'I'd miss Mother and Art and everyone... but, yes, I would love to work in London.' She turned to Polly. 'It must be so exciting, if you're in a big house.'

Polly shrugged. 'I worked in one for several years. It was the unhappiest time of my life. The mistress had a cruel nature, always picking on the servants. One of my jobs was to sweep the carpets in the drawing room. She regularly left pieces of paper under the rugs, to make sure I'd done the job properly.'

Flo frowned. 'So if the paper was still there she'd know you hadn't swept underneath.' She made a mental note to look out for such tricks.

20

'I hated the feeling of being watched and not trusted,' Polly went on. 'One day I left a piece of paper in its place after I'd written a big question mark on it. From then on I was left to clean in peace.'

Flo laughed, gazing at Polly in delight and astonishment. Polly gave a fleeting smile.

'It seems funny now but it felt uncomfortable at the time. She had her own back, of course, in the end we had words over some other matter and I was told to leave. Without a reference.'

It was the worst thing that could happen, Flo knew. No reference meant little chance of getting another place.

'My parents couldn't help me and I nearly ended up in the workhouse.' Polly paused, allowing those words to sink in. Then she added in a gentler tone, 'Luckily I found friends to stand by me until I got other work. But there's no excitement in London if you have no job and no money.'

Her voice was calm but there was suddenly such pain in her eyes that Flo looked away in embarrassment, as though she'd been caught prying into a secret.

'Come in!' called Edith from the doorway. 'It's time for the presents!'

These had been bought by Edith from the Army and Navy Stores: a tortoiseshell comb for Kate and some finely scented bath salts; pencils in an inlaid box for Joe; a little coat in cream serge for William.

'Too big for him just now,' said Edith with regret. 'I suppose he'll grow into it?'

'Very quickly,' smiled Kate, kissing her. 'And he'll look a picture. Thank you so much, Edie.'

Edith glanced at Flo. 'I haven't got you anything. I didn't realise you'd be here,' she murmured. But when Flo, pink and uncomfortable, said of course not and it didn't matter Edith sprang up and burrowed in her handbag.

'You shall have this, Flo. I do hope you'll enjoy it.' And she held out a book. It was *Diana of the Crossways.* Joe and Kate exchanged bemused glances and Polly looked a little disapproving but Flo was glowing now with pleasure.

'If you like that I'll bring you some more books next time I come,' Edith enthused and she took Flo off into a corner to discuss the novel with her.

Hugging Kate before she left Polly had murmured, 'You're looking very tired, dear. I'll talk to Arnold and see if you can bring William to Brighton for a few days. The sea air will do you good, I'm sure.'

Kate had smiled gratefully but knew the proposed visit probably wouldn't happen. Arnold Summers would find some excuse to put it off. What concerned her more was that she didn't care. A visit to the seaside was not what she needed.

They waved at the gate until the cloud of dust had dissolved into the late afternoon air, then Kate turned to Joe.

'I'd like to go for a walk.'

He nodded. 'Flo can mind William for a while. Shall we walk down to - '

'No. I mean I'd like to go on my own.'

He was silent and she added hastily, 'I've got a headache. I think a stroll alone would clear it.'

His eyes were anxious but he said easily, 'Yes, do you good to stretch your legs a while. We'll be fine.'

She knew he didn't really understand why she wanted to be on her own and she was grateful that he hadn't made it difficult for her. Shrugging into her coat she set off in the same direction the motor had taken.

Flo stared thoughtfully at her brother, aware of his puzzled concern as he watched his wife stride off down the track. She entertained a brief vision of herself striding thus, watched by a worried Sam Bundy. The vision shifted and Sam came hurrying after her. She breathed out quickly.

'You feeling all right? Making funny noises,' said Joe. She blinked and scuttled off to the kitchen.

******

It was dusk when Kate returned. She had stayed out too long, rambling the lanes, letting the freshening breeze make a mess of her hair, trying not to think. As she entered the kitchen she found Joe sitting in his chair by the range, the baby fractious on his knee and she realised guiltily that the child's feed was overdue. Joe made no complaint, however - probably because Matthew was at the table, a plate of bread and cheese and a glass of stout before him.

Matthew leapt up at once, took Kate by the shoulders and gave her a hearty kiss on the cheek, a custom he had begun on her wedding day. Kate hadn't seen him for some months and noticed that his face was thinner and that there were dark smudges under his eyes.

'I wish we'd known you were down here, Matthew,' she exclaimed. 'Did Joe tell you Aunty and Edie were visiting today?'

'And in the new car, I gather. I'm sorry I missed that. But I had to spend some time with James and Janette of course.'

'And is that all Joe's given you to eat?'

'It's fine, Kate. Honestly!'

She looked at her husband and he shrugged, holding William out to her.

'He stirred a little while ago, so I brought him downstairs. Flo wanted to fuss over him, but she's looking tired and a bit peaky, so I told her to go on

22

up to bed.'

Kate nodded. 'I'll feed him and settle him for the night. Matthew, you're not going just yet, are you?'

'And miss the chance of chatting to you, my dear? Of course not.' And he rose again to open the door for her.

When she returned Matthew had finished eating and had moved into the chair opposite Joe's. She cleared the table, listening to their conversation. It was obvious that Matthew was tired and depressed. He said that his course was tedious; that all he wanted was to begin teaching straight away. But although tempted to give up the training he had decided, reluctantly, to complete the course for which the government paid a grant to university graduates.

'It's supposed to be a generous grant, but if that's generous, well......' Matthew frowned. 'Still, I can occasionally enjoy myself. I was able to take Edith to dinner when we met in London. She was very kind and pretended not to notice that the cuffs are going on my jacket.'

'Do you have much studying to do?' asked Kate.

He shrugged. 'It's not like the easy-going university life.' He had come to the Hall this weekend for a rest, only to find himself in the middle of a dispute between Sir James and his wife. One of them wanted to holiday in the South of France while the other was determined on Switzerland.

'I honestly can't remember who wants what and I can't say I care very much,' said Matthew wearily. 'I just know that I was pig-in-the-middle. First James would ask my opinion and then Janette. At lunch today I lost my temper and started telling them about children in the East End who've never even seen the sea, let alone the South of France. That, of course, united them against me and I got hounded for letting down the family name and honour by wanting to do such a menial job as teaching.' He grimaced. 'No, that's unfair; Janette doesn't say that kind of thing. But she thinks I'd do better teaching at Eton. James just thinks I'm wasting my time.'

He finished his stout and Joe poured him another. There was silence for a moment, then Matthew glanced from Joe to Kate and began to laugh. They joined in.

'Well now,' said Matthew at last, 'that's got all the grumpiness out of my system. You can't imagine how good it is to come here and relax.'

They heard William crying upstairs and Joe said he would try to settle the child this time. Kate smiled at him gratefully. 'Yes, do. You've got the trick of it. He likes to have you tuck him up.'

She was feeling easier after her long walk. The uncomfortable sensations of the day were somehow blotted out for a while by the cosiness of this evening in the kitchen. As Joe went out he touched her arm, tenderly.

Matthew turned slightly in his chair so that he could look at Kate in her seat near the window while he talked. She saw him smile as she leaned forward to adjust the oil lamp.

'Kate, you remind me of a pre-Raphaelite painting,' he said gently. She was flattered but didn't let him see it.

'Had Edie met the Pankhursts when you saw her in London?' she asked and he smiled.

'Oh, yes. I got a full account of all that My Lady Christabel said and did.'

He paused then said more seriously, 'I hope Edith isn't going to get too involved. It would cause so many problems at home and not just for her.'

Kate agreed and explained Edith's plans to him. Matthew grew enthusiastic. He felt that a course of serious study would be ideal.

'She's interested in so many things and she tends to hop from one to another,' he said.

'And you think that studying would settle her down?'

Matthew grinned and Kate found herself disarmed, as ever, by his charm.

'I wouldn't want Edith to be too settled. Who would? But she has so much energy and life and if it was channelled in a really useful direction it would be wonderful.' The grin softened to a sad smile. 'She's my image of Cythna in that Shelley poem – "She moved upon this earth a shape of brightness".'

They were quiet for a long time after that. Occasionally they could hear Joe moving about in the room above. Kate took a sip of the drink Joe had poured for her. Usually she liked stout but tonight it tasted unpleasant to her, so she took it across to Matthew for him to try.

Standing beside his chair she suddenly burst out, 'Matthew, why didn't things go right for you and Edie? I was so sure they would.'

Then she went cold with embarrassment and tried, clumsily, to apologise. Matthew took her hand. 'Oh, Kate, don't worry. We've been friends long enough; you can say these things.'

He drew her round to face him, now holding both her hands in his.

'The answer is that I don't know and I wish I did. At first I thought she was falling in love with me as deeply as I'm in love with her. But when I decided to train for teaching... Well, it all seemed to fall to pieces.'

He fell silent, looking down at Kate's hands. After a moment she disengaged them from his grasp and went to fetch her workbox. When Joe came back she was busy with her darning, listening to Matthew's account of *The Arcadians*, which he had seen recently. He stayed for several hours and their talk ranged over many subjects but eventually, inevitably, settled on politics. Again the budget came under scrutiny and they wondered how much of it would get through the Commons. They spoke scathingly of Lloyd George and the other Liberals and praised the Labour politicians they most admired.

'This is pure self-indulgence,' Matthew laughed, but they agreed that it was a necessary boost to their morale.

'There aren't that many of us about,' grunted Joe.

At last Matthew left, promising to visit them again soon, and Kate and Joe went up to bed. As they passed Flo's room Kate saw a faint line of lamplight beneath the door. Flo was propped up against the pillow, drowsing over *Diana of the Crossways*.

'It's very late,' whispered Kate. 'Joe's gone on to bed.'

Flo looked guilty. 'I couldn't sleep so I thought I might read for a bit.'

'Are you enjoying it?'

The girl frowned then said carefully, 'Oh yes...'

'Not an easy book to get into,' Kate prompted and Flo nodded gratefully.

Kate looked at her more closely. 'You seem a bit pale. Are you not feeling well, Flo?'

'My monthly's just started,' Flo whispered, eyes lowered. 'I always feel strange, just for the first day or so.'

Kate fussed about her a little, asking if she'd like some brandy or some hot milk, but Flo was embarrassed by such attention and wanted nothing. With a sudden surge of affection which she could not explain Kate bent and kissed her sister-in-law goodnight.

She sat before the mirror, brushing her hair. Behind her, already in bed, Joe chuckled. 'You know that makes you look like a queen, don't you?'

Kate glanced at him over her shoulder. 'Am I so conceited?'

'Of course not, I didn't mean that.'

She laughed. 'Matty says I look like a pre-Raphaelite lady. He should see me when I'm all over flour, doing the baking.'

He drew her down into the depths of the soft mattress, running his hands through the hair she had just brushed smooth. He had left the lamp burning dimly on his side of the bed and now he gazed with pleasure at the sheen of her skin in the faint glow as he undid the buttons on her nightdress. Kate felt his hands on her body and a strange mixture of sensations swept through her. She could still feel the breeze on her face, out in the fields; the firm clasp of Aunt Polly's hand; the softer touch of Matty's long fingers twined in her own.

Joe kissed her breasts gently, too gently. William came into her mind and to shut him out she pushed her fingers into Joe's curls and pressed his

25

head harder against her until the insistence of his mouth made her groan with pleasure. For a moment she was back in the fields again, light as the wind, able to go where she pleased, and then she was bound down by his body and happy to be so.

Suddenly she was wide awake in the darkness. Joe slept heavily beside her and there was no noise from William in the room across the landing. What had roused her?

Gradually it came to her. Flo, feeling tired because her period had started. Kate pulled herself up against the pillow and began counting, knowing what the result would be almost before she began. Since William's birth she had been so regular. Her body blazed with the knowledge. Seven days late. A whole week.

When? When had it happened? She'd been so careful, and the new cap was supposed to be the very latest, the very best method... She groaned aloud. There had been one night, just like tonight, when she was too tired. No, not too tired for his love but too stupidly tired to be sensible.

She counted again, a different assessment now. If she was pregnant William would be only just over a year when the new baby arrived. The thought of looking after two very young children filled her with despair. Was it unnatural not to want another baby? She turned her head on the pillow in Joe's direction. She loved him but did she love him properly if she didn't want his babies?

She thought back to when she'd begun working at the Hall. She and Joe had caused quite a bit of gossip, the way they were so obviously attracted to each other, but they'd taken no notice of that. They became lovers almost at once, so far gone in desire for one another that they hadn't even thought about taking any precautions and the rest of that month they waited on tenterhooks. Somehow it didn't really matter. They both knew that they would marry; if Kate was pregnant that would simply put things forward. As it happened she was not, and, feeling rather smug, they got engaged at the end of that year, at the same time that Sir James married his heiress from the North of England.

Kate smiled in spite of herself, remembering their time as an engaged couple. It had been wonderfully happy - days in the country, rain and shine, days by the sea, days sometimes with Matthew and Edith coming along. It seemed, in retrospect, as though they had done nothing but enjoy themselves all the time. In fact they'd only been together on their days off and those were few as she'd been promoted to cook housekeeper by then and was kept busy. But the hours they snatched together were wonderful. Then she pulled a face at her own soppy thoughts. Beside her Joe grunted and changed position, butting his head more firmly down into the pillows.

The first months of marriage had seemed like the days of courtship, all run into one. Slower, of course, more gentle and easy now because they had time but just as intense and happy. The happiness had continued right through Kate's easy pregnancy. Then William arrived and life became different.

She shrank down into the bed, pressing her fists against her stomach. Perhaps it wasn't true, after all. And eventually, repeating this magic spell to herself, she drifted off into an uneasy sleep.

******

Just as she fed the soapy sheet into the mangle Kate heard William beginning to murmur. She groaned and wound the wheel vigorously. The iron frame of the mangle shook and suds churned back over the sheet as it was squeezed through the rollers. Scummy water splashed on her shoes and skirt and she cried out with annoyance.

In the kitchen William was crying too. Kate pushed the sheet, still slippery with soap, into the big wooden tub of clean rinsing water, then grabbed at a towel and hurried next door drying her hands as she went. Outside, a mild wind was blowing, ideal for drying if she could ever get the washing done she thought grimly, and she'd put William in his cradle near the range, expecting him to sleep for most of the morning. Yet here he was, crying for attention, and the washing not finished.

She gazed anxiously into his face, wondering if he might sleep again. It didn't seem likely. His cries ceased the minute she came into view and now he was beaming at her and reaching out to grasp the strands of hair which hung sticky about her face. Kate pressed her hands lightly against her breasts. No, she'd been wrong, there was nothing... She pressed again, harder this time, and knew she was trying to fool herself. Sore...... just the same as when she was starting with William. She jerked her head round, looking back towards the kitchen door, aware of the soapy mounds of sheets and shirts and napkins waiting in the scullery to be rinsed. And the kitchen to be cleaned... and Joe's dinner to get ready...

William, resenting the loss of attention, gave a little whine. Kate glared at him. Another seven months and there would be two children to look after. And less and less time.

The familiar sense of despair came down upon her and this time it brought tears with it. Kneeling beside her son she began to sob and William, after staring at her for a moment in complete surprise, wept with her.

'Kate! Oh dear, whatever's wrong?'

She was aware of Flo's plump arms round her shoulders, squeezing tight in a fierce attempt at comfort. The girl, squatting at her side, peered fearfully at her from under the brim of a new, beribboned straw hat. Kate

27

drew back a little, flushing; ashamed at being discovered like this by Joe's sister. But Flo was all concern.

'Are you feeling ill, Kate?'

Kate wiped her eyes and stood up, Flo supporting her with little murmurs of encouragement.

'I'm all right!' Her voice was sharp and Flo at once released her hold and stepped away uncertainly. Kate softened her tone. 'I'm sorry, Flo. I suddenly felt so tired... and William woke up, and I'm only halfway through the washing.'

Flo's face brightened. 'Oh, I can help you. I'll look after William.'

She swept the still howling baby up into her arms and the crying stopped at once and he gave Flo a damp smile. Meanwhile Kate was taking in her sister-in-law's appearance. After only a short time at the Hall the girl had filled out and was looking prettier, but her new taste in clothes left a lot to be desired. She was obviously trying to emulate Edith but the colour and style of her dress made her look far older than her years. Her hat was nice enough, but beneath it Kate could see frizzy wisps. Flo had tried for curls and her fine hair had rebelled against the attempt.

Trying not to smile Kate murmured, 'I'm better now you're here.'

Without William to worry about she soon had the clothes and sheets flapping on the line. She felt annoyed at giving way earlier. That was happening too often recently. She was snappy with Joe and had little patience with William. She must take herself in hand.

As she was wiping down the mangle, Flo put her head round the scullery door. 'I've made us some tea,' she said.

The two women sat at the kitchen table. Flo had covered the pink dress with an apron, but kept her hat on and William, sitting in her lap, tried hard to reach the ribbons.

'It's kind of you to help me, Flo,' said Kate, 'and on your day off, too. I'm afraid you'll be late getting to your mother's.'

Flo bent her head and tickled William's chin. 'I'm not going home,' she said carelessly. 'I told Mum last time that I'd most likely look in and see you and Joe today.'

She chattered on about events at the Hall. Kate smiled at her occasionally but knew she shouldn't be sitting here, drinking tea. The range needed cleaning - had done for days.

Suddenly she wanted to get right away from the house and interrupted Flo to ask abruptly, 'Shall we go for a walk?'

The girl seemed flustered, 'Oh, well ... Isn't Joe coming in for his meal?'

'It's cold meat today. I can leave that for him. He won't mind.'

'Oh...' Flo's voice was a whine of frustration. 'I'd like to, only... I don't want to miss Joe.'

Kate didn't believe her. 'Right,' she said coldly. 'We'll wait for Joe and all have something to eat and then go out together afterwards. Joe can spare an hour or so for his sister, especially as she's so anxious to see him.'

Flo's eyes registered panic then misery. She sniffed.

'I don't want to go out,' she muttered, bending her head down again so that Kate could hardly hear. 'I heard from Mr Bundy that he'll be coming over this afternoon to see Joe.'

'Who? Mr - oh, of course,' Kate gave a wry smile. She poured herself another cup of tea, saying, 'Sam Bundy, is it? How long have you been keeping company with him, Flo?'

The girl's face was bright red.

'I'm not, Kate,' she breathed. 'Well, not properly. But when I met him here that time he said if ever I was in Brighton I should call in at the shop because they had some very good lace ribbon at a reasonable price.'

Kate stared. 'And did you go?'

Flo nodded and Kate had to hold back a laugh. Shy little Flo was full of surprises.

'Not on my own,' the girl added hastily, blushing even more deeply. 'I took Sarah - she's the parlour maid - home to meet Mum and then the two of us went into Brighton to do our little bit of shopping. She was with me all the while.'

This time Kate had to laugh. 'I believe you, Flo, don't worry.' Then she went on more soberly. 'Mr Bundy seems a very pleasant person. Aunt Polly certainly likes him. But you're both very young - perhaps too young to be seeing much of each other.'

'He said my family might think that,' said Flo proudly. 'That's why he wanted to come over and see Joe today. To ask him if he wouldn't mind us walking out together.'

Kate finished off her tea and replaced the cup in its saucer before replying.

'Well, I don't mind Mr Bundy coming here this time Flo, but in future either Joe or I must invite him.' Her lips twitched. 'We don't want you two turning the house into a secret love nest.'

'Kate!' Flo's outraged tone and horrified eyes set Kate laughing but luckily William began to crow too and the girl was distracted by his beaming expression.

'Oh, isn't he lovely?' she said and Kate, leaning over to stroke William's round cheek, had to agree with her.

'I don't understand how anyone wouldn't want to have a baby,' murmured Flo, her gaze fixed on William. Kate said nothing, but she drew her hand away.

Flo lowered her voice. 'Sarah heard Lady Janette saying she didn't want children for a long time yet but she has a lovely house and lots of money...'

Kate didn't respond and Flo went on.

'Having quite a row about it they were Lady Janette and Sir James.' She saw Kate frown and added quickly, 'I told Sarah she shouldn't have been listening but she reckoned they were getting so snappy with each other that they didn't care who heard them. Anyway, Lady Janette said she didn't want children until she was at least thirty and that she'd make sure of it.'

There was a pause. Kate guessed what was coming next and she didn't really want to deal with it. And she was envious of Lady Janette. No chance that she'd forget to take the proper precautions. She had her own bedroom and bathroom at the Hall and plenty of privacy. No need to fumble about in the dark, in a hurry.

'What did she mean, Kate?'

Kate sighed. 'There are things a woman can use to help make sure she doesn't get pregnant if she doesn't want to. Men can take precautions too but they don't always want to do that.'

She caught sight of Flo's worried expression and added calmly, 'But there's no need for you to bother about such things now.'

Flo said thoughtfully, 'How did you learn about that?'

Kate smiled to herself. It was what Joe had asked and in almost the same slightly disapproving tone when, after their first scare, she had told him that she would use a cap until they were married. She gave Flo the same answer she had given then. 'My Aunt told me, when I started work. She explained everything to me very sensibly and carefully. You see she didn't want me to get into trouble out of sheer ignorance.'

Flo's eyes bulged again and Kate realised that she had put her answer badly.

'Oh, she never thought you'd - that you'd, you know, do it... before you were married!' Flo choked.

Kate struggled with her growing annoyance, tempted to tell the girl that she and Joe had been lovers long before their wedding, if only to silence her. Instead she said sharply, 'Of course not, but she had to tell me some time.'

Flo drew breath, another question ready, but Kate acted quickly to ward it off.

'Goodness, I've just remembered I'm completely out of black lead! Still, I've got time to get some from Mrs Halfpenny's, then I can clean the range before Mr Bundy comes.' She smiled at Flo. 'If you'll just look after William...'

'Yes, of course. But you don't need to worry, Kate.'

'Well, I don't want him thinking your sister-in-law keeps a dirty house. And I'm running low on flour, I'll bring some back, then I can make a cake for us all this afternoon. He'll stay to tea, of course.' Flo's obvious delight went some way towards easing her guilt.

Kate hurried off, her hat pinned on awry, her jacket unbuttoned, as though she feared something would happen to prevent her leaving. But once she'd gone the length of the dusty track and turned into the lane which led to the village she slowed down, tidied herself and, sliding her basket over one arm, adopted a more sedate pace. She wished there was time for a long ramble: still, it was something to be walking on her own to the village and Mrs Halfpenny, a great gossip, would be sure to have plenty to chat about. Since William's birth Kate had fallen out of touch with village happenings and weeks could go by without her seeing anyone but the child and Joe. He would occasionally bring some tit-bit of news from the Hall, but the very nature of his job meant that he too was alone for much of his working day.

She lingered, looking for signs of Spring in the hedgerows. It had all been so very different when she was working at the Hall. No shortage of talk there, though she had allowed no unpleasant gossip in her kitchen. All the girls worked well together and she remembered that the days had been lively and full of laughter. Of course there was hard work too. Mr Pearson had acted as valet to Sir James as well as butler and had been happy to leave most of the household organisation to Kate, once he'd seen how easily she could cope.

She heard the church clock strike, but missed the count. Never mind, there was plenty of time, she felt sure. As the first houses of the village came into sight she turned out of the lane and climbed over a small stile. Her path now lay across the church fields and she decided to go the long way round and walk by the stream for a while.

******

She burst into the kitchen, breathless after running the length of the track. Flo looked up quickly, relieved, but with a touch of resentment lingering in her face. She was hovering beside Joe, who sat squarely at the table, William on his lap, and some slices of bread and a wedge of cheese set before him. He eyed Kate warily but quickly sensed the buoyancy of her mood and, relaxing, gave her a broad grin.

'I'm late — I'm sorry!' She took off her hat and cast her coat over a chair, coming round the table with a light step to kiss Joe's cheek and take William up into her arms. Oh, it was so tempting to tell Joe now; to sit down

31

and spill out the whole marvellous plan she'd been building up all the way back from the village. But she resisted for Flo was there and this was for Joe's ears alone. In any case she wanted to go over it all again in her mind, for he'd be bound to have objections and she wanted to make sure she had the right answers to these. So she beamed at Flo instead and said she hadn't forgotten the flour and then asked teasingly if Joe knew about his visitor.

'Well, I told Sam that any time he liked I'd show him the woods and the covers, so that's why he's coming,' said Joe, giving Kate a wink. 'I've said to Flo that she needn't go thinking he's got any interest in her.'

'Ah now, don't tease your sister,' laughed Kate. 'Especially when she's gone to the trouble of feeding you in your bad wife's absence.'

Flo frowned. 'I remembered what you said about cold meat, Kate, but I couldn't find it.'

'Don't fret, girl, you've done your best,' smiled Joe. 'Why don't you sit down for a while and let Kate put the food out for us? And why on earth don't you take off that silly hat?'

The meal was a cheerful affair, made more so by the cider which Kate insisted on pouring for them. She caught Joe's pleased eyes on her often as she chatted happily with Flo, rocking William on her knee. They were still at the table when Sam Bundy arrived, early because he'd got a lift from Hassocks station on the afternoon milk cart. Flo was embarrassed at first but Sam seemed only too happy to sit down and eat with them though he refused the cider and drank tea instead.

As she spooned some mashed-up vegetables into William's mouth Kate asked Sam for news from Brighton.

'Mr Summers has bought up the property he's had his eye on and we're going to expand,' said Sam. In his grey suit he cut almost as smart a figure as in his chauffeur's uniform and Flo gazed across the table at him in open admiration. He smoothed down his already sleek black hair - slightly self-conscious.

'He's going to have a whole new section for ladies' gowns and another for men's clothing and he'll extend haberdashery.' Sam glanced warily at Joe. 'He says he wants to promote me.'

Flo turned an excited face to her brother.

'That's good,' said Joe, flatly, reaching for another slice of bread.

'If that happens, Sam, you can begin saving,' put in Kate in what she hoped was an encouraging tone. She liked his smile. The gap between his front teeth made him look quite cheeky. And although he didn't fuss over Flo his whole manner suggested that they were already a couple with a good understanding between them. Well, it happened like that sometimes. It had been the same with her and Joe.

When they finished eating, Joe went outside to sort out some traps and Sam took off his splendid jacket, rolled up his sleeves and set to on the washing up. Half scandalised, half bursting with pride at such unexpected behaviour, Flo hovered about him, drying up plates with trembling hands. Unable to contain her amusement Kate took the baby upstairs to settle him for a nap.

Her spirits were high all afternoon, though it became more and more difficult to contain the urge to speak about her plan. For it was a plan now, clear-cut and definite; worked out carefully while Joe and Sam were out and she and Flo baked scones and cakes for tea. As they ate the meal she found herself glancing often at the parlour clock and wondering when Sam would leave.

This time she refused his offer to wash up. 'We don't want to make you late getting back to Brighton,' she said and hoped her tone wasn't too dismissive. Sam fiddled with his cake knife.

'No, I mustn't miss the train. And I thought perhaps I should walk with Miss Flo back to the Hall, first......' He looked directly at Joe, waiting for his response. Kate saw Flo biting her lip anxiously and wondered what would happen in the unlikely event of Joe telling Sam to clear off and never speak to his sister again. She scrutinised Sam's face. The features were not strongly marked but there was a firmness about his mouth which somehow suggested he'd not give up easily and then there'd be no end of a to-do, especially as Flo –– for all her occasional silliness –– had more than her share of the Weaver obstinacy.

Joe leaned back in his chair and unbuttoned his collar. It was a good sign that he'd deigned to put one on before tea.

'If you can spare the time to take Flo back I'd be grateful Sam,' he said. 'It's good to know she's in safe hands.' He had dragged his tie loose now. 'And I'll tell Mother I'm happy enough for you to see Flo on some of her days off. I expect Mum'll be inviting you over there soon enough.'

******

'Really, it was almost feudal the way he sued for your permission to court her,' Kate laughed as she stood beside Joe in the doorway, watching the young couple stroll away arm in arm.

'Well, I like that in him –– shows he's serious,' said Joe firmly.

'You didn't ask anyone's permission,' she teased.

He turned quickly in the doorway and pulled her against him. 'Too late for all that the minute I first saw you,' he whispered and she felt the excitement surge between them. They hadn't made love for weeks. She had hated her treacherous body too much to let him touch it and so put him off with excuses that she was tired. Now her exhilaration made her body respond

33

to his. She wanted to talk to him but it could wait just a little longer. And if they made love perhaps he would be more receptive...... She kissed his mouth quick and hard, ashamed of herself for being so calculating. She had never used his desire for her against him, though she knew that some women bargained in this way.

They listened at the bottom of the stairs, hardly daring to breathe, but William was still quiet.

'Best not go up and risk waking him,' whispered Joe and he led her back into the parlour, closing the door while she drew the curtains across the window. After he had kissed her she was in as much of a hurry as he and together they threw cushions on to the rug in front of the empty grate and sank down there together.

'Did you have to drape my drawers over the fire irons?' she murmured as they lay quiet at last. When he denied it she forced his head round to look and they laughed together. Kate wondered aloud what Joe's mother would say if she paid them an unexpected visit but that broke the mood and his humour faded. She knew he was suddenly aware of his shirt up around his armpits and when the first loud wail came from upstairs he got up quickly and dressed.

'It's all right then, isn't it, love?' he said abruptly. 'About the baby, I mean?'

Kate felt her whole body stiffen. For a few precious moments she had forgotten the existence of the new, unwanted child and now here was its presence again, seeming almost as tangible as that of the boy bellowing out his hunger upstairs.

She pulled down her skirts and began buttoning her blouse, forcing herself to be calm. It would be worse than stupid to vent her anger on Joe -- she wanted him to agree to her plan.

'How long have you known?' she asked, congratulating herself on her light tone.

He had moved towards the window. 'Good Lord, woman, I live with you don't I? You decent again?'

She grunted, gathering up the loose strands of hair and fastening them in place with her comb. He drew back the curtains, revealing the warm, red-gold glow of the sunset.

'When you didn't say anything I thought you must be angry,' he added. 'You know -- because your what's it thing - ' he flushed and stumbled over the word, 'your cap...... because it didn't work.'

His embarrassment annoyed her, threatening the tight control she had on her emotions. Why did he have to seem so prudish at times? After such a love-making too!

'It does work,' she said sharply, 'but not when I forget to use it.'

He was a moment taking this in. Then with an odd kind of smile he said he would fetch William before the child brought the house down with his noise.

Kate cleared the parlour table, stacking the plates quickly and piling them on to a tray. Somehow the fine texture and delicacy of the china and the coloured pattern on cups and plates had a soothing effect. This was her favourite set — a wedding present from Aunt Polly — and was usually kept in the glass-fronted cupboard near the piano, for use only on special occasions. She thought that without realising it she must have been trying to impress young Sam Bundy today. Suddenly amused by her own showing off she smiled as she carried the tray carefully into the kitchen.

Joe brought down a red-faced but already smiling William and sat with him while Kate warmed some milk.

He said thoughtfully, 'It'll be nice having two, don't you think? Specially if the next one's a girl.'

Kate was about to retort that it would be more work for her but stopped herself in time. That was the last notion she wanted to plant in Joe's mind at the moment. So she agreed, keeping her voice as even as possible.

'Funny you forgetting, mind,' murmured Joe. He was smiling again and she realised he was pleased she'd been so carried away, that he had that effect on her. If William hadn't been sitting on his lap she could cheerfully have thrown the saucepan at him.

Joe stood William on his knee and the baby crowed and flexed his legs.

'Is he thinner?' asked Joe.

Kate shrugged. 'He's not wrapped up so much now the weather's warm.'

'You don't think you weaned him too early? Mum thought it might have been.'

She knew that in this mood everything he said would infuriate her, yet he did seem to be choosing the most vexing subjects.

'It's a good job he's weaned,' she responded, stretching a smile, 'now that there's another on the way.'

He accepted this piece of female lore without question and handed over the baby to be fed. Kate glanced anxiously at the mantelpiece clock. He'd be off soon on his evening tasks around the estate. She must talk to him now.

'Joe, sit with me a bit. I want to ask you about something.'

'Right you are, then. But only a little while.'

As soon as he'd got his pipe going and his feet up on the fender she said eagerly: 'I was talking to Mrs Halfpenny in the village shop today. She's going to sell up and move to Patcham.'

'That right? Going to her son's I suppose?'

Kate nodded. 'Her daughter-in-law is quite ill and likely to be an invalid for some time according to the doctor. Mrs Halfpenny's going to live with them and look after the children.'

'Be someone new at the shop, then. Mind you, it's time she gave that up. Must have been difficult managing on her own after Bob Halfpenny died.'

'Joe, listen...… She doesn't want much for the business. Why don't we buy it? We've a little saved - '

He gave a shout of laughter. William jumped and stared about him with large eyes and Kate patted the child's back to soothe him. She looked at her husband, hating his laughter, but forcing herself to keep calm.

'So you see us as a pair of shopkeepers do you?' he grinned. 'Oh, Kate, you do get some funny ideas.' And he swung his feet off the fender, about to get up and leave.

'No, listen,' she urged. 'It's a sound little business, Joe. She has plenty of customers and the stock's all good. There's a store at the back and she also keeps some things upstairs, but there's enough room: a parlour and a kitchen with a decent-sized scullery downstairs and bedrooms up above. We could make it really comfortable.'

'Kate, you can't - '

'And the beauty of it is that she's not asking a lot because she wants to leave soon. There's plenty of work to be done if you really wanted to expand the business, but we could do that. We could end up supplying the Hall. I was always saying to Mr Pearson that it was a pity we had to send all the way to Haywards Heath for what we needed.'

She paused. She hadn't run out of things to say but wanted to hear his objections so that she could counter them. She drew herself upright in the chair and settled William more firmly in her lap. He struggled against her tight hold.

Joe began the slow, deliberate business of knocking out and cleaning his pipe. She sensed that he was puzzled, rather than angry.

'We don't know anything about keeping a shop, Kate.'

'True -— but we can learn. You're head keeper on this estate and I've had charge of the household. We're not fools.'

He looked at her intently.

'I thought you were happy enough - specially now we've got this house.'

The reproach in his voice threw her off balance for a moment but she quickly recovered.

'I'm very happy, of course. But you've often said you'd like to be your own master.'

'Well... we've other responsibilities now. Think what a risk we'd be taking if I gave up this job. If you think about it seriously you'll see this isn't for us, love. I'm too much of a country clod to be comfortable running a shop!'

'You're no such thing! Just remember how many people value your opinion, turn to you for help with problems. Do you think Matty would still be friendly with a clod, even if he did run wild with you as a child?' She took a quick breath and hurried on before he could interrupt. 'Look at your own family. As far as your mother's concerned you're the head of it, even though Arthur's older than you.'

This drew a reluctant laugh from him. 'That's only because he's not married.'

'Maybe - but all the family come to you for advice,' she said, then added quickly, 'and your mother would like to see you in your own business.' Joe slowly nodded agreement and Kate's hopes rose. She could easily imagine Jane Weaver's pride and pleasure at having both her sons so well set up. She could almost see the small, round figure strutting down the village street and into her son's store to order her weekly groceries.

Joe jerked them both back to reality.

'Anyway, it's out of the question now we've another child on the way,' he said and stood up. 'I'm sorry I said that just now - about your crazy notions, love. I realise you want me to get on, for us and for our children, but you see - '

'Oh, Joe, don't dismiss the idea. Please say you'll think about it,' she pleaded. 'I can help in the shop till the baby's nearly due and I'll be able to do all the ordering and stock-keeping and the accounts. I had to keep the books at the Hall, so that'll be easy. And maybe when we've got the business going we'll be able to take on some help.' She meant help with looking after the children for she wanted above all things to be involved in the day-to-day running of the shop, but she decided to keep that to herself. Let him think for now that she'd be helping behind the scenes in between her housework and caring for the children.

Joe shook his head and bent towards her, resting his hand for a moment against her cheek.

'You haven't even considered the biggest problem. We've some savings, like you say, but nowhere near enough money to buy out May Halfpenny.'

He had turned away and was changing his coat for his working jacket before she found the courage to mutter, 'We could borrow it.'

'You know how I feel about borrowing money!' His face was red and sullen.

'It would be business, Joe. It happens all the while in business. And we'd pay off what we borrowed in next to no time.'

'Oh yes?' He laughed scornfully. 'And who do you think would lend money to the likes of us?'

She looked away from him. 'I thought... Arthur?'

'Don't talk stupid. All Art's money is tied up in the smithy. He has to take account of the times when there's not so much work about.'

She hesitated, then blurted out, 'Well, what about my Uncle?'

He came back to stand in front of her, very close, and she drew back into her chair, momentarily intimidated by his size.

'Well, this is a very different tune you're singing,' he said and his tone was far from pleasant. 'I wish I had a guinea for every time I've heard you speak out against that man - the way he treats your Aunt and spoils young Edith. Yet here you are saying you'll borrow money from him! I can't believe I'm hearing right.'

'You don't understand!' It came out as a kind of wail.

He sat down again, staring at her. 'Then make me understand.'

'It's business, like I said,' she told him, knowing the argument sounded lame. With shame she heard herself say, 'It doesn't matter that I don't like him - that we don't. That'll give us a real push to pay him off quickly.'

'No.' Joe shook his head. 'You can throw out your principles when it suits you but I'll not go to a man I dislike for money, even if that is the way business is done.'

He stood up again.

'I've got a good job and we're really comfortable now for the first time since we got married. Time enough to make other plans in a year or so, perhaps, when we've a bit more put by.'

She let go then, knowing she had lost, and poured out her anger in a harsh, accusing voice, calling him stupid and small-minded. William began to cry and the youngest dog yapped shrilly, excited by all the noise. Joe swore under his breath and pulled open the back door. As the dogs scrambled over his feet he turned back furiously.

'You just look after the house, woman, and stop worrying about how small-minded I am! You should spend less time gallivanting off by yourself thinking up ridiculous ideas and more keeping this place properly clean and your family comfortable!'

She stared at him open-mouthed and he slammed the door behind him.

The stairs seemed to tilt and shift beneath her and she leaned against the wall for a moment, fighting the dizziness, feeling the sweat grow cold on her face and neck. Then pain clawed at her again and she forced herself to go on down. Suppose he'd already gone? There was no sound from the kitchen. Perhaps she was alone in the house, with William and the pain...

She jerked the door open and slumped against the jamb, dizzy again and shivering. Joe was by the window, one foot on a chair as he fastened his leggings. She gave a sob of relief and he turned, startled. One of the dogs who had walked up to Kate suddenly turned away, whining, sensing something wrong.

'What is it?' Then he took in the white, pinched face and the blood on her nightdress and started forward. 'Kate, what's happened?'

'I thought you'd gone.' She was weeping now and the tears seemed to be draining her final strength. 'Joe, I think I'm losing the baby.'

He had her up in his arms in a moment and carried her back upstairs, putting her gently down in bed, brushing the hair off her clammy forehead. There was blood on the sheets too. She pulled herself together, muttering instructions and he ran to where she kept the linen and pulled out a pile of towels.

'The old ones,' she said weakly, but he snapped out that it didn't matter and did what he could to help with the bleeding.

'Now, lie still,' he told her, trying to keep his voice calm. 'I'll take my bike and go and get help. If William wakes take no notice: he's safe enough in his cot.'

She nodded, biting her lips against the pain. For a moment he held her and murmured fearfully that he was sorry and then she heard him pounding down the stairs.

Kate rode out the next wave of pain and realised the house was quiet. How long had he been gone? How long before there was no more pain? She pulled the covers up over her shoulders and lay shivering and afraid. And beneath the fear was guilt.

'This is all my fault,' she groaned aloud and her eyes filled with tears once more. The tears flowed, she thought, as easily as the blood. Yes, my fault because I wanted to pay him back for what he said. He'd no cause to complain about the way I run this house. I wanted to show him......

But that wasn't all. He had touched her on the raw when he criticised her for wanting to borrow money from Arnold Summers. It would have been very wrong and she knew it. She jerked her head from side to side on the pillow. Yet she'd not have suggested it if he hadn't been so adamant that Art had no money. His brother was as close as they come - always crying poverty

39

when the whole family knew he'd got a tidy sum saved. And Joe wouldn't even think about it!

It felt as though her limbs were burning. She jerked the covers back and then gasped as the pain seemed to pounce. She had cleaned the house yesterday from top to bottom to pay him back and now she was paying for all the scrubbing and polishing and all the anger that had consumed her. When he came in for his supper he'd pretended not to notice the sparkling surfaces and sharply tidy rooms, but she'd seen his embarrassment. It wasn't enough, though, and she had slammed about and sulked all evening and they had gone to bed in a grim silence. She groaned, clenching her teeth, willing the pain to stop. She must not die until Joe got back so that she could tell him she was sorry.

She was aware of someone else in the room, of firm hands raising her head and removing the damp pillow. She fought to hold her eyes open. It was a stranger. Dark hair and eyes and a beard. Fearful, she tried to call out.

'Mrs Weaver.' The voice was gentle but firm. 'I'm Dr Thomas. I've just seen your husband and he told me what's happening. He's gone to fetch his Mother and won't be long. Now, can you tell me - '

She clutched at his arm. 'No, tell him. Please tell Joe. It was my fault. Tell him I'm sorry.'

The dark eyes looked startled for a moment, then he began speaking again and his voice was comforting, though she didn't hear exactly what he said. She was aware, too, of an accent...… unusual… Not from round here…

******

Hearing her name repeated Kate opened her eyes. She hoped it wasn't time to get up because she really didn't feel like it.

'Oh, Kate, love.' Joe's voice was shaky with relief so she smiled to reassure him and he put his arms round her.

There was fresh linen on the bed and she had on a clean nightgown. But it hadn't been a bad dream. She knew, deep within her body, what had happened.

She tried to hug Joe but found she had little strength. He had his face against her neck and was muttering about how sorry he was and how he hadn't meant to upset her so much.

'It's not your fault.' She thought she had told him that already. Her mind was still muddled. 'Joe, please don't think that.'

He drew back a little, hearing the anxiety in her voice.

'Doctor says you'll be fine when you've had a good long rest.' He paused and struggled for the right words. 'I'm afraid -– the baby - '

'I know,' she said quickly. 'Is the doctor still here?'

'No. Gone long since. You've been sleeping quite a while. He said he'll look back in this evening.'

'What's all that going to cost us?'

'Good God, woman, that doesn't matter. I'm just glad I bumped into him - he was cycling up the High Street with his black bag in the basket. He's Warner's new partner.'

Kate nodded, then struggled to sit up. 'Whatever time is it? What about your dinner?'

'You're not to worry about anything. Mother's here and she'll look after me and William.'

She looked at him sharply, not too ill to feel slightly annoyed at having his mother take over.

He hastened to add: 'And she said to be sure and tell you that we've sent to let Aunt Polly know, so she's bound to come up tomorrow.'

Kate smiled then at his mother's kindness and immediately felt close to tears.

******

Jane Weaver watched her son as he wiped a chunk of bread around his plate to mop up the last of the gravy. Though pleased to see her cooking appreciated she also disapproved of this evidence of a hearty appetite in Joe while his wife lay exhausted upstairs. She shifted the sleeping William to a more comfortable position in her lap and took a swallow of tea. Time for her own meal after she'd got him off about his work.

'Well now,' she said in a no-nonsense tone, 'are you going to tell me what's been going on, Joe?'

The sudden guilt in his glance reminded her sharply of his father. She sighed.

'Don't pretend you don't know what I mean. You've been downright shifty ever since I got here. What's been happening between you two?' An unexpected fear caught at her and her voice dropped to a whisper. 'You've never been knocking her about, Joe?'

He swore at her then and though she took him to task for his language his outrage was reassuring. Both he and Arthur could break out angrily at times but she'd never known either of them to be physically violent.

'I'm sorry, Mum, but you've no call to suggest that,' muttered Joe. He paused then went on more slowly. 'We've been arguing, that's all. Both of us said some harsh things.'

She looked at him steadily. 'Harsh words don't bring on a miscarriage, as you very well know.'

'Well, I was out all day yesterday and when I got back everything was spotless. And she was tired out and bad- tempered.'

Jane gave an angry snort. 'She must have worked like a slave. What

41

on earth made her turn to like that – and in her condition?'

'I'd got angry...… I told her she should spend more time looking after the house…'

As his mother drew in her breath with a hissing sound Joe pushed his plate away and stood up.

'Now I know how wicked that was, Mum. Kate may have her faults but being a poor housekeeper's not one of them. But I've made my peace with her, so it's not your business to say anything more.'

He made a great fuss over checking his cartridge case and she smiled openly at his broad back. He was like his father in that too -– ready enough to admit it if he was in the wrong, as long as that wrong could be quickly put out of mind. Well, she would have to get the full story some other way. There was more to all this than a silly quarrel and she was worried that something had come between Joe and Kate. She said goodbye absently, only half listening to his orders to take care of his wife and be sure to fetch him if he was needed. Even then he wouldn't leave until he had told her exactly where he would be on the estate that afternoon. She gave a sigh of relief as the door at last shut behind him and poured herself another cup of tea.

She knew how much he cared for Kate. In the early days of their courtship it had annoyed her to see the way his eyes followed the girl whenever she moved away from him. Hungry eyes. She had guessed from that and from the way Kate seemed to light up in Joe's presence, what they were to each other. At first she had felt resentful of the young woman who had so enthralled her son. But as time went on she had to admit that Kate had more about her than any other girl Joe had shown interest in. Her domestic skills couldn't be faulted but that was to be expected given her work. It was her intelligence and self-confidence that Jane came to admire. She confessed to her eldest daughter, Nell, that it was a treat to listen to Kate talking with Matthew Hersey about books and politics and the like. Nell hadn't found that particularly impressive but greatly admired the way Kate managed to look elegant in even the plainest clothes. But what won Jane's reluctant but solid regard was Kate's attitude to Joe. At the tea Mr and Mrs Summers had given when the couple announced their engagement Joe, under Mr Summers' sharp questions, had admitted that he didn't want to be a gamekeeper all his life.

'I'd like to be my own master one day,' he muttered and then reddened uncomfortably.

'Of course you will be,' Kate had said swiftly. 'You'd be wasted otherwise.'

Jane had felt her heartbeat quicken at the words and from then on was fully aware of Kate's worth. Of course she'd never let on: it wouldn't be good for a daughter-in-law — it might make her conceited.

William woke up and beamed at his grandmother. Here was another Weaver male, she thought, full of charm and stubborn along with it. No doubt difficult to handle and hopeless at seeing his own best interests. With growing anxiety she wondered if Kate was finding the task of guiding Joe, without letting him realise it, too difficult. The girl was strong-minded, yet such strength could be worn down — she knew that herself, who better? Gathering William closer Jane tried to think of what she could say to Kate to comfort her and help persuade her not to give up that task.

******

Kate buttoned her nightdress, watching Dr Thomas rinse his hands at the washstand. She thought idly that his hands were like Matthew's, long and rather bony. But they were gentle — had to be in his work, she supposed.

'How do you pronounce it, again?' she asked. 'The name of your home town?'

He laughed, turning towards her as he dried his hands. She reminded herself to make sure Joe's mother had burned all those other towels. She smiled at Dr Thomas, liking the way his eyes were creased up by the laugh.

'You'll never get your tongue round it, Mrs Weaver. And it's not a town, it's a very small village, exactly like a lot of other villages in the Rhondda.'

'A mining village, then.'

'Oh yes.' He looked more serious now. 'The mine governs our lives.'

His words made her curious for he didn't have the air of a man who had stayed all his life in one place.

'You were born there?'

He nodded. 'I went away to train and I worked in London for a time. But I couldn't settle in the city - had to go back.'

'It must have made your family very proud, to have you setting up practice in the community you'd come from.'

Dr Thomas folded the towel carefully, giving her an appreciative look.

'Yes, they were all pleased, my parents especially. They gave me tremendous support and I needed that. There was a lot that had to be changed, you see.'

'Changed?'

'It's a poor area and the standard of health is low. When I - ' He stopped abruptly. 'Now I mustn't start off on that or I'll be here all day and you need to rest.'

But he had caught her interest. 'I'd like to hear about it.'

'Another time.' He came and stood by the bed and absently pulled

43

the embroidered coverlet straight. 'There was something I wanted to ask you, Mrs Weaver.'

He looked down at her and she could see he was wondering how to put his question without upsetting her.

'What is it, Doctor?'

'When I came here earlier you said something -— you were barely conscious -— something about this being your fault.'

Kate froze, knowing now the direction of his thoughts. He drew up a chair and sat down so that his face was closer to hers.

'Anything you want to tell me, Mrs Weaver, will stay completely private but it would be sensible to - '

'I didn't deliberately try to get rid of the baby, Doctor,' she said quietly. 'To be completely honest I didn't really want a second child so soon and I've been angry with myself for forgetting to take precautions but I wouldn't have taken or used anything to get rid of it.'

He looked at her with new curiosity and asked what method of birth control she used. When she told him, he wanted to know what size cap she had, where she'd bought it and how long she'd been using it. Her answers seemed to satisfy him.

'You're a sensible woman, Mrs Weaver. One of the very few in this area, I shouldn't wonder.'

Kate shrugged. 'Most women don't know what they can use, even if they could afford it.'

They exchanged a wry look, then he got up to go, urging her to rest. Kate liked the way he had treated her as an intelligent adult and not as a child who had to be reassured. He was a great improvement on Dr Warner.

Joe put his head round the door, asking if the doctor would like some tea. He refused, saying he was in a hurry but then, to Kate's amusement, he lingered suggesting that she try getting up in a day or so.

'But you're not to do anything,' he warned. 'Just rest.' He nodded towards the shelves by the bed. 'Make yourself comfortable with a book. I couldn't help noticing you've got a fine selection.'

'They should be in the parlour but we didn't have room for the bookcase after we'd got the piano in,' said Joe. 'Most of the books belong to my wife but the pamphlets are mine.'

Kate smiled to herself. The pamphlets had all been given to him by Matthew -— Joe was showing off.

Dr Thomas was scanning the titles. 'You're interested in radical reform?' His tone was eager, hopeful.

'We're both Socialists,' said Kate firmly and the doctor gave a delighted laugh.

'I can't tell you how refreshing it is to come across the pair of you. I've been here two months with Dr Warner and after the Rhondda it's like stepping into a different world.'

Joe put in, 'You must have known that this part of the country is hardly famous for fomenting revolution!'

'You're right. But I needed to get far away from Wales and I needed a job.' Dr Thomas smiled. 'And although we may not foment revolution I hope we can talk about it, Mr Weaver?'

'You must come to supper when Kate's better,' said Joe. 'It'll liven her up to talk politics with you. With luck Matty — er, Mr Hersey from up at the Hall — he'll be home soon and you'll meet him. Now he's one who does more than talk......'

The two men wandered out, deep in discussion. Kate lay back, closing her eyes and feeling more cheerful. The new doctor was an unusual man and with luck would prove an interesting acquaintance.

******

Polly took off her hat, stabbed the long pin back into it and laid it on the bed. Then she kissed Kate on both cheeks and gave her a brisk hug.

'You have been a silly girl,' she said.

Kate found she was near to tears. Dr Thomas had said this was a natural reaction to what had happened but the surges of emotion still took her by surprise. 'I'm so pleased to see you, Aunty,' she whispered.

'Now, come along.' Polly's voice also shook for a moment but she quickly got it under control. 'You'll be seeing more than enough of me, you know. I'm sending Sam Bundy back with the car as soon as he's had his dinner.'

The firm set of her Aunt's mouth told Kate the full story. Arnold Summers hadn't wanted his wife to come, so she'd given him the impression that she would only stay for the day. But doubtless a small suitcase had been smuggled into the car, perhaps with young Sam's help, and a message would go back to Mr Summers that the visit would be prolonged. Of course he wouldn't take his wife's defiance well, and there'd be recriminations when Polly eventually returned to Brighton but she obviously felt it was worth the trouble to be with Kate. For as long as Kate could remember, Polly had been forced to do the accounts of her personal life in this way; to weigh the effects of her husband's criticism or opposition against the importance of whatever it was she wanted to do.

Polly was saying something about sleeping in William's room. Kate jerked her mind back to the present.

'No, you must go next door, Aunty.'

'Mrs Weaver has that room, surely?'

45

Kate said that Joe's mother would be off home now but Polly wouldn't hear of it.

'You mustn't send her away, Kate; it would seem so ungrateful. You'd all three have been in poor straits without her.'

'I know,' Kate admitted, 'but she makes me feel uncomfortable. I call her Mother for Joe's sake but I don't find it easy.'

'Perhaps she's not at ease with you, dear. And that might well be your fault.'

The subject of Mrs Weaver was set aside and Polly proceeded to pass on her own news. First, though, there were Edith's messages, full of loving anxiety, and the gifts she had sent. While Kate untied the small parcels Polly produced from her bag she listened to her Aunt's account of Edith's progress with her university scheme.

'She keeps dropping hints to your Uncle, talking about young women from good families who are at university. He's not too quick at following her ideas but you know how he loves to hear her chatter and so he just sits there nodding and she's convinced he's taking it all in and will be perfectly amenable when she asks him outright on her own account.'

Kate unfolded a pretty, rose-scented handkerchief and showed it to her Aunt, who smiled.

'What do you think he'll say, Aunty?'

There was a sigh.

'I don't believe Edith realises how rigid her father can be. He's indulged her in the past but then she's never really crossed him. I know he wants her to stay at home until she marries. He's never been comfortable about her friendship with Matthew but he knows they're not as close as they used to be and so he's happy enough to let that continue because he thinks it takes Edith into the world of the aristocracy.'

Kate eyed her next gift - a tract entitled 'The Importance of the Vote' - then glanced up at Polly. 'So he wants a bridegroom from the gentry for Edith?'

'I'm afraid that's the way his mind is working. When he finds out what Edith's planning he'll be very disturbed.'

Kate put the pamphlet on the bedside table. She had hated her Uncle's bullying tone and the way he would use her own words against her, mocking her. She hoped Edith would manage better.

Polly changed the subject. Had Kate heard about the deputation of Suffragettes to Parliament and the arrests that followed? Clara Riseborough had been among those taken in custody.

'She was released at once,' said Polly, 'but she wrote that it was a horrible experience. Edith thinks she's a great heroine, which she is of course,

46

but - '

Kate smiled. 'I know what you mean.'

There was a light knock on the door and Jane came in with a tray.

'I thought you'd like something to eat up here, Mrs Summers,' she said. Her tone was uneasy yet polite. 'And that Mr Bundy is ready to go, if you've a message to send with him.'

Polly rose. 'I'd better come down, but do leave the tray here, Mrs Weaver. I'll be back in a moment.' She gave Kate a sharp look.

'Mother,' Kate said when Polly had gone, 'my Aunt would like to stay for a day or so. Will that make a lot of extra work for you?'

Jane folded her hands in her apron and looked at Kate suspiciously.

'But you won't want me here now Mrs Summers has come.'

'Oh, I will!' Kate's voice rose anxiously. 'You've looked after us so well and I know it's good for William to have you here.' She found unexpectedly that she meant what she said and she gave a weak smile. 'Do stay until I'm well again, if you can. It'll be such a weight off my mind.'

Joe's mother blinked and her round face filled with surprise.

'Well,' she said slowly, 'I'm glad if I can be of some help......'

The two women exchanged wary glances. Kate felt they had reached some kind of understanding and accepted that it would never be put into words between them. She sighed with relief and allowed Jane to rearrange the shawl about her shoulders and plump up her pillows.

A series of mild explosions from outside announced Sam Bundy's departure in the car and Jane moved to the bedroom window to watch.

'You know he's walking out with our Flo?' she murmured.

'Yes. He seems a very decent young man,' said Kate. 'My Aunt was saying that Mr Summers will have to hire a proper chauffeur soon as the haberdashery department doesn't run so smoothly when Sam's away. Apparently customers ask for him in person.'

Jane seemed well satisfied. 'That business is growing, so I hear. I suppose our Flo could do a lot worse.'

When Polly came back she had brought an extra teacup. 'William's still having his nap, so we can all have tea together. Mrs Weaver, will you pour out?'

It was like a drawing room party, Kate thought. The two older women settled themselves on chairs on either side of the bed and tea was poured, sandwiches passed and gossip exchanged. Polly took pains to draw Jane out on the subject of her children and was regaled with the latest news of Arthur, Nell and Flo. Of the last there was much to be said. Aunt Polly greatly approved of the attachment between Flo and Sam.

'He's doing very well for himself. His family lives in London, not well off but very respectable. They're Quakers, you know.'

There followed some debate on the philosophy of Quakers and Kate found herself joining in with enthusiasm. She was feeling stronger now.

The conversation tailed off as more tea was poured.

Uncomfortable with the silence Jane found a subject to fill the gap.

'I've heard Mrs Halfpenny wants to sell up her store in the village,' she said. 'Do you know the place, Mrs Summers?'

Polly nodded. She had shopped there once or twice on her way to visit Kate and Joe.

Kate found the words spilling out in a rush. 'It's a lovely little business. I wanted us to buy it, but Joe wouldn't listen to the idea.'

Jane gave a grunt of satisfaction. The puzzle had been solved, but she said nothing. Polly was not so reticent. 'Good heavens, Kate, that would be a huge change.'

Kate leaned forward eagerly and began to repeat the arguments she had used on Joe but quietly and firmly now.

'Of course money was the real problem,' she concluded. 'I made the mistake of suggesting that we ask Arthur to help. That upset Joe's pride, I think, though it might not have done if the idea had been his own.' She glanced at her mother-in-law who pulled a long face in agreement.

'So then I made matters worse by saying we might borrow from Uncle Arnold.' This time it was Polly who made the face but before she could speak Kate added: 'I wouldn't really want to take his money. I think I said that to goad Joe. I was - well, annoyed with him.'

She looked at her Aunt and at Jane. Polly was frowning, deep in thought. Joe's mother seemed to be intent on her tea. But then she put the cup down and looked squarely at Kate.

'Well, it's a pity you made a muddle of it, for I think it's a fine idea,' she said. 'I know Joe's a good gamekeeper but I'd as soon see him in some other job. His father started off fit enough but out all weathers and often at night...... it did him no good. He hadn't the strength to fight his illness when it came.' She paused and gave an approving nod. 'A little shop... well, that's comfortable and steady.'

She glanced at Polly as though expecting some contradiction but Polly had her eyes thoughtfully on Kate.

'You've really set your heart on this, dear?'

'Oh yes.' Reminded again that it was all too late, Kate found her voice shaking.

'I agree with all Mrs Weaver says,' Polly went on, reaching out to touch Kate's hand in a soothing gesture. 'But I certainly think it would be wrong for you to approach your Uncle for a loan. However, I might be able

48

to persuade him. Let me talk to him.'

Kate suddenly felt cold. 'Oh no, Aunty, I don't want you begging for us.' Polly flushed and Kate took her Aunt's hand into her own and gripped it tightly. 'He'd use it against you,' she said urgently. 'You mustn't. Please say you won't!'

It was Jane who broke the awkward silence. 'I'll have a word with Arthur,' she said in speculative tones.

Exhaustion overtook Kate. She lay back against the pillows feeling drained.

'You're both being very kind, but there's no point, Joe has said we can't even consider the idea.'

'My goodness me!' Jane rose briskly and began to collect the cups and plates. 'You mustn't give up so easily. He wouldn't be the first man in the world to change his mind.'

******

Joe climbed gingerly into bed beside Kate and when she turned automatically to rest against his shoulder he held her as though she was a piece of fine china.

'I won't break,' she grumbled, and felt him tighten his grasp warily.

'You're sure Aunt Polly will be all right in William's room?' Kate murmured.

'Good Lord, I should think so. My Mum's made up the bed like we've got royalty sleeping there. I caught her taking the quilt off her own bed and most of the pillows.'

'I hope you stopped her.'

'Have you tried stopping Mum when she's got her heart set on something?'

Kate snuggled closer against him and felt him relax at last.

'What do you make of the new doctor, Kate?'

'I like him. He told me where he comes from, but I can't say it.' She yawned. 'Is there a Mrs Thomas?'

'I don't think so. I wonder why he had to get away from Wales?'

'Is that what he said? Oh yes...'

Joe grunted. 'We had quite a long chat. He's a great one for politics. His family has known some hard times - strikes and such.'

Kate mumbled sleepily and Joe eased her into a more comfortable position. Then, unexpectedly, he gave a loud laugh.

'What is it?' she demanded.

'I asked Michael Thomas what he thought about Lloyd George and he said he wished we'd got the old devil on our side, fancy women and all. I reckon he's right.'

49

'Do you now?' She was roused to retaliate. 'Lloyd George relies on the Labour MPs and the Irish to get what he wants, but he takes all the credit. He'll use our people as long as it suits him but he won't give us anything in return.'

'No, but you wouldn't expect him to, would you?' said Joe in practical tones. 'This is politics, not chivalry.'

He sensed her growing annoyance then and quickly cast round for a less controversial subject.

'I wish I knew what my Mum and your Aunt are cooking up between them. When I came in tonight they'd got their heads together over the kitchen table, thick as thieves.' He laughed again, but softer now. 'And the old cat was sitting on the window sill between them, looking on, as if she was in on it too.'

Kate softened, lying warm against him. 'I expect they were just chatting. It's nice that they get on well together, isn't it?'

******

Joe offered Polly his arm from the kitchen door to where the car stood waiting at the gate. Kate would have walked with them but a light drizzle had begun and so they shooed her back into the house, where she watched from the window with Joe's mother and William.

Before reaching the gate Polly paused. Sam Bundy was no longer the chauffeur and she didn't want this new man to overhear.

'I'm sorry to be leaving so soon but Kate's up and about now and will be able to take over from your mother before long. I couldn't, in all conscience, delay going home any longer.'

He said nothing but they both knew she would not be received warmly by her husband. The note that came with the car had caused Polly to redden and bite her lip before consigning it to the fire in the range and hurriedly begin packing her few belongings. Her punishment had started with Sam's removal as her driver. One less friendly face about her.

Joe tried to say he hoped that she wouldn't get into too much trouble for staying with them but she knew it was difficult for him to find the right words and she shook her head, to silence him.

'I'm glad Kate has recovered so quickly - physically at least. Though she seems a little low in spirits still, don't you think, Joe?'

He frowned anxiously.

'Do your best to help cheer her up,' Polly went on. 'I'll send Edith over to visit you both.' And when Joe's eyebrows rose in surprise she added ruefully, 'Oh, once I'm home she will be released.'

Joe bit back an angry comment and instead bent to kiss Polly's cheek.

'Yes, send Edie, she'll do Kate a world of good,' he said. 'And come back yourself, as soon as you can.'

Long after the car had gone Kate stayed at the window looking out. Joe, lingering in the garden to repair one of the white fence posts, saw his wife's pensive face and gave her a cheerful wave. She pressed her hand against the window in vague acknowledgement. Her Aunt's departure and the manner of her going had distressed Kate, for she felt sad at being the cause of more trouble between Polly and Arnold Summers. For the first time since her childhood she found herself wishing that he might die and leave Polly, Edith and herself in peace.

Then she shook off the hatred. That was only part of her distress. However sorry she might be for Polly she was doubly sorry for herself and this frightened her. It was as though the frustration she had experienced before the miscarriage had soured away into a selfish misery that dragged heavily on her. Sometimes she was able to regain her old spirits and then she felt the weight lift and vanish. But it always returned. She moved away from the window with a shudder, wondering how long it would be before she was properly well again.

In the days that followed, Joe's anxiety about her also became apparent. He went out of his way to create a happy atmosphere in the house and she found him eager to do whatever she wanted - to finish any jobs his mother had not tackled, to talk with Kate on any and every subject, to entertain her and Jane with a sing-song at the parlour piano... And all the while Kate would see the concern behind his easy manner and ready laughter and she wished that she could respond in a way that would please him. But she could never be light-hearted for long.

She knew Dr Thomas wasn't entirely happy with her progress. Encouraged by Joe he came often to the house when his evening surgery was finished and proved an easy visitor, just as content to talk seriously about books or politics as he was to gossip over some small item of village news or lend his surprisingly deep bass to some musical endeavour. Yet Kate saw that he watched her too, concerned about her low moods.

Jane didn't mention the shop again and Kate tried hard to put the idea out of her mind completely. Nothing could come of hopeless wishing. But when her thoughts did stray in that direction she felt sick with frustration, knowing she could have run the business well and made a success of it.

Two weeks after Kate was on her feet again Jane announced that she would return home. Kate's initial sense of shock at the thought of managing on her own once more was quickly replaced by a despondent acceptance.

'Perhaps it will stop me moping, once all my time is occupied again,' she told Joe doubtfully.

He seemed heartened by the thought. Determined to create a

cheerful atmosphere he decided they would take his mother home in style, by horse and cart, and have a picnic with the rest of the family. Even Kate found herself cheered by the idea of an outing in the warm July weather and it was in a lively mood that they set off from the cottage on the following Sunday. Jane Weaver, her best black hat set squarely on her head, sat up beside Joe while Kate and William were made comfortable behind them on rugs and cushions. To mark the occasion Kate had put on the blue dress, trimmed with fawn silk, which she had made specially for William's christening.

The smithy was on the other side of the village so Joe took them on the back lane below the church fields. Kate saw that since the day she had hurried out to buy black lead and flour the Summer had advanced. The trees hung heavy and green-brown over the lane and the hedges were now thick with flowers.

'I might try making honeysuckle wine this year, Joe,' she called out. 'We've enough blossoms round the cottage.'

He glanced back and laughed. 'As long as it's weaker than your parsnip!'

Kate patted the basket at her side. 'I've put the last two bottles of that in here for Arthur. I know he likes it.'

Jane's rigid shoulders registered disapproval.

As the cart reached the smithy Flo came rushing out of the cottage next door to meet them. Kate saw the girl had abandoned the pink dress and was wearing a simple blouse and skirt. Her hair was dressed simply too and the general effect was pretty and pleasing. Nell came next, walking sedately down the path with her thin, wiry husband, Tom. Arthur was lurking just inside the doorway, red-faced and uncomfortable in a collar.

Kate found herself smiling as usual at the physical likeness between the two brothers, the golden hair and sharp, blue eyes and wide, charming mouth. But the similarity didn't extend beyond looks: Arthur was a slow, deliberate and shy man, but no fool for all that and Kate admired his steadiness. Now she noticed that he had on a new jacket and an equally new pair of boots and she found herself thinking sadly that he'd obviously done well this year and might have loaned them the money for the shop if Joe hadn't been too proud to ask.

Quickly she shook off those thoughts, handed William down to the excited Flo and allowed Joe to help her out of the cart. Jane, meanwhile, embraced her eldest daughter, looking hard at Nell's big, but well-proportioned figure. Kate guessed she was searching for signs of pregnancy as she'd done ever since Nell's marriage three years ago. None were apparent. Consequently Tom Green was greeted coolly as usual. By this time Arthur had ventured out on to the path and Kate, with sudden mischief, caused his red face to turn an even deeper shade by giving him a hug and a kiss on the cheek.

In the parlour Sam Bundy was pouring glasses of lemonade.

'We thought you'd like to refresh yourself, Mother, before we set off for the picnic,' said Nell, handing round the glasses. Kate liked her easy manner: Nell never seemed flustered or upset. At one time Kate had been puzzled as to how she had ever come to marry her skinny farm labourer with so little to say for himself. But she soon realised that Tom, whose pointed features seemed constantly to hover just behind his wife's right shoulder, was not only gentle and kind-hearted but believed Nell to be perfect in every way and was quite content to have her run his life for him. Nell could have gone further and fared worse.

While the others were chatting Kate drew Sam to one side.

'You're not driving my Aunt at all, now?'

'No. I was told Mr Mitcham had been taken on to do that so I'm back in haberdashery for good.' He gave a cheery smile. 'That doesn't bother me, though I'm sorry I shan't be seeing so much of Mrs Summers or Miss Edith.'

His obvious loyalty to her Aunt pleased Kate. Flo was lucky in her choice.

Eventually the gossip was halted, the lemonade consumed and the party set out for Ruckford Mill. This time Arthur took the reins, with Tom up beside him and the women, William and the picnic baskets in the cart, while Joe and Sam followed on their bicycles.

'Tell Mother and Kate your news, Flo,' urged Nell, unfurling a pretty parasol for all to admire.

Flo blushed, then blurted out that the Gales had finished buying and furnishing a house in London and would be moving in when they returned from a holiday abroad.

'And I'm to go there as parlour maid,' she gasped, still only half believing her luck.

Kate smiled at her. 'My goodness, you have got on well, Flo.'

Jane restricted herself to an approving pat on Flo's arm, but her face glowed with pride.

'Mr Pearson heard that Sir James offered Mr Matthew to live with them once the house is open,' said Flo. 'Apparently he just thanked Sir James very kindly but said it wasn't convenient for the East End where he's going to be a teacher.'

Nell sighed. 'Oh, it does seem a shame. Such a nice young gentleman having to work in such a horrible sort of place.'

'He doesn't have to - he wants to,' her mother told her sharply. 'And a very good thing too.'

'I can't believe I'm going to see London at last,' breathed Flo and Kate raised her head and smiled at the girl. She began telling her of places to visit in the city and what she might do on her days off.

'Drury Lane and the Royal Court,' she sighed, 'I used to save up to go. I saw *Major Barbara...*'

'That's nice,' said Flo politely, 'but I think I'll get Sam to take me to a music hall.'

Jane positively swelled with disapproval and for the rest of the journey there was a caustic lecture on the folly of spending hard-earned money on trivial activities. Nell and Kate tried to avoid each other's eyes and hide their smiles.

The party gathered on the grass near the mill pond, spread rugs and tablecloths and proceeded to enjoy the contents of the picnic baskets. When the food was eaten Flo and Sam wandered off together and as the other menfolk seemed intent on lighting up their pipes Kate and Nell decided to go for a stroll.

'Tom won't stir now until it's time to go,' said Nell. 'He gets so tired, out in the fields till all hours.'

They wandered over to the edge of the pond and looked across it at the mill and the house next to it. In the garden two little girls in clean white smocks were standing up against the fence, watching the picnic party. Kate waved to them and the girls giggled shyly and then waved back.

As the women walked on Nell said: 'Flo tells me Miss Edith has joined the Suffragettes. I hoped she wasn't arrested down in London?'

Kate was amused. 'Oh no. She supports them but she doesn't go to any of their meetings and she certainly wouldn't be allowed to join a deputation. But my Aunt's friend, Mrs Riseborough, was among the women arrested at the House of Commons.'

Nell looked interested and Kate explained that the women had been exercising their right as citizens to petition parliament on the vote issue. 'So Asquith was breaking the law himself by refusing to receive their deputation.'

Nell snorted. 'He'd not care about that, from what I've heard. Oh, it makes me so angry to think of decent women being shut up in prison.' She frowned at Kate. 'They're brave creatures, don't you think? I couldn't do it.'

'I'm not sure. Yes... perhaps.'

Jane watched the two women standing arm-in-arm, deep in conversation. 'Kate's been looking a lot more cheerful today,' she observed to Joe then added, firmly, 'That young woman needs something to take her mind off what's happened.'

Joe sighed. 'The doctor reckons it's too soon after the miscarriage for her to start another baby.'

'Oh Joe, that's not what I meant,' she snapped. 'It was probably too soon for her to have a second child anyway, with William so young. You should have thought of that. It's your responsibility.'

He gave an embarrassed smirk and was rewarded with a stern look.

'Now Joe, I want you to reconsider this idea of buying Betty Halfpenny's business.'

He flushed angrily but before he could speak she said quickly, 'Yes, Kate told me, but only in passing when I happened to mention that the shop was for sale. And you wouldn't even think about it! Now that's downright silly and you know it.'

She saw obstinacy replace his anger. 'Mother, we know nothing about running a shop. We'd make a mess of it and be left even worse off.'

'You're blind as well as stupid if you can't see that you've got the sort of wife who'll make a success of anything she tackles. Our Nell's like that too, only she's not likely to get the opportunity to make something of herself and her husband, more's the pity.'

'Well, I'm not like Tom Green! Do you want to see me running round at my wife's heels, acting as though she passes wine instead of water?'

'Joe!' His mother glared at him and he gave an apologetic grunt. She smoothed her hands across her lap and went on in a softer tone. 'Of course I don't want you to be like that. You're the man of the house, naturally. But I reckon you and your wife can work together.'

Joe shrugged. 'We haven't anywhere near enough money saved to buy out Mrs Halfpenny, so that's it and all about it.'

'You think it over again, Joe Weaver,' his mother advised. 'Money can generally be found for what you really want. Before you start going over all the reasons why you shouldn't do it, just think what it would mean to Kate if you do decide to buy the shop. She'd soon be back to her old self again.'

She said no more but turned away from him to dispose of an insect which was pestering William. From the corner of her eye she could see Joe frowning thoughtfully. He wasn't a petty man, she thought. He'd soon come round.

******

Kate lingered upstairs after putting William to bed and leaned out of his bedroom window, looking along the track towards the lane. The cat was stalking something in the grass by the hedge and Kate watched the delicate movements absently, while behind her William grunted and gurgled in his cot.

A good day and a happy one, she thought, though Joe had seemed preoccupied on the journey home. Perhaps, like the rest of them, he had just felt tired. The little girls in the mill cottage garden had long been called in for bed by the time the picnic party started back. Arthur had finished all the parsnip wine and, while Tom drove the cart, he sang and the others joined in.

Her eyes prickled with unexpected tears. Despite the pleasure of the day she felt discontent come upon her once more. She groaned and turned away from the window to hurry downstairs and occupy herself with something, anything, to keep from thinking. Joe was pottering about in the garden, but was bound to be in soon wanting a cup of tea.

The scullery door opened with a crash and Joe appeared carrying a basket of honeysuckle blossom. Kate stared in amazement as he put it on the kitchen table.

'What's this?'

'Well, you said you wanted to make honeysuckle wine, so I've just picked this for you.' He gave a beam of pleasure at his own forethought but all Kate could see was smugness in his face.

'You could have saved yourself the trouble!' she said coldly. 'I've changed my mind - I don't want it.' And she opened the tea caddy with a snap and ground the spoon down into the tea. Joe thrust a now aggressive face across the table at his wife.

'Do you know how long it's taken me to pick that lot?' he snapped. 'And now you say you don't want it?'

She scraped the spoon round the caddy, scowling. 'I didn't ask you to pick it.'

'Damn, I was trying to help!' He ran one hand through his hair, his anger tinged now with desperation. He stared at Kate and shook his head as if his wife was turning into a stranger before his eyes. She gave an infuriated cry and pushed the caddy away, scattering tea across the table.

'Oh, very well, I'll make the dratted wine!' She grabbed the basket and swung it towards her, showering honeysuckle on to the floor where one of the dogs sniffed at it hopefully.

Joe opened his mouth to roar out his frustration, but Kate's own howl of misery held him silent. Then she burst into tears, crying out that she was sorry and hearing the fear in her own voice.

'I don't know what's wrong with me,' she gasped out as he hugged her. 'One minute I feel happy enough, and then the next - '

'Hush, hush. You're tired,' he whispered but she could hear that he was frightened too. She forced herself to be calm and in a while detached herself from his embrace.

'Help me pick this up,' she said with a shaky smile, indicating the honeysuckle on the floor. 'I'll steep it overnight.'

His sigh of relief was painful to her.

******

56

'Well, I'm glad Joe's taken Matty off with him for a while. Now we can be comfortable.'

Edith sat back in the armchair and swung her feet on to the low stool in front of her, smoothing the folds of her skirt. She had changed her style in clothes. There were no rich lace trimmings, no trailing scarves. Instead Edith had arrived today in a severe, high-necked, white silk blouse and a plain, dark green skirt. A simple, broad-brimmed hat in light green straw had been removed to reveal the fair curls pinned firmly back off the face. Kate assumed that Edith was somehow attempting to show her father, and anyone else interested, the seriousness of her intent.

'I thought the atmosphere was strained,' Kate remarked, putting William down on the rug. 'Did you and Matty quarrel on the journey here?'

Edith was silent for a moment, looking at William as he laboriously pulled himself upright against his mother's chair only to slither down again, a frustrated little heap of crisp, white cotton.

'First of all he asked why I'd got myself up like an office worker,' she said at last.

Knowing what was expected of her, Kate tutted. She watched her son heave himself to his feet again.

'The fact that he's known me for so long doesn't give him the right to criticise what I wear,' Edith added hotly. 'Anyway, why should I always be in frills just to suit people like him?'

'You look very smart,' said Kate and Edith seemed soothed. William began to edge his way hesitantly round Kate's chair and the two women witnessed this new skill with approval. When he lost his balance and tottered, Kate caught him and placed him on the rug again. He considered his new location for a moment, while the crisp cotton grew somewhat limp, and then he began his expedition all over again.

Edith turned her attention back to Kate. 'And then we started arguing about the WSPU. Oh, he's all in favour of the vote and he positively worships Sylvia Pankhurst, but he hardly has a good word to say for Christabel.' Edith sat forward suddenly and her face lit up. 'Kate, I had a letter from Christabel recently, urging me to take every advantage of a university education! I'd written to her, you see, explaining my situation. I was so delighted that she had time to write back.'

Wondering exactly what impression of her 'situation' Edith had given, Kate said, 'Yes, that was kind of her. But don't you approve of the other Miss Pankhurst?'

'Yes, of course,' said Edith quickly. 'It's just that Matty was making so much fuss... Oh, they're all splendid people. I wish I could be active in the movement!' Then she laughed. 'But you can imagine how Father would react.

I'll have to wait until I'm at university.'

'I'm sure Matty approves of that scheme.'

'Yes, thank goodness, though he keeps saying I shouldn't be too disappointed if Father won't agree. Mother says the same thing. It's so pessimistic!'

'You think you'll be able to persuade him, Edie?'

The girl dismissed the problem with a gesture of her slim hands, then took her feet off the stool and stood up.

'I'd forgotten, there's a letter for you from Mother - all very secret! To be handed to you when Joe wasn't about.' She went to fetch her handbag from the table. 'I think it's to do with your shop plan.'

She thrust the letter at Kate, urging her to read it at once and then dropped down on the rug and tickled William's chin. Kate drew out a single sheet of paper, covered with Polly's close, neat handwriting. After enquiries about Kate's health her Aunt came quickly to the point.

"I have approached your Uncle about the possibility of a loan. I did not mention what the money was required for; perhaps I should have had some plausible reason ready. At all events he immediately assumed it was for my own purposes and refused outright. I am so sorry, my dear. However, I'm not without resources and I shall be able to advance you and Joe the money. I do hope that with the financial side of the matter no longer a problem you will more easily be able to persuade him into reconsidering the idea. It might be wise to speak to his mother on the matter. She is a most sensible woman, as I'm sure you realise by now, and has your interests very much at heart. Assure Joe, when you do broach the subject, that this is a loan and can be paid back over what period he chooses. If you are able to come to a decision while Edith is staying with you then she can bring back your answer."

Kate looked up and passed the letter to Edith, who read it through swiftly then folded it with a sigh.

'What's been happening?' Kate's manner was abrupt and Edith looked uncomfortable.

'I didn't know anything about this until I heard Father shouting at Mother one evening in his study.' She blushed suddenly. 'He was angrier than usual, Kate.'

'Was Aunty upset?'

'She came to my room later and she was perfectly composed, the way she usually is. She must have realised I'd heard the shouting and she told me why she'd asked him for money.' Edith smiled, hoping to relieve the tension. 'I think it's a fine idea, Kate.'

Kate ignored the comment and nodded towards the letter.

'But if he refused, how can she say now that she'll lend us the money?'

Edith thought for a moment. 'I suppose she could borrow from somebody else; Clara Riseborough, perhaps. Oh, don't look like that - they're good friends.'

'But I don't want Aunty borrowing from anyone on my account.'

'She could be selling some of her jewelry, I suppose.'

'No, she mustn't.'

Edith laughed. 'Heavens, it's frightful stuff. You know what appalling taste Father has.'

She looked up, saw the stubborn set of Kate's mouth and leaned forward eagerly. 'If Mother can raise the money you must take it, Kate. I only wish I could help.' She sighed. 'I'll be a very rich woman some day, according to Father. Pity I can't get my hands on some of it now.'

'Well, I'll not touch a penny that comes from him, however indirectly,' said Kate firmly.

She fetched paper, pen and ink from the sideboard and soon the reply to Polly was written and Edith had reluctantly tucked it into the depths of her handbag. She watched as Kate cleared the writing things away and guessed that despite her apparently strong resolve it had taken some effort to refuse Polly's offer.

Lifting William into her arms and planting a kiss on top of his silky fair hair Edith cried cheerfully, 'Now come and sit down again, Kate, and tell me all about this Dr Michael Thomas. He's coming today, isn't he? I'm longing to meet him.'

******

Joe went off to unload his gun and Matthew sat down beside Kate on one of the chairs set out on the lawn. He leaned back, his eyes on Edith who was walking William alongside a flower bed. She held both his hands so that he could walk without falling but he was eager to reach out and grasp the flowers and was struggling to get free.

'Did you go along to the rookery?' asked Kate, looking up from the bowl of peas she was shelling, and Matthew nodded.

'The fields are full of buttercups; it's all green and gold as far as you can see.'

'And the woods are cool and slightly gloomy.'

They exchanged smiles, but his soon faded. She sat quiet, waiting for him to speak.

'I've been desperate to get away from London,' he said. 'Looking forward to this day in the country.'

And now Edith's coolness had marred it for him, she thought.

'Well, it's lovely to see you again, Matty. You're always a welcome visitor.'

The warm reassurance in her voice seemed to ease him. When he spoke again he was brisk and cheerful.

'Joe's been telling me about this shop idea. I'm on your side, Kate. I think it would be the right thing for both of you.'

She listened to him carefully. It seemed that Joe had been scornful of the image of himself as shopkeeper, making up packets of tea and slicing cheese for the old ladies of the village.

'I told him it's a worthwhile occupation, not to be looked down on,' Matthew went on, 'and I reminded him that when you move into trade you move into an area of some influence. Well, look at your Uncle, Kate - the good burghers of Brighton pay a lot of attention to what he says. It's only a pity he's a Liberal.'

'Michael Thomas thinks Joe should be on the parish council,' Kate agreed regretfully. It was good of Matty to have spoken so frankly to Joe, but she didn't need to ask what the response had been.

The sun was hot now and Matthew asked if Kate would mind him taking off his jacket. She frowned as he rolled back his shirt sleeves.

'You're very thin,' she said.

'Oh, I eat well enough, but London's not a healthy place to live in, at least not where I am. We're all a pale-looking lot. I try to get up to one of the parks every Sunday to see some trees and a bit of grass.'

'And your teaching?'

His face immediately lit up. 'It's very different when you're actually doing it, Kate: different from what they try to tell you in the training. My class is a really mixed group. Some very clever children, others slow, others downright stupid it seems! It's wonderful when the clever ones quickly grasp what you're telling them and get on with their work and get it right; but when you finally get through to the others and help them understand something they didn't understand before... Well, that's the finest feeling imaginable.'

'Oh, it must be,' Kate beamed. It was good to see him happy for the first time that day.

'I wanted to tell Edith what I've told you,' said Matthew, drily, 'but somehow we didn't get round to it. I always seem to say the wrong thing.'

Kate glanced at his gloomy face and quickly changed the subject. 'What about your lodgings? You were pretty disgusted with them when we last saw you.'

Edith and William settled themselves by the hedge, picking daisies. Matthew put his head back and squinted upwards into the tree above them.

'Oh, I'm wonderfully comfortable now. Edith's mother wrote to Clara Riseborough and within a week that well-organised lady had whisked me off to excellent rooms in a very respectable household.' He lowered his head suddenly. 'I can't see.'

'Your eyes are dazzled by the sun.' She finished the peas and put the bowl on the grass. Matthew rubbed his eyes and Kate looked at him with amused concern.

'Tell me about this respectable household, Matty. Do you feel at home there?'

'Are you mocking me? It's run by a widowed lady who cooks almost as well as you, though without your inspiration. The other two lodgers are young gentlemen in the lower ranks of the legal profession, I think. It's a bit like something out of Dickens.' Matthew raised his head. Though watery, his eyes were mischievous. 'And there's a daughter, Kate.'

'Indeed?'

'Indeed. Both she and her mother support the WSPU and the daughter is very active in the movement.' He wiped his eyes and explained that he had recently helped with the printing of a pamphlet on the vote issue. 'Written by Miss Wilson - that's the daughter - and very well written too. It's just for distribution locally among women who might be interested in joining the movement but she and her friends took great care with the production of it. I helped with an old press they'd got the use of. And I really enjoyed it,' he went on reflectively, putting his handkerchief away. 'The women were all at ease with each other, happy in each other's company and somehow I felt included in that. I felt their strength too... very different from male strength. I think I envied it.'

He looked quizzically at Kate who smiled thoughtfully.

'You should certainly tell Edith that,' she said.

'Yes, I intended to but we started arguing about Christabel Pankhurst and somehow the opportunity was lost.'

Kate pulled a face and Matthew sighed.

'Joe says Edith rides roughshod over me,' he said and Kate gave a snort of laughter.

'There's the pot calling the kettle black!'

They looked at each other in surprise, aware that they were both being unusually candid.

'He'd never deliberately hurt you, Kate,' said Matthew with sudden urgency. Kate shrugged, wondering how on earth he could be so sure of that, but all she said was, 'I know Joe has a poor opinion of Edith. He thinks she's spoilt.'

'She's fussed over, perhaps, but that's not surprising with such a doting father,' Matthew smiled. 'Even you and your Aunt join forces to shield her from anything unpleasant.'

61

Kate shrugged, feeling embarrassed now. He suddenly sounded patronising, talking about Edith like this and she was about to make a critical retort when she heard him draw a sharp breath. He was watching Edith as she knelt beside William in the grass and at that moment she turned her head in their direction. Edith's curls had broken free of their restraining combs and tumbled about her face which was pink and smiling. Matthew sighed softly and Kate looked away, saddened by the pain in his eyes.

******

Michael Thomas, when he arrived, immediately set himself to be amusing and Kate thought he took a certain manipulative pleasure in making them all respond to him. This aspect of his character interested but did not surprise her. While the others made themselves comfortable under the tree she sat a little apart from them, holding William in her lap and giving him sips from her lemonade glass. Her mind kept returning to Polly's letter and she wondered if it would have worked out as her Aunt had hoped - that Joe would have agreed to buy the shop if there was no immediate financial barrier. Judging by his complaints to Matthew it seemed unlikely.

'What do you think, Kate?'

Edith was looking round at her expectantly. Kate apologised for not listening and Edith laughed. She was sitting very close to Michael Thomas, Kate noticed.

'You're daydreaming! We were just talking about flying and how it's put the Great British nose out of joint to have a Frenchman fly the Channel first.'

'I expect so,' said Kate vaguely.

'It's something I'd like to try,' Matthew enthused and Joe said he wouldn't mind seeing an aircraft close up and finding out how it worked.

Michael shrugged. 'Small chance of that, Joe. It's a rich man's sport, not for the likes of us.'

There was a note of disapproval in his voice and Kate saw that Edith was watching him thoughtfully. After a moment the young woman said: 'And a male sport, Dr Thomas. I don't suppose that Madame Bleriot - if there is one - has an aircraft of her own.'

Joe gave a choking laugh, but Michael remained perfectly serious. 'I'm sure you're right, Miss Summers. Kate has told me about your interest in women's suffrage. I'd be very glad to hear your views on the subject.'

Edith went pink with pleasure and immediately began to talk about her meeting with Christabel Pankhurst. After a while Joe yawned loudly and asked Kate if she needed any help preparing the meal. She quickly rose and led the way into the house. He had never before been so pointedly rude about one of Edith's enthusiasms and Kate was glad the girl was too busy talking to take much notice. Matthew had realised, though, and been surprised.

Once inside the house Kate shoved William into Joe's arms and reached for her apron. 'You can look after your son while I put the potatoes on,' she snapped.

'Oh Lord, what have I done now?' But as she slammed the heavy saucepan on to the range he shrugged apologetically. 'If I've heard Edith's lecture about the Pankhursts once I've heard it a dozen times.'

There was another crash as the oven door was pulled savagely open. Kate prodded at the meat sizzling inside.

'I'm sorry, Kate.'

'And how many times have I had to listen to your Flo's silliness?'

He looked taken aback and she was at once ashamed of using Flo, for she was fond of the girl, but that only made her more angry.

'You'd soon be up in arms if I said something rude and walked away from her, wouldn't you? But it's all right for you to behave like that to one of my family.'

He was spluttering with sudden anger. 'You make it sound as though I regularly go out of my way to be offensive. And what's all this about Flo being silly? I've never expected you to put up with stupid behaviour from her, or any of my relatives for that matter!'

William began to cry, waving his arms about in distress.

'Oh, look what you've done!' cried Kate, fully aware of her own unreasonableness, but past caring.

'What I've done!'

A quiet, sad appeal broke into their noisy exchange.

'Please stop. Please.'

They turned to see Matthew in the doorway, lemonade jug in hand. His manner was uncomfortable but determined.

'It's horrible to hear you quarrelling like this,' he said.

Kate lowered her gaze, feeling like a chastised child. Joe pacified William and did not look into Matthew's face.

'I came in to see if there was any more lemonade,' Matthew said after a moment or two. 'Edith and Dr Thomas are thirsty.'

When he'd gone with the refilled jug they were silent for a long time. Then Joe cleared his throat and said firmly, 'We must talk things over, Kate, as soon as we're on our own.'

She busied herself putting plates to warm and did not look at him.

'Yes,' she said, wondering, miserably, what there was to talk about.

But over the meal she took her cue from Joe and kept her conversation lively and was glad to see the relief in Matthew's face. He had obviously been too concerned about her and Joe to pay much attention to

Edith and Michael, and Kate wondered when he would realise that these two had already progressed from being mere acquaintances. They weren't exactly flirting but occasionally their gazes would interlock and stay that way for much longer than was necessary.

As so often happened these days talk soon came round to Lloyd George.

'Too many people are seeing him as the saviour of the working classes,' said Michael. 'The People's Budget, indeed! No help for those who are still without work?' He glared round suddenly. 'And what, come to that, is the Parliamentary Labour Party doing for those people?'

Matthew grew defensive. 'Our Labour MPs are working men themselves. They're not slow to press that issue.'

'Some are conscientious, I agree. I'm thinking of Victor Grayson especially.'

Edith said quickly, 'Tell me about him.' She was rewarded with one of Michael's gleaming smiles.

'He's the man who interrupted business in the House a while back, demanding a debate on unemployment. Of course they threw him out but not before he'd called them a House of Murderers.'

Edith looked impressed and Kate found herself exchanging an amused glance with Joe. She didn't remember she was cross with him until it was too late.

'Grayson's a troublemaker.' Matthew pronounced the criticism in a reasonable tone. 'People don't like seeing a party turning on itself.'

The doctor's smile had gone and his voice rose. 'I think you exaggerate. Honest self-criticism does a party no harm.'

There was an uneasy silence then Kate said, reflectively, that it was worrying if the Labour Party had no remedy to offer for the problem of unemployment.

'The remedy, of course, is Socialism, Kate,' said Michael stoutly. 'True equality. The throwing down of class barriers.'

Edith looked at him curiously. 'You really believe that can happen, Dr Thomas?'

He slewed round in his chair to face her. 'I couldn't function properly as a human being if that belief wasn't always at the forefront of my consciousness,' he told her, with a burning look which, Kate thought with some disquiet, could easily be misconstrued.

Matthew seemed alert to the situation at last, for he skilfully directed the conversation into a different area, by talking about the production of *Strife* which he and Edith had seen in London. 'I expect you've seen it Dr Thomas? No? That's a pity for you'd have enjoyed it I'm sure. It's about a strike in a

Welsh tinplate works.'

Kate gazed at Joe happily, remembering their first visit to the theatre together, not long after they became lovers. For a moment she felt their mutual need for each other like a live thing, linking them in an exclusive intimacy. She lost the thread of the discussion and Edith steered it towards women's suffrage, inviting the doctor's opinion which he was only too pleased to provide. And when the meal was finished and cleared away he led Edith to the piano and insisted that she demonstrate the skill he had so often heard praised. Kate shot Matthew a sympathetic look. He had stretched out in one of the armchairs and appeared to be comfortable and relaxed but his thin hands were clasped too tightly across his stomach for that to be true.

Kate excused herself and went out into the kitchen to clear up. After a while Joe joined her.

'Duets now,' he said morosely and Kate looked surprised.

'Don't you want to listen? Go back and keep poor Matty company.'

But he stayed where he was, chewing on his thumbnail and getting in her way until she asked snappishly what was wrong.

'Do you think Edith's taken a fancy to Michael?' he muttered.

'Why are you whispering? They can't hear. She may have done, or she may just be teasing. You know Edith can be a bit silly sometimes.'

Kate felt glad she had used the word silly. It somehow cancelled out her thoughtless remark about Flo earlier on.

'Yes, but suppose he's taken a fancy to her?'

'Well, that would be sad for Matty but things seem to be at a standstill between him and Edie, don't you think?'

Joe sighed. 'I should have said something before... It was some time ago. Michael mentioned his wife.'

Kate bit her lip but kept her anxiety in check. 'Perhaps he's a widower,' she declared hopefully. But they were uncomfortable with this conclusion. In the village it was widely accepted that Dr Thomas was a single man. Certainly none of Dr Warner's servants contradicted this view.

Kate grew agitated. 'You must find out, Joe. Edith's not likely to do anything silly, but he's paying her a lot of attention and she'll be hurt and embarrassed if it turns out that he has no right to do so.'

'I can hardly ask him,' Joe grumbled.

'Why not?'

There was another argument, this time conducted in whispers, which resulted in Kate declaring that she would deal with the matter herself. Her chance came when the music had finished and she asked the doctor if he would mind looking at William who wasn't settling to sleep and seemed hot and fretful.

Upstairs she stopped him on the landing outside the bedroom door. She was slightly taller than he was and felt at more of an advantage.

'There's nothing wrong with William - I just wanted to speak to you privately,' she said brusquely. 'Joe says you once mentioned your wife, Michael. Are you still married? You've been behaving like a single man with Edith ever since you arrived.' There was a flash of anger in his eyes, but then he spread his hands in a self-deprecatory gesture.

'Have I? If you say so it must be true, though I wasn't really aware of it. I was just enjoying the company of a very pretty young lady.'

He gave a hopeful smile but Kate shook her head.

'I think you know quite well what you were doing,' she said. 'Edith may seem very adult, but she has little experience of life. Someone like that can be easily hurt.'

This was delivered on a chilly note and Kate moved to go back downstairs.

'Ah no, let me explain myself. Please.'

His voice was bleak and when Kate turned she saw that he had gone pale.

'Don't think badly of me, Kate. I'd do anything rather than lose your regard and Joe's. If I've acted wrongly towards Miss Summers I'll put it right, of course I will.'

His agitation was real enough. 'I'm still married,' he admitted, 'and I have two young children. They live with my wife in Wales, in the village I told you about.'

There was an uncomfortable silence which Kate broke by asking: 'Will your family be coming to join you, once you're established here?'

'No.' Michael shrugged. 'I may as well tell you the whole thing. I know it won't go beyond you and Joe.'

He lowered his head wearily.

'My wife has refused to live with me again, though she accepts my money for the children, which I have to send through my mother. She won't let me see them or write to them.'

Kate's immediate reaction was of outrage against such a harsh ruling but she knew it was unwise to jump to speedy conclusions, so she held her tongue. Michael looked at her, perhaps expecting her to speak. When she didn't he continued more hesitantly.

'Oh, I suppose she's right. If I can't be a proper father to them it's better that they forget me.'

'That depends on the circumstances,' said Kate evenly.

He shrugged again. 'It was my own stupidity.'

She murmured hurriedly that he didn't have to tell her but it was too late to stop him now.

'There was a girl in the village who had an abortion,' he said harshly. 'Unmarried, of course. I was called in when it was too late. She was dying. I was angry, Kate, very angry. She was a lovely girl, with all her life before her and it had been destroyed by some greedy oaf who couldn't keep his hands off her. I made her tell me who the man was and then, like a fool, I told her she should have come to me when she knew she was pregnant - that I would have helped her.'

Kate thought sadly of the dying girl. 'That can't have been much comfort to her.'

'I know. Instead of keeping my feelings under control I behaved like a fool and I paid for it. Someone overheard what I said. One of the women I suppose. There were women in and out of her room all the time.' His voice had a sharp edge to it.

'Perhaps they were trying to help too,' said Kate.

'One of them had done that well enough, that's sure. I let my anger have its head and after she was dead I found the man who had raped her and gave him a thrashing.'

She looked at the delicate hands, trying to imagine them laying into another man. The set of his mouth convinced her. Even though time had passed he still seethed with violent anger against the guilty man.

'That was stupid too,' he went on, after a while. 'In a village like that, where the girl was popular... Well they'd have dealt with him in their own way. It wasn't my business to do anything, so when I did there was some feeling against me. Then what I had said to Eira became known and gossiped about and after a while there was more gossip that I was really the father of her child.'

Kate sighed. It only took a slanted comment or a downright lie and in small communities reputations could be destroyed. And yet...

'Surely your wife didn't believe it?'

His face was a sickly grey. 'I'm afraid she did.' He twisted his hands together then gripped them tightly. 'I'd been stupid once before... well, twice in fact. It meant nothing and Gwen always forgave me. But this time she wouldn't even listen.'

Kate knew he wanted to go on talking but she didn't want to hear any more.

'I'm very sorry for you and your wife,' she said, 'and especially for your children. Don't you think that one day - '

Michael shook his head abruptly. 'My mother sends me news of them. I have to be content with that.'

Although the doctor appeared cheerful enough for the rest of the evening Kate was aware that the edge had gone from his pleasure. It was as though he drew apart from them a little: certainly he no longer dominated the conversation.

As far as Edith was concerned he kept his word. Subtly his attitude towards her changed. He spoke to her and to Matthew as though they were a couple. Once he mentioned the satisfaction of living alone and having no responsibility for dependents: it was cleverly done in the context of a discussion about children, and the other two men scarcely made note of it but Kate saw Edith glance at the doctor sharply and then shift uncomfortably on her chair.

It was early evening when Michael left, declaring that it had been a delightful day, and carefully avoiding Kate's eyes. Matthew stayed a while longer and it seemed that for the first time that day he and Edith were relaxed with each other. They didn't say much but sat together at the parlour table while Kate poured glasses of elderberry wine.

'Are you expected at the Hall, Matty?' asked Kate. 'You know you're welcome to spend the night here.'

'Thank you but I must go. James will be waiting for me with brandy and cigars in his study and no doubt I'll have to hear all about the new house. Then I'm supposed to go with them to church in the morning. Oh, has Edith told you she's lunching with us at the Hall tomorrow?'

Kate smiled her approval. 'But you'll both come back here for tea, won't you?'

Reluctantly Matthew finished his wine and rose to go.

'I've enjoyed myself,' he said. 'Your friend Dr Thomas certainly provides some lively conversation.'

'A pity he's so self-opinionated,' said Edith coolly. 'I'll walk a little way with you, Matty. I want to hear about your teaching.'

******

Yawning, Joe pulled back the covers and climbed into bed. He propped a pillow against the brass rails and leaned back against it, still listening to Kate's story. When she finished he puffed out his cheeks with a disapproving breath.

'Sounds as though he's been a bit of a philanderer, that doctor.'

Kate laid down her hairbrush. 'I think he used to be. Unfortunately his wife judged him on his past behaviour, even though he hadn't done anything wrong with the girl.'

'Do you believe that?'

'Yes, I think so.' She got into bed beside him. 'Are you going to sit up like that all night?' she asked sharply. But she wasn't really angry with him any more and he knew it.

'I was thinking we ought to go to church tomorrow,' he said.

'Why? Edith's perfectly capable of going on her own and meeting Matty and the Gales there. If we go too I'll have to get up early and iron William's coat - he's nothing else fit to wear.'

'If we go we're bound to see Betty Halfpenny; she never misses a Sunday. If she's willing we can walk back with her and have a look at the shop.'

Kate stared at him in amazement. 'Are you joking with me?'

'I should think not!' he grinned. 'I hope you're not going to say you've changed your mind?'

She felt the excitement bubbling up inside her. 'No, of course not, but - '

'Now look, just because we're going to see it doesn't mean to say we're going to have it. If it doesn't turn out to be suitable or if we can't raise the money we'll have to let it go. Do you agree?'

She could see that he was wary, wondering if she would break into some fresh argument, so she forced herself to appear calm and satisfied. And she was, at heart. It was enough for the moment that they were going to see the shop; that they would discuss the idea between them and come to a joint decision about it.

'Aunt Polly's offered us the money,' she said as Joe slid down into the bed and she told him about the letter Edith had brought and of her own reply, refusing the loan.

'If she sells something he gave her then it's his money,' she frowned. 'Was I right, though?'

He was silent much longer than she expected. Then he gave a reluctant grunt. 'Yes. It's a pity, the way things are at the moment. But, yes, that was right.'

They talked for a little longer before putting out the lamp. In the room next door Edith lay sleepless in the dark, listening to the gentle murmur of their voices. She had been aware at odd moments during the day that all wasn't well between Kate and Joe and it was comforting now to hear them at ease with each other. She turned on her side and Michael Thomas's face floated momentarily before her. The slow heat of embarrassment took hold. She'd not misjudged him earlier in the day, she was sure of it. He had been attentive, interested in what she had to say, eager to talk to her. After a while the messages in his eyes had become clearer and clearer: admiration, excitement and something more.

She pulled her fingers angrily through the tangle of hair on her pillow. There were few young men in her life, her father saw to that, but she was well aware of the effect she had on those she knew. Look at Matty. A frown and a sharp word from her today and he had been cast down into the depths, while her smiles this evening had drawn delight from his eyes. Some time ago, when she had thought herself in love with him, she had once let him kiss her and the warmth and wetness of his mouth had amazed and excited her, and frightened her a little. Today she had found herself wondering what it would be like to let Michael Thomas kiss her. He would have been only too willing, she was sure... sure... So why had he changed? She had felt his withdrawal from her as though he had physically got up and left her side. So it had all been a game. He wasn't really interested in what she said or in her ideas. She turned over completely and buried her hot face in her pillow.

******

Kate left Joe talking to Betty Halfpenny in the yard and slipped through the kitchen and back into the shop. With an almost sensuous pleasure she sniffed again the mixture of smells - everything from coffee and spices to soap and metal. She knew it well, of course, as a customer, but today it seemed positively intoxicating in its strength.

She laughed at herself for being so silly and William, balanced on her hip, looked up and laughed too. She startled him by giving him a sudden, urgent hug,

'Oh, William! Isn't it lovely?'

She checked that he was dry and then sat him on the gleaming mahogany counter and looked round the shop for the first time as an owner might do. From here she could see out into the village street through the one large window on the left of the door. Kate frowned. There was no reason why the shop window should seem so empty. Betty displayed very little and would probably argue that all her customers knew what she had in stock but Kate remembered some of the pretty displays she'd seen in London shops and thought she would like to have her window looking attractive.

Inside she would rearrange the stock. The tall canisters on the shelves behind her, containing rice, tea and other dry goods would stay, but all the cleaning materials - soap and blue, starch, bath brick and the rest - would be together over near the door. Betty kept them too close to the dried fruit. In fact that area by the door could be completely given over to items for the house - nails and tools and cutlery, and things like toys and writing paper too, which Betty kept in all sorts of odd corners of the shop.

William stretched out his hands towards the big coffee grinder at the end of the counter and when Kate wouldn't let him touch it he screwed up his round face in annoyance. Kate glanced at the clock above the door and realised with a start that it was long past dinner time. Then her eye caught sight of the boxes piled on the shelf below the clock. Those were the cheap

70

cotton and woollen goods Betty stocked, most of them hopelessly out of fashion and only bought by the old ladies of the village. Well, that was something else that would have to be changed.

'I thought you must have come back in here.' Mrs Halfpenny walked in smiling. 'Mr Weaver's just having another look round at the back.'

Kate smiled too. Joe's interest was a good sign.

'We'll have to go soon,' she said. 'William's getting hungry.'

'Ah, the little angel!' Mrs Halfpenny stroked the boy's hair. She was a small woman, very thin, and her black dress made her look even thinner. She wore, as always, a rather top-heavy hat with a narrow brim which gave her grey head a fragile air as though, any minute, it might topple forward off her tiny neck. Her husband had been a big, robust man and it had come as a surprise to the entire village that he should die before his wife.

'What do you think of the rooms upstairs, Mrs Weaver? Of course you may want to rearrange them but we always liked to use the big one at the front as our parlour, with the others as bedrooms. We liked to have somewhere we could sit, away from the shop if you see what I mean. Oh, we used the kitchen down here at the back most of the time but it was nice to have somewhere a bit special.'

Kate nodded agreement. The parlour was much too cluttered for her taste at present but once Mrs Halfpenny's furniture had gone there would be far more space than they were used to at home. She could have her bookshelves on display at last.

There were only two bedrooms of reasonable size and two that were smaller. William would have one, of course, but she had plans for the other. Why not move the kitchen upstairs, so that all the ground floor of the building could be used for the shop? As they walked home she toyed with the idea of mentioning this to Joe, but decided against it at present. He was enthusiastic about the garden which lay beyond the yard.

'I didn't realise it was there. Her son must have done a bit to it and I can soon get it shipshape again. We ought to be able to grow enough to keep ourselves in vegetables, like we do now.'

'And perhaps there'll be a bit of grass for William to play on?' That had been one of her worries about moving into the village High Street.

Joe nodded absently. 'But what about that kitchen, Kate? The range looks a bit old-fashioned.'

'I've cooked on far worse!' she declared. Then she stopped and caught his arm. She smiled into his eyes.

'Listen to the way we're talking, Joe. We've decided, haven't we?'

He gave a reckless laugh. 'I suppose we have. Though Lord knows where we'll get the money, or what kind of a mess we'll make of being shopkeepers.'

'We'll be fine. We must talk to Mrs Halfpenny properly about the stock and suppliers and that kind of thing. I know she'll help us. Didn't she say she'd be glad for the shop to go to local people?'

They stood beaming at each other, until Joe noticed that William had pulled part of a flower off Kate's hat and was chewing it contentedly.

'Poor lad, he must be starving,' he laughed, as Kate hooked a finger into William's mouth to extract the pulpy mess. She cast an amazed glance at Joe.

'Another tooth!' she whispered. For a moment everything else was forgotten as they smiled in shared pride upon their son, now opening his be-toothed mouth to give a hungry howl.

******

Polly was waiting on the platform at Brighton station for Edith's train. 'Mitcham's here with the car,' she murmured as she kissed her daughter's cheek, 'but I thought we could send him back with your bag and go for a stroll along Madeira Drive. It's so pleasant now.'

Once the car had gone they turned down Queen's Road at a comfortable pace and Edith eyed her Mother's three-quarter length coat with approval. 'Is that new?'

'Your Father and I went to a fund-raising event out at Rottingdean the other day,' Polly explained, almost guiltily. 'I felt I should have something different.'

'Oh, Mother, you are silly! It's as though you feel ashamed of spending money on clothes. Yet you always know exactly what suits you. I just love the braid on the cuffs - it looks so smart.'

She lifted her head and caught a glimpse of the sea, like a blue satin ribbon.

Polly fiddled with the handle of her parasol. 'Did you give Kate my letter?' she asked at last.

'I did, and I've brought back her answer.' Edith's steps slowed a little and in spite of her best efforts she found her voice growing sharper. 'They're going to buy the shop, Mother, but not with Summers' money.'

She handed her mother Kate's letter and waited while she glanced quickly at the contents. When they walked on Polly was silent, thoughtful, and Edith gave her a sharp look.

'Mother, do you suppose that Kate is jealous of me?'

'Jealous?' Polly's tone was cautious.

'I've never felt it before. Kate always seemed to accept our situation without question. I've felt guilty because I had the better education and didn't have to go into service like her. I remember when we first met Joe and Matty

I was going through that phase of actually calling Kate my sister. I only stopped because it made her embarrassed having to explain how things really are.'

Polly gave a wry smile. 'Yes. That was a little embarrassing for all of us, you know.'

'Father wasn't embarrassed, just angry,' Edith retorted. 'Anyway, that's not the point. I always believed that I felt the difference between us much more acutely than Kate did. But the other day, when she told me she was refusing your offer... Oh, it sounds silly, but I wonder now if underneath she wasn't actually pleased to be doing so.'

She frowned, perplexed, and was glad when her mother clasped her hand and squeezed it gently.

'I can't imagine that Kate was really pleased; she very much wants the shop, you know. But you can surely understand why she would refuse money that came from your father, even indirectly. She doesn't like him and has never pretended otherwise. But she loves you, dear, and I don't think she's at all envious.'

'I suppose she might be jealous that you're my real mother but not hers,' went on Edith thoughtfully. Then she saw Polly's eyes narrow and added hastily, 'Oh, you've always been equally loving to both of us, but Kate must feel it - not knowing who her real mother was.'

'Whatever Kate feels about that is nothing to do with you,' said Polly crisply. 'I worry about you, Edith: your head seems to be crammed with so many foolish thoughts and half-formed ideas.'

They reached the sea front and stopped for a while to look back along the beach. Near some bathing machines, pulled down to the sea's edge, a group of young women and children were plunging through the waves with piercing squeals of excitement.

Edith sensed her mother's reluctance to continue their conversation and decided to change the subject.

'Matthew and I went to lunch with Sir James and Lady Janette and their house guests from London. I can't tell you how tedious that was! All we heard was gossip about the King's health and the latest fashions and visits abroad.' Then she added more fairly, 'Actually, I had a chat with Janette afterwards and she's not at all as light-headed as she appears. She even apologised for changing the subject when I mentioned the suffrage campaign over dessert.'

Polly sighed and Edith said sharply, 'Mother, don't look like that - why shouldn't women talk about politics too?'

'No reason, dear - though time and place are important.'

There was silence for a moment then Edith said briskly, 'Mother, I

73

want to study, seriously. I've made up my mind that I'll ask Father today if I can go to university. You will back me up, won't you?'

'Oh, dear!' Polly looked harassed. 'It really isn't a suitable time, Edie. Your father's in a bad mood. There's been some sort of difficulty at the shop.'

Edith shrugged. 'He'll be over that by the time we get home, surely?'

'This is more than a minor annoyance,' said Polly. 'He was reprimanding one of the junior assistants in the haberdashery department and Sam Bundy took the young man's part. I understand that he said your father was being unfair.'

'He's not given Sam notice, surely?'

'No. Luckily no-one else was about when this happened, and your father knows very well how valuable Sam is to him. But he came home in one of his tempers and that hasn't improved since.'

Edith gave her mother a teasing smile. 'Don't worry; I can always coax him back into a good humour. Now don't fuss any more, dear. Let's go and look at the electric railway.'

******

Arnold Summers pushed his plate away and glared across the table at his wife.

'I thought you were going to speak to the cook,' he snapped.

'I did so,' Polly responded calmly. 'Is there something wrong with the meat, Arnold?'

'Over done! Now that I've at last persuaded you to order more expensive cuts we don't want them ruined by an incompetent cook. I suppose I'll have to do your job for you and see her myself. Edith, ring and have this cleared away.'

Edith obeyed in silence. Now that he had vented his anger on Polly Mr Summers leaned back in his chair, looking more satisfied. He smoothed a hand over his thick, iron-grey hair, and then ran his palm down the front of his jacket with a preening gesture. Edith bent her head to hide a smile, thinking that her father looked for all the world like a pouter pigeon, flattening ruffled feathers. He favoured dark grey cloth for most of his suits and had a neat, dapper appearance that was almost bird-like. Not when he was angry, though.

The maid cleared their dishes and brought in a baked raspberry pudding. Edith saw that Polly was holding her breath, expecting Mr Summers to send the food back with another outburst of rage. Perhaps he was aware of that too, for he chose to praise the pastry and demand a large helping.

'And how are Sir James and Lady Janette?' he asked Edith. 'Entertaining a good deal at this time of year, I suppose. Was it a big house party, my dear?'

Edith recounted her visit to the Hall - not as she'd done for her Mother but putting in all the little details she knew he loved to hear: what the ladies had worn; what people had talked about; the quantity and quality of glass and china on the luncheon table and exactly what they had eaten. He was fascinated by the Gales' forthcoming trip to Biarritz and his eyes lit up when he heard that they had bought another car.

'Sir James drove Matthew back to London in it,' said Edith. She liked to introduce his name into these conversations whenever possible. Her father would often forget that it was only because of Matthew that she was also counted as one of the Gales' circle of friends.

'Drives fast, does he?' Mr Summers chuckled, his tone suggesting that Sir James was an old acquaintance and could therefore be mocked a little. 'Well, well...'

Edith decided to wait a while after the meal before speaking to her father, knowing that he liked to doze in his study, as he called the small room off the front hall lined with books which she and her mother had chosen for him and which they were sure he had never opened. She prowled around the drawing room thinking, and not for the first time, how little she liked this house. During her childhood the family had lived above the shop and although their living quarters were separate they weren't cut off from the activities below. She and Kate knew all the assistants in the shop and they had their favourites. Mr Summers worked alongside his employees in those days and at particularly busy times such as stocktaking, Polly, who had an excellent head for figures, would always lend a hand.

Her mother had gone upstairs to change for an evening visit to Mrs Leigh. The invitations usually came for Polly alone these days and Edith guessed this was because she had spoken dismissively of her mother's Liberal friends. But she had to admit that life was even more tedious without these outings - she was getting tired of spending so many evenings at home. Well, that wouldn't matter for much longer. It was time, she thought with a smile, to beard the pigeon in his lair. She darted a quick glance in the mirror to see if her curls were flattened and tidy, then she crossed the hall and tapped on the study door.

There was a considerable amount of cigar smoke in the room and a glass of whisky on her father's desk. He beamed at her.

'Come in, my dear. You can open the window a little, if you wish. I know you ladies don't like too much of a cigar!'

Edith relaxed. He was in a good mood, so her task should be easy. She resisted the temptation to slide the window fully open and instead raised it an infinitesimal amount. Her father was always anxious about the damaging nature of draughts.

'Come and look at this,' he invited. 'Final plans for the new shop. 'I intend to be open by Christmas, you know.'

She stood beside his chair and bent over the papers laid out in front of him, murmuring appreciation as he described where the different departments would be. But she wasn't really listening. Her mind was going over what she would say to him, polishing the fine phrases, so that he would be immediately impressed.

Mr Summers sat back in his chair and looked up at her.

'It's going to be marvellous, Father,' she said warmly.

He gave a satisfied nod and began to fold up the plans.

'We've certainly come a long way since the old days at the original shop,' he said.

'Yes, I was thinking that just now.'

'You were?' He beamed again. 'Do you remember when I bought the property next door and began to extend? You were too young to appreciate what a risk that was, my dear. There were plenty who thought I'd lose everything I'd put into the business! Some of the fine folk who are only too pleased to come here now and eat my dinners would have turned their backs on me then if I'd failed.'

'Oh Father, I'm sure there was never any question of you failing.' She kept her voice light and a little teasing. He wasn't foolish enough to succumb to any heavy-handed flattery.

'And did you know, Father, that Kate - ' she broke off quickly, furious with herself. She had nearly given away the secret and while there was no reason why her father should object to any plan of Kate's now that she was married, it was certain he would take exception to this and probably be irrationally angry.

'What about Kate?' Mr Summers demanded.

'Oh, nothing... When I was there she and I were talking about living over the shop...'

He gave a disparaging grunt and began to complain about feeling cold. Edith hurriedly closed the window.

'Could you pour me another whisky and soda, my dear?' her father asked. 'You know how I like it.'

As she replenished his glass she recalled how proud she'd been as a little girl when he showed her how to make this drink for him; always eager to do it. Now, catching that self-satisfied eye upon her, she realised how much he enjoyed having her wait on him in this way. The knowledge made her feel uncomfortable and she splashed a little of the soda water on the floor. The eye grew disapproving.

'Well now,' he said as she handed him the glass. 'What did you want to see me about, Edith? Money is it? You need some new clothes?' He looked her up and down critically. 'You certainly seem to be wearing some very plain things these days. Is this your way of letting me know that you've spent all your allowance and can't afford anything pretty?'

She didn't join in his laughter.

'I want you to let me go to university, Father.'

No: it was not the right time to ask. The comfortable atmosphere of just a few minutes ago had gone. Then she saw his face and realised that there would never have been a right time.

'Whatever nonsense is this?'

'I want to study, Father - to improve myself. You've always said that's a good thing.'

'But you have studied. Good heavens, I sent you to the best school in Brighton and you could have gone to one of those finishing places only you made out you'd be homesick - '

'Yes, I know. You've done so much for me. That's why I felt sure you'd approve of this idea.' She grasped at something he would understand. 'I want to continue my education so that when I do marry...'

He softened, as she knew he would. 'Oh Edith, you get some funny ideas into your head. So you think you'll make a better match with a fancy education behind you?'

He was laughing quietly now as he held out his hand across the desk. Reluctantly she took it and he drew her round to him, pulling her down so that she had to perch uncomfortably on the arm of his chair, leaning against him.

'My dear, don't you realise that you've got everything a decent husband will be looking for? You've got good looks and you dress well - though you're a bit expensive there: still, men expect that kind of extravagance - and you mix in the best kind of society and can talk with the best kind of people as an equal. On top of that you've got money, my money. I've told you I'll be generous when you marry, and when I die everything will go to you, apart from your mother's legacy, of course. Believe me, Edith, you don't need anything more.' He kissed her cheek, 'Now put all this silliness out of your head.'

He released her and she stood up, hating herself for being too cowed to answer him. He took her silence for agreement and became expansive. 'I expect you're finding things quiet here,' he said, 'especially after visiting the Gales. It's high time we did more entertaining and invited some younger people, particularly some young men.' He gave her a roguish glance. 'I'll have to get used to the idea of eventually handing over my little girl to someone else.'

Edith suddenly felt her anger rising. 'I'm not a parcel or a piece of property!' she snapped.

He was staring at her, momentarily at a loss, his mouth open.

'I shall go to university,' she declared, shakily. 'And one day you'll be glad and proud that I did.'

Mr Summers had regained his self-control. He glared and thumped a fist on the desk. 'This is all falling into place! It's that Matthew Hersey, isn't it? I've heard rumours about his political notions but I refused to believe them. After all, he's Sir James's relative, even though he is choosing an odd way of earning his living. I can see now I was mistaken. I should have taken note. He's infected you with his radical ideas.'

He sprang up and began pacing about.

'You're not to see that young man again, Edith. I absolutely forbid it. And I shall have a serious talk with your mother.' His face darkened at the thought. 'I may support the Liberal Party but I don't go along with all the views their members express. It wouldn't surprise me if she's exposed you to some wrong-thinking women!'

'It's nothing to do with Mother or with Matthew,' cried Edith in alarm. 'It's all my own idea.' But she could see he had made up his mind and wouldn't listen to her. Tears of frustration filled her eyes and splashed down on to her hands.

'Edith, Edith...' Having allocated the blame to his own satisfaction he could now afford to be generous. 'Don't cry. I shouldn't have been harsh with you, but I wanted to get to the truth of this.' He put an arm round her shoulders.

'I know this idea seems important to you at the moment, but it won't last, you'll see. As soon as you make some new friends you'll find plenty to occupy yourself until the time comes to marry.'

He drew her to a chair by the window and sat her down, making soothing noises. Gradually she stopped crying and sat staring dully at the handkerchief clasped in her fingers.

'Of course I don't want you to think you've got to get married all in a rush,' her father went on. His hand, heavy on her shoulder gave a firm squeeze. 'I want you to be able to choose from the very best.' He smiled, reflectively. 'That's what my mother always wanted for me, Edith. You know what a struggle she had to bring me up and educate me and I'm only glad she lived long enough to see our name over the shop. It's sad that she never saw her granddaughter, but I know she would have wanted the best for you too: a husband with the right sort of background.'

Edith stood up and turned to leave and he added: 'Send your mother to me.'

The words and the unpleasant tone in which they were uttered shook her calm.

'She's gone out to Mrs Leigh's for the evening,' she said quickly, but the sound of Polly's voice in the hall, talking to the maid, gave the lie to her words. As she fled past a surprised Polly and up the stairs Edith heard her father call his wife into the study.

Polly pressed her back against the study door. She knew Arnold would not strike her. He had once done so, long years ago, raising a bruise on the side of her face, and she had threatened that if ever he did it again she would leave him, no matter what scandal ensued. He was always fearful of damage to his good name and to the business; she knew that to her cost. It was the only weapon she had against him. But there were other kinds of violence and he could employ his loud voice to strong effect, battering her with insults and accusations.

'I suppose all this university nonsense is your idea? Well?'
She shook her head and tried to keep her voice steady.

'To be honest I think Edith would have difficulty getting through the entrance examination.'

That threw him off track and while he blustered defensively about Edith's intelligence Polly added quickly: 'If she did get in I think it would do her good, keep her occupied. And her fellow students would be from the very best families. She would make some useful friends.'

He paused for a moment, brushing his hand over his hair. When he next spoke his voice had lost some of its aggression.

'Well, that's as may be, but I don't want that for my daughter. If she needs something to occupy her get her involved in charity work.' He frowned. 'And another thing, Polly, she's not to see Matthew Hersey again. He's a bad influence on her.'

'It's through Matthew that she mixes with the Gales and their set. I thought you wanted that.'

'She's close with Lady Janette now and doesn't need that young man any more,' countered Mr Summers with an air of triumph. 'He can come here to visit occasionally, when you and I are present - I suppose we can't cut him completely. But there are to be no more of these little outings. And she's not to visit Kate if he's going to be there.'

Polly sighed and moved away from the door. It seemed that his anger was spent and although his final rulings were harsh some way around them might be discovered in time.

'I'll go up and see Edith,' she said, knowing what he wanted to hear. 'I must be more firm with her in future.'

Her hand was on the door when he called out for her to wait. His voice was hesitant as though he was working something out in his mind.

'That money you asked me for,' he said thoughtfully, his eyes hard. 'Was that something to do with Edith's scheme?' His anger grew again with his suspicions. 'Some sort of fee perhaps, in case I didn't agree, so that she could go to university in any case?'

He grasped Polly's shoulder and turned her to face him. 'If I find you've been plotting behind my back...'

'Of course it wasn't for that!' She pulled away from him, rubbing at her shoulder where his fingers had dug in. 'Women can't buy their way into Oxford or Cambridge, you small-minded creature!'

She had the brief satisfaction of seeing sheer amazement in his eyes at the insult before the hard look returned and he began the old diatribe which she knew almost by heart.

'How dare you speak to me like that - you of all people! Small-minded am I? But not too small-minded to rescue you from the gutter and give you a decent name and a decent home and decent clothes on your back. Where would you have been without me...?'

Once these words had carried the power to hurt her but the love and respect of friends like Clara Riseborough, of her daughter and of Kate and Joe had long since made her aware of her own worth. When he was silent at last Polly nodded, almost politely, and turned away.

******

Polly returned late from Mrs Leigh's even though she hadn't intended to stay long. Edith's sullen silence had made it impossible to offer any comfort or sensible advice and so she planned to go to her daughter's room once again when she got back home. After an evening alone Edith might be more in a mood to talk about her disappointment and listen to her mother's advice and reassurance.

But it was so pleasant at Mrs Leigh's; the women relaxed yet lively and the conversation interesting. They had talked about Mrs Garrett Fawcett's suffrage campaign, comparing it in detail to that of the Pankhursts.

When she eventually glanced at the clock and exclaimed over the lateness of the hour Polly realised she had put events at home completely out of her mind. For a few precious hours, during which she was treated as a sensible human being with views worth listening to, she had forgotten her husband's loud rudeness and her daughter's discontent. Now, as she closed the front door quietly behind her, she felt guilty. Poor Edith! This was the first time she had come into real conflict with her father, for it was the first time she'd asked for something he wasn't prepared to give. That would have set her back, perhaps made her hopes seem futile. If she wasn't already asleep Polly felt she must talk to her and try to rebuild her self-esteem.

Arnold stepped out of his study into the hall. His face was set into harsh lines. 'Edith's gone!' he hissed.

Polly felt her stomach turn. 'What do you mean?'

He waved a piece of paper in her face. 'It must have been while I was out. I had to see my architect - some small point...'

Polly clenched her hands. Even at such a moment he couldn't resist showing off. "My architect" indeed!

'When I got back I went up to Edith's room. I thought she might be calmer; ready to listen to reason. I found that she'd packed a bag and gone. There was this note.'

Polly's eyes flew over the few lines and relief flooded through her. Edith had gone to Kate's. She raised an untroubled face to her husband.

'She'll be all right, Arnold. A few days in the country and she'll be bored again and missing life here. We shall have her home in no time.'

She realised, too late, that he'd come to that conclusion already, otherwise he would have had the car brought round long ago and gone off in pursuit of his daughter. It would do his temper no good to hear her placidly confirm this decision: indeed his face was already changing colour. He grasped Polly's arm and pushed her into the drawing room.

'Well, I'm glad this doesn't ruffle you,' he sneered. 'Perhaps if you'd taken the trouble to stay at home tonight you might have noticed your daughter running away. I presume you would have stopped her? Or would you have helped her to pack?'

Polly raised a hand to her eyes which were beginning to feel sore and tired.

'There's no need to be so sarcastic. Even if I'd been here I couldn't have watched over her all the time.'

'She obviously waited until the house was quiet. If you'd come home at a respectable hour you might have caught her.'

She had a vision of a dramatic tableau. Edith tiptoeing down the stairs, bag in hand, to find her mother barring the way like the angel at the gates of Eden. On the verge of laughter she pulled out a handkerchief and covered her mouth.

'It's too late for tears now!' he snapped. 'You're a bad mother to that girl and it's time you admitted it.'

All laughter died in her. She stared at him angrily. 'That is a lie, Arnold, and you know it.'

'Do I? You've been taking her into some pretty strange company just lately, without my knowledge or approval.'

She could tell from his uncertain tone that he wasn't sure of his ground. She turned away and crossing to the fireplace began to unpin her hat, watching their reflections in the mirror above the mantelpiece.

'These women you're forever visiting - '

'The members of the Liberal Women's Association?' she murmured. 'Yes, what about them?'

'Oh, don't you look so innocent, Polly! Some of them are in that votes for women crowd, aren't they?'

She laid her hat carefully aside. 'Yes, I believe one or two of them belong to the National Union of Women's Suffrage Societies, but - '

'I thought so!' His eyes narrowed in triumph. 'And you think women like that are suitable company for Edith?'

'Good heavens, Arnold; calling for the vote is hardly evidence of moral collapse.' She smiled suddenly. 'But I can assure you that Edith has no time for Mrs Garrett Fawcett's campaign.'

He paced across to the piano and stood drumming his fingers on the polished lid. 'I'm not so sure,' he muttered. 'Round at Marsh's this evening we got talking about her group. Did you know that their secretary was at university?'

His look held a mixture of anxiety and suspicion. Once she had found his ability to detect conspiracies where none existed mildly amusing. But that was long ago.

'Are you suggesting there is some wicked female plot and that Edith is being dragooned into going to university by suffragists?' Polly snapped. 'That's an extraordinary notion, Arnold.'

Her tone stung him. 'I don't know what I think, yet,' he blustered. 'But you can be sure that I'll keep a closer watch on my daughter in future. She's been getting these strange ideas from somewhere, and I won't have it!'

******

Polly woke early the following morning. Although she had gone to bed in a calm frame of mind, assuring herself she wasn't worried about Edith or about her husband's stupid allegations, she had not slept well. It was difficult to see where this sudden rift between father and daughter would end. Up till now Edith had been the little princess of his life; nothing was too good for her. There were occasional upsets, of course, small disagreements, but Edith's boast was correct - she had always been able to coax back her father's good temper.

She sat up in bed and reached for her favourite white woollen shawl to wrap round her shoulders. It wasn't an elegant garment but she preferred it to the silk one which her maid left out hopefully from time to time. She would also have worn plain, comfortable nightdresses, instead of these fussy, frilled creations but there was always a remote chance that Arnold would come into her room and it would anger him to see any lack of ostentation.

Perhaps that was what had always angered him, she reflected. Well, not at first: then he had admired her thrift and her ability to feed and clothe the two of them and later Edith and then Kate on very little, so that as much money as possible could go into the shop. Yes, there had been admiration, in spite of the odd nature of their marriage and he'd relied on her too, though he would never have admitted it. She felt that if they could have stayed like that, mutual respect might have deepened into affection. But it was pointless to wish for the impossible. The business had thrived, they had moved out of the rooms above the shop and into a different kind of society. Now Arnold didn't want her to be thrifty any more, but to spend his money and let others see that she was spending it. She had tried, hesitantly, to explain why she found it so difficult; that the early poverty and insecurity of her life had left careful habits ingrained. But he was embarrassed by that and wouldn't listen. So she had become the butt for his sharp remarks and occasional more unpleasant outbursts. It didn't matter, she was no longer hurt, but she didn't want Edith to suffer in that way. She must try to smooth over this situation.

Agitated by her thoughts Polly slipped out of bed and went to the window, drawing back the curtains a little. In the distance the sun glinted on the sea, and fishing boats, their sails filled out by a good, brisk breeze, seemed to skim across the water. In the street below maids were scrubbing front door steps, heads down, suds splashing, eager to be done. For some people the day was already well advanced.

Polly turned away letting the curtain fall. She would suggest to Arnold that the three of them go for a holiday abroad. Of course he would refuse on his own account, being too busy with his plans for the new store, but she was sure he would agree to mother and daughter going on their own. With luck, by the time they returned to Brighton Edith would have forgotten all about university, and life could resume its normal, quiet pace.

She could hear Arnold moving about in the room next door and she toyed briefly with the idea of going to see him at once about the holiday plan. Then she decided against it. He had too much on his mind now: the evening was a better time.

She picked up a book from the table near the window and got back into bed. Arnold had always liked to be up early and she was able to use that as an argument for them having separate rooms when they had moved to this house.

'I want to be able to enjoy the luxury of sleeping late, now that we can afford it,' she had told him. It wasn't true, she rarely slept on, but the flattering suggestion that now his wife could behave like a great lady persuaded him. She soon trained her maid to bring tea and then leave her alone for an hour, so that she could use the time for reading or writing letters.

And having a room completely to herself meant that Arnold no longer came to her at night. He had never been of a particularly amorous disposition and it seemed that the idea of tiptoeing between their rooms deterred him completely.

She heard him go downstairs and leaned back against her pillows and opened her book at the marked page. Soon the maid would come in with her tea and hot water and she would dress and write to Kate. She would have to say something about this business with Edith, but the main purpose was to persuade Kate to reconsider taking a loan to buy the shop. Polly frowned, then dragged her mind away from this new source of concern and back to *The Pickwick Papers*. She was soon involved in "Another Awkward Situation".

Heavy footsteps stumbling up the stairs and along the landing broke her concentration. The door burst open and she looked up, startled. Arnold slammed the door shut behind him and leaned against it, his face dark with fury.

'I've been seeing wicked female plots where there are none, have I? Well, I'm no fool, woman, and you've treated me as one for the last time. I know what this is all about. You've always been jealous of Edith so now you're trying to turn her against me with the help of your fine friend Mrs Riseborough. Yes and Kate's in on it too, I'll be bound!' He gave a kind of sobbing gasp and she was amazed to see his mouth quiver. 'But you won't do it! You won't come between me and my daughter ever again. I'll see to that!' And with a gulp of self-pity he was gone.

Polly carefully placed her bookmark between the pages and laid the book aside. Then she got out of bed and began to set out her own clothes, her face calm, her mind in a frenzy. What on earth had happened to spark off that strange outburst? She couldn't imagine that he had brooded on this all night and waited only until now to come and relieve himself of his feelings. Her heart began to thump. Suppose Edith had not gone to Kate's at all but spent the night wandering the streets... She struggled into her lace-trimmed combinations, her fingers suddenly clumsy.

The maid slipped into the room with a tray, her face full of barely repressed excitement. Obviously all the servants knew what was going on, so Polly asked her outright if Edith had returned and the girl shook her head.

'The master's gone out, just this minute,' she volunteered. 'He had the car brought round.'

'I see. Help me with this, will you? And then tell cook I'll have breakfast straight away. Something very light will do.'

Once downstairs she learnt that her husband had driven out of town on the main road, confirming her suspicion that he'd gone to fetch Edith. She went into Arnold's study, with the vague idea that there might be some clue as to his fury and his speedy departure. Perhaps a note from Edith - though how she had sent it...

The letter lay crumpled on his desk.

"My Dear Polly..." It was a quick and brief response from Clara Riseborough to Polly's letter of a few days ago. She would be only too pleased to lend Polly the money, especially as it was for such a good cause...

Automatically Polly straightened out the creased page. For Arnold to open her letters was nothing new. He usually did it when he was angry with her, to reassert himself she supposed, and it only lasted a while. Her correspondence was of little interest to him. But today he had chanced upon this note. Coming on top of everything else it must have confirmed his suspicion that she wanted money to forward Edith's university plans. He had mentioned Kate in his garbled accusation: he must think her party to the plot. And so he'd gone rushing off to vent his anger on her and to drag Edith home.

She paced over to the window, thinking furiously. It would cause embarrassment, yes, for Edith and for Kate to have him arrive at the cottage and play out a dramatic scene, but Joe's presence would surely prevent any real unpleasantness. Unless Arnold planned to do more than create a fuss. What had he said? Something about her not coming between him and Edith again. Was there real spite behind his words? If so, he had it in his power to cause considerable trouble and hurt.

Polly's face drained of colour and she ran to the door. She must get to Kate's as soon as possible. If Arnold decided to speak out now, after so many years of silence, he could do irreparable damage.

******

Joe got out of bed quietly, hoping not to wake Kate, but as he turned to rearrange the covers over her she opened her eyes and smiled at him.

'Sleep on for a while,' he murmured. 'We were late to bed last night.' But she shook her head and scrambled out beside him.

'I must get on with the baking,' she said, giving her husband's cheek a warm yet brisk kiss. He caught her and turned her mouth to his and her body relaxed against him. It was as though the past weeks with all their awkwardness and anger had never been.

Kate drew away from him, laughing, putting the bed between them before she pulled her nightgown over her head and began to hurry into her clothes. He stared at her long white body and she smiled to show him there would be plenty of time tonight to finish what they had begun between them this fine August morning.

She ran lightly downstairs, full of a new vigour. It was because she'd got her own way about the shop, of course - she admitted that. Now that she could start making her plans the world was a happier place. She hadn't been at all put out when Edith arrived the previous evening and in great distress. She simply sat her down, plied the girl with tea until she was calm again and then settled herself to listen to Edith's story.

Joe had quickly made an excuse to get out of the house with the dogs at his heels and hadn't bothered to hurry back. But after seeing Edith off to bed with a hot brick for her feet, Kate waited up until her husband returned. As he drank a glass of stout Joe was given the full story behind Edith's unexpected arrival. At the end of it he groaned.

'I suppose that means old man Summers will be here tomorrow to fetch her home again,' he complained. 'Well, I'll make myself scarce; you know I can't abide the man.'

'No more can I,' said Kate. 'I gather there were some unpleasant things said between them. He may decide to leave Edith alone for a while.' She added, frowning, 'What really worries me is how this will affect Aunty. He usually takes his temper out on her.'

Joe swore, his own anger flaring all at once. 'I wish she would run away and leave him,' he snapped. 'She could always live with us, and welcome.'

He was all but smothered by Kate's violent hug.

'You're a good man,' she murmured tenderly. Then she sighed. 'But while Edie's single Polly will stay at home. After that too, probably.'

Now, as she set slices of crisp bacon on Joe's plate Kate wondered whether he would find it easy if they had to have Edith as a guest for any length of time. As though reading her thoughts he looked up and asked, with a casual air, which didn't fool her for a moment, what Edith's plans were.

'I told her we'd be pleased to have her until she felt she could go back,' said Kate firmly, filling his mug with hot tea. Then, seeing his glum look, she added with a twinkle, 'She can make herself useful. I'll get her to mind William this evening when we go over to see Arthur.'

They smiled at each other knowing that even Edith's problems must take second place to their plans for the shop. Joe had put aside his doubts about the venture and was as eager as she to persuade Arthur to lend them the money.

'You're sure Betty Halfpenny knows we really want the shop?' asked Kate anxiously, and Joe nodded.

'She obviously took a liking to us, for she's giving us first go,' he said. 'I told you she's had some people over Hurstpierpoint way interested, though.'

'Oh, I hope Arthur won't let us down.'

'Well, Mother's been working on him. If anyone can help loosen his purse strings it's her!'

In his exuberance he jumped up, grabbed Kate and swung her off her feet. They were still laughing, with the dogs leaping and barking about them, when they became aware of Edith, standing in the doorway, a silent and accusing figure.

'Oh, Lord!' Joe released his wife hurriedly. 'I'd best be off.'

Edith sat down at the table and when Kate returned from saying goodbye to Joe, she murmured, 'I don't think he likes me being here.'

'That's silly,' Kate responded sharply. Then she gave Edith an affectionate look and touched her shoulder. 'Do you still enjoy making bread? If so you can help me this morning.'

Edith's smile was strained. 'Should I write to Mother, do you think? Let her know how I am?'

'Yes, you should.' Kate cleared Joe's plate and cutlery and began to lay a place for Edith. 'She might think you're still angry with her.'

'But I wasn't,' Edith protested. 'I was upset at what Father said and I didn't really want to hear Mother telling me we must wait until he's in a better mood and then try to get round him. Honestly, Kate, that's what she always says. It seems as though her whole life with him is built on compromise.'

'I know,' said Kate, sadly.

Edith's chin rose. 'I'd never let my life become like that!'

Afterwards, when she thought of that day, Kate always remembered how they had enjoyed the bread making. Edith soon cheered up and they chatted light-heartedly as they worked, laughing a lot and getting themselves and William covered in flour. Then, when the dough-filled bowls were set to rise, Edith wrote to her mother.

'I'll walk into the village now and post it,' she said, 'and be back in time to get the bread into the oven.'

'Wipe your face first - you're white as a ghost!' Kate laughed.

It was some time after Edith had gone that Kate heard the noise. It seemed vaguely familiar and she stopped what she was doing to listen. Then she frowned and picking William up hurried out into the garden.

'It's the car, lovey. Let's hope it's Aunty come for Edith.'

But in spite of the dust she could see that the upright figure beside the driver wasn't Polly. She sighed then opened the gate and stepped forward with a polite smile as the car halted. Arnold Summers did not smile back. He looked hot and uncomfortable which was hardly surprising, Kate reflected, as he'd chosen to wear a dark tweed overcoat. He nodded a greeting, muttered some instructions to the chauffeur, then stood back to allow Kate to precede him into the house. She tried to show him into the parlour, but he stood squarely in the middle of the kitchen, stripping off his gloves and frowning as he looked about him.

'I'm not making a social call,' he snapped. 'Where's Edith?'

'She's gone to post a letter, Uncle, but she'll be back very soon. Won't you sit down and let me - '

'Letter, eh? That wouldn't be to Clara Riseborough I suppose?'

His voice was harsh. She was aware, suddenly, that he was quivering with suppressed fury. This unnerved her and she hugged William closer.

'She's written to Aunty,' she said, trying to keep her voice level. 'She thought you might be worried about her.'

'I can't answer for your aunt,' he grated, 'but certainly I am very worried.' He came closer to her and lowered his voice. 'You'd do better to tell the truth, Kate. Don't try to cover anything up. I know what's been going on.'

She backed away, alarmed by his strange manner.

'There's nothing being covered up, Uncle. I'm sorry you and Edith have had this disagreement.'

His sharp laugh cut across her words. She watched him pace to and fro in front of the range and wondered uneasily what would happen when Edith returned.

'Well, if you won't have a cup of tea at least sit down, Uncle,' she said in what she hoped was a soothing tone. 'I must get on with the baking.'

He spun round, glaring. 'You're taking this very calmly, young woman,' he snapped. 'Perhaps you don't understand. I know what's been going on. This business about the money. You've played a part in it, haven't you?'

She flushed at the mention of money and he gave a triumphant cry and waved a finger in her face.

'Yes I was right. You're in it too!'

She said quickly: 'Uncle, if you mean the money that Aunt Polly asked you for then, yes, that was going to be for me. But I didn't want her to ask you and I certainly wouldn't have taken it if you'd agreed.'

She saw that he had no idea what she was talking about and she cursed her stupidity in saying too much, but there was no way to put it right.

'She wanted that money for you?'

Kate nodded. 'Joe and I are hoping to buy the village shop.'

He was silent for a while, digesting this new information. Then he stepped away from her and gave a sly smile.

'Well, well... So you and your husband want to rise in the world, do you? That's what the money was for.' His eyes narrowed sharply once more. 'Do you think your Aunt might have written to Mrs Riseborough asking her to lend you what you needed?'

'I suppose that's possible,' Kate answered warily.

Again that uncomfortable silence. Then another question, shot out at her, making her jump.

'And it really has nothing to do with this business of Edith going to university - the money I mean? It's not to pay for her to get in?'

Kate looked at him. Of course that was how he would think - that a place could be bought for whoever wanted it. She knew that her face must betray how much she despised him, but she didn't care. She was unprepared for his shout of fury and the unleashing of his anger.

'Don't you look at me like that! That's just how your aunt looked at me; supercilious, as though I was so much dirt under her feet. I'll not be treated like a worthless imbecile by the two people who owe me so much. I'll not have it! Do you hear?'

William gave a howl of fear and burrowed his head into Kate's shoulder. She cried out for Arnold Summers to be quiet but he was beyond listening. Fists clenched, eyes bulging with rage, he went on shouting at her - an incoherent catalogue of all that he had provided for her since he had taken her into his home.

Once more she tried to interrupt, to shout him down, but it was impossible. With William sobbing in her arms Kate ran to the kitchen door. As she fumbled with the latch his words suddenly rang clear.

'Not many men would adopt their wife's bastard daughter and bring her up with their own child!'

It seemed to Kate that a long time passed before she released her hold on the latch and turned back to face him. But William was still crying; Arnold Summers, though silent now, was still red with rage.

'What do you mean?' The voice sounded too calm to be her own. Yet, as she stepped away from the door and drew a chair forward to sit on, her movements were smooth and unhurried. Only the fierce, almost overwhelming beating of her heart betrayed the effect his words had upon her.

She sat down and made William comfortable on her lap, reaching for a spoon from the table for him to play with. His tears stopped and he began to beat the spoon against his knees.

Her apparent composure had thrown Arnold Summers off balance. He seemed unsure of himself again and was trying to edge his way to the door. She held him with a fierce, questioning gaze.

'It's true,' he said brusquely, trying to gather some shreds of dignity about him. 'You're Polly's daughter. She had you about two years before I married her.'

It was what she had always wished - and it was true.

Arnold had fallen silent.

'Go on,' she urged. 'You must tell me everything now.'

He unbuttoned the overcoat that had become stifling and stood by the table, looking thoroughly uncomfortable.

'I met your Aunt... I met Polly not long after Mother died,' he said. 'It was at a Liberal Party meeting in Brighton: she'd come down to visit some friends - or so she said. She was working for Clara Riseborough in London and I was impressed by the way Polly spoke of her, as though she was a friend rather than an employer. Well, I found out that she came to Sussex whenever she had a day off and so we began to meet after she'd seen her friends. She spent nearly all the time with them, though, and I started to resent that. I was beginning to think she was the sort of woman who'd make a good wife.'

He gave a bitter laugh and Kate started.

'Once I made my intentions clear I soon found out the truth of things. She had an illegitimate child - you. That was why she came to Sussex so often, to visit the couple who looked after you. Oh, it all came out. She was honest enough, I'll give her that. Apparently Mrs Riseborough befriended Polly when she got into trouble and helped her find a place for you and gave her a job into the bargain.'

Arnold squared his shoulders, straightened his cuffs and smoothed a hand over his hair. His self-confidence had returned.

'Well, that shook me for a while, as you can imagine, but after I'd given the matter some thought I decided to go through with my original plan. I persuaded Polly to take me to meet Mrs Riseborough. They were both delighted when I said I'd take you into the family as soon as Polly and I had children of our own.'

Kate felt sickened by his smug tone.

'You know the rest,' he concluded carelessly. 'After Edith was born and the doctors said Polly couldn't have any more children I kept my side of the bargain and you came to live with us. You've had every advantage, Kate, you can't deny that. Very few illegitimate children get such a start in life.'

Her mouth was dry and her voice scarcely rose above a whisper.

'Do you know who my father was?'

'Ah, well...' the knowing look in his eyes made her feel unclean. She lurched to her feet.

******

Edith saw Joe come through the gate and shout at his dogs to stay where they were. He had remembered that Kate was baking and wouldn't want the animals indoors under her feet. Was it the baking they'd been so busy with? Edith looked vaguely down at her hands. No sign of the flour. No, of course not. She'd washed her hands before she went to the village. And her face. Kate had teased: 'You're white as a ghost.'

'Edith, is something wrong?' Joe was standing beside the bench and she raised her head, looking at him in confusion. 'I came back for my cartridge case,' he went on. 'I saw the car as I came down the lane. Is it your father?'

His sympathetic tone touched her and tears started in her eyes. She clutched at his arm. 'I listened outside the kitchen door,' she gasped. 'He was talking to Kate. Telling her things about Mother. I can't believe it, Joe!'

He freed himself from her clinging hands. 'Now don't get upset, Edie, there's a good girl. I'll go in and see what's happening.'

Then they both heard Kate's voice, hoarse and ferocious. 'Don't you dare speak about her like that!'

As William began to wail Joe pushed open the door and Edith followed him in. Arnold Summers was cowering beside the range while Kate stood in front of him and seemed about to strike at him. Joe was at her side in a moment, his arms around her and the child, drawing them away. When Kate turned to him Edith saw that her face was streaked with tears. In a few choking words Kate told him what had happened.

Joe made her sit down, standing behind her chair so that he could keep hold of her. Kate's face was grey now, her eyes dazed. Edith wanted to take hold of her hand and receive some comfort herself, but she couldn't move.

Joe was talking to her father, ordering him to leave. When Arnold Summers began to bluster Joe's tone rose in fury.

'If Edith wasn't here I'd have knocked you down long since. You'd better go, Summers, while I still have hold of my temper!'

'Edith?' Her father jerked round, rigid with dismay as he saw her in the doorway. 'Edith!' He started forward, hands shaking as he reached out to her, but she stepped away from him.

'Father, I heard what you said to Kate. Is it true?'

His face creased with despair. 'I didn't know you were there, Edith. I didn't know.'

'It doesn't matter! You've got to tell me if it's true.'

His eyes darted about the room as though he was looking for some way of escape. But there was none. His hands dropped slowly to his sides and he nodded.

Edith drew a deep breath. 'Now, do as Joe says and go away.'

He hovered a little longer as though trying to decide if there was any way to redeem the situation. Then he picked up his gloves and went out.

Edith began to shudder, hiding her face in her hands. She was alone with her misery only for a moment and then she felt Kate's arms about her.

91

She clung on fiercely and began to sob.

It was a long time before Edith was calm again and by then Joe, somewhat hampered by a fretful William, had made tea and set the pot and cups on the table. Kate and Edith drank their tea in silence and Joe sat with William on his knee, watching his wife. Kate gave him a puzzled look. 'Why didn't she tell me?' she whispered.

Joe shook his head, but it was Edith who spoke, her voice sharp. 'Why didn't she tell us?' She gave a shaky laugh. 'You remember how angry Father used to get when I called you my sister? Mother always told me not to upset him. Why couldn't she have told us the truth then?'

Kate didn't respond. She was still trying to come to terms with what she'd heard. Edith's tears had given her something to cope with but now that small crisis was over she felt dazed. She watched William spill tea on the table, as though looking on from miles away. It was Joe who answered Edith with some annoyance, as if she was a child being a nuisance.

'It's my guess your father made her keep silent. He probably never intended the truth to come out. Today he spoke out of anger, to punish her, and hurt Kate.'

Edith shook her head, still mystified. 'But how could any mother keep the truth from her own children?'

'Out of shame,' said Kate, her voice flat. 'That's what he told me. Because when she was a housemaid no older than Flo she had so many lovers coming to her, night after night, that when she found she was pregnant she didn't know who was responsible.'

Edith made a choking sound. Joe stared at Kate.

'Do you believe that?'

She eyed him blankly and he suddenly thrust his face close to hers and raised his voice. 'Kate! Do you believe that?'

He was through to her at last. She gave a gasp and her mouth began to quiver. 'No, I don't! He's a wicked, wicked, liar.' She sprang to her feet. 'But I wish she'd told me. Oh, I wish she had!'

She pushed back her chair. 'I have to go out,' she muttered and when Joe tried to stop her she shook him off. 'I want to be on my own.'

Edith also rose. 'Let me come with you, Kate?'

But Kate turned away, shaking her head.

When she had gone Edith looked at Joe helplessly. He said, 'She's not taken it all in. Best we leave her be for a while.' But he was equally uncertain and after a while he put William into Edith's arms and went out into the garden. Edith felt deserted.

She looked down at William who was dozing, his face pink and relaxed. Rocking him gently she tried to imagine her mother before her marriage. She had carried with her, for so long, the idea of Polly as an indispensable servant to a wealthy family, leaving only when offered a better post with Clara Riseborough and finally giving up that life altogether for marriage. Now, that no longer fitted. Instead the indispensable servant became - what? A teasing housemaid who had all the men below stairs wild for her? And the master and his sons too, perhaps?

Edith shivered. No, her mother couldn't have been like that. Kate was right - her father had lied. But what was the truth? Gradually she began to weave another picture. Her mother, young and beautiful, loved by the youngest son of the house, a man like Matthew perhaps, for whom the barriers of class meant nothing. He knew his family would object but he intended to defy them and marry the girl he loved. So sure were they that nothing could prevent their marriage that they let their passions carry them away. Then, when Polly found that she was pregnant...

'Edith.'

She turned. Her mother came into the room, looking dishevelled, as though she had been hurrying. But her face was pale and fearful. Buoyed up by her romantic dream Edith gave her a glowing smile and reached out a hand.

Polly listened carefully to Edith's account of all that had happened. 'So now you know everything,' she said, unpinning her hat. Edith shook her head.

'We just know Father's side of the story,' she insisted and her mother gave her a grateful look.

'I'm sorry it should all come out like this, in anger. When I realised your father was coming here I thought he might have this mischief in mind. I got the first train from Brighton but I guessed I'd be too late.'

'I'm glad we know,' said Edith firmly.

'But what about Kate? How did she take it?'

Edith felt a stab of jealousy. 'We were both very shaken,' she muttered. At once aware of her feelings Polly leaned forward and hugged her protectively.

Kate hadn't gone far, only across the track and into the field where she sank down in the grass, already warmed by the sun. Polly had kept the truth from her all this time, so was it anger then, this hot, choking sensation in her chest? Was she furious that Polly had deceived her? No - there were no real lies. Polly had loved her equally with Edith and if she had never been able to own the relationship with her elder daughter she had at least made it clear to Kate that she was valued as much as a daughter would be. So when the tears came they were not for herself but for her mother, forced to maintain the deception for so long.

After a while she wiped her face and went back towards the house, calm now, but with hundreds of questions rattling round in her head. Joe was hovering by the gate, his eyes screwed up with anxiety and she smiled at him, the smile broadening when he told her Polly had arrived. He put his arms about her, murmuring words of comfort which she did not really take in, though she was grateful for his reassurance. He dropped behind a little as they went into the kitchen.

Polly looked up anxiously and Kate paused, not knowing what to say. Then Edith gave a loud sob and William began to squirm on her lap. Kate automatically moved forward and put her arms round her mother and sister and William gurgled with pleasure. Polly smiled at last and the three women clung together.

'Kate's father was a gentleman who came as a guest to the house where I first worked, in London,' Polly began.

The three of them were sitting round the table. Joe had taken William out and could be heard singing to him in the garden.

'But why didn't he help you when he knew you were pregnant?' asked Edith.

Her mother gave her a puzzled look. 'He knew nothing about it,' she replied and seeing Edith's frown she waited for another question, but Edith was silent.

'When I was about three months gone my mistress found out,' Polly went on. 'Of course she said I'd have to go and because she'd never liked me she made a real scene about it - called me some vile names.'

'That's horrible,' murmured Kate, clasping Polly's hand tight in her own.

'Yes, but fortunate too,' Polly smiled. 'I think she made such a to-do because she wanted to impress Clara Riseborough who was there on a visit. Of course she misjudged her guest. Clara took me on one side before I was put out and asked if my parents were able to help me. I said I wasn't sure and she made me promise that if I found myself with no support I'd go to her.'

Polly paused to emphasise her next words. 'Clara never asked me how it happened. I knew she believed I wasn't at fault and that gave me real strength in a very desperate time.'

'What about your parents?' Edith asked and Polly shook her head. She had gone home and told them the truth only to find herself shut out of the house. 'I think my mother might have helped me, if it hadn't been for Father. He was a tyrant - no other word for it - and she didn't have the courage to stand up to him. She knew he would have turned her out too.'

Edith stared, amazed. 'But how wicked!'

'Well... perhaps, but he'd been ill you see, and couldn't work and there was so little money. I think that made him hard and humourless and my mother was too timid to ever cross him.'

'We know what damage poverty can do to people,' said Kate, 'but he shouldn't have turned his back on you. Don't find excuses for him, Mother.'

The name came easily off her tongue and for a moment her confusion returned. Polly's warm smile settled her.

'Well, there I was with no-one to help me. I did my best to help myself, but I had no reference and my condition was beginning to show so I certainly couldn't get another job in service. So eventually I went to Clara.'

Kate watched her closely. How much time had passed before she gave up the struggle to support herself and what had she been through? Her mother's face gave nothing away.

'She was so kind,' said Polly. 'We soon became real friends. Clara arranged for me to come down to Sussex to have you, Kate, and I stayed with the Morrisons at Pyecombe. When you were weaned I left you with them and went back to work for Clara. Officially I was her maid and companion but she treated me like a younger sister. It was a difficult time for her as her husband was very ill. I was able to help them both and I like to think that in that last year before he died I did something to repay Clara for the kindness she'd shown me.'

Edith asked bluntly, 'Was it because of her friendship that Father decided to marry you?'

Polly flushed. Though Edith might sometimes be full of idealistic notions she also had the ability to cut sharply through to an uncomfortable truth.

'I think so,' she admitted. 'He was very pleased with what he called my connections and even more impressed when Clara made us quite a substantial gift of money on our marriage, which he was able to put into the business. I think he saw that as a reward for his Christian charity.'

Kate snorted and with no attempt to hide her disgust described Arnold Summers' self-congratulatory manner when he told her that part of the story.

'I suppose he held it over your head all the time?'

'Oh, it wasn't quite like that, dear. I was fond of him and grateful too - especially after Edie was born and he agreed to adopt you. Of course I was upset that he insisted that we hide the truth of the matter, but I could understand his point of view.'

'There you go again, Mother!' The reprimand came from Edith. 'You're making excuses for Father. The way he's put me above Kate all this time has been absolutely hateful.'

Polly sat up straight, suddenly determined. 'Well, Arnold has broken his side of the bargain now so I feel quite justified in making it known publicly that Kate is my daughter.'

'No, you can't do that,' said Kate sharply and when the others stared at her in surprise she added, 'It will cause so much gossip.'

Polly blinked, but before she could speak Edith rushed in.

'But Kate, we can't leave matters as they are! I want to be able to tell everyone you're my sister - don't you want that too?'

'As long as we know what does it matter? Can you imagine what a meal the Brighton gossips would make of all this? Not to mention folk round here.'

'I don't care,' snapped Edith.

'Maybe not - but I do. I care for you and more especially for Mother!'

There was an uncomfortable silence then Polly murmured doubtfully, 'I suppose I could say I was married before...' But Kate shook her head.

'Let it be,' she said, trying to soften her tone. 'We'll just tell those we love and trust.'

She looked at them both and read agreement in their faces. Edith's came reluctantly, she knew, but she felt sure her mother was relieved by what they had decided.

'Mother...?' Edith found herself suddenly shy. 'Did you... did you love Kate's father very much?'

Amazement filled Polly's face, but it was quickly replaced by understanding. She sighed and gently, almost pityingly, stroked her youngest daughter's cheek.

'Edie, dear, I think you haven't quite grasped what happened. As I said, he was a guest in the house, a young man who'd come as a member of quite a large party. They were celebrating the engagement of my mistress's son. They had quite a lively evening with a good deal of wine. Later that night this young man suddenly appeared in my bedroom. He was drunk, but not too drunk to see that I was very frightened.'

She had begged him to leave, but he wouldn't go. Any other night she would have been safe for she usually shared the room with another servant.

'Only she had a bad cold and the mistress moved her into a separate room up in the attic,' Polly explained. 'That wasn't out of kindness, I may say, but because she didn't want me to get ill as well and have two maids off sick. So I was alone.'

She had threatened to scream and call for help but her unwanted visitor only said that if anyone did come he'd say he was there at her invitation and who would believe her word against his? Far better to keep quiet and take off her nightdress like a sensible girl.

Unaware of the pleasant dream Edith had woven Polly completed its destruction as she added in unemotional tones, 'I was just glad it was over quickly and that he didn't hurt me very much. He obviously hadn't realised I was a virgin because when he saw the blood he seemed ashamed and even tried to comfort me in a clumsy sort of way.' Polly raised her head. 'I spat in his face. I've always been glad I did that.'

Edith's face was red. She opened her mouth but Kate spoke first. 'Yes,' she said firmly. Then she added, 'I'll make us some tea.'

Joe came in just as Kate realised that the fire in the range was nearly out and the dough not yet ready for the oven. At once a great bustle ensued and it wasn't until early afternoon that they all sat down for a meal.

******

Sitting before the mirror that night Kate felt a great weariness overtake her. So much had happened today. It had taken all afternoon for her to catch her breath after the morning's events and then the evening had brought more surprises.

She and Joe had decided to postpone their visit to Arthur, but Polly urged them to go.

'What's happened today mustn't affect your plans,' she said, earnestly. 'If Arthur can help, that will be splendid. And I know Clara would be only too glad to support you.'

'Well...' Kate hesitated, looking anxiously at Joe. He gave Polly one of his sweetest smiles and said with mock docility, 'Why anything you say, Mother-in-law.'

Polly laughed at that and told him not to be saucy. Then she grew serious again. 'I want you to tell your mother what's happened today, Joe. Tell her everything, please. She's a fair-minded woman and I know she won't think badly of me.'

Kate wondered if Polly was right, but it turned out as her mother had anticipated and Jane clucked her tongue in sympathy throughout the re-telling of the morning's events. Then she turned to Kate and patted her arm.

'There's some men not fit to live in decent society,' she asserted, her mouth grim. Then she softened. 'But you can be proud of your mother, Kate. I'll come over and call on her and your sister tomorrow, if that's convenient.'

Kate and Joe exchanged relieved glances. As far as Jane was concerned all was well.

Then they heard Arthur coming in from the forge and sat forward expectantly on their chairs. He did not bother to come right into the kitchen, but stuck his head round the door.

'Evening Kate; Joe.'

Joe cleared his throat and looked awkward and Jane raised her

97

eyebrows. 'Come in, Art, do. You know they want to talk to you.'

Arthur reddened and his big hands clutched the door against him as though for protection.

'Oh... It's about the money isn't it? Well, that's all right Joe. How much do you want?'

Kate, seeing Joe's mouth fall open in amazement, choked back a giggle. Joe blurted out the sum and Arthur looked pleasantly surprised. 'That's less than Mum said. Still, you can have it and welcome. Now come out the back, Joe, will you? I've a new ferret to show you.'

When they'd gone Jane rose, shaking her head. 'I shall never understand men,' she had said in despairing tones, 'not if I live to be a hundred. Art's been saying all week that he doesn't have a penny to bless himself with and moaning on about how you shouldn't lend money to family - and now look at him! Kate, I think I need a little drop of my sloe gin. Will you take a glass?'

'In the end I took several,' said Kate, laying down her hairbrush and smiling ruefully at Joe who sat on the bed unlacing his best boots.

'I don't blame you. I could have done with something to brace me up after Art said his piece. I'm beginning to wonder if I know my own brother as well as I thought.'

'Families are strange sometimes,' murmured Kate, enjoying the warm surge of contentment these words caused. Then she laughed. 'It does seem silly, Joe, but I keep wanting to tiptoe across the landing to see if Mother's really there. It's the way I felt after William was born. Remember how I kept peeping into his cradle to make sure he was still breathing?'

Joe smiled. 'So did I, when you weren't about,' he confessed. 'But don't worry, love. Your mother's here, asleep in her grandson's room and your sister in the room next door. All your family safe.'

They got into bed and she laid her head on his shoulder.

'But they're going back to Brighton tomorrow,' she said, her voice troubled.

'I know, and I think they're right. Things have to be sorted out between your mother and Summers and the sooner that's done the better.'

'You didn't seem so very surprised that Polly's my mother, Joe.'

'I think I've suspected all along that she was more to you than she made out but I knew she'd only keep silent about something so important if there was a very good reason. Perhaps Mum felt the same.'

'Maybe.' Kate yawned. 'Anyway, I'm glad they're good friends.'

'Friends and plotters. They got all this loan business neatly tied up between them, didn't they?'

But she knew from his tone that he didn't resent what had happened.

Settling into his arms she listened with a glow of pleasure while he talked about the arrangements that must be made and how he would go to see Mrs Halfpenny first thing next day. He fell asleep halfway through some complicated calculation of repayments and she kissed his face tenderly before turning down the lamp.

******

Polly and Edith stepped into the drawing room.

'Well, at least our belongings weren't piled up on the front doorstep,' Edith murmured and her mother gave her a scandalised look.

Edith crossed to the mirror and examined her reflection. She felt that after the events of the last few days she must surely look older, more worldly even. She was disappointed to find no obvious change. While she was engrossed the door opened and her father came into the room.

'Ah, you're both back. That's convenient - I've just rung for tea.'

He seemed smaller, Edith thought, as though he had withdrawn into himself. The preening pigeon had become some lesser bird. He was looking at her anxiously as though fearing what she might say or do. Edith approached him and pressed her cheek against his with cold politeness. The anxious look remained.

The maid came in with the tea tray and was sent off again for extra cups and plates. While she was gone they sat in strained silence, their chairs drawn up towards the fireplace even though no fire burnt in the grate. Edith waited hopefully for her mother to speak out but Polly said nothing. Her father kept his eyes fixed on the tray.

At last the maid returned, tea was poured and handed round and they were left in peace. Arnold Summers gave a dry cough.

'Edith, I've been thinking about this idea of yours for going to university. I may have condemned it too hastily. A business associate of mine - you wouldn't know him - well, his daughter won a scholarship to Cambridge last year and he speaks very highly of the place. Perhaps you and I should talk this over again.'

The awkward little speech ended on a pleading note and Edith felt her eyes prickle with angry tears. He was trying to bribe her - trying to get her back on his side, after all the damage he had done. She could hardly believe it.

Polly's voice was sharp. 'Edith, answer your father. It's good of him to reconsider what you asked.'

She stared at her mother. Surely she wasn't going to take his part? Pretend that nothing had changed? She'd been so sure that Polly would treat him differently; would be angry with him, or hard and cold at the very least. There must be some revenge taken for what he'd done. She was determined to do her part by showing her Father no scrap of affection.

99

'Edith,' her mother prompted.

She put down her cup. 'Thank you, Father,' she muttered. Then she stood up. 'But I've changed my mind - I don't want to go to university. If you and Mother will excuse me I'd like to lie down for a while. I have a headache.'

Polly watched her leave the room and sighed. She knew exactly what Edith had expected on their return and was acutely aware that the girl felt let down. She'd been so full of anger on her mother's behalf.

'She's very upset, of course,' said Polly. 'It will take her time to recover.'

Arnold nodded. He replaced his cup carefully on the tray then looked her in the eye at last. His face was grey and tired.

'What are you going to do?' he ventured.

She knew how much he feared what people would say if the truth came out: knew, too, that she could pretend, just for a while, in order to pay him back. Edith would want that. But she thought Kate would understand what an empty triumph it would be.

'We've decided that only close relatives need know that Kate is my daughter.'

His face seemed to melt with relief and Polly went on quickly, 'But you must allow me to visit her whenever I wish and let Edith do the same. I don't think Kate or her family will want to come here.'

She poured out more tea and then handed him his cup.

'Now, tell me how the arrangements are coming on for the new shop, Arnold. Will it really be ready so soon?'

He was grateful for the swift change of subject and got caught up in recounting how he had dealt with a recent minor setback. Before he knew it he had launched into the pros and cons of buying materials and furnishing fabrics from a new supplier and because she knew the business inside out she was able to offer her own views. So they sat for some time over the teacups, engrossed in plans. Polly thought wryly that it was a prosaic conclusion to the drama of the last few days, but she preferred that to further scenes of violent emotion.

Arnold gave a start. 'Look at the time - I've an appointment with the solicitor in half-an-hour.' As he stood up he added gruffly, 'Are they going into business - Kate and her husband? Well, make sure they get proper legal advice. I'll give you the name of a man at Haywards Heath they can deal with - very reliable. No need to say it was my recommendation.'

After he'd gone she rang for the maid. Not a bad man, whatever Edith might think, only proud and rather stupid.

'But then, when you get a lot of proud and stupid men together badness can easily find its way in.'

The maid, gliding into the room, stopped and stared.

'I beg your pardon, Madam?'

'Oh, nothing,' Polly sighed. 'I was talking to myself.'

******

Kate looked up from the china plates she was wrapping as Joe came in. 'Any chance of a cup of tea?' he asked, brusquely.

'Wouldn't you prefer beer, or cider?' Her back was aching but she got up quickly, with a cheerful smile. Since they'd begun packing for the move, now only hours away, Joe had grown quieter and quieter. Today, clearing out his shed, he was thoroughly morose and Kate knew that if she let her own weariness show he might sink into an even worse mood. He couldn't call off their venture at this late stage, but he could make the start of it a thoroughly miserable process. She wondered why on earth he didn't accept that moving house was a difficult business and then just get on with it. She was tired of having to smile and feign a cheerfulness she was far from feeling.

Matthew put his head round the door. 'Beer for me, please,' he called. 'Less trouble than tea. Kate, you look full of energy.'

'Really? I've been up since dawn,' but she was smiling in earnest now. Perhaps Matthew would cheer Joe up. She found the beer and rummaged to unwrap glasses already packed away. The men had sat down on the bench outside the back door and Kate could overhear their talk.

'I didn't realise I'd collected so much stuff,' said Joe. 'And we've not been here that long. It seems like only yesterday I was crowing over having a decent shed to keep things in.'

Matthew laughed. 'When do you go?'

'The carter's coming here for the furniture first thing tomorrow.'

'Well, if you've got such an early start wouldn't it be better if I took Edith to the Hall to stay tonight? You can't really want visitors here.'

'Don't you let Kate hear you suggest that. She wants you both to be here. And in case you've not noticed you're not here to enjoy yourselves. You're meant to help me out here and when Edith arrives she'll be on china packing duty indoors.'

Kate glanced out of the window. The ground outside the shed was covered with piles of tools and pieces of wood, sacking and string. She smiled to herself, wishing she could see Matthew's face.

When she went out with glasses of beer on a tray Joe seemed more at ease, smoking one of Matthew's cigarettes and talking quite cheerfully about his plans for the new garden behind the shop. Kate handed Matthew his glass and he asked after William.

'Joe's mother is looking after him today, and he'll sleep there tonight,' she said. 'All the bustling about was upsetting him.'

101

Joe remarked that William wasn't the only one but Matthew just laughed at his friend and told him to stop moaning and drink up.

'What have you been doing with yourself, Matty?' Kate asked. 'We've not seen you in ages.'

He launched into an enthusiastic account of his teaching, the school and of the headmaster who was known as a man with progressive ideas.

'Adam Grenville: I like him. But you should see some of the children. Thin, sickly looking little things.' Matthew dropped his cigarette end and ground it angrily into the grass underneath his shoe.

'Well, that's the case round here too, don't forget,' said Kate thoughtfully. 'Poverty's not confined to the cities.'

Matthew nodded. 'It's easy to forget that, when you come out of London and find yourself among trees and in fields, breathing fresh air. It seems so different, but it's not of course.'

Kate settled down on the grass with her drink. The men continued to talk about Matthew's new job but she took no part in their conversation. Her mind was ranging over the tasks still to be done before the day was out. Then she realised the talk had come round to Edith.

'I haven't seen her since your news,' said Matthew. 'I suppose it all came as an awful shock to her.'

Before Kate could speak Joe muttered, 'Oh, I'm out of patience with Edith. Apparently she's making life very uncomfortable at home and it's Polly who suffers.'

Kate put down her glass. She didn't want Matthew to hear only Joe's version.

'I think Edith disapproves of Mother's attitude towards Mr Summers,' she explained. 'She thinks Mother's too... oh, well, too kind to him, I suppose.'

'And he doesn't help,' put in Joe. 'Polly thinks it would be better if he was his old, bad-tempered self, then there'd probably be a row and that would clear the air. But instead he grovels to Edith.'

'He's trying to win back her affection by giving her everything she wants,' said Kate. 'Mother says it's pitiful to see. Well, I can't be sorry for him but I can understand how worried Mother is on Edith's account.'

Joe wiped a trace of beer froth off his moustache. 'I'm glad Kate's had our arrangements for the shop to keep her mind off all this,' he said piously. 'Though I know you get anxious, don't you love?'

She felt like snapping back that she worried most about him, but she only nodded.

Suddenly they heard the furious yapping of a motor car horn and as it rolled up at the gate they saw with some surprise that Sam Bundy was at the wheel. Edith sprang out before he could get to the door, and enveloped Kate in a hug.

'Oh, darling, I'm such a beast for staying away so long! Do you forgive me?'

Her voice was light and brittle and, Kate thought, not completely sincere. When she looked into her sister's eyes she saw the unhappiness there. Edith's curls were back in evidence and she was wearing a hat so wide-brimmed that it made her head look fragile. Her short-waisted jacket and skirt were in the latest fashion and Kate could only guess at the cost of the entire outfit, from the feathers on the hat to the high, buttoned boots.

With a wry smile Kate handed Edith on to Matthew and suggested they go in to get a drink for her sister.

'And lemonade for Sam,' said Edith, waving towards the young man who stood beside the car, turning his cap in his hands. 'I insisted that he drive me here,' Edith added. 'I thought he could help us with some of the loading tomorrow and I also hoped that Flo might be about.'

Feeling uncomfortable at Edith's grand tone, Kate looked anxiously at Sam. 'I don't think Flo can manage much time off at the moment,' she said. 'The Gales' house in London is being opened next week.'

'I know,' said Sam quietly. 'But I'll be glad to help here if I can.'

Matthew and Edith went into the house and Kate and Joe hung back, waiting for Sam who was bringing a suitcase from the car.

'I daresay if you go over to the Hall, later on, you might get the chance for a few minutes with Flo,' said Joe. 'The housekeeper's a decent enough soul.'

'Flo and I don't need anyone to arrange our courting, thank you,' said Sam and Joe was taken aback.

'No need to rear up at me like that.' Then he grinned at Kate. 'He sounds a real Cockney when he's in a temper, doesn't he?'

Sam grinned in spite of himself. 'I'm sorry to be rude, Joe.' He closed the gate behind him and rested the case on one of the posts. 'I'm just a bit put out at the moment.'

'Has my sister done something to upset you?' Joe's tone was anxious. Kate knew he'd be really pleased to have Sam as a brother-in-law and she was glad when the younger man shook his head firmly.

'In fact we're planning to get engaged on her next birthday. We want enough money saved before we get married, but we also want everyone to know we're serious.' Then he pulled a face. 'But I don't think I'm going to get that promotion at Summers' after all. Miss Edith prefers me to drive her, not Mr Mitcham, so Mr Summers has had to give responsibility for my work to someone else.'

Joe shoved a hand through his hair in exasperation, making it stand up in a tangled crest. 'Drat that girl! Doesn't she see the trouble she's causing?'

Kate frowned at him and Sam drew in a sharp breath. 'I'm sorry. I shouldn't have said anything.'

'No, it's all right,' Joe shrugged. 'We'll keep quiet about it. Now come in and have that lemonade.'

Kate looked at Sam and smiled. 'If you do find yourself without a job we'll always have a vacancy for you at our store.'

The laugh she had expected didn't come. 'Are you serious?' asked Sam, urgently.

Joe's face brightened. 'Well, we could certainly do with having someone like you around.'

Kate nodded. 'But I don't think Uncle would really want to lose you, Sam. We're a very small business in comparison.'

The gap-toothed smile appeared for the first time since Sam's arrival. 'I've seen your shop and I'm sure you'll do well. If you employ me you can just give me enough to pay for lodgings in the village, until things get going.'

Joe chuckled. 'Well, Kate, it seems we've hired an assistant.'

'But you must think it over carefully Sam,' she insisted, 'and talk to Flo about it. Even if you do want to leave Summers you can get a much better post elsewhere.'

'I'd prefer a job with a bit of a challenge and to work for people I like,' said Sam, his jaunty air fully restored.

Joe went back to his packing in a far more cheerful frame of mind and had his shed cleared in no time. Sam, his uniform jacket cast aside and sleeves rolled up, flashed about the house, emptying cupboards and filling boxes with speed and efficiency. The others were spurred on by his example and by the time they came together again at midday to eat a meal of bread and cheese in the kitchen the packing was well advanced.

'Matty, you'll take Edith for a walk, won't you?' asked Kate. 'And I'm not letting either of you off work. There are some old clothes I've sorted out which you can take down to Mrs Parry near the common.'

******

The sun was warm outside but in the Parry's cottage the air felt clammy and there was a sour, damp smell. Edith refused an offer of tea and waited near the open door while Matthew exchanged a few remarks with Mrs Parry. As she stood looking out to where a group of grubby children were stirring water from jam jars into a pile of ash a little girl sidled up to her and gave her a lopsided smile. Edith looked down into the girl's face. It was smeared with dirt.

'You've got a lovely hat,' the girl whispered.

Edith took it off. She was about to put it on the girl's head but after a surreptitious glance at the matted hair changed her mind. Instead she removed one of the feathers and, taking a hairpin from her curls, she fixed the feather behind the girl's ear. With a beam and a triumphant cry the girl rushed off towards the ash pile. As Matthew and Edith left the cottage garden the children were gathered round their oddly adorned comrade, murmuring enviously.

Edith swung the hat in her hand. 'It's so warm - shall we walk back through the church fields? We can sit by the stream for a while.'

Matthew nodded absently. 'The roof on that cottage hasn't been mended for ages,' he muttered. 'James ought to get someone to go round and see to things like that, instead of trying to manage the estate himself. Good God, he can afford to employ a man now he's got Janette's money.'

'Yes, but they're spending a lot on this new house in London,' said Edith tartly.

'Well, the Parrys can't go through another winter with their cottage in that state.'

'Then tell him,' she suggested.

Matthew nodded. 'As soon as we've got Kate and Joe settled in above the shop tomorrow I'll take a walk round the whole estate. There could be a lot that's been overlooked.'

His concern pleased her and as they walked she asked him about his work. He responded hesitantly, ready to change the subject quickly if it bored her. But she was interested and asked a lot of questions, wanting to know about the teaching and what the children and the members of staff were like. They settled themselves beside the stream, in the shade of a tree, and Edith felt happier than she had for a long time. It seemed that their relationship was, all of a sudden, back on the old, friendly footing and she realised how much this meant to her. Matthew took off his jacket and folded it to make a cushion for her back, against the tree, and then he lay down on the grass beside her.

Edith undid the tiny pearl buttons at her throat and loosening the collar of her blouse raised her face towards the sun. 'Matty, I'm sorry I haven't answered your letters,' she said, unhappily. 'I've been feeling so wretched - '

'It's all right,' he put in, raising himself to look at her. 'I understand.'

'Do you? I wish I did,' she responded with a grimace. 'I'm beginning to wonder if it's all self-pity.'

He waited for her to go on and she knew, with a flood of gratitude, that he was prepared to sit and listen to her for as long as she wished.

'When Mother told us about Kate I was appalled at what my father had done,' she explained. 'I think it's unforgivable and yet Mother went back home, to their life together, as though she did forgive him.'

He chose his words carefully. 'I suppose it's up to your mother to decide how to treat your father.'

'Yes, I realise that now. But I can't behave as though nothing has changed.' She clasped her hands round her knees. 'When I was a child I thought he was so splendid. He was always giving me little treats: it was so exciting. As I got older I was aware of his bad temper and silly ways, but I suppose I still loved him in spite of that. Now I can't even think back to my childhood and say that he was nice then, because I know that all the time he was cheating Kate out of so much happiness.'

She gestured down at her new clothes. 'He's trying to buy back my affection. I've only got to mention something and he gets it for me. He's even agreed that I can try for a university place. And everything he does makes me hate him!'

Matthew picked a long piece of grass and began stripping the stem. 'Have you talked to your mother about how you feel?'

Edith shrugged. 'She's tried to talk to me but I can't seem to say the right thing.' She raised her hands helplessly in a gesture of despair. 'So I'm being unpleasant to her as well as to my father. But I can't seem to help it.'

She turned a miserable face towards him and saw that his eyes were full of tenderness.

'Perhaps you're angry with her, Edie?'

She started. 'With Mother? No - she's suffered so much.'

He pressed on with growing confidence. 'But all that's been about Kate. Maybe you resent sharing your mother with a real sister.'

'What an idea!' Yet his words had struck home and she fell silent, thinking furiously. She'd been reluctant to visit Kate lately - that was true enough.

When she finally spoke her voice was hesitant. 'I'll think about what you've said, Matty, and try to talk things over with Mother.'

Matthew stroked the length of grass across the back of her hand.

'Don't look so cast down. It won't be difficult to put things right with both of them.'

She nodded and felt her spirits rise a little.

'Thank you for listening to me,' she said gratefully. 'You're a good friend.'

He wanted to be more than a friend, she knew that. He'd never given up wanting her. But when he turned away, lying back on the grass and staring up into the tree, she felt a sudden sense of rejection. She didn't want him to withdraw the care and concern that had enveloped her so warmly ever since she'd started talking about herself.

She looked down at him as he chewed on the grass stem and asked what he'd been doing recently apart from teaching.

The smile returned. 'Oh, you'll be pleased with me, Edie.' He sat up and leaned next to her against the tree. 'I've mentioned Miss Wilson, my landlady's daughter, I think? I've been helping her with printing pamphlets for her suffrage activities. She and her mother don't have a great deal of time to themselves but are as active as they can be.'

Edith was aware of a growing sense of disquiet. 'Miss Wilson sounds... an admirable person,' she said and Matthew nodded enthusiastically.

'She's marvellous,' he agreed. 'You must meet her, Edie, I'm sure you'd like her.'

She was sure she would not and knew that the irrational annoyance building inside her was prompted by jealousy. Matthew yawned suddenly and stretched his arms above his head, saying that they ought to go.

'Oh, not yet,' she said, quickly. 'Kate's turning out her linen cupboard and I'd prefer to miss that experience.' She forced a laugh. 'And I'm sure you've had enough of packing boxes for one day?'

He groaned. 'Well, if I'm honest...'

She tweaked the piece of grass out of his fingers and tickled his nose with it. There was a swift, laughing tussle and then he recaptured it and stuck it in his mouth.

'You look like a ploughboy,' she teased and he grinned.

'A poet ploughboy, I trust?'

Their contact had excited her and she let that feeling take control. She plucked the grass from his mouth and, leaning close to him, rested her lips briefly on his. His eyes widened with amazement and he pulled her against him for a longer, harder kiss. He was trembling, his whole body trembling and she felt a glow of pleasure. He lifted his head, his eyes full of hope and she smiled at him, moving so that she was lying across his lap. He bent his face down to hers once more and this time when he kissed her she opened her lips and drew his tongue into her mouth.

As they walked back along the lane Edith thought that if she wasn't holding his arm he'd probably be turning somersaults. His pleasure gratified her and the devotion in his eyes when he gazed at her gave her a warm feeling of her own worth. It was wonderful to be able to please someone in this way. For the first time in weeks she felt at ease. Matthew's comforting presence today had begun to loosen the tension but his kisses and the security of his arms about her had done the most good. The love in his eyes and the warmth of his mouth had restored her. Already he had spoken of love, as they reluctantly gathered up their things and left the shade of the tree.

'You know how I feel about you, Edie. That's not changed since we first met.'

But she wasn't so far gone in her need for him to lie. 'I don't quite know what my feelings are, Matty. But I care for you very much.'

That seemed to more than satisfy him. He walked beside her with a light step, exuding happiness.

'I hope there's some tea left,' she said quickly, to distract herself from a sudden sense of guilt.

'We're probably in disgrace for being away for so long,' he grinned. 'Nothing for us!'

But when they got back Joe and Kate were drinking tea with Sam in the kitchen.

'Sorry we've been so long - Mrs Parry kept us talking,' said Matthew. 'She needs a new roof on that cottage, you know.'

'The whole family needs more than that,' grunted Joe.

Edith sat quietly in her chair, watching the others. They seemed infected by Matthew's happy mood and even Sam, who rarely aired his opinions in public, was drawn into a discussion about farm workers' housing.

After a while Edith touched Kate's hand and murmured, 'Shall we get on and leave them to talk? I've hardly done a thing all day.'

Up in William's room Kate sorted through a pile of blankets, coverlets and linen.

'I've already made up your bed next door,' she said, 'but if you could put some fresh sheets on this one for Matty that would be a great help. I'll take the rest of the blankets downstairs - Sam's going to sleep on the sofa in the parlour tonight.'

Edith gathered up two pillows, then abruptly laid them down again.

'You know I've been so stupid,' she said, and had to stifle a giggle at Kate's startled look. Whatever did her sister think she was going to confess?

'Making things horrible for Mother by my behaviour at home and then staying away from you... It's been childish of me.'

'No, I understand,' said Kate firmly. 'It's all been very muddling.'

'Yes, it has,' said Edith, gratefully. 'I always wished you were my real sister but when that wish was granted I behaved horribly. It's completely irrational.'

Kate nodded. 'But I think you must try to find a way of getting on with your father for Mother's sake, even though it won't be easy.'

'She's unhappy for him too and that makes me even more angry. Kate, I think I'll have to go away.'

'To university, you mean?'

Edith shrugged. 'Perhaps. I'm not really sure that's what I want any more.'

'You can come and stay with us.'

Edith gave a strained laugh. 'I can see Joe loving that!'

'I'll make him understand,' said Kate firmly and the next moment she was wrapped in a fierce hug.

'Oh Kate, I'd not let you upset Joe on my account - but it's wonderful to know you would!'

They drew apart, laughing, and Kate gazed at her sister, taking in the flushed cheeks and sparkling eyes.

'You know, Edie, you've been looking a lot happier ever since you got back from your walk. What else did you and Matty talk about?'

To cover her confusion Edith reached across the bed and grabbed at the sheets.

'Don't say anything else,' she murmured. 'You might break the spell.'

******

Kate stood beside her husband at the garden gate, looking out towards Wolstonbury as dusk fell. Giving the excuse that they needed to check there was nothing forgotten they had left the others in the parlour and gone together through the house, looking into each room, before slipping out of the kitchen door and into the garden.

'Was there enough for supper?' Kate asked. 'I hadn't counted on Sam being with us.' Joe put an arm round her shoulders.

'Good Lord, woman, you did us proud. In any case Edie only had a titchy little helping - and she just picked at that. What's she up to now, do you think?'

'It's been a very difficult time for her, Joe. Don't be so critical.'

'Well, it's difficult for you and your mother, too.'

Kate watched the hill gradually disappearing into darkness. 'I was wondering if there's something between her and Matty,' she said, tentatively. 'She's been so nice to him this evening.'

'Don't try match-making, love. That was all over long ago.' But he pulled her closer to him in a warm hug and for a moment she leaned her head against him. Behind them they heard a strong voice launch into a popular song and they both turned quickly towards the sound.

'Matty can't hold a tune to save his life, so that must be Sam,' said Joe. 'He's singing for his supper!'

Sam entertained the company with a few more songs then they all took a final drink together. Joe banked up the fire in the range. After breakfast the following morning it would be allowed to go out for the first time since he and Kate had moved into the cottage.

Sam took himself off into the parlour, candle in hand, his shadow small and gnome-like against the wall. Joe and Kate led the way upstairs, then said goodnight to Edith and Matthew who suddenly started up a conversation about Sam's impromptu concert.

'I didn't think Quakers were allowed to have so much fun,' Edith murmured and Matthew laughed.

'Oh, they're not a rigid sect. I went to a Quaker meeting once. Can't remember where - or why. I think I was visiting one of my old nurses and she took me along...'

Joe grunted and muttered something about having to get up very early and ushered Kate into their bedroom. Once the door had shut Matthew lowered his voice but continued his description of the Quaker meeting, while opening his bedroom door. He put his candlestick on the floor by the bed and looked back anxiously at Edith. She gave a loud yawn.

'Matty, you can tell me all about the Quakers tomorrow, I promise,' she said, raising her voice a little. 'But I'm almost asleep. Goodnight!' And she opened the door of her room, closed it briskly then stepped across the landing and into Matthew's arms, narrowly avoiding singeing his ear. He pushed the door to and stood against it, holding her close.

'Put that wretched candle down somewhere and let me kiss you properly,' he whispered.

******

Edith leaned on the window sill, watching the first strands of daylight spread delicately across the sky. Then she went over to the bed and began to fold up the unused sheets and blankets, knowing there was a foolish smile on her face as she did so. She hoped that Matthew was still sleeping, just as she'd left him, spread naked beneath the sheet, one arm across his face as though shielding his eyes from a bright light. He had fallen asleep an hour ago and she had kept silent vigil beside him, leaning on one arm and watching his face which seemed so vulnerable in repose. It had been difficult to slide out of bed and dress and she thought that if he'd woken she might have stayed, risking their being found out. But he slept on and she left him at last.

She had wanted them to make love properly last night, to take him inside her and experience what she felt sure would confirm that her feelings for him were true and right. But even though she clutched him against her, whispering her longing, then kissing him again and again, he eventually held her away.

'Edie, we can't,' he groaned. 'If I make you pregnant - '

'We can marry,' she whispered and gave an excited laugh.

'And can you imagine the scene when I go to your father and explain our situation and ask his permission? What he'd say and do - and what your mother would think?'

She had shivered suddenly and Matthew stroked her hair, already free

110

of its pins and combs.

'Do you really want to marry me, Edie? This afternoon you said you weren't sure of your feelings.'

'I love you,' she said, then jerked her head back and stared into his face. 'Why? Do you think I'm not worthy of you now, because I want us to be lovers?'

'Oh my darling, of course not! I want you too, you must know that. And I want you to stay with me tonight. But we have to be careful.' He kissed her mouth again, gently and slowly. 'And we can make each other happy. Let me show you.'

She went back to the window sill. Now the dawn was sliding into being and she opened the window to catch the first fresh breeze of the day, as delicate on her face as Matthew's fingers on her body. They had undressed each other, slowly at first, then with increasing excitement gazing, touching and kissing. In the small bed they had to press close together and feeling him so hard against her she hoped dizzily that he would give way and was annoyed to find her mind wandering into the mundane realm of how to deal in the morning with bloodstains on the sheet beneath them. But instead he showed her how to hold and stroke him and give him his pleasure and afterwards he did the same for her.

And watching the trees become clearer as the light grew she admitted to herself that she was glad they had made love in that way. They talked in whispers for a long time afterwards, making plans for a shared future which filled her with excitement and happiness. And then he had kissed her face and breasts and, shockingly, all the way down her stomach until she had to push the sheet into her mouth to stop herself crying out.

The sound of muffled conversation, doors opening and closing, and footsteps on the stairs told her that Joe and Kate were going down for breakfast. And now she heard Matthew moving about next door. She went out on to the landing and waited anxiously for him to appear. After what she had done last night would he still feel the same about her?

She needn't have worried. He admitted to being as fearful and they laughed guiltily together as they hugged and kissed.

'Let's go and tell them we're engaged,' she whispered and he took her face between his hands and smiled happily.

'Edie, it's obviously escaped your notice, but I haven't proposed to you yet.'

'Oh dear. Then we'll tell them I'm your loose woman.'

'Shall I go on bended knee here? On the landing?'

'Why not? If I know my sister the floor is spotless!'

'Engaged!' Kate dropped the bread knife and darted round the table to hug her sister. 'Oh, that's marvellous! When did this happen?'

'I proposed on the stairs just now,' Matthew grinned. Joe stopped chewing his bacon and stared up at his friend in disbelief, while Sam Bundy hurriedly swallowed a mouthful of tea and offered his congratulations.

Kate kissed Matthew's cheek. 'I'm so pleased for you both,' she said and cast an imploring gaze at her husband. Joe flexed his shoulders, as though shaking off doubt, and stood up to shake hands with Matthew.

'We want to keep this secret for a while,' said Edith firmly. 'I'll tell Mother, of course, but we'll have to pick the right time to break the news to my father. We want to wait until Matthew is properly established as a teacher.' She sat down at the table. 'I'm famished,' she announced. 'Can I have some bacon too, Kate?' Joe rolled his eyes at his wife and she feared that he'd suggest Edith cook it for herself. But next minute they heard a cheerful shout from outside.

'It's the cart,' said Joe, with a wide grin. 'No time for breakfast!'

******

'Oh, your hat!'

The young woman next to Edith made a vain attempt to reach after the hat as it rolled along the ground, but she too was pinned fast by the crowd. Edith watched the dainty brown and white creation disappear under many pairs of scuffling feet, with little regret. She had felt, rather than seen, the placard swooping down towards her, snatched from someone in front by one of the policemen, and she was only thankful she'd lost nothing more than her hat.

'Are you all right?' asked her neighbour. 'It only just missed your head.' She rescued the hatpin dangling behind Edith's ear and Edith put it in her handbag.

'I'm sure that policeman threw the placard deliberately,' Edith said shakily. The young woman gave her a sympathetic look.

'Don't expect them to behave like gentlemen. As far as they're concerned we are no longer ladies.'

At that moment the crowd surged forward again and she was jostled away. Edith tried to struggle after her but was at once swept back again and almost fell. She clutched at the nearest arm to regain her balance and was briefly aware of an unknown woman's smiling face and a hand steadying her. Then someone shouted that the police were giving way and there was triumphant laughter all around her and a sudden concerted advance.

Not for the first time that day Edith wished she was taller. Near the back of the crowd, waiting to march on Parliament, she had been unable to see the deputation led by Mrs Pankhurst. They were trying to get into the House to demand a meeting with the Prime Minister but Edith didn't know if

Clara Riseborough was with them or not. She got only an occasional glimpse of the police and couldn't tell if they were arresting women at the front. She felt helpless, able only to move with the mass of women about her, and then not far. It was not what she'd expected.

'My dear, it won't be what you expect.' Clara's words, spoken disarmingly over breakfast that morning were now recalled with a grimace. 'Mrs Pankhurst will read out Asquith's latest statement on the Conciliation Bill and then I expect we'll march on the House. There won't be a great deal of socialising.'

Edith, put out, had responded sharply: 'I don't want to come for the gossip, Clara. I want to support whatever action is taken.'

Mrs Riseborough had set down her cup with a clatter. 'Edith, dear, I'm sorry! I don't mean to imply that your motives are trivial. But I promised your mother not to get you involved in any public activities of the WSPU. And imagine what your father would say!'

Edith thought of the current newspaper image of the Suffragette - hard, loud-voiced and ugly - then smiled, for Clara was the exact opposite of that false vision. Though somewhat older than Edith's mother and widowed for many years Clara still took great pains with her appearance and even at breakfast was dressed as though expecting a Royal Visit. It was unlikely, though, that the new King would be as eager to call on attractive women as "Good old Teddy" had been.

Ever since she came to live with Clara at Elm Square Edith had been well aware of the woman's power over men. At her regular dinner parties and evening gatherings - for Clara entertained a great deal - Edith watched her smile and flatter and win her way with many gentry, politicians and businessmen. They all knew about her involvement in the women's suffrage movement; knew also that behind the pretty face lay a sharp mind. Yet it was the charm they succumbed to when she urged them to lend their support to the cause.

Over the breakfast table that charm had been directed at Edith.

'I'll invite Emmeline and Christabel for dinner one evening next week,' Clara smiled. 'Yes, I know I'm fobbing you off, darling, but I really can't let you come with me today. Besides, aren't you going to visit Margaret Wilson - taking those books you sorted out for her?'

So Edith had put her new hat on her head and her books in a bag and hurried away to where she usually caught the omnibus.

Now, without the hat, the bag of books long since jettisoned because it had become too heavy, she wondered if it would have been more sensible to take that omnibus after all, instead of letting it go by and setting out on foot in the opposite direction.

No. She tucked her handbag more firmly under her arm and settled her feet apart, ignoring the ache in her ankles. She was glad to be here, to be part of this protest. As the women marched on Parliament Square they linked arms, even though many had never seen each other before. Edith guessed it must feel like this marching to war in a just cause. All around her she had sensed, with exhilaration and growing excitement, the combined strength of the women.

Now there was another movement in the crowd and Edith saw a small gap open up on her right. Without hesitation she slipped through, pushing her way forward, using her height and build to advantage at last by wriggling under restraining arms.

'Come on, now!' Two hands grasped her upper arm so tightly that she cried out in pain. The policeman released her at once but with a shove that sent her staggering backwards against those behind her. She realised that she was right at the front.

Two other women rushed forward into her place and the policeman struggled to hold them both. One pulled away from his grasp but another officer restrained her, clasping the woman under her armpits and hauling her off her feet. Edith saw her face twist with pain. She was thin and fragile; the policeman big and broad, his shoulders and arms stretching the heavy serge of his coat. He had no need to hold her like that; he could have moved her easily aside. But he was grasping her tight, squeezing the breath out of her, so that she couldn't even cry out. Edith felt a cold rage possess her. She darted behind the policeman and struck at his back and shoulders, using her handbag as a weapon. She knocked his helmet forward and he had to release his captive to push it back from his eyes. To Edith's relief she saw that the woman, though shaking, was able to stand and she hurried to support her.

A hand grabbed the back of her coat, just below the neck, halting her in mid-stride. She had time to register the grateful glance of the woman she'd helped, then she was swung round to face the policeman. His other hand gripped her shoulder, bunching the material and pulling upwards, so that she was forced up on tiptoe as he marched her away. Was he arresting her?

He pushed her backwards and she fell against something hard - a tree, or railings, she couldn't be sure - and shoved his face almost against hers.

'You bitch!' he hissed and shook her again and let her fall back. She felt pain in her shoulders and the length of her spine. 'Votes for women, is it? I know what you need and it's not the vote!' The hands reached for her again and the shaking was repeated. She found she could hardly breathe. The angry face jerked forward again. 'You need a thorough good hiding!'

The face was red and sweat-soaked now and the eyes full of hate. She felt helpless terror before that hatred. She couldn't escape.

In her dazed condition she thought for a moment that she had uttered the terrible scream which cut like a knife through the turmoil all around them. But the policeman was looking away, over to the right, his eyes gleaming. She didn't know what was happening but it gave her the chance she needed to summon up her failing strength. As he turned back to her she struck him with her bag, full in the face.

It wasn't heavy, did little damage, but the surprise was enough to send him staggering sideways and he lost hold of her. She drew back her hand and dealt another blow. This time he cried out and the fury in his face turned to amazement. He clapped his hand against his chin and she saw blood oozing between his fingers and guessed that the hatpin had driven through the cloth and cut him. Before he could move to grab her again she turned and ran.

There was a wide-open space before her now but she had no idea where she was. All she knew was that she must keep on running and running so that he would never catch her. So she didn't see the horses until she was amongst them and was too frightened to take in the warning shouts of the riders. She was saved by the quick action of two young women who pulled her to safety and was just able to gasp out her thanks before she fainted.

******

Clara Riseborough hovered beside the bed watching as Alice, her maid, rubbed ointment into Edith's back. Clara's full mouth clenched into a hard line as she saw the bruises on the young woman's shoulder blades. She had returned to the house only half-an-hour ago to be met by Alice, wringing her hands and wailing that Miss Edith had been brought home almost unconscious but was refusing to let a doctor be called. Convinced there had been some accident at the Wilsons Clara took a little while to uncover the true story.

'Edith, you must let me get Dr Jensen. You look dreadfully pale,' she murmured.

'No.' The voice was a little muffled by the pillows, but the refusal was firm enough. Edith twisted her head round to look at Clara. 'I just need to rest.' Then she smiled. 'This ointment is doing me good.' Alice clucked and muttered and smoothed more over Edith's shoulders.

'And you say it was a policeman who did this to you?' Clara sighed. 'Well, I'm afraid that doesn't surprise me, my dear.' Her voice hardened. 'They behaved like brutes today. A lot of women were badly hurt.'

'Not you?' Edith struggled to sit up. 'You're not injured?'

'No, no.' Clara smiled in spite of her weariness and leaned forward to help Alice ease the nightgown back over Edith's shoulders. 'Like you, I just need to rest. Alice, will you bring us some tea up here, please? Then I'd like

115

my bath.'

When the maid went Clara sat down on the bed and arranged the covers more cosily about her charge.

'It's no good my being angry with you for going on the march today,' she said. 'Too late for that. But suppose you'd been badly hurt, Edie? Or been arrested? How could I have faced your parents?'

Edith flushed. 'I'm sorry,' she said, 'but you weren't to know how violent it would be.'

Clara shook her head. 'It was appalling. I don't think I'll ever feel the same way again about the police. They're supposed to uphold the law!'

Edith remembered the sweaty face and the hate-filled eyes so close to her own and began to shudder uncontrollably. With an anxious murmur Clara sprang up, hurried out of the room and was back in a moment with a decanter and glass.

'Brandy,' she explained as she poured out a large measure. 'I keep some in my bedroom - as a treatment for colds, you understand.'

She held a glass between Edith's chattering teeth and tilted it so that she could take a sip. After a while the shuddering stopped and Edith had regained enough strength to push the glass away.

'I don't really like your cold remedy,' she said and gave a shaky laugh.

'Nor I, but it does the trick,' smiled Clara and she swallowed the brandy left in the glass.

Edith leaned back against her pillows. 'The women who brought me home - they were so kind,' she murmured. 'They only stayed long enough to make sure I was in good hands and I forgot to ask their names.'

'I think that many strangers would have found themselves supporting each other today, without expecting any thanks.'

'Yes,' Edith agreed. 'It felt as though we were all working together. That part of it was good.'

Alice came in with a tray. Edith saw there were sandwiches and cakes as well as tea and realised she was ravenously hungry.

'Mr Matthew's downstairs,' reported Alice with a disapproving sniff. 'I told him what had happened but he won't go away. It was all I could do to stop him rushing up here.'

Clara frowned. Alice was loyal but far too ready to gossip. 'You'd better let him see you, Edith, or he'll plague us all.' She poured herself a cup of tea. 'I'll take this with me and get changed. Don't let Matthew stay too long, mind. You need some sleep.'

Although she was munching her way through the sandwiches when he appeared it took Edith some time to reassure Matthew that she wasn't seriously hurt. He tried to hug her but the tray on her knees was in his way, so he contented himself with holding tight to her hand.

'When I got back from school Margaret told me she'd been in the Square and what happened,' he gabbled. 'I came round to see how Clara was. I never dreamed you were there too.'

Edith dismissed his anxiety, explaining what had happened. She was more concerned to hear about Margaret Wilson. During the past year in London she had got to know the young woman well and to admire her commitment to the WSPU. She admired, too, Margaret's artistic talents and wished she could have the chance to use them instead of devoting her life to her mother. They had discussed that many times, but Margaret always insisted that her mother must come first.

'She's been a widow since I was very young and she's always done her best for me,' she said. 'I'm perfectly happy with the way things are, Edith; helping her with the boarding house. I used to have more time for painting but that's mostly taken up with the suffrage movement now.'

Matthew smiled at Edith. 'Margaret's fine; though somewhat buffeted about I think.' His face darkened. 'She told me how the police behaved. Oh, love, are you sure you shouldn't see a doctor? Alice said you were badly bruised.'

'Mind the tray, Matty!' She rescued her cup and saucer. 'No, don't fuss.'

He drew away a little and Edith, seeing his hurt expression, felt the now familiar guilt and the usual sense of annoyance which always followed.

'How was school today?' she murmured and had the satisfaction of seeing his face brighten.

'You remember those two lads I told you about? They've certainly buckled down to their arithmetic since I started giving them extra time after school. They're very bright really but you can't expect them to keep up when they have to work as well to help their Gran.'

He talked for a little longer about the boys whose parents, despairing of the poverty of their life in London, had recently scraped together enough to buy a passage to America, promising to send for their children as soon as they got settled. Matthew wondered if the summons would ever come. 'People think there's easy money to be made over there, but I can't believe it's much different,' he said.

He took the tray off her lap and moved closer to her.

'I'm so tired,' she murmured, feeling suddenly and surprisingly nervous.

'I know, and I promised Alice I wouldn't stay long. She'll soon be in to chase me downstairs.'

The gentle voice, the smile, were so familiar and should have been

117

soothing, but as his face came nearer and his hands reached out to touch her she felt her heart begin to thump. Panic set in and as his fingers rested on her shoulders she gave a cry and shrank away.

'What is it?' Matthew's face was full of dismay. He moved back and she began to take control of herself again.

'I - it's my shoulders - the bruises...'

He was immediately contrite and then swiftly angry over what had happened to her. His protective manner pleased and comforted her and she was able to take his hand again and hold up her face to be kissed. His mouth was soft on hers and she knew he was restraining his feelings. Well, that was no bad thing.

After he'd gone she lay back and tried to work out if her feelings for Matthew were changing. They had felt most strong during her first weeks here with Clara. Her father, in his new, acquiescent mood, had been easily won over to her plans for staying in London and had even been persuaded to let Edith go on seeing Matthew in company. Edith had soon let her mother into the secret of their unofficial engagement and was pleased with Polly's response.

'He's a fine young man, Edie, and he'll make you a good husband. But it's sensible of you both to wait a while before thinking of marriage.'

So Polly had agreed that Clara should also be told and authorised to allow the couple some time on their own. As far as Clara was concerned this meant that Matthew could visit Edith regularly at Elm Square and take her out to the theatre or dinner.

When Edith had last visited Kate Matthew arranged to be at the Hall and had come over to stay the night. When everyone was in bed he went to Edith's room but almost as soon as they began to kiss and touch each other William woke up. They lay together, rigid with fright, listening to doors opening and closing and Kate's low voice soothing the tearful child in the room next door. Eventually, everything was quiet again but neither of them could relax and so Matthew left. Back in London they were rarely on their own in private for long and their few intimate moments were hurried and not always satisfying.

Edith's mind came back to the usual conclusion - that everything would be all right once they were married and living in their own home. But she couldn't avoid the fact that she'd begun to feel differently towards Matthew, uneasy at any physical demonstration of his affection for her, and guilty because she felt like that.

She groaned as she eased her body into a more comfortable position in bed and then she closed her eyes. For a long time before she slept the vision of a hate-twisted face was sharp against her eyelids.

Matthew found Clara was waiting for him in the drawing room, clearly anxious still.

'Matthew, you do understand that I had no idea what Edith was about today?'

He quickly reassured her and she sat down in one of the fireside chairs, indicating that he should take the one opposite.

'What are we going to do?' she murmured. 'If she insists on getting more and more involved she could find herself arrested.'

He couldn't help but smile. 'This from a woman fully prepared to throw missiles at erring politicians and risk imprisonment for the cause!'

Clara smiled at that, shrugged and spread her hands and he remembered Edith telling him about all the admirers who came visiting. 'And she's older than Mother,' Edith had added, with a touch of amazement.

'That's a different matter, as well you know,' Clara said. 'I think I can cope with Arnold's outrage if Edith does something stupid but not Polly's pain. I should send her back to Brighton, of course, but I don't want to deprive you of her presence, dear, and I know how difficult things have been for her there.'

Matthew nodded. 'We really appreciate being able to meet here, without risking gossip,' he said.

'Perhaps if you could announce your engagement...?' Clara looked at him hopefully.

'Edith doesn't want that yet. She thinks if I complete this year at Shrub Grove and show I'm really serious about teaching that could help ease matters with Mr Summers.'

'Well, what can we do in the meantime to distract Edith a little from the Suffrage cause so that she doesn't get into any more serious trouble? We need her to be involved in something worthwhile but which doesn't risk her being arrested. What a pity she decided against trying for university. I've raised that with her again but last time I did she snapped out that her only real talent is playing the piano.'

He sighed. 'Well, that's not true - ' Then he broke off and gave a broad grin. 'Oh, Clara, you clever creature. You've just reminded me of a way to resolve all this. Let me explain, and then you can advise me on how to present this idea to Edith.'

******

Edith walked into the school hall, at Adam Grenville's side, watched suspiciously by the children. Their teachers, Matthew included, hushed enquiring voices and the headmaster quickly got on with the business of wishing everyone good morning and introducing Edith.

'Miss Summers has very kindly agreed to play the piano for our

119

hymns this morning,' he explained. 'I know that since Miss James left us to become Mrs Morrison we've missed her in our assemblies.'

Edith held back a smile. 'It's been appalling,' Matthew had told her. 'Anne James was a really good teacher and her musical skills were outstanding. Jane Monk, who's replaced her, is a fine teacher but she doesn't play piano and no-one else has the right skills, so in assembly each morning we bash away at the hymns without accompaniment and make the most awful racket. Graham Maynard booms out but always in the wrong key, and the rest of the staff are too busy trying to keep straight faces. By lesson time the children are practically spinning like tops - takes an age to calm them down in class. Edith, if you could come and help out for just a while it would be wonderful.'

'Your Mr Grenville wouldn't mind?'

'He says he'd be forever in your debt!'

She had laughed at that, then added more sharply, 'Doesn't Margaret Wilson play? She lives nearer the school - I'm sure she'd be only too pleased - '

'Edith, you've much more skill, and you get on so well with children. Please say you'll help.'

Sitting at the piano now, and playing the introduction to the first hymn, she wondered if she'd made the wrong decision. As the singing began she was convinced she had. The adult voices were ragged and overpowered by a fiercely tuneless tenor she could only assume belonged to Mr Maynard. Some of the older girls were doing their best but the boys either warbled away with little enthusiasm or laughed outright at Mr Maynard. She groaned inwardly. She shouldn't have come - it was a stupid idea. She was a fool to have listened to Matthew and Clara. She stopped playing, stood up and turned round and the voices trickled to a halt.

One of the boys grinned at her. But she thought he wasn't mocking, merely waiting for her to correct matters.

'Well, that wasn't very tuneful,' she said, with a smile. 'Hymns are meant to be sung to praise our Lord, but I think if he heard that he'd stick his fingers in his ears - don't you?'

There were a few laughs and some gasps and she wondered if she'd gone too far.

'So let's do it better, this time. I want all the girls and the lady teachers to come forward and stand at this side of the piano and we'll have all the male voices on the other side. And, Mr Maynard, I'd be so grateful if you would be my music-turner, so I can watch our choir properly. All ready? Right, we'll try again.'

It wasn't a lot better, she thought, giving an emphatic rendition of 'O

120

worship the King' but with Mr Maynard otherwise occupied, and looking rather smug while at it, the voices had a better chance. She moved quickly into the other designated morning hymn and then everyone went back to their seats and Mr Grenville led prayers.

'And before you go to your classes I'm sure you'll want to say thank you to Miss Summers for playing for us this morning. I hope she'll do so again.'

Edith found herself touched by the chorus of thanks and the smiles from the children. During prayers she'd had the chance to look at the assembled youngsters properly. None was in rags and most had reasonably clean clothes and wore boots, but their faces were thin and some had dark rings round their eyes as though they slept little. She thought of the Parry children and understood why Matthew was so concerned about the family.

Once the hall had emptied the headmaster smiled at her. 'We really are grateful, Miss Summers. Do you think you could do this again - can you bear to come back to play for our morning assemblies?'

She'd liked Adam Grenville at once, just as Matthew had said she would. He was a tall man, with a long but well-shaped face and a full moustache, touched here and there with grey like his thick, close-trimmed hair. She knew he'd been a widower for some years and looked for signs of neglect about his clothes but he was as neatly turned out as her father always was, though his suit was nowhere near as expensive as those Mr Summers bought.

She found herself saying she'd be pleased to do so, at least until they found a teacher who could take over the task.

'I have a full complement of staff at the moment.' He frowned. 'Look, I'll be frank with you Miss Summers. It would be a tremendous help if you can play some mornings and also for our weekly country dancing classes. And the youngsters have a choir which should rehearse in the dinner hour some days, but without Miss James it hasn't been singing together at all. I can rearrange the timetable so that you'd not need to be in every day and I'll make sure you're properly remunerated, of course. I just think children need music in their lives, don't you? These youngsters don't often get that at home.'

Edith nodded and he asked if she'd like time to think about his suggestion.

'No: I'll do it. I'll be happy to.'

'That's splendid.' He smiled broadly. 'But in future perhaps you could refrain from speculations on the Lord's reaction to our singing in assembly?'

On the omnibus Edith was in good spirits. It would be interesting to see what she could achieve at Shrub Grove and already she had ideas for organising the school choir as well as tunes in mind for country dancing.

121

Then she remembered the letter from Kate which had arrived that morning and which she'd been too full of nerves to read. She took it from her bag, skipped the greetings and enquiries about health, and was soon immersed in Kate's news.

"Our regular order from the Hall is getting larger week by week and we can only assume they are stocking up for Christmas well in advance. According to the gossip Sir James and Lady Janette are entertaining on a grand scale this year. I suppose they expect to couple the religious festivities with a celebration of great Conservative gains after the General Election! We're sure, though, that the Liberals will hold on and, of course, they'll get the support of the Labour MPs. Michael Thomas, who comes to supper with us once a week now, has been very excited about the Bill limiting some of the power of the House of Lords. He'd like to see that chamber completely abolished and I agree with him, but Joe isn't so sure.

"It was after one of our more lively debates, a week or two back, that Joe said he'd really like to know more about politics, not just what's happening now but the background to political thought. So he's enrolled for an evening class on philosophy, out Cuckfield way, and is attending every week. Sam goes with him. They've missed a few meetings, starting so late on, but the tutor has loaned them some books so they can catch up. You know I can't let books alone, so I've been reading too. Now, once we've cashed up at the end of the day and had our supper the three of us discuss the ideas of people like Locke and Burke and Godwin and sharpen up our wits!

"Sam is such a help to us. He saved us from making lots of mistakes in the early days here and we still turn to him for advice. He's always so cheerful and never too busy to take an interest in William, who is always running in and out of the shop and trying to "help" us.

"Now that we're settled and doing good business I've been thinking that we should begin to expand. This is just my secret plan as yet, I haven't mentioned it to Joe, so not a word to anyone, Edie. But our next door neighbours have been talking for some time about finding a smaller house now their two girls are married and yesterday I heard they may have got what they want. So their present property could be empty soon. I want to persuade Joe to rent it so that we can move next door and put shelving and counters in our present rooms over the shop. Then we could use the upper storey for selling materials and a much wider stock of haberdashery items. I'm sure we'd do well with that. Our nearest competitors would be at Haywards Heath. Do write and tell me what you think.

"Joe and I both hope that you and Matty will come here for New Year. Sam will be with his family for Christmas, of course, but he's coming back on the 30th and Flo is able to join us then, so we should be quite a lively party. Michael has said he'll call in and Joe is even trying to persuade Arthur to come round. We've heard rumours that he's walking out with someone from the village and hope we'll get the chance to meet her (if she exists).

"William wants his tea and I must get on with the book-keeping soon so I'll close now. Our love to Matty and best respects to Mrs Riseborough..."

Edith smiled. So Kate already had plans to turn the shop into much more than a village store! Well, she'd probably get her way.

******

'...so I hope you'll agree that I should take this chance to help out and put my musical skills to good use. You and Father can think of me conducting my young ladies and gentleman in some lively singing.'

Edith looked across the room to where Clara lounged in a froth of white lace on the sofa.

'Is that appropriate do you think?'

'Perfect, my dear,' Clara replied with a smile. 'You make Shrub Grove School sound like a most select establishment.'

Edith chuckled. 'Well, that's what I want Father to think, but I'd not like Mother to feel I'm just doing this as a diversion.'

Clara shook her head. 'Don't forget your mother knows London. She won't mistake helping out at Shrub Grove as nothing more than a pleasurable distraction.'

Edith smiled and Clara rose and went to her writing desk at the window. 'I've written to Polly myself, reassuring her about this work,' she said. 'You see how seriously I take my role as guardian, Edith? I've been to considerable trouble ferreting out information about your Mr Adam Grenville and his school.' She held up several sheets of notepaper and added reflectively, 'His ideas seem very sound.'

'He's also good looking and a widower,' put in Edith slyly. 'You must meet him, Clara.'

'For heaven's sake don't start match-making, dear,' laughed Clara. 'I'm too old for such matters. But do read my letter and pop it in with yours. And hurry up! We must go and dress. You've not forgotten that Matthew is taking us to *The Quaker Girl* tonight?'

Edith had not forgotten. She blushed but kept her voice steady.

'I won't be able to go, Clara. I'm sorry but I really must prepare myself for getting started with the choir on Monday. I'll explain to Matty when he comes - I know he'll understand. There's no reason why you two shouldn't go without me.'

'No reason at all,' said Clara lightly. 'I certainly don't want to miss the performance and I enjoy Matthew's company.' But at the drawing room door she paused and looked back at Edith quizzically. 'You've been spending less time with him lately. Is everything all right between you?'

Edith laughed. 'Of course! We've both been busy that's all. And don't forget we'll be seeing each other much more in future.'

When Clara had gone Edith sealed both letters in an envelope and addressed it. Her father's feelings mattered very little to her but she was anxious to reassure her mother, even to impress her. She turned the letter over in her hands. By the time it reached her parents she would have started work at Shrub Grove. The knowledge exhilarated her and her mind raced ahead to what she'd be doing with the youngsters on her first day at the school.

The front door bell and the sound of voices in the hall interrupted her thoughts and she gave an agitated sigh. It was Matthew, arriving far too early, and she wondered what she should say to him. He'd been looking forward to the evening so much.

******

Edith hurried along the narrow street, too anxious to be aware of the clammy November morning. She felt sure she was late, that the journey from the other side of London had taken more time than she had so carefully allowed.

She found herself wishing she'd agreed to Matthew meeting her off the omnibus as he'd done the first time she came here. She'd banned him from fussing over her but now, with growing panic, she realised that all these streets looked drably similar and without him as guide she might well take a wrong turning. Then she saw her destination ahead. Edith sighed with relief, slowed her pace a little and took the chance to look about her.

Everything seemed grey, and the dampness that wasn't quite rain hung in the air and blurred her vision. The street was dirty and cheerless, the buildings on either side layered with grime and their windows pokey. But even in bright sunshine this street and all the others leading off it would wear an air of shabby depression.

There were few people about. Some women, hugged into thin shawls against the chill, made their way to a shop on the corner. She heard one of them laughing and the sound echoed by a companion. Edith glanced round, amazed that they could find something to amuse them in a place like this. She thought of Clara's elegant terrace house, with the wide street outside and the trees and bushes thrusting against the park railings opposite; thought too of the quiet, pretty square where her parents lived and the view of the sea from the windows. She had always known she lived a privileged life - Matthew had made the point often enough - but walking the length of Shrub Grove she began to appreciate more clearly what that privilege meant.

She reached the gates. The school, grimed like the houses nearby, was surrounded by a high brick wall which enclosed the playgrounds. Matthew was lurking just inside and his presence seemed to dispel the ugliness around her.

And he was waiting, discreetly, to walk with her to the omnibus stop at the end of the day. She had seen him once or twice about the school and they'd exchanged polite nods and even now they walked well apart. But she could tell that her happiness touched him at once.

'It went well, then?' he smiled and Edith nodded, swinging her music case.

'Well, I could see everyone trying a bit harder in assembly this morning,' Matthew went on, 'but what about the country dance class and the choir?'

'Oh, there's a lot of work to do of course, but they all seemed to enjoy what we did today. Young Wilf Malone - apparently his family is Irish? Well, he's a real star at dancing. And your two lads whose parents are in America: they sing so well. And most of the girls in the choir are really keen. I'm a bit concerned about the Jessop lass - do you know her? She's very quiet. It took a lot of encouragement from me before she'd sing her solo.'

'You got shy little Anna Jessop to sing a solo? Edie you're a born teacher!'

She went on talking about the choir and when he saw her on to the omnibus her mind was still busy with plans for tomorrow. Once home she found a willing audience in Clara who was eager to hear all that had happened. It was at dinner that the tiredness hit her. One moment she was tucking into roast lamb and holding forth about Wilf Malone's jig and the next she was almost asleep in her chair. She wasn't sorry when Clara hurried her off to bed, though she felt guilty because she'd planned to write to Kate. But she would tomorrow, if only a teasing reply about the store soon rivalling Selfridges.

******

'In fact I still haven't written!' And Edith pulled a doleful face to make her mother and Clara laugh. She had come downstairs, yawning, on Saturday morning to find the two women chatting by the fire in the small drawing room. With a cry of delight, Edith had rushed to greet Polly.

'Have you been here long? Oh, I'd have been up much earlier if I'd known!'

Smiling, Polly shook her head. 'When Clara told me how tired you've been this week I was quite content to wait.'

'I'm ashamed of myself for feeling so weary. Matthew and all the other teachers do far more hours. But I suppose this is my first experience of real work!'

125

While Edith chattered on about school Polly eyed her daughter thoughtfully, seeing the dark rings round her eyes, yet also aware of a new, purposeful air about her.

She explained that she was in London with Edith's father for the weekend only.

'He's seeing some supplier at the moment but he'll be here shortly and we'll all go out for lunch. Then he insists that you and I go shopping to get you some new clothes. He thinks you'll need a decent number of hard-wearing but smart dresses.'

Edith gave a wry smile. It was her father's way of offering his approval of what she had done - to reward her with gifts. At lunch he would listen politely to her account of the school and what she did there, and he would urge her to spend whatever amount was necessary to buy anything she needed. She, in turn, would be courteous and friendly and keep her conversation safely neutral. She sighed, thinking that she would almost prefer his anger.

'And we thought we could all go to the theatre tonight,' Polly went on. 'Your father wants to see a comedy. He's even suggested that as Matthew is now one of your colleagues you might like to invite him to join us.'

Edith stared at her mother. 'He said that?' And when Polly nodded she bit her lip. 'You've not told him about Matty and me?'

'Of course not, dear. I expect he just wants to impress Matthew. Maybe he's imagining our outing will be talked about at your school, so the other teachers will get to know what a fine family you come from.'

Edith joined in her mother's slightly mocking laughter, but felt uncomfortable. 'It's a lovely idea, but I think I'd rather have the two of you to myself tonight.'

In avoiding her mother's eye she found herself looking at Clara. The elegant eyebrows lifted slightly, then came together in a puzzled frown.

******

There was nothing in Matthew's manner to tarnish the bright pleasure of Edith's first two weeks at the school. Each day he behaved towards her in much the same way as with the other members of staff. When he accompanied her to the omnibus his attitude was still that of a colleague, though his eyes caressed her at every parting and his voice grew especially soft as he said good evening. But he didn't press her to go out with him, or expect to be invited to Clara's house.

Then, at the end of the third week, he asked her to go with him to the theatre.

'Something nice and light-hearted,' she said cheerfully. 'We ought to celebrate the 42 Labour seats we've just won.'

Edith, who had been only vaguely aware of the General Election agreed with an enthusiasm she did not feel. The play they saw was the one she had been to with her parents but Matthew didn't know that and it made that part of the evening easier for her. She didn't have to bother about following the story yet could discuss it perfectly well during the intervals.

Afterwards they decided to walk for a while and although the night was growing murky they became so involved in discussing school activities that they scarcely noticed the weather. When they reached the Embankment fog was already swirling in from the river and the yellow light of the lamps battled ineffectively against it.

Matthew took advantage of the gloom to hold her close and kiss her gently. For a moment she relaxed against him, feeling safe and comfortable.

'If you'd told me a month ago that after an evening at a play we'd spend so much time talking about school I wouldn't have believed you, Matty.'

He laughed. Then his arms tightened about her. 'But I don't really want to talk about work, Edie.'

He undid a button on her coat and slipped his hand inside, stroking her breast through the material of her dress. She had to stop herself pulling away and in that moment confronted the truth. She didn't want this with him any more. She didn't want his hands travelling down her body in the old, familiar way. She didn't want the way this always ended.

'Matty, don't. Not here.'

He stopped at once. 'I'm sorry,' he whispered. 'But I love you so much, Edie.'

She groaned, knowing she should be honest about her feelings and her confusions. But it was impossible. And he thought her just as frustrated and stepped away from her, repeating that he was sorry.

'We can wait - we must,' he murmured. Then his tone lightened. 'You'll be chilled to the bone, dear. I'd better get you back to Clara's or I'll miss the last omnibus.'

He lifted her face and kissed her mouth softly and she smiled in relief. They parted warmly in Elm Square, with another light kiss, and Edith went to her room feeling as though a weight had been lifted from her. She felt sure there would be no repetition of what had happened tonight unless she wanted that. She would have time to find the right words and the right way to tell Matthew... To tell him what? She looked at her own anxious face in the mirror. Did she want to break their engagement? Had it come to that?

She dreaded seeing him at school again on Monday morning, but by that time there were other matters to occupy them both. One event dominated conversation and had the children whipped up into a state of feverish excitement. While investigating a burglary in Houndsditch five policemen had been shot and three were now dead. Another man, a foreigner, was also found dead of a gunshot wound. Some arrests had been made but the police were still hunting for a band of Russian anarchists.

Mr Grenville urged his staff to exercise their common sense and take no notice of wild rumours or the equally sensational stories put out by some of the newspapers.

'There's a lot of bad feeling building up,' he warned. 'We're a rag-bag of races in this district and though people usually rub along together pretty well it doesn't take much to spark off trouble. I've already overheard some nasty talk among local people against all "foreigners". Let's try to prevent that taking hold in this school.'

But Edith found herself facing trouble as the choir assembled during playtime. Anna Jessop slumped in her seat, her face streaked with tears and a great bruise on her forehead. Edith knew little about Anna, only that her mother was dead and the child was often kept at home to look after a father in poor health; but the girl had a pleasant nature and a lovely singing voice.

'What's been going on?' Edith snapped and when no-one seemed likely to answer she added, 'If you don't tell me I shall make sure the whole choir is punished.'

She thought none of them would break the unwritten law of not telling tales so was surprised when Wilf Malone raised his hand. 'The others were getting on to Anna,' he said, boldly. 'Her Mum was Russian, Miss, and they're saying her family must be anarchists.'

'They're not, Miss Summers, they're not!' cried Anna and burst into tears again.

An angry muttering broke out, some of it directed at Wilf and some at Anna. Edith called for silence in a voice that made them all jump and then sit rigid. Up till now they'd experienced only her mildness and good humour.

'Well, I'm ashamed of you,' she said coldly. 'We all know about the terrible things that happened over the weekend. There has been horrible violence and four people have been killed. Yet here you are using the same kind of violence against someone you sing with every assembly. Oh, yes' - she raised her voice against a murmur of protest - 'yes, it is the same, you know. One of you picked up something, a stone perhaps, and hit Anna with it in anger. Supposing that instead of a stone that person had a gun. I want you to think for a moment what might have happened then.'

She held the silence for a painfully long time, looking from face to face, seeing from their shocked eyes that her message had gone home. Then she drew a deep breath.

'Luckily Anna isn't very badly hurt. Now, Lizzie, please take her to bathe her head. Wait a moment - I'll give you a clean handkerchief to use.'

After the girls had gone out Edith sat on the piano stool.

'It was stupid to pick on Anna, wasn't it?' she asked in a more reasonable tone. 'I know the police say the criminals are Russian but that doesn't mean all Russians are criminals. Just because Dr Crippen killed his wife it doesn't follow that all doctors are murderers.'

The children laughed nervously. In the back row a hand went up.

'Everyone's saying it was anarchists who shot the policemen, Miss Summers. What does anarchist mean?'

Edith suppressed a sigh and explained as best she could. Another hand flapped tentatively. 'So were they trying to take over the country, Miss?'

Before Edith could answer another voice chimed in. 'My Dad says all the foreigners would like to take us over if they could. He says there are too many round here and they should be sent back where they came from.'

Wilf Malone rounded on the speaker in sudden rage. 'Some of them might be killed if they had to go back!'

Edith looked at the aggression on the faces in front of her and felt suddenly out of her depth. She forced herself to remain calm.

'That's quite right,' she said. 'A lot of people have come to this country to escape persecution. Who can tell me what persecution means?'

Slowly and carefully, through questions and answers, she got them to think about the people who lived in their own streets, their own buildings, in the rooms next door; people they knew as neighbours, part of the community even though they might not have been born where they lived. Gradually the anger in their faces disappeared as they discussed Irish, Russian, French... the list seemed endless.

Edith was smiling at them at last. 'And if we tried to send all the foreigners home - all the real foreigners that is - why, most of us would have to pack our bags.' And she launched into an account of the Roman conquest and Viking invasions. Anne and Lizzie came back into the classroom, Lizzie shepherding the younger girl along in a motherly way. The other children either looked uncomfortably at Anna or pretended to ignore her. Edith soon had everyone laughing as they examined each other for signs of a Roman nose, then, before they got out of control she handed round the song sheets she had prepared and launched into a rehearsal of 'Greensleeves'.

'Well done,' said Matthew when she talked to him at recreation time. 'It could have developed into a nasty situation.'

'They said such horrible things,' sighed Edith.

'Don't judge them too harshly. They're just repeating what they've heard their parents say. And you've given them something more to think about now.'

Mr Grenville hurried in. 'I can't believe Miss Roberts has run out of ink again,' he groaned. 'Does she make the children drink it?' He glanced at Edith. 'I heard about Anna Jessop, Miss Summers. I believe you handled that well.'

Edith smiled. Then she asked what he knew about Anna's family.

'Very little, I'm afraid. The father is English but all the children were born in Russia and the family hasn't been here long. Mr Jessop is a sick man and I've only met the eldest son. He and his brothers work locally. They seem decent people.'

'Not anarchists, then,' smiled Edith, but Mr Grenville did not smile back.

'I've not heard that they're involved in any of the political groups that flourish here among emigres. But... I don't know. Some who have left the country have been active against the Tsar...' He shrugged, then hurriedly opened the store cupboard, muttering about the ink.

'What about Wilf Malone?' Edith persisted. 'He spoke up for Anna.'

As he burrowed into the shelves Mr Grenville's voice was muffled. 'Yes, he probably would. The Malones are from Ireland, of course, and rumour has it they had to leave in a hurry after some very unpleasant business in Belfast. I wouldn't want to enquire into that too closely.'

He emerged from the cupboard, holding the great stone bottle of ink.

'You'll get to know family histories very soon, Miss Summers. In the meantime let's hope the police conclude this case quickly, so that we can all get back to normal.'

******

Edith's hands trembled as she opened the piano. It was the final assembly before the school closed for Christmas - the Carol Service. She had rehearsed the children well and knew they would give of their best but still she felt as nervous as if they were performing to a paying audience at the Albert Hall.

Having to change things at the last minute had upset her, of course. When she got to school Wilf Malone was waiting at the entrance with the news that Anna Jessop couldn't come to school that day. 'Her Dad had a coughing fit after breakfast, so she had to stay at home,' Wilf confided. 'His chest's that bad, Miss. He brings up blood sometimes.'

Edith groaned. The programme she had devised had a solo by Anna as a high point and there was no time to rehearse with another singer. Wilf looked at her expectantly.

'We'll have to do "The Holly and The Ivy" as choir and congregation,' she said quickly. 'Get the choir together will you, Wilf? We'll give it a quick run-through before the rest of the school comes in.'

'We've not rehearsed that, Miss.'

'No, but you can all sing like angels - tell everyone I said so.'

And now all was going well and she could sense the pleasure generated in the hall as everyone joined in with a will. She wondered what kind of Christmas the children would have. There would be few treats, few presents - some would go without altogether. Yet their thin, pale faces were all alight with expectation as though Christmas Day was going to bring all manner of wonderful surprises and a positive banquet of delicious food. Not for the first time she found herself admiring their resilience.

The choir stayed behind when assembly finished, crowding round the piano.

'What now?' she asked, assuming a blank stare.

Some of them looked concerned.

'Its Cards, please Miss Summers,' ventured one of the girls.

Edith clapped a hand to her mouth. 'Oh, my goodness! I knew I'd forgotten something!'

Faces fell. But she had reckoned without Wilf.

'Ah, go on, Miss - you're having us on!' The rest of the choir joined in the merriment. It was a good joke, one they could relay to their parents. How Miss Summers pretended to forget and how they had all known, really... Eagerly they reached to take the envelopes as she moved among them. These would not be opened now but on the day itself.

There was one card left.

'I can take that to Anna if you like, Miss Summers.' Edith wasn't surprised that Wilf volunteered and she smiled as she shook her head, saying she would deliver the card herself.

'Right, off you all go,' she ordered. 'Your class teachers will be waiting. Let's hope they've all got cards for you.'

There was laughter as they filed out, each handing Edith a card and wishing her a happy Christmas. When the hall was empty she examined some of the offerings and was touched to see how much trouble had been taken with the drawing of pictures and inscribing of greetings in best handwriting.

She closed the piano lid, put the sheet music into her case and shrugged into her coat. She felt weary, physically and mentally, and looked forward to the holiday almost with desperation.

It hadn't been an easy first term. For some time after the Houndsditch killings the school was unsettled, reflecting the mood of the whole area, for Mr Grenville's hopes were not realised. The police failed to capture the men they were seeking and feelings continued to run high against all immigrants in the East End. There was no further serious trouble in the choir but elsewhere in the school children who had previously got on well suddenly turned on each other and friendships were broken up overnight. The teachers realised they were helpless against parental influence and that the best they could do was maintain order until the trouble died down.

Despite all this Edith had enjoyed the work. She'd made mistakes and had some problems but hadn't been afraid to ask Mr Grenville and her other colleagues for help and advice and they had responded generously.

Where Matthew was concerned Edith felt far from content. Though he seemed relaxed in her company, both at school and when they were on their own, she could tell he was often anxious about their relationship yet fearful of expressing that anxiety.

As she entered the dark, foul-smelling hallway of Shrub Mansions, where Anna Jessop lived, and eyed the narrow staircase that led up into the shadows, Edith found herself wishing she had let Wilf deliver the card. As she hesitated she heard voices echo down the stairs - a man's angry tones and a woman's voice, harsh and miserable. A stale smell of cooking and soapsuds permeated the air - that and the sour, damp smell she had become accustomed to on the children's clothes at school.

She heard a rustling sound behind her and spun round, heart thumping, expecting to see someone come lurking out of the gloom. Then she realised it was probably a rat and this sent her stumbling up the stairs.

Several doors led off the first landing but there was no way of telling who lived where. Then one of the doors flew open and a woman's red face appeared, the mouth open and bellowing, 'I told you what I'd do if I caught you at it!' Abruptly she clamped her mouth shut and stared at Edith who had started back in fright.

'I'm sorry, ma'am.' The voice dropped to a normal level at once and the face broke up into a smile. 'I heard a noise and thought it was them boys again. They sneak up and bang on my door and run off. I thought I'd got them this time.'

Edith laughed with nervous relief.

'I'm sorry I disturbed you. I'm looking for the Jessop family.'

'Oh.' The smile vanished and the woman sniffed and eyed Edith suspiciously. 'They're up on the top landing. We don't have nothing to do with that lot any more.'

Edith turned away from the narrowed eyes and began to climb on. On the top landing one of the doors was standing slightly ajar. Edith knocked timidly and immediately a man's voice called out cheerfully in a language she didn't recognise. While she hovered, wondering whether to knock again the door was pulled open and she saw a dark-haired, bearded man, whose face wore a wide, welcoming smile. But the smile was quenched at once and the face became defensive.

'Excuse me. I was expecting a friend.' The words sounded like an insult and Edith flushed.

'Mr Jessop?' It did not matter about seeing Anna. She would leave the card with the girl's father and go.

He nodded and she launched into a hurried explanation of who she was and why she had come, at the same time fumbling for the card in her handbag. As she did so it occurred to her that this man bore none of the marks of a consumptive: in fact he looked in remarkably good health. Her voice trailed off in confusion.

'You have come to the wrong room,' he said. As he spoke, the vowel sounds seemed to roll round his mouth - the only indication that English was not his first language. 'I'm Anna's brother. She's across the landing with my father. Come.' And he closed the door behind him and led the way.

To step from the gloomy landing into that comfortable living room was like entering another world, she thought. The furniture and carpets were not new but everything was clean and cared for. There were pictures on the walls and shelves of books. The insidious damp smell had not penetrated here - instead there was a delicate fragrance of dried flowers, mingling with a pleasantly spicy aroma which came from a covered dish left warming by the fire. The room was cramped - it also housed an area for cooking and washing, partially curtained off - and the windows were small but the panes shone. Someone worked hard to make this a welcoming sanctuary. It was as though the rest of Shrub Mansions did not exist.

Anna's brother motioned Edith to sit down by the fire then crossed to one of the doors leading off the main room, tapped gently and went in. Left alone Edith walked over to a bookshelf and examined the contents. There was a mixture of books, mainly Russian she supposed but some in English, French and German. Most of the English books were collections of poetry but she recognised some works of politics and philosophy that she'd seen on Kate's shelves. There was no trace of dust on the books, nor anywhere else in the room it seemed. She guessed that all this neatness was the result of Anna's hard work and wondered if the child ever had time to play.

'Hello Miss Summers.' Anna had slipped quietly into the room. She was wrapped in a large apron that had once belonged to someone much bigger and she greeted her teacher in a matronly fashion. 'Would you like some tea?'

Edith shook her head. 'No thank you, Anna. Tell me how your father is.'

Anna glanced anxiously at the bedroom door. 'Bram's sitting with him, but he should go to sleep soon. He's had such a bad day, Miss Summers,

133

otherwise I'd have come to school. I'm so sorry I wasn't there for my solo. I let you down.'

'No, it couldn't be helped, Anna. Please don't worry. Here, I brought you this.'

There was a squeak of delight and Anna suddenly reverted to being a little girl. With sparkling eyes she took the envelope over to the mantelpiece and tucked it behind a small china vase.

Edith resumed her seat by the fire and patted the stool beside her. 'Now, come and sit down for a moment,' she said. 'I'm interested to hear about your family, Anna, if you'd care to tell me.'

The story came out somewhat muddled but Edith was able to piece it together as Anna went along. Her mother had been a maid in the home of a wealthy St Petersburg family which also employed Mr Jessop as English tutor to their sons. But when the English tutor fell in love with the maid the family had disapproved, turning the couple out. They had survived and lived a poor, but happy existence in the city for many years. There were three sons - Bram, the eldest, then Alexei and Peter.

'I was born much later,' said Anna. 'About the time Bram got married.'

Edith nodded thoughtfully: she had been wondering about the brother's age. Probably a few years older than Matthew.

Anna's voice dropped to a whisper. 'I don't really remember Bram's wife, but she was a heroine. She died in Father Gapon's march on the Winter Palace.'

Edith frowned at the girl. 'I'm sorry, Anna - can you explain that to me?'

'My wife was murdered, Miss Summers.' Bram Jessop had come silently up to them and his words made them both jump. His voice was hard and bitter.

'Thousands of us marched to petition the Tsar for proper elections and decent wages - among other things. We weren't armed. Some of the people were even carrying pictures of the Tsar and singing an anthem: but the soldiers opened fire, just the same.'

Edith could think of nothing to say. Expressions of regret would seem trite. And she wanted to ask Bram Jessop what the situation was now - had things improved or had his wife and others died in vain? But clearly this wasn't the time.

'Is Father any better?' asked Anna and Bram turned to her, smiling now.

'He's sleeping, Anna. That's the best thing for him. Why don't you make some tea? The doctor promised to look in and you know how he loves a glass.' Bram glanced at Edith. 'When you knocked at my door I thought it was him, Miss Summers - that's why I gabbled at you like a heathen. He's another who has fled the Tsar's oppression.'

While Anna busied herself in the tiny kitchen Bram spoke to Edith in a quieter tone.

'She's very worried about Father, of course. Our mother died of the same disease, only a year after we came here.'

'I see.' Edith gestured vaguely about her. 'So Anna is mother to you all, now?'

'And very competent she is, too.' He gave a half-smile and looked slightly shamefaced. 'I'm afraid we take her hard work for granted.'

'I think that's the fate of many women,' said Edith, more sharply than she'd intended and at once he closed against her.

'Oh, some women do well enough,' he said. 'Those with money and position...'

'It depends what you mean by well enough, Mr Jessop. In this country a woman isn't deemed worthy of voting no matter how much wealth she has or what position she holds.'

She knew her voice had become shrill but she was glad to have spoken out. He was at last looking at her with some interest.

'You support the good, middle-class ladies who have deserted their drawing rooms to - ' He stopped abruptly and spread his hands in an apologetic gesture. 'No: I was about to say something grossly unfair. Ignore my rudeness, Miss Summers.'

Edith nodded, feeling some relief. She wasn't sure she would hold her own very easily in a debate with this man. She gathered her things together and Anna came running back to say goodbye and apologise for not having made her a Christmas card.

'Good heavens, Anna, I can see you've been much too busy for that sort of thing,' said Edith, briskly. 'You keep house for your father and brothers very well. My mother used to be a maid but I don't think even she could have got her fire irons sparkling like yours.'

The little girl beamed with pride, but Edith was more aware of her brother's puzzled frown. He followed her to the door and said he would accompany her downstairs.

As they descended Edith realised they were being watched. On each landing doors were eased ajar as they passed and sometimes a face would bob out, only to be hastily withdrawn.

'Our kind neighbours like to know what we do and where we go,' said Bram, wryly.

'Such touching concern for strangers in their midst,' said Edith and was rewarded with an amused laugh.

'Exactly so, Miss Summers. That reminds me that I must thank you for what you said and did when Anna was bullied at school.'

'I believe there's been no more trouble since then.'

'At school - no.'

'But here?'

'Yes - and for my brothers at their work. We're no longer half English. We're half Russian. Here, let me take your arm, Miss Summers. The treads are loose.'

His hand under her elbow was broad and bony. Not a comfortable hold but she felt more secure.

Out in the street she looked about her uncertainly, suddenly unsure of her way.

'Where do you live, Miss Summers?'

She told him and added quickly, 'I'm staying with a friend - she was my mother's employer, which may sound strange - '

He cut her short. 'You're lucky to live in such pleasant surroundings. I know that part of London well. I like to sketch there when I have the time: such beautiful buildings.'

She tried to mimic his mocking tone. 'You're an artist, Mr Jessop?'

He gave a sharp laugh. 'Only when I have a little leisure and that's not often. I work for a chemist, making up medicines.'

'A pharmacist, then.'

'Oh, too grand a title. I had my own business back home - ' He broke off sharply as though afraid of saying too much. 'Where do you get the omnibus, Miss Summers? The Commercial Road? I can direct you.'

On the journey home Edith sat alone, staring out of the window but not taking in the passing scene. Her mind was crowded with ideas about what she could have said to Bram Jessop and what he might have replied. She feared he might think her shallow... She lowered her head. Ridiculous to be concerned about that. What did it matter what he thought?

******

'So, as I understand it the uprising achieved precious little. They did get a parliament at last - a Duma they call it - but from what I've heard it's very weak and doesn't have much control over the Tsar.' Joe smiled at Edith. 'So perhaps it's not surprising your friends left to come here.'

'They're not my friends,' said Edith, quickly. 'The family of a pupil who's in the school choir.'

She sat back with a troubled frown. Joe's account of what had happened in Russia since 1905 had been succinct and interesting but she was more concerned at the moment with the way she'd contrived to bring the

Jessops into the conversation. It seemed they had been on her mind all over Christmas. She'd talked about them to Clara, to her mother and now here.

She was sitting beside the fire in the pleasant living room above the shop. Opposite her Joe had turned his attention to lighting his new pipe - a Christmas present from Polly. Kate sat next to him, busy with some mending and Matthew lounged in the fourth chair, sipping a glass of elderberry wine. The four of them had just finished a filling supper and were now waiting for midnight and the arrival of the New Year.

'I suppose there's been more antagonism towards foreigners in London since the funeral of those policemen,' said Kate.

Matthew sighed. 'Oh yes - and some newspapers are having a fine old time stirring up anti-Semitism under the guise of concern for public welfare.' He leaned forward, adding bitterly, 'And the Tories are saying the Liberals have made it easy for anyone to get into the country - as if all immigrants are criminals.'

A heated discussion on this was halted by the sound of feet pounding up the stairs. Sam and Flo appeared, swathed in scarves against the cold, their faces pink and shiny. They had walked from Jane's and brought exciting news.

'Art had a guest to supper, Joe,' Flo giggled. 'It was Miss Johnson from the Post Office! When we left, the two of them were sitting side by side on the parlour sofa, prim as you please, with Mother keeping a sharp watch on them!'

'I'm sure she is,' Joe laughed. 'In case the young lady makes a bolt for it! Poor old Art - Mum'll push him up to the altar rail yet!'

Sam pulled off his coat. 'We passed Dr Thomas on the High Street and he said he might be late. He's been called out to Mrs Parry's.'

Kate frowned. 'I hope everything's all right with the children. She's expecting another in six months or so.'

'Another?' sighed Joe. 'But she's not long lost her youngest.'

Edith scarcely heard the exchange. She had caught Matthew's eye and blushed, knowing that he was remembering the day they had gone down to the Parry house and what had happened on the way back. She didn't want to dwell on that now. She sprang up.

'Can we have some music, Kate, or will that wake William? Flo, come and help me choose something.'

Flo had changed a good deal during her time in service, becoming more self-confident and able to speak out on her own behalf. But her admiration for Edith had not altered or lessened and now she hurried to assist.

Kate glanced at Sam. 'If you've got a moment we could sort out that delivery problem,' she said. 'I really think we must try another company for the dried fruit.'

Sam nodded eagerly. 'I've remembered the name of those people I mentioned - not long started up. I could go and see them if you like?'

Kate looked towards Joe for his approval. He was still struggling to get his pipe going properly.

'What do you think, Joe?'

He sucked in hugely and choked on a lungful of smoke.

'Oh, you and Sam see to it!' Still coughing he reached for his glass of beer on the mantelpiece. 'And if you two are going to talk about the business I think I'll take a turn along the High Street. I need to stretch my legs. Like to come for a walk, Matty?'

As the two men rose Kate asked, tentatively, if Joe would mind moving some of the sacks in the storeroom before he went out. She was worried about mice. She saw a flash of temper on his face before he nodded agreement and hoped none of the others had noticed. As the door closed behind the two men Edith began to play a lullaby.

Flo, sitting beside Edith at the piano, watched without envy as the pale hands moved across the keys. Then she glanced at Edith's face and, seeing the frown creasing her forehead, wondered if anything was wrong. But it was rude to stare, so Flo glanced around the room. Kate had got it looking really smart and there were new curtains at the windows. It was right what Sam said, the shop was proving a little gold mine. Kate and Joe had paid off what they owed to Art and were now able to give Sam a good wage and enjoy a better life themselves. She wondered, hopefully, if she and Sam would one day be able to get a business of their own, like this.

The music ceased. 'That was lovely,' said Flo politely.

Edith let her fingers drift, vaguely picking out a tune. 'Are you staying at the Hall for a while now, Flo?'

'I think so. Of course we'll be back in London for the Coronation but after that Lady Janette wants to go cruising in the Mediterranean. They've got a yacht now, you know. She thinks that she and Sir James will need a good rest by then.'

Edith burst out laughing. 'I've never heard anything so ridiculous,' she said. 'You and all the other staff are the ones who'll deserve the rest.'

Flo hung her head. 'Sam said something like that,' she muttered, 'and Kate was quite rude.' She sat up defiantly. 'I know all of you are right in a way, but they're really good employers. I get top wages and you should see my room in the London house. I mean, I could just about weep when Mr Matthew tells us about the children in Stepney and those other places and how the rich are responsible for all that poverty. But I just can't dislike Sir James and Lady Janette. They're not bad, Miss Edith. I think they just don't

138

realise. Oh, I'm not saying this right.'

Edith gave her a smile. 'I think you've said it all perfectly well and I know how you feel, Flo. But they're not fools: they understand how things are. It's just that they don't care enough to do anything.'

'Sam says things will be different once the Labour Party comes to power,' said Flo, thoughtfully. They were silent for a while as Edith tried out another tune. Then she said, with studied carelessness, 'Did I tell you about the little Russian girl in my choir at school? Well, she's half Russian really...'

Kate waited eagerly for Sam's response. She hadn't intended telling him so much but after sorting out their immediate problem their talk moved to future plans for the shop.

His first question wasn't unexpected. 'What does Joe say?'

Kate fiddled with her wedding ring. 'I've not spoken to him yet, Sam. I want to choose the right time - when we can sit down and work it all out. It's difficult with visitors here but I'll talk to him after New Year.' She paused, then added slowly, 'I think it would help if he knew you approved of the idea. He has great respect for your judgement.'

Sam leaned forward. 'It's just that I get the feeling he doesn't have as much interest in the business now as he did at first.'

'That's another reason to expand,' Kate nodded. 'Joe's happy enough serving in the shop but he's leaving everything else to us more and more. If we have another department he could take charge of it.' But she could hear the doubt in her own voice. Joe was good with the customers, straightforward and at ease with everyone - from those who came in for a little tea in a screw of paper or a farthing candle to the owners of the big houses at the other end of the village, whose orders were gratifyingly large. But Joe was at a loss when it came to figures and finance. It was Kate who ran the business side of things and they all knew it.

'I'm sure there'd be the custom for drapery and haberdashery,' Sam said, avoiding the problem of Joe for a moment. He glanced around. 'And these rooms could easily be converted. Nice big windows... plenty of light. We could have displays of material.'

Kate's eyes sparkled. 'I've got so many ideas, Sam...'

Edith had begun to play again. 'When are you and Sam getting married?' she murmured, making sure her voice didn't rise above the music. Flo blushed.

'We're still saving. But I've met his parents now and been to their Meeting House.'

'Really? So you'll become a Quaker, Flo? I've never been to a Quaker wedding.'

Joe was in a livelier mood when he and Matthew returned and Kate thought, with relief, that the walk and Matthew's company had done him good. They were all talking cheerfully when Kate's new pendulum clock began to strike the hour.

'Quiet!' cried Matthew. 'Listen!'

They were silent for a moment then Kate quickly handed round the glasses - fruit cup only for Sam and Flo - and they raised them in a toast to the New Year. Amid the laughter the door swung open and a sleepy William tottered into the room.

'What?' he demanded truculently. It was the most heavily used word in his present vocabulary. Kate laughed and swept him up, carrying him around the room so he could have his share of kisses.

'So, it's 1911,' said Joe. 'I wonder what changes we'll see this year?'

Sam and Flo exchanged smiles. With luck they would be married before the end of it. Matthew looked at Edith by his side and smiled, hesitantly, raising his glass to her. Gently she took his hand and his smile broadened.

'Votes for women, perhaps - eh, Edie?' Joe teased.

Before she could answer they heard a banging at the street door. Joe hurried downstairs and came back with Michael Thomas. Cheerful greetings and good wishes died away as they saw his face and Kate took William back to his bedroom.

'Mrs Parry's dead,' said Joe. 'Miscarriage.'

'Only it wasn't really,' muttered the doctor. 'She did it herself with a knitting needle.'

Edith and Flo both gasped aloud and Michael Thomas eyed them blearily. 'My apologies, ladies. I had a drink or two before I came here and now - '

Joe silenced him quickly. 'What arrangements have been made for the children? Can we help? We can make room here.'

The doctor seemed to pull himself together. 'They've gone to a neighbour. Joe, could you go and see Jack Parry tomorrow and find out what help he needs? He's probably got nothing put by for funeral expenses...'

'I'll go,' said Matthew, quickly. 'And I think you should sit down, doctor. You look done in.'

Kate came back into the room and Michael Thomas turned to her. 'It was wrong of me to come here and spoil your evening...' but his voice dropped to a mumble and he swayed a little. Joe moved quickly to steady him. The doctor gave a weak smile. 'A bad night: I couldn't save her.' Then his eyes blazed suddenly. 'Waste of a life! She must have been desperate. I'd warned Parry that she shouldn't have another child and I told him what to do about it. But he wouldn't listen, damn him! Oh, he's sorry now, of course, but it's

140

too late for that.'

Kate caught Joe's eye and jerked her head towards the door. 'Get him into the spare bed,' she snapped. He and Matthew helped the doctor out and Kate followed, saying she'd get him a hot drink from the kitchen. Edith went with her and fetched a saucepan and some milk.

'Matthew was to have that room tonight,' said Kate, 'but I daresay he won't mind sleeping on the couch in the parlour.'

Edith wasn't listening. 'To do something like that to yourself...' she whispered and tears began to trickle down her face, tears of anger and frustration which took her by surprise. Kate put an arm round her shoulders, stroking the fair curls tenderly, but with rage in her eyes.

'Votes for women,' she muttered. 'Oh, Edie, how can that be our goal when so many don't have even basic rights yet?'

1911–1912

'What a terrible thing to happen,' said Polly sadly. 'Who has care of the children now?'

Edith replaced her cup and saucer on the tea table and helped herself to another cake.

'An older sister who's in service at Wivelsfield has come home to look after them,' she said. 'Joe went to see her and managed to get some money from a local charity to help with the funeral expenses, because Mr Parry had nothing saved.' She popped a piece of the cake into her mouth and added indistinctly, 'Joe's been really splendid, Mother. He's so good at helping people.'

Polly smiled and poured herself another cup of tea. She was enjoying this time alone with Edith. Her daughter had arrived back in Brighton earlier than expected and it would be another hour or so before Mr Summers returned so the two women had shut themselves in the drawing room.

'You sound surprised at Joe helping the Parrys,' she murmured.

Edith shook her head. 'Not that he did it but the way he did it. Well, it's obvious that in the shop Kate organises everything and Joe lets her get on with it - '

'But in this instance he was the efficient one?'

'And compassionate too, without being maudlin. Not like the vicar's wife who went down to the cottage and drooped all over the little ones and just made them cry.'

Polly nodded and there was a companionable silence for a while. Then Edith wondered aloud what Joe would make of Kate's new ideas for the shop. Her mother frowned.

'I'm surprised she hasn't told him yet. But he'll surely see the sense of expanding, now the business is doing so well.'

'I suppose so.' Edith shrugged. 'Kate's very excited at any rate, so Joe's bound to realise something's up, sooner or later.'

Polly was troubled and to change the subject asked after Matthew. 'I thought he might come here with you, Edie.'

'Oh, Janette and James wanted him at the Hall to make up numbers for a party,' said Edith, hastily. 'I went over there for dinner and, honestly Mother, all they talked about was the King and Queen. I kept wanting to say we should abolish the monarchy. Joe says that's what the people in Russia want.'

'Now you're not going to tell me that grisly story about your pupil's brother and the Winter Palace again, are you?' murmured Polly. 'It was quite enough that we got it with our pudding on Christmas Day.'

Edith laughed to hide her embarrassment. She was annoyed to realise she'd been talking about Anna Jessop's family so much. She stood up and stretched, crossing to the window. The sea was grey today, reflecting a sky heavy with snow.

'You're looking so much better now, Edith,' said Polly approvingly. 'Teaching music at Shrub Grove clearly suits you. Though I do wish you had a longer holiday.'

'But we can talk more often now,' Edith laughed. 'Telephone me at Clara's at any time!'

Polly knew her daughter was teasing and gave a wry smile.

'Well, I'm sure telephones are useful at your Father's workplace but I can't see why we need one here in the house. I think he's only had it installed to be like the rest of his business friends.' She sniffed. 'I shall only use it in an emergency. These machines will ruin people's ability to write proper letters, you know.'

Edith looked out of the window again. 'Oh, Father's just coming in,' she sighed. 'Isn't he early?'

'Yes indeed. I hope nothing's gone wrong at the shop.'

They exchanged wary looks. Dinner would be an uncomfortable meal if Mr Summers was in a bad mood. But he came into the drawing room in a state of great excitement and Polly's offer of tea was waved impatiently away.

'I've brought the newspapers for you to see,' he said and when they only looked puzzled he added, triumphantly, 'They've taken those villains - the Russians who shot the policemen.'

Polly raised her eyebrows. 'Well, that's a very good thing.'

'Let me finish.' Arnold flapped a newspaper at her. 'There was a siege - in London! The men were trapped in a house, surrounded by the police, but they kept up a positive barrage of fire so no-one could get into the building. The army was called in and Mr Churchill himself went down to direct operations!' He sank into an armchair. 'My goodness,' he murmured. 'I wish I could have seen it.'

Polly had taken up one of the newspapers. 'Sidney Street,' she exclaimed. 'And it says here the firing was "tremendous and almost continuous". How terrible.'

Arnold began a detailed account of the siege and Polly realised he had the newspaper story almost by heart.

'Hundreds of police,' he crowed. 'Not to mention a detachment of Scots Guards. What a sight that must have been!'

'And all to capture two men,' murmured Polly, with an edge to her voice.

'Oh no!' Edith's exclamation startled her parents. She looked up from the newspaper she had been reading and stared accusingly at her father. 'You said they were taken!'

He did not meet her accusing gaze but mumbled vaguely. Edith held out the newspaper at arm's length as though it was contaminated. 'The house caught fire and the police let it burn with the men inside!'

Arnold blustered that the fire had started by chance - 'Not surprising with all that shooting going on!'

'But to let them burn to death, Father!'

'They could have come out. They chose to die in the flames. It's just the sort of thing these extremists would do.'

'Extremists?' Edith almost shouted the word at him. 'There's not even proof that they were the wanted men!' She jumped up and hurried out of the room. Upstairs, she sat on her bed, shivering. Pictures flooded into her mind: the policeman in the square who had thrown her down; soldiers shooting unarmed supplicants to the Tsar; police and soldiers firing into a blazing house; the darkness of a landing and the support of a strong hand.

She went back to London nursing her anger and eager to see Matthew again, sure he would share her feelings. He was round at Elm Square almost before Edith had unpacked, but it wasn't until the day before they were due back at the school that she had the chance to talk to him alone. He had suggested a stroll in Kensington Gardens but in the event it became a brisk walk, for the snow just after New Year had brought colder weather in its wake.

Matthew gazed somewhat sadly about him and talked about the Summer days when they had sat by the Serpentine under a cloudless sky. Edith gave an exasperated sigh, snuggled more closely into her new coat with its flattering, fur-trimmed collar, and clasped Matthew firmly by the arm.

Her sudden closeness seemed to take his breath away and she had to repeat her first words, but then he was all attention as she talked about her growing feelings of discontent.

'Matty, I've never felt so angry before! The pattern is repeated, over and over again. Men oppress women, the rich oppress the poor, the powerful oppress the weak. It's got to stop - and I want to be part of changing things!'

She saw him bite his lip and thought he was trying to hold back laughter.

'You're not taking me seriously, are you?' she accused, pulling away from him. 'You think this is just another of my fads!'

'No, I don't think that,' Matthew protested, but with a guilty air. 'I'm pleased you've seen the light at last, Edie.' He blinked at her furious look and added quickly before she could speak, 'Yes, that sounds patronising - I'm sorry. But if you're interested in supporting the Labour Party at last you need to understand that it's not our policy to overthrow the state. We're not anarchists. We intend to achieve Socialism gradually, by taking office and using the parliamentary system for the people of this country, rather than against them. I hope you'll come with me to meetings, Edie - I'd love that. But it's only fair to warn you that we don't sit around plotting bloody revolution.'

Edith nodded, saying quietly that she understood but not bothering to conceal her discontent. His caution had crushed her enthusiasm.

She glanced at him as they walked back, fancying that there was a severity about his mouth that she hadn't seen before. She had felt so sure they would be drawn closer together after this talk. Instead it seemed that a gap had opened up between them.

******

The bell rang for recreation time and as Edith closed the piano lid the children scrambled to get to the end of the room where, in cold weather like this, they were allowed to huddle round the stove. She watched them jostling each other. The boys, of course, forced their way to the front to be nearest the heat but they were generous enough to make spaces through which the girls could warm their hands.

Seeing the children coming into school these mornings, their faces pinched with cold, hands blue, with no proper coats and their shoes often falling to pieces, Edith had all but wept for them and was glad when Mr Grenville made a general announcement that all pupils could stay indoors at break times until the weather became warmer. She took to wearing one of her oldest coats on the days she went in, ashamed of her latest fur-trimmed luxury, yet knowing this was a pointless gesture - of no benefit to the youngsters.

Anna Jessop was hovering at the edge of the group by the stove and Edith remembered that she wanted to talk to the girl, so she called her away and drew her out into the empty corridor. It was easy to see that Anna was one of the luckier ones. Her boots were old and looked too tight, but they were still sound and she had good, thick stockings to keep her legs warm. Like most of the girls she was wearing a shawl over her shoulders with the ends wrapped cosily about her waist and tied at the back. But Anna's shawl was bulky where those of most of her classmates were worn thin.

Edith smiled at the girl's anxious face. 'I just wanted to ask how your father is, Anna - particularly now the weather's so bitter.'

'Thank you for asking, Miss Summers. Actually he's always a bit better when it's really cold. It's the damp that gets on his chest and upsets

145

him.'

'And your brothers?'

'Yes, very well, Miss, thank you.' But the girl looked anxious still and Edith asked what was worrying her.

'Oh - it's nothing, Miss. Well, I mean...' And suddenly the girl was crying and saying she had done very badly in her reading test that day and that Mr Maynard had said he'd need to speak to her father if things didn't improve.

Edith bit back an angry remark about Mr Maynard and gave Anna what she hoped was a reassuring smile.

'I was always hopeless at reading tests – well, at any test,' she said cheerfully. 'My sister was a much better scholar.' Then she added, more slowly, 'So she used to help me, out of school. She'd read with me or make sure we could practise sums together... Anna, would it help you to stay after Monday choir practices so we can read together?'

Anna stared. 'Just me, Miss?'

'That's right. Your father won't mind, will he? I'll write him a note.'

Anna's eyes sparkled with pleasure. 'I'm sure he'll agree, Miss.' Then her face fell. 'But I really ought to be back home directly after school to get his tea and then prepare the evening meal for Bram and Peter and Alexei. Father goes out before they come home - to teach his evening classes.' She saw Edith's frown and added quickly, 'We don't want him to, Miss, but he says he feels better and must do his bit towards the savings.'

Edith stopped herself from asking what the Jessops were saving for. Really it was none of her business. Perhaps they wanted to move to better lodgings... somewhere more healthy...

'Well, suppose I come home with you after school? You can see to your father and then we can work together until it's time for you to start cooking for your brothers.'

The girl was beaming and nodding.

'Good - then ask your father tonight and let me know after Country Dancing tomorrow. Now go back in and try to get warm!'

As Anna hurried away Edith realised she hadn't told the girl to keep the idea to herself but somehow knew that wasn't necessary.

******

Anna led the way to the top floor of Shrub Mansions and pushed open the door. The man sitting by the fire rose at once and Edith was introduced to Anna's father. She was surprised by his fair colouring: light brown hair, greying in places, and pale blue eyes. His daughter and his eldest son must take after their mother in looks, yet Edith could see something of Bram Jessop in this man's thin face.

'It is kind of you to give Anna help with her reading, Miss Summers,' he murmured in a friendly voice, handing her into a comfortable chair. 'I'm afraid she may have fallen behind her fellow pupils as she's been away so often, looking after me. But I'm on the mend now and when the Spring comes I shall be restored to full health again.'

Edith saw Anna beaming and smiled herself, but with difficulty. She had little experience of illness but could see that Mr Jessop was unlikely to make such a recovery.

Anna said she would make tea and heat her father's meal.

'Tea by all means, dear - I'd like a hot drink and then I can rest before I go out. But I've already had that splendid stew you made for me so you don't need to worry about that.'

The girl scolded her father, sure that he must have tired himself getting the meal but he teased her gently for fussing and shooed her away.

'She worries about me,' he said to Edith.

She lowered her voice so that Anna, setting out cups in the kitchen alcove, would not hear. 'I think someone needs to worry about you, Mr Jessop.'

If her directness surprised him he did not show it. 'Ah now,' he smiled, 'it's somewhat too late for that, Miss Summers, as you clearly see. But I honestly feel a good deal better than when you were last here. I'm sorry I wasn't able to get up to speak to you then.'

The curtain across the alcove was drawn back and Anna struggled towards them with a full tray. Edith jumped up to help and soon the three of them were sitting before the fire with tea, talking cheerfully. Then the table was cleared and Anna fetched her reading book. Mr Jessop urged them to start work at once. He was going to rest in his room.

Edith found it hard to concentrate. The coughing began almost as soon as Mr Jessop closed the door behind him and Edith felt her body tense up as each spasm was succeeded by a new and fiercer one. She realised, sadly, that Anna was used to this now. The girl read steadily through each piece Edith gave her.

Soon Mr Jessop reappeared, smiling, wearing a thick, warm overcoat with several scarves about his neck. Anna ran to fetch his hat and gloves and he delivered a mock reprimand for her temerity at leaving her books without permission. 'I think Miss Summers will have to bring her cane in future,' he said and Edith forced herself to join in the laughter. He bowed in her direction - a sudden reminder that he had lived much of his life in another country - and asked, rather stiffly, how much she wanted to charge for Anna's lessons.

For a moment Edith did not understand him and then she said, hastily, 'Oh, there's no charge, Mr Jessop. I'm not a qualified teacher - I just go to Shrub Grove for a few days each week to give music lessons and work with the choir.'

'And country dancing, Miss. That's such fun with you,' beamed Anna and her father smiled at Edith.

'Thank you, Miss Summers. If my eldest son comes home before you leave and makes any mention of this please tell him I am content with our arrangement.'

When he had gone Edith was able to turn her full attention to Anna's reading. The girl managed most of the words before her but there was little expression in her voice.

'Don't you read much, here at home, Anna? Fairy stories, perhaps?' Edith asked and was not surprised when the little girl shook her head.

'Mother used to tell me stories and sing to me,' Anna sighed. 'Father still does - when he's feeling well enough.'

'Would you like me to bring you some books? I've still got some of the ones I enjoyed when I was your age. You could read to yourself - when you have time, of course.'

They heard the clump of heavy boots on the stairs and Anna sprang guiltily off her chair.

'Miss Summers, can we stop now, please? My brothers are coming and I haven't got the potatoes on yet. Oh dear!' and she scuttled off behind the curtain.

With a wry smile Edith closed the book and reached for her coat. She was pulling it on when the door opened and Bram Jessop came in, followed by two younger men. Bram's face was as she remembered it, closed and slightly sullen, but his brothers smiled when they saw her and greeted her cheerfully. These two had inherited their father's colouring and something of his friendly manner. They called out a greeting to Anna, whose harassed little face popped out from behind the curtain, then disappeared again.

'I'm afraid your meal may be slightly late,' said Edith. 'I forgot to take account of the time.'

One of the young men gave her a grin. 'Anna, no need to hurry,' he called. 'Peter wants me to cut his hair before we eat!'

The two men laughed and Peter, who possessed a fine head of elegant, if somewhat lengthy curls, aimed a mock blow at his brother's shoulder. There came an echoing laugh from behind the curtain and even Bram's face lightened a little. Peter's hair was obviously a family joke.

Edith nodded to the others and called goodbye to Anna and when the little girl appeared, smiling, repeated her promise about the books.

'I'll bring them to school on Wednesday and we can begin work on them that evening.'

Bram stepped forward. 'I'll see you down, Miss Summers,' he said coldly. 'We must talk about these extra lessons for Anna.'

In fact he said nothing as they stumbled down the stairs but his silence only made her anxious. At the bend where the treads were loose he automatically took her arm and she was glad of the darkness, for the pressure of his hand sent a quiver through her body that made her face grow hot. Anger at her own stupidity turned into annoyance with him and once they were outside the building she took the offensive.

'I've already explained to your father that I don't expect payment for giving Anna some help and he's perfectly happy with that - he asked me to tell you so.'

To her satisfaction Bram was taken aback.

'Well... well thank you. We're very grateful. But you mentioned books, Miss Summers. We have books.'

'I know that, but Anna tells me she doesn't read very much so perhaps those books don't really interest her.'

He shrugged, his manner suddenly insolent. 'Or maybe she isn't really interested in reading, Miss Summers? Anna is, perhaps, the kind of child who is happier with the practical rather than the creative side of life.'

Edith stared at him, her anger bubbling up and the words were out before she could stop herself.

'You mean she should only be occupied with cooking your meals and cleaning your home and nursing your father? She's a little girl, for goodness' sake. Why are you trying to turn her into a woman before her time?'

His face was dark and his eyes frightened her. 'Miss Summers, you're Anna's music teacher. Her family and her role within it is not your concern and if you want to continue coming here to help her with her reading you will not presume to make it so.'

They stared at each other, both breathing heavily, then Edith lowered her head.

'You're right,' she muttered, hot with shame. 'That was unforgivable of me. I'm very sorry.'

'No... no. It's...' His voice was softer now and when she looked up again he gave a slight smile. 'It's not surprising you said what you did. It must seem to you that we treat Anna unfairly but that's really not the case, Miss Summers. After my mother died we all shared household work between us but that upset Anna - she thought we didn't trust her to look after things. But you must believe we all keep a careful watch on her and make sure she doesn't do too much or get too tired. We're quite skilled at looking after ourselves and yet pretending it's all Anna's doing.'

Edith nodded and he gave a weary sigh that made her want to reach out and touch him.

He went on, quickly, 'Just lately too much of a burden has fallen on Anna because of Father's illness. She has been at home looking after him and worrying over him far too often. I should have done something about that sooner. We can afford to pay someone to come in and sit with him when he's unwell so that Anna can go to school.'

'Not one of the friendly souls here in the Mansions?' said Edith quickly, trying to lighten the mood and she was pleased when he smiled.

'No, no! But we have friends living not far away - I'm sure they will help.'

His change of mood encouraged her. 'And I can lend Anna some books?'

'Of course. I'll see she has time to read them and that she takes good care of them. But don't expect too much of her, Miss Summers.'

That seemed to be all. They were both shivering now, having stood still for so long, and Edith reluctantly decided it was time she left. But as she began to say goodbye he gave her a bow, just as his father had done, and said he would walk with her to the omnibus stop.

'I don't like to think of you alone in these streets,' he said.

'No indeed,' she responded lightly as they set out. 'I might get attacked by a crowd of armed policemen.'

He laughed at that then said sharply, 'You have a poor opinion of your city's police force, Miss Summers?'

She found herself telling him about her experience in Parliament Square, saying far more than she'd ever done to Clara or Matthew. He listened carefully, then said, 'And have your injuries healed now, Miss Summers?'

For a moment she was puzzled, then realised there was a deeper meaning to his words.

'The bruises went long ago... but sometimes it's as though I can still feel his hands crushing my shoulders and the pain in my back,' she murmured. 'Will that fade too, like the bruises?'

'Better it does not,' he responded and his tone was hard.

As they neared the stop Edith felt confident enough to venture a different sort of question.

'Will you tell me more about your country, Mr Jessop? My brother-in-law has been trying to explain to me about the... well, the political structure of Russia, but - '

'Is he an expert, this brother-in-law?' Bram asked sharply and Edith gave a nervous laugh.

'No. He and my sister keep a village shop in Sussex. But they're both really interested in politics and they read widely. They're Socialists, of course,' she concluded, self-consciously.

He laughed. It was an attractive sound.

'You speak as though all keepers of village shops in England are Socialists, which I feel is far from the case,' he smiled.

'Yes - that sounded silly.' Edith looked at him boldly. 'But will you tell me about Russia? Please?'

'Very well,' he said. 'But only if you first explain yourself to me, Miss Summers.'

'Explain myself?' He was straight-faced enough but she thought she saw a glint in his eye.

'When we first met you were wearing a coat that would not have looked out of place if you had been visiting your King George. The one you wear now is older, I think, but was obviously made for you by an expensive tailor. Your whole manner is that of a refined upper class young lady and you live in a part of London that perfectly suits that image. Yet you teach music at Shrub Grove School; you support the Suffragettes and you mistrust policemen. And you state that your mother was a parlour maid and your sister keeps a shop. You must admit, Miss Summers, that there is much about you that is contradictory and somewhat puzzling - especially to a poor, foolish immigrant like myself.'

They were both laughing now and Edith saw his whole face relax and change, becoming almost handsome. With a mixture of regret and relief she saw the omnibus drawing near.

'I'll explain everything - next time I'm here,' she said as she stepped up on to the platform.

'No. I should like to hear now.' He was beside her and to her amazement followed her inside, sat down next to her and insisted on paying for her ticket as well as his own.

'Your meal - ' she protested but he waved that away. So she talked about herself, awkwardly at first and then more easily - about her father and his business, how it had grown and changed their lives, and about Kate and Joe, even Flo and Sam Bundy. And when they reached the stop where she got off to walk a short distance and catch another 'bus that would take her almost to Elm Square he stayed with her, listening to her describe her admiration for the Suffragettes.

'So now you know everything about me, Mr Jessop,' she concluded, well aware that there was one person she had not mentioned. But she quickly put that out of her mind and insisted, with teasing charm, that he fulfil his part of their bargain and tell her about Russia.

'Well... the politics I will leave until another time. I think I will

151

describe to you the city I come from, for parts of it are very lovely.'

His voice, his face, everything about him grew happier as he spoke and he often lapsed into Russian and then corrected himself in English with an apologetic smile. She watched and listened, fascinated, and when they eventually reached Elm Square she blinked about her, confused, half expecting to see the quayside he had conjured up so vividly for her, with its statue of a sphinx, brought there long ago from Egypt.

She told him that and he was pleased. Then he looked around and realised where they were.

'I didn't mean to come so far. Fortunately there is no-one about.'

She protested fiercely that it didn't matter, that she didn't care and neither would Clara. 'You must come in and meet her - and have something to eat.' But he shook his head. 'I'm sure it is as you say and that Mrs Riseborough would indeed make me welcome. But I don't really care to go visiting in my working clothes and boots, you know.'

Edith blushed and tried to apologise but he was smiling again and bowing and then he was gone, leaving her feeling strangely lost.

At dinner that evening she was quiet and ate so little that Clara grew worried, asking if she was feeling ill. At that Edith grew suddenly lively, expressed her intention of visiting St Petersburg one day and launched into a lengthy description of the city. Clara watched her, half reassured, half exasperated and - not for the first time - relieved that she had no children of her own to fret over.

******

As the audience began to applaud Edith sat up with a start. That was the second or third time she had lost track of what the speaker was saying. She realised, guiltily, that she'd not taken in a great deal of the speech at all. And Matthew had been so pleased when she suggested accompanying him to this meeting.

Beside her he was clapping enthusiastically and so she joined in. She hoped he wouldn't quiz her about the speech afterwards: she was sure to say the wrong thing.

The speaker sat down and the chairman rose to thank him and ask for questions from the audience. There were few enough in the hall and Edith thought smugly of the women's suffrage meeting she had attended recently with Clara - how crowded it had been.

'The gentleman at the back, I think?' murmured the chair.

'Yes, thank you. Surely a consolidated union such as the speaker suggests would require very careful arrangements for coping with individual problems in the different sections...'

Edith, who had recognised the voice, lost the rest of the question in her own confusion. It was Bram Jessop who had spoken: he must have come in after the meeting began - had been there all the time without her knowing. Had he seen her?

Matthew, interested in the point raised, swung round in his chair to look at the questioner. Somehow his action annoyed her and she shrank down in her seat, glaring furiously at her boots.

Gradually the questions petered out and the speaker was thanked again and the audience rose in ones and twos and trickled away. By pretending to have mislaid a glove Edith kept herself and Matthew in the hall for some time and when they eventually made for the door she was relieved to see they were the only ones left.

'Good evening, Miss Summers.'

He was lingering on the pavement as though waiting for an omnibus. The working man had vanished and in his place, in a well-cut tweed overcoat, was a man of business, perhaps, or a member of some profession.

'Oh, Mr Jessop - were you at the meeting?' Edith's voice was high and bright. 'Most interesting, wasn't it?'

She was aware that the two men were eyeing each other thoughtfully and added quickly, 'Mr Jessop, this is Mr Hersey who teaches at Shrub Grove. Matthew, Mr Jessop is Anna's brother.'

They shook hands, both smiling now. Edith glanced swiftly from one to the other, wondering what each was thinking behind the polite facade.

'I believe your father has been very ill, Mr Jessop,' said Matthew. 'I hope there's some improvement?'

Bram answered briefly, but seemed grateful for Matthew's interest. And then, to Edith's surprise, they plunged into a discussion of the meeting, arguing cheerfully, ready to talk all night it seemed. After a while she announced sharply that she was getting cold and managed to draw Matthew away.

'He's an interesting fellow,' said Matthew. 'We could do with more like him.' And somehow this threw Edith completely out of temper.

******

By the time she was due at the Jessops' home again she had talked some sense into herself and faced the awkward fact that she found Bram attractive and that he probably felt the same about her. Why else would he hang around outside the meeting hall to see her, even though she was in another man's company?

Having confronted this she felt well able to cope with it. They were both sensible adults - good heavens, he was a widower - and quite capable of controlling their feelings, which really amounted to very little in any case. She would give the lead by being friendly and polite but distant, when they next

153

met.

So she didn't quite know how it was that on Wednesday evening she came to be dancing a breathless polka around the Jessops' living room with Bram's arm firm about her waist while Alexei whirled round with Anna and Peter played a lively tune on his guitar.

She had taken tea with Mr Jessop and Anna as usual and after he had gone they worked on Anna's reading. Edith felt there was some improvement and perhaps because of this she felt well in control of herself when the three brothers appeared, greeting Bram in a friendly fashion and making a well-rehearsed remark about the pleasant coincidence of their last meeting.

Then Peter produced his guitar. At last he'd been able to afford to have it properly restrung and he wanted Edith to hear it. So she was persuaded to stay a little longer and listen and at first was glad she'd done so. Peter sang a mournful Russian song in a clear, true voice and his playing was delicate and sweet. Edith was delighted and urged him to sing again and this time Alexei and Bram joined in and the song was much more lively.

'Miss Summers, would you sing to us, please?' asked Anna and her brothers supported the timorous appeal and Edith found she couldn't refuse. She began strongly enough and Peter managed to follow, but after the first chorus she caught Bram's eye upon her and in trying to fathom his look she wavered and stopped.

'Peter's more at home with raucous male voices,' laughed Bram, covering her faltering apology. 'Come on, Peter - give us something we can dance to!'

Their merry-making was abruptly ended by a furious banging on the door and a harsh voice shouting angrily. Alexei flew to the door, but the complainant had already slipped away downstairs.

'Whatever we do is wrong as far as our neighbours are concerned,' he grumbled. 'If we're quiet we're being secretive. If we make a noise we're a nuisance. You should hear some of them on a Saturday night, Miss Summers - drunken brawls out in the street and up and down the stairs - yet they call themselves respectable and call us - '

'Miss Summers doesn't want to hear all that,' muttered Bram. 'Put the guitar away, Peter. We've danced enough.'

Edith shared that view, though not because she cared about the neighbours. Her heart was still thumping with excitement and her face tingled where his beard had brushed against her cheek as he swung her round. She could still feel the closeness of his body. There had certainly been enough dancing.

She was silent as they paced along the street together. Bram looked at her once or twice and then, to her dismay, began to talk about Matthew.

154

'I'm surprised that Mr Hersey is a Labour Party supporter. Isn't he related to Sir James Gale?'

Edith nodded hurriedly, wondering how she could change the subject.

'Matthew's been a Socialist for years.'

'And he's an old friend of yours.'

She stopped and turned to him. She knew now how dangerous the emotions were which he aroused in her when they danced together and this stifling sensation when he questioned her was too much to bear. Better to tell the truth, even if it meant -

'Yes, I've known Matthew for a long while. He is godfather to my sister's son and a good friend of Clara Riseborough and of my mother.'

She paused and he laid a hand on her arm as though urging her to leave nothing unsaid. She couldn't raise her eyes to his face but concentrated on his hand, seeing the thin blue veins standing out under the white skin.

'He wants me to marry him. We're unofficially engaged.'

'I see.' The hand was quickly removed. Now she looked at him and his face was once more closed against her. She wanted to cry out that she didn't know if she really wanted to marry Matthew, but knew it was too late.

She didn't see Bram alone after that. He rarely came home with his brothers and it was Peter who escorted her down the dark staircase and she made her own way to the omnibus stop. She put up with this until the end of February and then told Anna that there was no longer any need for their lessons. It was the truth in any case: she had helped Anna improve her reading as far as was possible.

The news upset the girl. 'You will come to see us sometimes, won't you Miss Summers?' she urged and Edith had to agree. She could visit once or twice perhaps before Bram got back from work.

She made sure she kept busy so that there was little time in which to brood. She went to more and more Labour Party meetings with Matthew - warily at first, dreading that Bram might be there. But he didn't appear again. She also increased her involvement with the WSPU and found some comfort in the company of Margaret Wilson. And, for a while, the love and attention poured out upon her by Matthew helped restore her self-esteem. But in time his devotion became annoying and there were quarrels between them. Then Clara stepped in, limiting strictly the number of times Edith could see Matthew out of school.

'I'm sorry to seem a stuffy old bore, but I must insist,' she told the two of them, seriously. 'Matthew, you can see how tired Edith looks. She's doing too much. You two will have plenty of time together in the school holidays.'

155

Matthew was contrite and agreed at once. Edith felt a mixture of relief and shame and realised, bitterly, that such feelings now seemed to sum up her relationship with Matthew.

******

Edith pushed her plate away and smiled across the table at Margaret. 'I think that was the best breakfast I've ever tasted.'

Margaret nodded and laughed. 'We've earned it. We must have walked for miles - all the way from Trafalgar Square.'

Edith nodded and finished her cup of tea. She thought that it would be wonderful to move to one of the armchairs in the Wilsons' cosy parlour, but then she heard noises from upstairs and realised that some of the lodgers were getting up.

'I'd better be on my way back to Elm Square,' she murmured. 'It was kind of Clara to let me come here with you for breakfast but she looked very tired when we left her, don't you think? I want to make sure she's getting some rest.'

'Won't you wait until Matthew comes down?' Margaret asked. 'He's bound to want to know how we got on last night.'

Edith stood up. 'I'll be seeing him this evening - Clara's invited him for dinner, I think. But do tell him all about last night, Margaret and reassure him that we all came home unscathed!'

She set a brisk pace towards the omnibus stop. It was early still and there were few people about. Looking up to check her direction she found herself walking towards Bram Jessop.

'Miss Summers?' The surprise in his face was almost comical. 'You're out early.'

They stopped awkwardly and she waited for her own reaction to his presence. It was over a month since she'd seen him. Would there be pain? Anger? But she found herself too buoyed up still by the excitement of the night before to experience any of these emotions.

'I've been up all night, Mr Jessop, along with hundreds of other women. We were abstaining from the census because our government won't give us the vote.'

'Ah... census night.' He looked at her with admiration. 'And you defied it?'

'That's right. "No Vote No Census" - that was the slogan.'

'Yet the government may prosecute?'

'Well... if that happens it will be Clara who suffers. She's the householder - the one supposed to fill in the census paper.' She flushed but gave him a direct look. 'So I haven't really done anything very courageous, Mr Jessop.'

156

'You've given your support and that's important,' he responded, gently.

'It's certainly been a marvellous experience.' Edith's voice rose again with enthusiasm. 'There were so many women out: walking around Trafalgar Square. Some of them went skating at an ice rink, others just stayed in groups, talking, singing. We felt so strong.'

'Yes - good!' He had caught her excitement. 'That's how it should feel when there are many of you, bound together by a common purpose. I have missed that.'

She wanted to ask him what he was remembering. Political meetings in his own country? Secret gatherings with fellow activists? She gazed in admiration, imagining his involvement in the struggle to free his people.

His face was alight with enthusiasm and he smiled at her. 'You are on your way to Elm Square? Perhaps you would have time to come home with me first - we've some very good coffee. I think we would all like to hear about your sleepless night!'

Edith smiled back, confident enough to agree. Seeing him again like this was the best thing that could have happened to her, for she felt it somehow purged her of her infatuation. She would prove it by accepting his invitation.

As they walked she asked why he was out so early.

'I was at the hospital.' He gestured back the way they'd just come. 'One of our neighbours got so drunk he swallowed disinfectant by mistake. His wife came to me, thinking I'd know what to give him. But he was too far gone for simple remedies and I had to help get him to a doctor.'

Somehow the pleasure had gone out of the morning. Edith walked beside him now with her head lowered, depressed by what he'd told her. They went up the stairs together and in the gloom her confidence was slowly ebbing away, leaving only agitation.

The main room was dark and empty. Bram turned up the lamps to dispel the gloom and muttered that he was surprised no-one else was up yet. 'It must be earlier than I thought - my watch isn't very reliable.' She sensed, with his every jerky movement, that he was regretting his invitation.

'Perhaps I should go,' she said softly. 'We might wake your father.'

He saw that she was shivering. 'At least warm yourself at the fire for a moment, Miss Summers.' And so she sat down quickly, took off her gloves and held out her hands as he stirred up the coals.

She saw him casting about for some topic of conversation.

'Er... how is Mr Hersey?' The question was blurted out before he realised what he was saying but she could not help drawing back.

'He's very well,' she said slowly, looking down at her hands. Then she added, wearily, 'I'm not going to marry him, you know.'

He leaned forward. 'Why not?' His voice was shaking.

Edith blinked. 'Because I don't love him enough.' How simple it was. She could have told him that long ago and saved so much pain.

She stood up, looking around her in a dazed fashion, feeling vaguely that now she had cleared the air between them it was best to leave. Bram seemed unable to move and she was nearly at the door before he came to life again and started forward. She flowed into his arms and he clutched her to him as though afraid of losing her and kissed her.

Her arms were tight about him. Neither of them could speak for happiness and relief. They could only kiss each other again and again.

They froze as soon as the fierce coughing began and drew clumsily apart. Even before they heard Anna's sleepy voice calling out to her father, Edith had the door open.

'I'm here, Anna, don't get up!' Bram cried. 'I'll go to Father.'

He bundled Edith out on to the landing and gazed at her in desperation. 'We must talk properly,' he whispered. 'Shall I arrange somewhere we can meet, and write and let you know?' Another bout of coughing started and Edith quickly took a card from her handbag.

'This is Clara's telephone number - I wrote it down because I keep forgetting it.' She pushed it into his hand. 'Is there a telephone where you work?' And when he nodded she smiled. 'That will be quicker than writing.'

'But why would I - '

'To thank me for helping Anna with her reading?'

He nodded, turned to go, then spun back, grasping her hard by the shoulders and kissing her mouth. It was Edith who pulled away first, in control of herself at last.

'Go to your father now.'

                                    ******

Edith tossed the newspaper aside and glanced across the drawing room at Clara. 'I think I'll go and sort out my clothes. I really don't need all those blouses.'

Clara looked up from her book. 'I thought you did that yesterday. Your room was at sixes and sevens all evening.'

Edith reddened. 'That was my shoes.'

'Oh yes - you tried to pass on those dance slippers to Alice. What were you thinking, dear? That she'd break the habit of a lifetime and go out and enjoy herself?'

Edith gave a wry smile. 'Yes - that was silly. She looked so disapproving.'

Clara closed her book and leaned forward. 'It was a little thoughtless,

Edith. You do seem very unsettled at the moment - and you were rather brusque with your mother when she telephoned yesterday evening. That's so unlike you.'

'Well, it's difficult to have a proper conversation. I think Mother holds the telephone at arm's length!'

Clara laughed. 'Well, yes - I know what you mean. But I'm still worried that your teaching work is tiring you out, dear.'

Edith shook her head, smiling to cover her anxiety at Clara's words. She had certainly been on tenterhooks since parting from Bram only two days ago. Would he telephone, or had she imagined the tenderness and the passion between them - misunderstood a moment's flirtation? At all events it wouldn't do for Clara to become suspicious. She cast around for some kind of excuse and lighted on an idea she'd been mulling over before census night.

'No I'm not at all tired, Clara, but I've a plan to arrange a concert at the school - something all the children can take part in and present to all the teachers and perhaps any parents who can come along. I think I've been a bit distracted because I'm trying to get it sorted out in my head before I put the idea to Mr Grenville.'

'Oh, that sounds splendid!' Clara was all smiles now. 'It will be a lot of extra work for you, but a great achievement, I'm sure.'

And it would mean, Edith thought, that Clara wouldn't have to worry so much about her charge being drawn into further action for women's suffrage.

There was a knock at the door and Alice came in.

'Telephone call for Miss Edith,' she said, disapprovingly. 'Says he's a Mr Jessop - about some books.'

Edith forced herself to stand up slowly. 'That must be Anna's father.'

'The little girl you were helping with her reading?' said Clara with a puzzled frown. 'How does he have my telephone number?'

'Oh - I gave it to him. When he wasn't well. In case it was inconvenient for me to go round there... I'll just see what he wants.' And Edith hurried out, hoping her words didn't sound as feeble as she feared.

But once back in the living room she was herself again, controlled and careful, as she settled herself opposite Clara.

'I gave Anna some of my old books but it seems I didn't make it clear that they were a gift. Mr Jessop was wondering if Anna should bring them to school for me, tomorrow.'

'So I gathered,' smiled Clara. 'You're a fine one to complain about your mother shouting on the telephone!'

Alone in her room Edith pounced on her notebook and quickly wrote down the details Bram had given her for tomorrow while she had been apparently conducting a conversation with his father.

'We'll meet there as if by accident. Perhaps you could dress plainly, my love? It's a poor area.'

'Of course, Mr Jessop,' she had trilled. 'Please don't worry about it. I hope you're well.'

'I'm in torment,' he had muttered. 'I can't sleep for thinking of you.'

'Oh, I'm sorry to hear that,' she responded, glad there was no-one to see her doting smile.

'But if you change your mind I'll understand, Edith. You must not come if you have any doubts.'

She lay back on the bed. Doubts? Of course there were doubts. She wanted to know - now, this minute - that he loved her enough to make all that she was risking worthwhile. That his torment was as real as hers had been. That his sleepless nights had been filled with visions as tender and as disturbing as hers.

******

Adam Grenville looked at her thoughtfully. 'A concert? Well, that's an ambitious project, Miss Summers. We've not done anything like that in school for quite some time. And it wouldn't just be the choir, you say?'

'I'd like the country dance classes to show what they've achieved.'

'But that involves most of our pupils.'

'Taking it in turn. So we'd start with some songs from the choir with the rest of the school in the audience and then each class would come forward in turn for the dancing. And there'd be some solo performances - the Malone lad is a wonderful little dancer and so are Katie Wayne and Poppy Burley. There's a lot of musical talent in this school.' Mr Grenville nodded and Edith decided to risk a joke. 'In fact, I'm sure Mr Maynard would be the star of the show!'

He tried to hold back a laugh but failed. 'And I'm sure Mr Maynard will be too busy helping behind the scenes to take part.'

Edith smiled back at him. 'You're right.' Then a thought struck her. 'The scenes... Do you think some of the youngsters could make some scenery, Mr Grenville? That would really make it a splendid show.'

He raised his hands - warding off her enthusiasm, or perhaps in a gesture of surrender. 'Let's see how things progress, Miss Summers. I'll make an announcement to the staff this morning and just test the waters, shall I?'

She was glad she had raised the matter with him early in the day as plans for the concert kept her mind occupied when she wasn't concentrating on lessons and playing. She needed a distraction from thoughts of Bram and their meeting later that afternoon. And the project gave her something to talk about with Matthew, when they met between classes.

160

'It's a splendid idea,' he told her, with a proud smile. 'From the reactions when Mr Grenville discussed it with us earlier you'll have plenty of support from the other teachers.' And his smile broadened. 'And I suppose you might need to come into school more often, each week, for rehearsals? Now that Clara is keeping us at arm's length it's good to know I might at least see more of you here.'

Edith reddened, her mind immediately conjuring the chance of more opportunities to see Bram, but Matthew assumed she was blushing with pleasure at his words, of course.

After choir practice at midday she got a message summoning her to Mr Grenville's office before she left and, though not surprised, was glad to get his agreement to her plan.

'The staff are all pleased at the idea of a concert and some of them came up with additional suggestions,' he told her. 'Miss Milton thinks that some of the girls in her sewing classes could make those - er - handkerchief things for the dancers to wave. And Mr Maynard thinks scenery of some kind could be made in carpentry.'

'Oh, that's wonderful,' Edith smiled. 'And would you be happy with me perhaps coming in occasionally for some extra practice work with the children Mr Grenville?'

He nodded. 'As long as you don't take up too much of their playtime, Miss Summers. They need a break from school work - as we all do.'

His smile was warm but she felt a sudden shame at using his generosity to further her own plans. As she left the school and walked towards her meeting place with Bram she determined that the concert would be a perfectly splendid event. Then she saw him briskly crossing the road and all thoughts of school and concerts fled. They exchanged polite greetings and Edith asked directions to a friend's house. Bram led her down a narrow alleyway, then turned off into another, even smaller, and finally into the doorway of an apartment building. Only then, and when he was sure there was no-one about, did he take her into his arms and they clung together like the survivors of some great ordeal.

'I've been swinging between heaven and hell every minute of every day since I last saw you,' he whispered and she could only nod agreement. The feel of his body against hers took her breath away and the world seemed to be spinning. Then he kissed her, tender but demanding, and the spinning stopped. She was on firm ground, safe with him, part of him. He told her he loved her and she leaned against him, full of happiness, repeating the declaration, word for word.

Then she drew back a little, smiling, teasing - 'But I think you disliked me somewhat when we first met.'

161

'Oh, Edith, I found I liked you too well. I've tried not to fall in love with you - I thought you realised that.'

'Because of your wife?' she asked hesitantly and was shocked when he laughed.

'You thought I was trying to keep true to Sofia's memory? No, it wasn't that. I guessed what it would be like to love you and be loved by you.' His arms tightened about her. 'I would be bound to you.'

There was such helplessness in his voice and his eyes that she felt strangely fearful, but he bent to kiss her again and all anxiety vanished.

Some noise further along the street disturbed them and he quickly ushered her into the building and led her up the deserted staircase to a room on the first floor, explaining that it belonged to a friend who'd agreed he could have it as often as he wished.

'He thinks I'm going to use it as a studio - for my painting.'

They looked round the bleak interior and Bram said he'd already tried rearranging the few pieces of furniture - the table, two chairs, washstand and bed - to make the place seem less cold and bare but had only succeeded in stirring up a good deal of dust from the carpet on the floor.

Edith eyed the carpet with some amusement. 'It looks so thin I'm surprised there's anywhere for dust to lurk.' She smiled at him encouragingly. 'Don't look so woebegone, Bram.'

'We could light the fire,' he murmured, his face still morose, and she agreed, cheerfully, holding down a surge of exasperation. What did the room matter? And why didn't he kiss her again?

'I'll bring some flowers next time,' she said, stripping off her gloves as he bent to set light to the paper and wood in the fireplace. He groaned. 'Oh, Edith - I've longed to spend every penny I could lay hands on to make this place fit for you. It should be *filled* with flowers!'

She was about to comfort him but realised this would be wrong.

'Nonsense,' she said lightly, moving about the room and giving it a careful inspection. 'This will do splendidly. An excellent little love nest.'

Her mocking tone drew a reluctant laugh from him and he set the poker aside and took her in his arms. She felt his tension ease as they kissed. She took off her jacket and crossed to the window. From here she could see only an alley at the back of the building.

'It leads into another court,' he said. 'I'll come in that way and you must always use the front entrance. After today we should never be seen entering or leaving together.'

'Like spies!' she laughed, turning towards him.

'Yes, like spies,' he said gravely.

He took her hand and made her sit by the fire in one of the stiff

162

armchairs, while he sat opposite. Edith grew anxious. This was not how she had imagined their meeting.

'Edith, I've got to be honest with you. I can't marry you - not yet. I may have to go back to Russia.'

She laughed with relief. So that was all. He thought she would not want to leave England with him.

'Of course, Bram: it's your home.'

'No, you don't understand.' He leaned forward eagerly and she melted with love at the intense seriousness in his dark eyes.

'We left Russia in a hurry to escape arrest, or worse. All of us - apart from little Anna of course - were involved in trying to change this corrupt system.'

Edith gave an excited laugh. 'You're revolutionaries,' she breathed.

Bram frowned. 'If you like... At all events I have to return. We still have friends there who are able to let us know what's really happening. So when I'm needed - '

She sprang up. 'Oh, my love - do you think I'd try to stop you? I'd never stand in your way!'

He gave a sigh, then stood up and drew her into his arms. When he kissed her again it was different - fierce and demanding making her tremble with desire. She knew now that there was no going back and that this would be more than anything she had experienced with Matthew. But when they pulled off their clothes and sank down on to the narrow bed the sight of a deep, livid scar on his left shoulder and arm brought her back to her senses. Lying against him she touched the puckered red and grey tissue, so vivid against the paleness of his body, and suddenly felt out of her depth. This man had the marks of a terrible violence upon him and an unbending commitment to a cause she barely understood. What on earth was she doing getting involved with him? She gazed at him in bewilderment and found the selfsame look in his eyes. With a great shudder she turned in his arms, pressing her face against his chest to blot out the image of those uncertain eyes and, as though this was a sign he had been waiting for, he started to touch and kiss her and it was too late for rational thought.

It was late afternoon when she got out of bed and reluctantly began to dress. Bram propped himself up against the thin pillows, his eyes following her every movement. He would not leave for another half-an-hour, he said.

'Shall I take the sheet?' she murmured. 'There's room in my music case.'

'No, leave that: I'll get rid of it.' And he gave her a wry smile. There had not been much blood but it had shocked him. He had not realised she was a virgin and he held her tenderly, apologising again and again for hurting her. But it had been pleasure, not pain, that made her cry out so wildly and she guessed that he knew that and was not as sorry as he seemed.

'When can we meet again?' she asked urgently. That afternoon had shown her a side of herself she'd not truly been aware of - driven by desire, shameless. And she was only able to accept such a humbling revelation because he had made her know that it was just the same for him.

'Whenever we like. I'm renting this room from Stefan. It's ours to use as we wish.'

She gazed at him, one arm in her blouse, the other reaching out to him.

'But when?'

His fingers locked painfully into hers. 'When are you next at the school?'

'Not until the end of the week - but I can tell Clara I'm going in to make some arrangements for rehearsals. Oh, don't look puzzled, Bram - I'll tell you all about that next time. But it's the perfect excuse. We can meet tomorrow.'

'The day after. I can probably make an excuse and get an hour or so off work.' He drew her into his arms. 'Yes, we'll meet then. I can't go too long without you.' Then he pulled her down beside him, whispering in Russian the words of love and desire he had already taught her.

'Once more, Edith,' he gasped. 'Please?'

She needed no urging but was quickly out of the few clothes she had on, moulding her body to his and feeling their mutual hunger taking swift and absolute command.

After that they both dressed quickly. Then Edith put her arms about him.

'I love you,' she said. She had cried out those words so many times that afternoon in frantic joy, but now her voice was calm.

'And I love you,' he responded, gravely. 'But we must be sensible, Edith, and not let this get out of control.' Yet he clung to her as though she was the one with strength enough to restrain them and for a moment she felt terribly afraid.

******

'A letter for you, Edith.'

Clara passed the envelope across the breakfast table as Edith slipped into her seat and reached hurriedly for the toast.

'From Kate: I'll read it on my way to school.'

Edith felt guilty at not having been in touch with her sister for such a long time. It had been a month, a whole month, since that first time with Bram and now they were meeting briefly twice a week and spending time

164

together on Sundays. That was when Clara thought she was meeting Margaret Wilson and her mother for tea. Indeed it had been a month of increasing deceit - with Clara lied to and, of course, Matthew. She now had the excuse of concert preparation for going into school more often but claimed she could not often stay to spend time with him as Clara needed her back at Elm Square. They could meet, with Clara's approval, on Saturdays. Edith knew she had to be careful, though, about showing affection for him. Bram's love had released something powerful in her that Matthew responded to with an excitement that was difficult to contain.

Bram hated the idea of her seeing Matthew at all and their only disagreements were caused by his jealousy.

'I have to keep up the pretence,' Edith told him. 'If I break with Matthew now Clara's bound to allow me less freedom.' In her exasperation she had glared at him challengingly, wishing he would say that they must come out into the open at last. Instead he had caught her to him and soon they were naked in each other's arms.

Edith blushed at the memory and put aside her toast untouched.

Clara glanced at her across the table. 'They're releasing Olive from prison at the beginning of next week,' she announced and after a moment's confusion Edith realised she was referring to a suffragette friend in Holloway. She made what she hoped was a suitably sympathetic noise.

'Poor soul: her health's not good at the best of times. Now she's in a very bad way...' Clara frowned for a moment then said, decisively, 'I'll take her away for a complete rest.'

Edith leaned forward. 'Away?'

'To the sea, I think. The East Ccoast shouldn't be too crowded and the air will do her good. It's the least I can do for her.' Clara smiled. 'We can drive there and put my new car to good use. At the moment it spends most of its time shut away.'

Edith was nodding eagerly, her thoughts a jumble of possibilities.

'But I wouldn't be happy about you being on your own here,' murmured Clara. 'Shall we ask your mother to come and stay while I'm away?'

'No!' She knew it had come out too strongly and she went on hastily, 'Father's been unwell lately, remember? He'll get so fussed if Mother leaves him on his own.'

Clara agreed and Edith hurried on, 'I can ask Margaret Wilson to come and keep me company for a while. How long do you think you'll be gone?'

'Well, about three weeks, I should think. But Margaret is such a sensible creature - she'll be an ideal companion if that can be arranged. Shall I write her a little note?'

'No, I'll sort things out, dear. You concentrate on looking after poor Olive.'

Edith was on the omnibus and halfway to school before her mind stopped racing. There was a lot to organise and she must make no mistakes. She'd have to put up with Margaret's company at Elm Square for at least a week and that would mean losing time with Bram after school. But once that little game was played she could tell Clara and the Elm Square staff that she would be staying some nights with Margaret or with one of the women teachers at Shrub Grove - to make it easier to go into school for the concert rehearsals. In fact she would be with Bram. For the first time they would have whole nights together.

It was a precarious scheme but worth the risk, surely? Edith clutched her handbag against her and tried to restrain her jubilation.

She remembered Kate's letter, thrust into the bag as she hurried out of the house. She smiled as she opened it, but as she read the single page all contentment vanished.

"I've been hoping I need not write this letter, Edie, but now it seems things will not change in a hurry, so I must tell you what has happened before you hear some garbled gossip.

"The truth is that Joe has left me. Although he seemed to like serving in the shop he'd been growing more and more unsettled. That's why I put off telling him about my plans to expand the business and in the end our neighbour let slip that I'd approached him about renting the house. Well, then the fat really was in the fire!

"We had a furious argument and he said he wished we'd never taken on the business and that he'd like to sell up and go back to being a gamekeeper. You can imagine how strongly I argued against that. In the end he just walked out, saying he'd only come back when I saw sense. He's been living at Nell's for the past week or so and he refuses to see me unless I agree to give up the shop. I feel so miserable, Edie. Can you come down - just for a day or so? I've no-one to talk to. I'm writing to Mother now and I expect she will get in touch with you."

Edith read the letter through once more, then folded it and put it back in her bag, seething with resentment. How cruel of Joe to put Kate into such a position, leaving her with William to care for and the shop to run, not to mention facing all the gossip his behaviour was bound to stir up in the village. Her lip lifted in a sneer. Of course he'd be hoping Kate could not cope and would capitulate.

'Why should she have to give up what she so enjoys?' Edith demanded of Matthew at lunch time that day. He was supervising in the noisy playground so there was no chance their conversation would be overheard.

166

Matthew sighed. 'It seems hard, but I know Joe has been very unhappy for a long time. He must have been pretty desperate to do this, Edie. He loves Kate dearly, and William too of course.'

'If he's been so miserable why not talk about it with Kate before now?'

Matthew looked at her with some concern. 'Honestly, we shouldn't take sides, Edie. Don't judge Joe too harshly. And don't forget he owns the business and he could have sold up without even consulting Kate. Instead he's allowing her to make the choice.'

Edith snorted angrily that it was a poor sort of choice for her sister.

'Well, the way he's behaving may seem ill-advised to us, but - '

'Ill-advised!' Edith's tone was heavy with sarcasm. 'You sound like some simpering vicar, Matty. He's been hurtful and malicious to Kate and we both know it!'

He turned towards her so that his anger was hidden from any prying eyes. 'No, that's unfair. I know you're angry on Kate's behalf but that kind of accusation does no good and she'll not thank you for it.'

She stared belligerently at him for a moment, then lowered her eyes. She'd not often seen Matthew roused to this cold anger and she found it alarming.

'I'm sorry,' she murmured, shaken, and his manner softened at once.

'Will you go down to see her?'

'Yes - at the weekend, so I won't be able to meet you on Saturday, after all. I'm sure Mother will come too.'

After school that day she found herself close to tears as she explained to Bram why she would have to miss their Sunday rendezvous. He was concerned on Kate's behalf but made no judgement against Joe.

'From all that you've told me they have had a good marriage up till now,' he said. 'With luck it will prove strong enough to survive this disruption.'

'Was yours a good marriage?' she asked, hesitantly. It was the first time she had mentioned the subject and she waited warily for his response.

'I think it was good of its kind,' Bram said, slowly. 'I did not feel for Sofia what I feel for you, my love, yet I was happy with her. She was a good friend.'

Edith had the sense to suppress her sudden burst of jealousy.

'She shared your political beliefs? Oh, yes - she must have done. You told me how she died.'

His mouth tightened into an ugly line. 'The waste of those lives! And what have we to show for their sacrifice? But the time will come...'

Her eyes lit up in fascination. 'You really believe there will be a

167

revolution, Bram?'

He sighed, then grinned lazily at her. 'Russia is a million miles away and we are here and you have to leave in a little while. Lie down again, my love.'

But she refused. 'You don't want to discuss political matters with your whore?'

He reared up, grasping her by the shoulders. 'Don't dare to call yourself that, Edith!' Then he looked at her closely, saw she would settle for nothing but plain speaking and so drew her down beside him.

'I can only tell you what I hope,' he said. 'I'm in touch with groups working secretly in my country. Stolypin - the Prime Minister - suppresses anything that smacks of protest, so the message has to be spread slowly and carefully. Those of us in exile can do very little at the moment but eventually our help will be needed.'

Edith laid an arm across his chest and pulled him closer.

'And then you'll go back and work with the revolutionaries and overthrow your corrupt rulers,' she said fiercely. 'Oh, that will be magnificent!'

Bram stroked her hair. 'You make it sound a great adventure but - '

'I wish I could be part of it too,' she interrupted, her eyes sparkling. He pressed his fingers against her mouth.

'No more of this,' he said. 'We can't make plans for the future, Edith. If you can accept that it will be the best way you can help me now.'

She knew she had said the wrong thing and so laughed a little and kissed him and then said, teasingly, 'Well, there's something that can help us both here and now. Soon we'll be able to have a whole week to ourselves - more if I can manage it!'

As she explained her plans she held him close. Surely he would soon realise that they must be together, always.

When she got home Clara was hovering in the hall.

'Thank heavens you're back, Edith. Your mother has been telephoning all afternoon!'

******

Sam Bundy beamed a welcome and pulled up the heavy wooden flap so that Edith could step behind the counter.

'Well, I'm certainly pleased to see you, Miss Edith. Kate said to go on up - she's getting William's tea.'

But the shop was empty of customers so Edith paused a moment.

'Have things been difficult, Sam?'

He shrugged, rubbing his hands down the front of his apron.

'When the gossip started up we could hardly move for people coming in to buy something and have a good old nose round. Now trade's falling off,

168

though. Kate's worried but I tell her things will pick up again. Our regulars are sticking with us and the others will drift back when they're tired of having to go much further for their groceries.'

'What hypocrites!' said Edith, hotly. 'As if having your husband walk out makes you incapable of serving a pound of cheese!'

'Yes, but you know what people are like.' And Sam gave a wry grin. 'Joe hasn't been back at all?'

He shook his head and lowered his voice. 'Kate's been over to the smithy several times, but he won't see her. He's being stiff-necked and proud and I've told him so to his face. Makes no odds, though.'

They might have said more if Kate had not called from upstairs. 'Was that the bell, Sam?'

Edith answered cheerfully. 'It was and here I am!' Then she fixed a smile on her face and mounted the stairs.

'You look like Daniel entering the den,' chuckled Kate, leaning over the banisters. 'Don't worry - I'm not going to collapse in floods of tears.'

As they embraced Edith relaxed a little, realising Kate was right. Yet she could see from the dark rings under her sister's eyes that there had been plenty of sleepless nights when tears, no doubt, were shed. Her own eyes grew wet as William came running up to her. She thought that his little arms clung about her tighter than usual and she held him close, wondering how much he understood of what had happened.

'I had a lovely letter from Mother this morning,' said Kate.

Edith sighed. 'She was so disappointed she couldn't come here with me. Trust Father to be unwell now.'

'She seems very concerned about him,' Kate put in charitably but Edith shrugged.

'I think that now he knows he can't bully Mother he uses the excuse of poor health to keep her by him. But she's promised to come over next week, even if it means hiring a nurse to fuss over him.'

They had supper and then Edith claimed the privilege of putting William to bed. He was flushed and excited so she sat with him for a while, telling him a story to calm him down. His eyelids were drooping long before the end, but when she smoothed the covers over him he suddenly looked straight at her, wide-eyed and worried.

'Daddy's gone to work with Uncle Arthur.'

'Yes, I know,' said Edith with a smile. 'It's kind of Daddy to help Uncle when he's so busy.'

The little boy seemed satisfied with her response and said no more. Edith went on with the story for a while until he was asleep at last and then she tiptoed out of the room. Kate was tidying the parlour.

'Sam's closed up and gone,' she murmured and seeing Edith's look of concern added quickly, 'Is William all right?'

'He said Joe's working for Arthur.'

'Oh yes,' Kate shrugged. 'Joe's been earning his keep at the smithy. Art said Joe told him he's not been so happy since he gave up gamekeeping.'

Edith saw Kate's lips tremble and her own anger with Joe hardened. She asked what William had been told.

'Only that Joe is helping Arthur. Sam's very good and takes William over to mother-in-law's on Saturdays so that Joe can see him.' Her voice dropped. 'I took him the first time but Joe wouldn't come into the house. His mother was furious with him.'

Edith nodded approval of Jane Weaver and her admiration increased as Kate told her how Joe's mother had announced that he could only enter her cottage for the purpose of seeing his son. At all other times, though he might be working next door, his presence at the family hearth was forbidden.

'So Joe's lodging with Nell and his mother only allows that on condition he pays rent as well as his keep.'

Edith held back a triumphant laugh. Kate was too obviously upset.

'I hate the trouble all this has caused Jane and the others,' Kate said. 'I've even had Art round here, red as a beetroot, reassuring me that giving Joe work doesn't mean he approves of what's happened.'

'But that's good,' said Edith, earnestly. 'It means they care about you Kate and don't want you and William hurt. Why should you blame yourself for the mess Joe has made?'

Kate sighed. 'It's not as simple as that, Edie. I helped make it too.'

They sat at the table and Kate talked quietly about what had happened. She had decided that she and Joe must resolve their differences: living with her husband's sullen silence, lying sleepless at his side at night, had fast become unbearable. So she'd arranged for them to visit Jane one Sunday, for tea, and then suggested they take a walk while William stayed with his grandma. But this strategy had annoyed him in itself and he strode along the road towards Hassocks at an angry pace and she struggled to keep up with him.

'We must talk, Joe!' she panted. 'I know you don't want to expand the shop further and I don't want to go against you. I'm prepared to forget the whole idea.'

Her choice of words had exasperated him. That was magnanimous of her, he growled, considering it was his shop to do with as he pleased.

She bit back an angry response, saying instead that she would do all the business side in future. 'You can deal with the customers - you know you enjoy that.'

'A pretty state of affairs when the wife's running things and the husband's working for her!'

She grabbed his arm, forcing him to stop and in the shade of a tall hawthorn hedge confronted him coldly.

'What's all this, Joe? I thought we were working together.'

He looked put out and muttered, 'Well, I know... but people talk.'

'And when have you taken notice of stupid village gossip?'

'Since we moved off Sir James's estate and into the village,' he snapped. 'It's no good pretending we can ignore what our neighbours think - '

'The few prejudiced busybodies who still think a woman shouldn't stir out of her kitchen!'

Kate looked at Edith sadly. 'I thought that would make him laugh - would somehow clear the air between us. Instead he said that if he could get another job gamekeeping he'd sell up. That running the shop had come between us and that he wanted us to go back to the way we were. Well, you can understand how I felt at that moment!'

'Oh, I can,' said Edith, stoutly.

'Things were no better after that. I felt powerless.'

'You should have written to me then,' said Edith grimly and Kate smiled for the first time since she had begun her tale.

'So, when does your punishment end, Kate? When you express due repentance? And how's he supposed to know if he refuses to see you?'

'He doesn't really know what he's doing, poor soul,' Kate murmured. 'At the moment he's afraid I'll break his strong resolve - get him to change his mind, if he sees me.'

Edith raised her eyebrows. 'Could you do that if he's so set against you?'

Kate gave her a straight look. 'I'd use every way I know to make him come back to me.'

It was obvious what she meant and Edith did not blush. She knew too well the power of sexual attraction. If there was any fear of losing Bram...

'You'd even agree to give up the business?'

Kate's sigh wrung her heart.

'Oh, Edie, I can hardly bear it without him.' The lovely face was twisted with pain. 'But I can't bear the thought of losing all this either. I love the work and I do it well. If I have to give it up I'm afraid I'll feel so dissatisfied. What good will that do our marriage?'

Edith went to her sister, putting an arm round her.

'No good at all. You're right to hold out for what you want!'

******

Edith slept late the next morning and was eventually woken by the

171

sound of anxious voices on the landing outside her door. She pulled a shawl round her shoulders and looked out to find Sam trying to calm an agitated Kate.

'Oh, Edie, you're awake,' said Kate, relieved. 'Can you sit with William for a while? He's not very well and I'm going to get Michael Thomas to call in. Sam has to serve downstairs.'

Edith dressed quickly. William was lying in bed, unusually still and quiet, his colour high and his forehead hot.

'He says his throat is sore, so I've made up some lemonade,' whispered Kate, bringing in a jug and cup. 'I'll get you some tea before I go, Edie.'

'Don't worry about me.' Edith leaned over the bed and brushed the little boy's hair out of his eyes. 'I expect it's just a chill Kate. My children at school are forever getting them.'

In spite of her concern Kate found herself smiling at Edith's motherly and knowledgeable manner and she went downstairs feeling a little more cheerful.

Michael Thomas cheered her even more when he called later that morning by confirming Edith's diagnosis. He left some powders, to be stirred into William's lemonade, and said the little boy should be kept in bed for the rest of the day.

He greeted Edith politely enough and they talked briefly about her work at Shrub Grove. Somehow she felt uncomfortable in his presence and uneasy with the way he seemed to be looking at her. His smile, as he turned to go, made her shiver. It was as though he knew about Bram.

Edith took a turn in the shop so that Kate could wash William and change his sheets. Sam went to leave a message for Joe and confided in Edith his hopes that this would bring Joe home.

'You know how he feels about William,' he said and Edith agreed eagerly.

'Put it on a bit, Sam. Give the impression William's worse than he really is.'

Later Sam confessed that he'd probably overdone things and made Joe suspicious, for when he returned he only had Nell with him. Edith was serving the vicar's wife and the woman's eyes gleamed with curiosity as Sam ushered Nell upstairs.

'I see Mr Weaver's sister has come,' she said, unnecessarily, and before Edith could reply added, 'To see how the little boy is, I suppose. Goodness, I do think it a shame that his father isn't allowed here. So sad when a disagreement between parents hurts the child, don't you think? Right, that's all I need, Miss Summers. The maid will come to collect it all this

172

afternoon.'

Edith realised, astonished, that the woman thought Joe was banned from the house. She started to put the story straight, but then abandoned the attempt. No doubt all manner of tales were flying around the village. She wondered, suddenly, what would happen if her own secret got out and she felt cold with apprehension.

Nell closed the door of William's room and went back to Kate in the parlour.

'He's sleeping, so I didn't disturb him,' she said. 'He looks very flushed, doesn't he?'

'Dr Thomas says he'll be over it in a day or two,' said Kate, coolly. 'Make sure Joe knows there's nothing he need worry about.'

The other woman's eyes filled with sudden tears.

'I couldn't believe it when he said it was just a trick to get him back. Lucky Mum wasn't about or we'd have had ructions! But I told him a thing or two, believe me.'

Kate softened and smiled. It was unfair to be short with Nell because of her brother's behaviour.

'He doesn't know when he's well off,' Nell went on, sharply. 'There's some would dearly love a little son like William.'

Kate guessed she was referring obliquely to her own childless state and was aware of the frustration beneath Nell's apparently placid exterior. So she made them both some tea and asked about Joe. It seemed he was enjoying work at the smithy but for the rest of the time was morose and uncommunicative. The only time he seemed cheerful was when Sam brought William for the day.

'Then tell him that in future William can stay on Saturday nights and have his Sunday dinner with you all - if that suits you too, Nell,' said Kate. Her voice faltered a little as she imagined solitary weekends for herself but when Nell protested she stood firm. William missed his father and it was only right that he should see him as much as possible.

'Oh, that brother of mine! He's too proud and stubborn to admit how stupid he's being. You're going to have to make the first move, Kate, and agree to give up the shop. I know you've got the strength to do it.'

Kate felt herself waver. So much had happened this morning to make her acutely receptive to Nell's urging. She had been almost sick with fear when she discovered William was ill. On the rare occasions in the past when there was something wrong with the boy Joe's calm good sense was always there to support her. She not only felt afraid without him but was worried that she'd be blamed for failing to care for William properly.

She looked up and saw her sister's eyes upon her. Edith had slipped quietly into the room and her presence reminded Kate of all the arguments against giving in.

'That wouldn't be any good for either of us, Nell,' she said softly. Then she rose, suddenly brisk and active.

'I must get dinner ready: we'll all be hungry!'

William slept for most of the afternoon and woke up with an appetite, which everyone thought was a good sign. His temperature was down and when Michael Thomas returned he needed only a brief look at the boy to confirm his recovery.

After the shop was shut, Sam gone and their evening meal eaten, Edith urged Kate to go to bed but her sister shook her head.

'Not yet. I sleep so badly now and usually wake up early. Can we talk for a while, dear, if you're not too tired? Not about all this - tell me what's happening in London.'

'Only if you tell me about Sam and Flo. I didn't like to ask him when they're getting married, but I can't imagine she'll want to wait long.'

'She'd like it to be before Christmas, but Sam wants them to have a place of their own so he won't agree to fixing a date until that's all arranged.' She sighed. 'I keep forgetting they'll be affected by what happens to Joe and me. If the shop's sold Sam might have to look for another job.'

Edith began to point out that this was another good reason not to sell but Kate cut her short.

'We're back to the same old subject again, Edie. That's a new blouse, isn't it? And so is the dress you had on yesterday. I imagine Matty approves - you told me once that he prefers you in frills and furbelows!'

Edith drew a deep breath. 'It's nothing to do with Matty,' she said sharply. 'I've fallen in love, Kate - with someone else.'

She had expected some kind of sharp response, knowing how fond Kate was of Matthew, but her sister leaned forward, smiling.

'And you're happy, Edie,' she murmured. 'I can see that. Will you tell me about him?'

The words came pouring out. Edith hadn't realised how much she wanted to confide in someone and now she couldn't stop talking. Even when concern replaced the sympathy in Kate's face she didn't check herself. At last she talked herself to a standstill. Kate's eyes were grave.

'Oh, Edie, I'm so afraid for you. It seems you're risking everything while he... And what if you fall pregnant?'

'We're so careful, Kate.'

'Even so... Bram's said he can't marry you.'

'Not yet,' said Edith firmly. 'He wants to, I know, but he has to go back to Russia - '

174

'Yes, you've explained that. But it might not happen for years. And you surely can't mean to deceive Matthew for much longer?'

'I know - I know!' Edith gave a groan. 'It's so wrong! But I can't face up to all that just now. It's enough that I can be with Bram! Please say you understand.'

Kate sighed. 'Edie, you've seen what's happening with me. You know I understand you.'

******

Glancing out of the carriage window Edith realised her train was fast approaching Victoria station. She closed her book and pushed it to the bottom of her bag and as she did so her fingers touched the political pamphlet Bram had given her to read and which had remained unopened. Well, on a train journey it was easier to concentrate on George Eliot.

She realised with some surprise that she wasn't glad to be back in London. Yet she was longing to see Bram and knew how slowly time would pass until tomorrow evening. But there was something...

Kate had been wonderful. She asked questions about Bram and his family, allowing Edith the blessed relief of being able to talk about the man she loved just as if theirs was an ordinary, acceptable courtship. And over breakfast on Sunday morning the sisters had gossiped over Mr Jessop's health and whether or not Peter had the makings of a serious musician. It had all seemed so normal.

As the train jerked and thumped to a halt Edith thought wryly that she and Kate had kept up the illusion pretty well, never once letting the unpleasantness of reality intrude on their time together. They had parted with smiles as Edith set off for Hassocks station.

Now, as she walked towards the barrier, she heard her name called in a voice so low she did not recognise it at first. Then, even before she turned to face him, she knew it was Bram. He took her arm and quickly drew her out of sight behind a pile of crates. She smiled at him, speechless with pleasure, all depression dispelled by his presence. He smiled back, yet hesitantly, as though unsure of himself.

'I had to see you. I couldn't wait until tomorrow. Edith, I've hated every minute you've been away - I wanted only to be where you were.'

She felt triumphant and at the same time chastened. Everything about him, from the defeat in his voice to the trembling of his body as he clung to her told her he would not be satisfied until she was his wife. She was sure that if she urged him he would even give up all his involvement with the Russian cause and arrange for their marriage at once.

She moved her head to press her mouth against his and her desire fired up in the excitement of their kiss. She would not urge it. Now that she

175

knew beyond doubt that he could not do without her she could afford to be patient. They could take time to prepare their families before announcing their engagement and there would be no question of marriage until Bram returned from Russia or she joined him there.

She laughed breathlessly as he released her. 'Oh, I love you,' she whispered. 'I wish I didn't have to go back to Elm Square.'

But her recklessness alarmed him. 'Don't be foolish, Edith. We must get you a cab.'

Quickly she laid a reassuring hand on his arm and nodded to show she would not try to take advantage of his need for her. He looked relieved and they kissed again, but briefly this time. Then they stepped out of hiding to walk the length of the platform, making polite conversation, like acquaintances who had met by chance.

******

Edith left the door open and, crossing to the window, opened it and drew the thin curtains back. But nothing dispelled the dusty heat in the room. With a sigh she took off her broad-brimmed hat and undid the top buttons of her blouse. Already people were saying this was an unnaturally hot Summer and predicting dire consequences. Lying on the bed she thought back over the past weeks. Nothing had worked out the way she had expected, even though the omens at first had been so positive.

Her time with Bram, while Clara was away, had been completely happy. As her eyes traced the now familiar pattern of cracks on the ceiling she pondered on that word. It seemed too simple a way of describing how their days together had felt, when they made this room a temporary home, living, eating and sleeping together. But she thought there had been precious few times in her life when she was conscious of being so deeply content.

Bram had felt the same, she knew it. He laughed more and when he made love to her he was less intense, making time for gentleness as well as satisfaction. And as they sat together after a meal he would draw, using a thick pencil on rough sheets of paper. Nothing he had done had really pleased him but Edith insisted on keeping a sketch he made of her. Raising her head she could see it now, propped up by a jar on the mantelpiece. He had thrown everything else away but she wouldn't let him destroy what she saw as a symbol of their happiness.

When it was time to go back to Clara's and the old way of life she had been distraught and Bram pale and miserable.

'We must be married,' he said firmly. 'I shall make my father understand that it won't change my determination to return home when I'm needed. As soon as I've told him we'll go to Brighton and see your parents.'

But on the following day Mr Jessop was ill again, too ill to be

176

worried, Bram said. In her frustration Edith sometimes wondered if Mr Jessop was using his illness in the same way as her own father. Mr Summers had become increasingly sickly and Polly wasn't able to spend too long visiting Kate. But Edith said nothing of her suspicions to Bram.

She swung her feet off the bed and sat up, reaching for her handbag to find a comb. There was some comfort to be had in the knowledge that Bram wanted her to tell Matthew the truth.

'Explain to him that we'll see your parents as soon as my father is better,' he urged. 'Hersey doesn't sound the sort of man to go running to your mother or Mrs Riseborough with tales, out of spite.'

She crossed to the fireplace and stared into the mirror, then pulled the comb through the damp curls at the side of her face. Bram was right about Matthew, of course. He would be hurt, badly hurt, if she told him what had happened but he wouldn't try to hurt her in return. So why did she keep avoiding telling him the truth?

She put down the comb, sure she had heard a sound in the yard, and flew across the room just in time to see Bram coming through the back door, taking the usual careful look behind him as he did so. She waited to hear his footsteps on the stairs and found that instead of filling with thoughts of love her mind was drawn to the state of the sheets on their bed.

'What do you mean? Buy clean sheets?' Bram was striding about the room waving his arms as he always did when angry or excited. 'Are you mad, Edith?'

'Well I can't take them home with me to be laundered!' She was wondering helplessly how the argument had started. One moment she had been in his arms, smiling a welcome, and the next aware that those arms were empty.

'I know, I know! I meant to take them for Stefan's mother to wash as usual but I forgot!' Bram flung back the bedcovers. 'These are all right. What are you fussing about? Anyway, you're usually too busy enjoying yourself to notice what state the bedclothes are in.'

She bellowed at him in pure rage, hurling her handbag at his head. Then her anger died at once and she stared at him in horror. But Bram was laughing.

'Oh, Edith, we'll make a Russian of you yet. That was a fine display of temper. Not at all like an English young lady.' And he pounced on her and pulled her towards the bed.

Edith allowed herself to be pulled. 'I didn't mean to get cross,' she murmured. 'It's the heat - and you were so late again.'

'I had to spend time with Father. You know we take it in turns to sit and fan him to keep him cool.'

177

Guilt made Edith feel uneasy and she drew away again. 'I wish I could help. Tell him about us, Bram. Then I'll be able to come to visit and lend a hand.'

'Edith, I'm tired of telling you that as soon as Father recovers we'll make our plans known. Don't keep on about it, please.'

There was a terrible weariness in his manner and she felt a cold touch of fear, her mind fastening on his first words - 'Tired of telling you...' Tired of that and what else? Was he tired of the situation they were in; tired of their relationship; tired of her? Suddenly she was shaking, unable to calm herself.

'Have you changed your mind? Don't you want to marry me?'

He clapped his hands to his head and gave a roar of frustration. 'Don't be so bloody stupid!'

She had not seen such rage before and felt as though he had hit her - in the stomach, for that was where the sick churning was beginning. He was coming at her, all concern now, knowing he had scared her, but she turned and rushed out of the room, clattering down the poorly lit staircase.

There was a figure at the bottom of the stairs - someone looking up: a black, forbidding silhouette. She halted, leaning against the wall, gasping for breath.

'Edie! What's happened?'

He was up the stairs and beside her in an instant, putting out a hand to support her. She shrank away.

'Matty? Why are you here?'

'Tell me what's happened.' He had hold of her arm now. 'Is Jessop up there? Has he hurt you?'

'I'm here, Mr Hersey.' Bram came down quietly from the landing. 'I'm afraid you've interrupted a foolish quarrel. A lovers' quarrel.'

Matthew released her so abruptly that she slipped on the stair. Bram steadied her.

'I went to Elm Square,' Matthew snapped. 'Clara was surprised to see me but said I'd be sure to find you at the Wilsons.' He drew a shuddering breath. 'When I got there Margaret was surprised too - you'd just that moment left her to meet me. I said I must have mistaken our arrangements and I got to the end of her road just in time to catch a glimpse of you, Edie. So I followed you.'

His voice broke and Edith looked away, not wanting to see him hurt. But he quickly regained control of himself.

'I've been waiting outside, wondering what was happening. I didn't see you come in, Jessop. I thought that perhaps, after all, I was wrong.'

Edith moved away from Bram. 'No, you weren't wrong, Matty.' She was surprised to find her voice steady. 'I shouldn't have deceived you. It was

178

wicked of me.'

He looked at her almost pityingly. 'You didn't - well not for long. I saw both of you at Victoria one evening. I went to meet you but he was there before me.'

'We're to be married,' said Bram. 'My father's illness has delayed our plans.'

'Ah, yes. I see.' To Edith's amazement Matthew managed a lopsided smile. 'Another secret engagement, Edie.' Then he moved back towards the street door. 'I'll leave you to continue your lovers' quarrel in peace.'

Suddenly she did not want him to go and called his name with such urgency that he turned back and looked sharply from her to Bram.

'Edith... If you want to come with me...?'

She felt a shudder run through Bram and heard his quick gasping breath.

'Matty,' she murmured, 'you won't tell anyone, will you?'

His sudden gentleness was replaced by bitter resentment.

'That doesn't deserve an answer, Edie. But I'm not going to cover up for you. When you lie to Clara and Margaret don't use me as an excuse any more!'

She winced at his words and then again as he slammed the door shut behind him, the noise thudding up the stairwell. Bram took her hand.

'Is there a quarrel?' he whispered.

She shook her head, unable to speak. Even if she could find the right words she didn't think she could make him understand how bereft she suddenly felt. It wasn't just that Matthew had gone out of her life, probably for ever, but that something was lost between her and Bram. Not everything, of course - otherwise she wouldn't be climbing the stairs, leaning against him, feeling his arms tighten about her - but some precious piece of the pattern of their relationship. She wasn't sure if their love-making would wipe out this strange sense of loss.

******

Kate dropped the *Daily Herald* on to the table and looked out of the parlour window. Outside the village street was deserted, save for one or two dogs, lying in the gateways of houses, panting in the heat. She toyed with the idea of sitting in the garden for a while or going for a walk. As it was Sunday William was still with his father, and Sam and Flo wouldn't bring the boy back until early evening. Hours to go yet. But when she moved it was to sit back in her chair and reach for Edith's most recent letter.

It had been a difficult Summer for her sister, too. She had come down to Sussex, guilty and distraught, soon after Matthew discovered her relationship with Bram.

179

'He's given Mr Grenville his resignation,' she told Kate. 'I never dreamed he'd do such a thing! Of course I told him I'd give up my music work with the children so he could stay on, but he said if I did that he'd tell Clara and my parents everything. He wants to leave and that's that!'

It had taken Kate some time to calm her sister and make her see that under the circumstances Matthew's behaviour might not be kind but was certainly sensible.

'If you're both careful you can make sure your paths don't cross at school, Edie, until the end of term. You need to concentrate on how you're going to explain to Mother and Uncle Arnold about Bram.'

Edith had nodded, pulling a face. 'As soon as school finishes for the Summer I'll go down to Brighton to prepare the way and then Bram will join me and face Father. I'm dreading that. I know Father will raise every kind of objection.'

'And if he does?'

Edith's head had jerked up defiantly. 'We'll announce our engagement just the same and live together. I think that might change Father's mind.'

Kate read through her sister's letter again. Poor Edith: the deception had not ended. Only days before she had planned to go home and confront her parents she was urgently summoned to Brighton. Mr Summers had collapsed with violent stomach pain.

Edith found her mother in despair. Mr Summers was refusing to take proper medical advice even though his own doctor, after giving him something to ease the pain, had urged him to consult a specialist. Arnold wouldn't hear of that, insisting there was nothing seriously wrong and prescribing for himself regular doses of some patent medicine designed to soothe digestive problems. But he was often in severe discomfort and Polly grew more and more anxious about him.

It was impossible for Edith to break her news under these circumstances and she had written miserably to Kate, predicting a wretched Summer for herself, stuck in Brighton, helping her mother with nursing duties and unable to see Bram.

That prediction turned out to be false. After only a week or so of what she counted as dreary imprisonment Edith was packed off back to London. This time it was Polly who wrote to Kate.

"I know Edith is unhappy about the break with Matthew but I feel sure her heart isn't truly broken and I can't stand her mooning about the house all the time and shutting herself up in her room.

"Your Uncle is a very difficult patient and I would be glad of Edith's help, but if I ask her to sit with him for a while she just fidgets him with her restlessness. I wish she could come to you, Kate; then at least I would know you had some company. But of course Edith refuses to visit Sussex now that Matthew is there. So I've no choice but to ask Clara to have her again."

As it was so unlike her mother to complain about Edith Kate knew matters must have become very difficult. She, too, was unhappy about Edith going back to London for the Summer for she knew from her sister's now ecstatic letters that she had resumed her meetings with Bram.

It was a change in Matthew's fortunes which had resolved matters for Edith. Sir James had urged his cousin to apply for the newly vacant post of headmaster at the village school and had brought his own influence to bear to get Matthew appointed. Soon after the Summer holidays began Matthew moved into the adjoining school house.

'I'm preparing properly for when school starts again,' he assured Kate on one of his rare visits to the shop. 'But I don't plan to be here for long. I want to earn enough money to travel abroad.'

She had felt deeply depressed by this. Yet another part of her once stable world was breaking away. Soon there would be nothing but separate pieces.

She got up, suddenly restless, and went to the window, but the view had not changed. It was only at weekends that the loneliness frightened her. During the week, with William here and the shop to occupy her, she was scarcely aware of the isolation. True, it felt a little uncomfortable when Sam locked up each night and set off down the street to his lodgings, but she had the supper to prepare and she often kept William up so that he could eat with her. When he was in bed she would cash up and make ready for the following day and as often as not go to bed early herself, with the newspaper or a book to read. She had fallen into a routine of sorts and it grew easier as the days went by.

And William was more settled, too. After his Sundays with Joe he would tell Kate what they had done together but during the rest of the week he never mentioned his father and if Kate did he would try to change the subject. She had expected regular tears, tantrums and bad behaviour but not this calm, self-contained acceptance of the situation. If it had seemed that William was suffering she felt sure she would have gone to Joe for their son's sake. William had not given her that excuse.

There was a knock on the street door and she went down to find Michael Thomas in the porch, mopping his face.

'I thought I'd look in to make sure William isn't suffering too much from this heat,' he said. 'A lot of the village children are dragged down by it.'

'William's with Joe - he goes every Sunday,' she said, with a touch of annoyance.

'Oh, of course: I forgot. The heat is frying my brain.' And he pulled a clown's face which made her laugh in spite of herself.

'Then you'd better come up and have some tea,' she said. 'So you won't have had a completely wasted journey. And for heaven's sake if you're so hot take your jacket off, Michael: you're not visiting the vicar's wife.'

They talked, as she had expected, about the strike and the men killed as rioters in Wales, but she was aware all the time of a restlessness in him. That only increased her own fatigue and she soon found herself longing for him to go.

'I must get on with the accounts soon,' she murmured but he ignored the hint.

'I heard some odd news about Joe today,' he said abruptly. 'I gather he's thinking of going into partnership with his brother.'

Kate's mouth was suddenly dry. She tried to speak, but could not and had to take a swallow of tea.

'He told you that?'

'No. Some friend of Arthur's mentioned it.'

She was appalled. Was it true? Would he really set up in business with Art? She clenched her fists. How ironic that would be for the man who seemed to hate the business he had set up with his wife!

For a moment anger buoyed her up but then a new thought struck her. Joe would need money to go in with Arthur. He would sell the shop, whether she agreed or not.

She burst into tears. It was a long time since she had cried so fiercely and once she started she couldn't stop. She was aware of Michael talking to her, trying to comfort her and then giving up and simply sitting beside her, holding her against him while she sobbed.

At last she raised her head, accepted the handkerchief he offered and detached herself from his hold, trying to think more clearly. She didn't want him fussing over her now and she jumped up.

'I must write to his mother - she'll know what's happening.' And she turned away, intent on starting the letter at once.

She felt his hands on her and turned back, wondering what on earth he was doing and he got his arms about her and she found herself crushed against him with his face, hot and damp, against her neck.

'For goodness sake!' She was more annoyed than anything and tried to push him away, but he had her arms pinned tight.

'Kate. Oh, Kate.' His lips seemed to burn her neck where they touched and she jerked her head away.

'Let me go, Michael! Stop this!'

'You must know I love you, Kate. I can make you happy, if you'll let

182

me. So happy!'

Downstairs someone knocked on the door and they both froze. For a second she felt guilty but this was quickly replaced by anger that she should feel responsible for what had happened. She pulled herself free and without another look at him went out. Matthew was at the door, smiling cheerfully.

'Kate, I know the shop's closed but do you happen to have any curtain rings? Mrs Bartley - she comes in to clean for me - says she'll sew them on tomorrow so I can have curtains in my kitchen at last.'

As they climbed up the stairs Michael Thomas appeared on the landing and Matthew stopped abruptly. There was such pain in his face that Kate couldn't help grasping his arm.

'What is it? Are you ill?'

He gave a harsh laugh and shook his head, watching as the doctor came down, coat buttoned and bag in hand. Michael did not look at Kate but murmured a greeting in Matthew's direction. Kate hurriedly repeated the excuse Michael had given for his call. It seemed lame to her now.

'I'd forgotten that William is with his father today,' said Michael sharply. 'Thank you for the tea, Kate - very refreshing. I'll let myself out.'

There was a moment's confusion as he passed them on the stairs, with Kate and Matthew shuffling together against the wall. Then, with another muttered farewell, he went out.

'Our doctor friend doesn't seem to be in a very cheerful mood,' said Matthew as he followed Kate into the parlour.

'Annoyed about his wasted journey, perhaps,' she said, brightly. 'Now, I'll make a fresh pot of tea, Matty, and then look for curtain rings. We can get some from the shop if I've none to spare. And if I know Gertie Bartley she'll take a month or more sewing them on. Why not let me do that - I'm always after things to keep myself occupied.'

They looked at each other and he nodded soberly. She guessed he felt the kind of loneliness she was experiencing and the need to fill empty hours with some sort of activity.

'Edith hasn't been down for a long time and Mother is occupied nursing Uncle Arnold,' she went on, unable now to halt the flow of self-pity.

'And I suppose Joe's folks are all afraid of appearing to take sides? Oh, Kate, I'm sorry. I've used that as a reason to keep out of things too. I've been a bad friend to you.'

'Well, you've enough worries of your own - ' she began but he shook his head saying she shouldn't defend his thoughtlessness. Then he smiled.

'Come back to tea with me now, Kate. Mrs Bartley might not be a speedy sewer but she's a prolific cook and she's left me a big fruit cake to be eaten. It won't be up to your standards of course...'

Kate laughed. 'Oh, Gertie's fruit cake is always delicious. Just let me find those curtain rings and I'll be ready. Nell won't be bringing William back until five.'

She locked up and they walked the length of the High Street and turned off near the church and up a shady path to the school. She saw the eager look in his face as he surveyed his new domain and asked if she might see inside. He hurried to unlock the door and she stepped into the coolness of the infants' classroom and saw that the place was newly painted. So this was how he had been spending his days alone up here.

'I've done my classroom out in the same way,' said Matthew, leading her into the adjoining room. 'Do you think Miss Crosby will be pleased? She's on holiday at her sister's, so I haven't been able to consult her.'

Kate smiled at the thought of the soft-spoken infants' teacher making any kind of objection and was able to reassure Matthew. In his classroom the walls were covered with new maps and pictures and she guessed they had been paid for out of his own pocket. She realised all his talk of this being a temporary post was not to be believed. His commitment to his new job showed through clearly.

By contrast he had done little to brighten the house next door. The rooms were clean enough but the old-fashioned furniture gave the place a sombre look and Kate thought the parlour horribly cluttered and gloomy.

The kitchen was brighter, though, and so Kate worked there, stitching on the curtain rings while Matthew prepared the tea. They talked easily about various political matters, but once tea was over and the curtains hung Kate found her thoughts returning fretfully to the gossip Michael had relayed.

'Matty, I heard something strange today... that Joe's thinking of going into partnership with Art. Has he said anything to you?'

Matthew pulled a face. 'So that's what Michael Thomas was up to - making mischief! I knew he'd upset you somehow.'

'Then it's just gossip?' She felt suddenly light with hope and leaned forward in her chair, looking for a cheerful smile from him. But there was no answering smile.

'Well... I don't know...'

'He'd have to sell the shop to do it.'

Matthew came to sit beside her and took her hand. 'He'd never do that without your agreement, I'm sure.'

'I'm not!' The tears began now. 'It's been so long since I've seen him and he won't answer my letters. I don't know what he's thinking.'

Matthew put an arm about her. 'Kate, dear, don't cry.' But his voice seemed as shaky as her own and it seemed her misery had loosened a flow of sorrow within him.

'Oh, I'm being selfish, Matty. You're unhappy too, of course. Edie's hurt you so much.'

'I saw them together,' he muttered and then everything flooded out from seeing Edith and Bram at the station to finally confronting them. She knew from the halting way he spoke that this was the first time he had managed to put his feelings into words.

'When she walked back up those stairs with him I could have killed them both, without regret,' he muttered. 'Since then, though, I've come to hate myself far more than I could ever hate Edie. I think I knew the first time he made love to her - I could sense what had happened to her in the way she moved, in everything she did. It was as though she was lit up from inside, Kate. But I couldn't admit it to myself. We were never lovers, you see - not properly. I thought we should wait...'

He had his eyes tight shut but it was too late to stop the tears or the sobs which tore him. Kate was alarmed for a moment, but was reminded of William who also cried in this fierce, rending way when his child's sorrows became too much to bear. So she responded in the best way she knew, pulling Matthew against her so that she could fold her arms tight about him until the storm of grief had passed.

She found part of her mind reflecting that his hair smelt fresh as though newly washed. Almost absently she pressed her face against it and at the same time he gave a low murmur and turned his head into the softness of her breast. She felt her heartbeat quicken, then thump erratically. Matthew sat upright and kissed her mouth. It was a lover's kiss, lasting a long time. It took all her strength to pull herself out of his arms.

'We can't do this. We mustn't,' she whispered, moving quickly to put the table between them.

'But I love you, Kate. I wish I'd loved you long ago.'

She shook her head but knew it was pointless saying this was not love he felt - that they both felt.

'I must go,' she said with deliberation. 'I promised to make William jam tarts for his tea. We usually play for a while on Sunday after he gets home and then I read him a story...' Her voice died away as she saw how much she was hurting Matthew.

'No,' he muttered. 'You and William must come away with me. We'll set up house together. What is there for us here, Kate?'

She pressed a hand to her forehead. 'Oh, stop it, Matty - please! Don't you see how difficult this is?'

There was a long, raw silence, then he gave a shiver despite the warmth of the room.

185

'I'm sorry, Kate. I don't mean to hurt you.' But as she reached the door and grasped the handle he added with an edge to his voice, 'I'll be here, though, if you change your mind.' She stood still for a moment and then looked back.

******

The words spun round in her head as she walked home, forcing herself to take a slow, steady pace in case she was a focus for prying eyes. Back in the kitchen she began the cooking but couldn't concentrate, re-living his embrace and her own frighteningly passionate response, remembering him standing in the school house kitchen, begging her to stay with him. Tears ran down her face and dripped into the bowl of flour on the table in front of her and then she gave a great shudder and swept the bowl aside. It rolled into the corner of the room before breaking, spreading a trail of flour across the floor.

Kate stared at the mess, calm at last. There was no reason why she should bear this weight of misery and guilt alone. She left things as they were and went into William's room.

When Nell arrived with the boy Kate had his meal ready as usual. But she was brisk in her manner and, as she had planned, Nell did not linger. As soon as she had gone Kate washed the jam off William's face and fetched the case she had packed.

'We're going on a journey,' she said and when he began to bounce up and down on his chair with excitement she felt her own heart lighten. She hugged him, but carefully, so that he would not be aware of the intensity of her feelings and be alarmed. She was sure now that this was the right thing to do.

******

Polly heard the confusion at the front door and hurried up behind the maid to find out what was going on. It was important that Arnold's sleep should not be disturbed.

Over the girl's head she saw Kate hovering on the doorstep with William and she gave a cry of delight. Kate looked relieved.

'I'm sorry to arrive so late and without any warning...'

Polly hurried forward, kissed her daughter and lifted the sleepy William into her arms.

'Don't be silly; it's lovely to see you.'

Kate gestured towards the cab at the kerb.

'I thought that if it wasn't convenient for us to stay because Uncle's unwell we could go to lodgings - I told him to wait.'

'Lodgings!' Polly was genuinely shocked. 'Whatever are you talking about? Doris, send the cab away and bring in Mrs Weaver's bag, there's a good girl.'

Kate was grateful for her mother's swift acceptance of the situation. Polly asked no questions but hurried them into the drawing room.

'I'll ring for a tray,' she murmured. 'Sit down, Kate. You look tired out.'

Now that she had reached the end of a journey which seemed to have taken so very long Kate did indeed feel an overwhelming weariness. She took off her hat and sank on to the elegant sofa, while William made himself thoroughly comfortable on Polly's knee.

'You're sure we won't disturb Uncle?' Kate asked and Polly shook her head.

'We've had his study converted into a bedroom for him so that he doesn't have to go up and down stairs too often. I'll put you and William together in Edie's room on the top floor.' She gave Kate a reassuring smile. 'And Arnold's feeling much better this week.'

'He won't be angry at us staying here?' Kate's voice shook and her mother reached out and touched her hand.

'You mustn't worry, dear. He's changed a lot, you know, since his illness. He'll understand that this is an emergency.'

Kate nodded. 'Oh yes - it is.'

Her mother didn't press the matter but talked about how much William had grown. Soon the maid came in with tea and sandwiches and Kate realised she had eaten very little that day. The food revived her and she went upstairs with Polly to put William to bed. The little boy was tired and was asleep before his mother and grandmother left the room.

Polly drew Kate into her own bedroom. 'Now, if you're able, tell me what's happened, dear. You're obviously very distressed.'

Kate had thought she would be able to speak about all that had taken place that afternoon but realised now that she could not. So she focused instead on the news about Joe and how much this had hurt her. Polly hugged her daughter and kept one arm close about her and Kate felt herself relax at last. She would not find an easy solution here but at least she had a temporary haven where she could gather her strength again. She went to bed that night in her mother's house feeling calm for the first time that day and she slept without dreaming until William woke her, late the following morning.

******

'So, have you left your business to run itself?'

Arnold Summers pulled the rug closer about his knees and gave Kate a severe stare. As a child she had feared him in this kind of critical mood; as a young woman she had despised him. Now she felt only pity for him. He had changed greatly since their last, memorable meeting and seemed to be shrivelling up.

187

'Sam Bundy always opens up in the morning and I left a note asking him to take charge and saying he can take on more help if he thinks it necessary.'

Her uncle gave an unexpected snort. 'Oh, Bundy can manage a place that size on his own. You've a good man there.'

Kate nodded. Arnold looked around, muttering something about a draught, so she rose to shut the window. It would make the room stuffy and probably give her uncle a headache but she had promised Polly to do everything he asked. Kate could understand her mother's look of relief when she offered to sit with her uncle that afternoon.

'Would you, dear? If it wouldn't be too much trouble... It would be so nice to get out into the sunshine and I can take William for a walk along the front.'

Arnold sniffed. 'I don't know all the ins and outs of this trouble between you and your husband and I prefer not to; but I gather there's some talk of him selling up. Is that right?' He leaned forward in his chair. 'Well, let's see shall we?' And in a firmer voice he began questioning her about profit and stock and the running of the shop. She drew her chair nearer to him, setting her mending aside, answering him in detail and listening carefully to his comments and suggestions. She had never imagined talking to him in this way and it wasn't until she heard the front door open and William's excited voice in the hall that she realised how much time had passed. Arnold sank down into his chair, but there was still life in his voice.

'He'd be a fool to sell now and I don't think that husband of yours is a fool. Take my advice and expand as soon as possible - your profits are good and you can afford to take the risk.'

Then he began to cough and Kate went to the sideboard to pour him a glass of water.

'If we keep the shop I'll certainly do as you say, Uncle,' she said firmly. 'I'm very grateful for your interest and advice.' She put the glass into his hand and saw how slack the skin hung between his fingers.

'Will you take some advice from me in return?'

He looked up, startled and she added quickly, 'Please see a doctor, Uncle. You shouldn't be stuck here like an invalid. You've your own business to run.'

She saw the flash of panic in his eyes and knew that what prevented him from seeking help was fear of what might be discovered. But this was replaced by a more reflective look. He said nothing and waved her away and then Polly came in, smiling and refreshed, to say that William was ready for his tea and waiting for Kate in the drawing room.

Arnold suddenly spoke up. 'I suppose I shall be allowed to see the

188

boy? Or have you made me out to be such an ogre that he's afraid to come in here?'

Polly gave Kate an astonished look. 'Of course you can see him, Arnold,' she stuttered. 'We'll bring him in before his bedtime.'

******

'I'd never have believed such an evening possible,' laughed Kate some hours later as she and her mother shared the bedroom mirror to tidy their hair before dinner.

William had behaved perfectly, sitting on a stool by Arnold's chair and making his somewhat limited conversation in a clear voice. He was much impressed with the gold watch Mr Summers had fished out from beneath shawls and blankets and listened with evident awe when it was made to strike prettily.

'I was rather afraid he might not give it back, mind,' smiled Polly.

Luckily good manners had prevailed and the watch was returned to its owner. Soon afterwards Mr Summers announced that he was tired and the audience ended.

'Now both children are tucked up in bed and we can relax,' said Kate without thinking. She flushed as soon as the words were out and looked apologetically at her mother's reflection. Polly gave a sharp grimace.

'You're quite right - Arnold can be very childish at the moment. Sometimes I could scream at him for being so silly. But he's often in great pain, you know.'

There was a tap at the door and the maid appeared, her eyes wide with anticipation.

'There's a Mr Weaver downstairs to see Mrs Weaver,' she hissed. 'I've put him in the drawing room.'

Kate's flicker of hope died in a moment.

'It'll be Arthur,' she said, flatly. 'Jane must have guessed I'd come here.'

She pushed a hairpin into place and turned away from the mirror, almost casually. Her mother thrust her towards the door.

'Go down Kate - hurry,' she urged. 'Doris, you stay here a moment.'

Kate descended reluctantly into the hall and Polly watched from the top of the stairs, trying to will into being the hope she had been nursing all day. Kate opened the drawing room door, gave a cry and vanished inside. Polly found herself smiling, wide-mouthed and foolish with relief.

******

He had tried to hold her off, she knew that, but at the same time she saw the longing in his eyes. Then he gathered her into his arms, clasping her tight. She was shuddering and laughing and murmuring his name until he

189

silenced her with a hard and hungry kiss.

'Joe...' She had to break away from him; she couldn't think with his mouth on hers.

He stroked her hair and touched her face gently, then quickly released her as though he too needed to put some space between them. His face was brown but thinner than she remembered and his moustache needed trimming. She saw that he had put on his best suit. That made her cry, and she must not cry...

'I'll come back to the shop,' he burst out. 'I'll do whatever you want Kate, only don't go away from me. Don't take William away.'

She could not bear the defeat in his voice and his eyes. She heard herself exclaim the very words she had sworn she would not utter.

'I don't care about the shop! I'll give it up, if that's what you want. Just stay with me, Joe.'

They stood in what seemed like endless silence, horrified at having forced each other into submission. Then Kate moved to him and they held each other once more but tenderly now.

She did not know if it was the right moment to speak but an instinctive sense of self-preservation forced the words from her.

'Can't we compromise? Won't you let me run the shop while you work with Arthur? Do you have to sell up?'

'No - we can keep the shop and do as you say.' He gave a shaky laugh. 'It's all so simple, really.'

She felt the load slip away from her. All so simple, so easily resolved.

'I can't believe... after all this time - ' She broke down, crying and he pulled out a handkerchief and pushed it into her hand. Her weeping ceased at once. 'Joe Weaver! What on earth is this?'

He stared at the frayed and filthy piece of cloth with a distaste that matched her own. 'Oh Lord - I must have been using that in the forge,' he said, guiltily.

'Whatever would people think - ' she began, but then the laughter came in great, uncontrollable waves. As she clutched at him, gasping, she saw his face redden with mirth and her love and longing for him overflowed.

They sat together on the sofa, calmer now, and Joe explained how frightened he had been when Sam Bundy arrived at the smithy that morning with the note Kate had left.

'I just didn't think that you'd come here. I was in a complete panic - sure you'd run away where I couldn't find you. I rushed off to see Matty. I hoped you might have told him where you were going.'

She leaned against his shoulder so that he shouldn't see her face and her heart thumped fearfully.

'Of course he knew nothing about it,' Joe went on, 'but he gave me a rare old talking-to. Said he'd not blame you if you ran off to Timbuctoo. Made me see how stupid I've been. Well, I wish he'd been so outspoken long ago. And he guessed you'd come here, first off at least.'

He turned to her and put his hand under her chin to raise her face.

'I can't believe we've been apart for so long for such a daft reason.'

She gave a sad little smile and he kissed her. She forced herself to relax in his embrace. It would be easy to protest that if he had agreed to see her, or had answered any of her letters... No; the faults, the stubbornness were not all on his side. She'd not taken enough notice of his feelings about the shop... Now there must be no recriminations.

They sat together in warm silence for a while longer and then went to join Polly in the dining room. She kissed Joe warmly on both cheeks, said she was glad to see him and then hurried them to the table.

'I've kept dinner back as long as I could but Cook's meat pie will be a disaster if we don't eat it now!'

They took their cue from Polly and there was no further mention of their separation and reconciliation. Instead they discussed politics and Lloyd George's behaviour towards the railway unions. Polly rushed to the Chancellor's defence and the debate grew heated. It was just like old times, Kate thought, with a mixture of happiness and relief.

'I like the way your mother can argue her corner and yet harbour no ill-feeling if someone disagrees with her,' said Joe, later, when they were alone together in the guest room. Kate had already taken him in to see William, but the boy was fast asleep and Joe would not wake him.

Joe had brought nothing with him so Polly found him a nightshirt of Arnold's and now he stripped to his underwear and held it against him. It was far too small and they both laughed immoderately.

Kate turned to the mirror to undo her hair. Matthew's face seemed to flicker before her eyes and she forced herself to reject that memory. She didn't bother with her nightdress but slipped naked into bed before Joe and then let him pull back the covers and just sit looking at her.

'In the beginning I missed you most at nights,' he murmured. 'I ached for you so much. Somehow that made me angry. Perhaps I'd have come back sooner if it hadn't been for all that anger.'

Kate stroked his chest. 'It was like that for me, too,' she said. 'The first night I didn't even go to bed. I walked about the house; walked and walked, all through the upstairs rooms and then down into the shop, round and round the storeroom. I was crying and raging, all at the same time.'

He groaned and clasped her against him and she clung to him in a turmoil of desire and relief. The hands which caressed and opened her were calloused and a little clumsy, but she knew she wanted no other touch upon her.

******

Edith ran up the stairs, found the key in their usual hiding place and unlocked the door. The room was still warm from the late afternoon sun but she shivered as she lit the lamps.

She knelt before the empty fireplace and began to clear away the ashes. She liked to have the fire lit and the kettle boiling before Bram arrived but concert rehearsals had kept her later at school than expected.

The flames were licking about the kindling as he came in. She went to him at once and they clung together, saying nothing for a moment. It was often like that now, she reflected, as though they greeted each other in desperation rather than joy. She drew back and looked at him.

'You've changed out of your working clothes.'

Bram shrugged. 'I've not been to work today. Father is ill again - I've spent the whole day with him.'

'Oh, I'm sorry.'

She made him sit in the fireside chair while she bustled about with the tea things. Though the room was hot now, he kept his coat wrapped around him. He seemed distanced from her - concerned for his father she supposed - and this made it difficult for her to say what she had planned. So, when the tea was poured she sat opposite him for a while and they drank in silence. Like an old married couple, she thought, with nothing to tell.

At last he stirred himself. 'Is anything wrong, Edith? You're very quiet. All's well with your sister, I hope?'

'Oh yes - she's busy with the shop and Joe is thoroughly enjoying working with his brother. They've come through their crisis and are stronger for it, I think. No...' she hesitated, then plunged on, 'No, it's my parents. They're arriving at Clara's tomorrow. Father's agreed at last to see a specialist about his poor health.'

'Ah.' He dropped his gaze and it was as though a great weariness came over him. Edith slithered to the floor, kneeling before him on the hearth rug.

'Bram, please let me tell Mother about us. I can't bear this secrecy any longer. We can't approach Father while he's still unwell, of course, but if my mother knows we're engaged that will make things so much easier.'

Bram touched her hair with his free hand and then leaned forward to kiss her cheek.

'If your father is ill this is surely not the moment...' He spoke vaguely as though his mind wasn't really on the subject and she knew he was deeply troubled. At any other time she'd not have pressed him further but somehow

192

she felt the matter mustn't be put off.

'I'll make it right, Bram. Will you agree to my telling Mother about us? Please?'

He said nothing and she realised with amazement that he wasn't listening to her. Holding back her anger with difficulty she shook his arm and repeated her question. He looked down at her as though dragging his mind back from some distant place.

'Edith, your father is ill: nothing has changed there. Your mother will be too worried about him to have any interest in us.'

She shook her head. 'I'm sure the specialist will set Father's mind at rest. We may even be able to break the news to both of them while they're here. But I want to speak to Mother first.'

Bram shrugged, then stood up abruptly, pulling off his coat.

'As you wish, Edith.'

She gave a laugh which shook with relief. He dropped his coat in a heap on the chair and turned to her, his eyes suddenly bright, almost frightening in their intensity. He caught hold of her and pulled her to his feet and into his arms.

'I don't want to talk any more, my love. For God's sake let's forget everything else for a while. Do you want me?'

Her arms wrapped about him and her mouth pressed hungrily to his were answer enough. When they made love he was fierce with her and she responded with an exultant ferocity of her own, marking his body with her teeth and nails.

'The devil's in us both tonight,' he gasped and she laughed. But there was something desperate about the sound and she felt a chill of fear. Then his body slid over hers again and the fear was forgotten.

******

'Miss Summers! Oh, I thought you weren't coming!'

Edith stopped and smiled down at Anna who had apparently been waiting in ambush just inside the school entrance.

'Yes, I'm late. I missed my omnibus this morning. But we've a few moments before assembly. Is something wrong?'

'Father said I must be sure to find you and ask if you'll come back with me after school today. He needs to see you - it's very important.'

Edith's heart gave a jerk. Bram must have acted first: he had told Mr Jessop of their engagement and, not surprisingly, his father now wanted to talk to Edith in person. It would be awkward this afternoon. Her parents were arriving in London today and her father was going straight to see the specialist, so they would both be waiting for her at Clara's. Perhaps she could reorganise the planned concert rehearsal and leave school early... She glanced

193

at Anna who was hopping from one foot to the other.

'Thank you, dear. Of course I'll come to see your father. Now, let's go into assembly together then you won't get into trouble for being late.'

Anna gave a sigh of relief but her face did not lighten and Edith asked what was wrong.

'I don't really know, Miss. Bram and Father were talking together until ever so late last night and Bram had gone this morning when I got up. And now Peter and Alexei seem so miserable. I don't know what's happening.'

Edith gave an involuntary shiver. Mr Jessop disapproved - that much was clear. Bram must have sat up late trying to win his father's approval for the engagement. The fact that Bram had gone to work early and that his brothers were disturbed suggested that there was a serious rift between father and son, affecting the whole family. And now she had to face Mr Jessop. Bram would be there, of course, and the engagement could not be stopped but she was still concerned about causing strife in the family.

She quickly pulled herself together. 'I'm sure there's nothing seriously wrong, Anna,' she said firmly. 'Let's go in now.'

It was difficult to keep her mind on her work that day: she found herself busy assembling her arguments for Mr Jessop. It was vital to convince him that she was well aware of Bram's commitment to his country and that she would work at his side wherever the cause took him.

Country dancing had only just begun when a boy came into the hall with a message that Edith was wanted in Mr Grenville's office. Mr Maynard was waiting outside the door and murmured that the headmaster had someone in with him. They craned to hear the rise and fall of voices from inside.

'Is it a parent?' Edith whispered. 'Oh, heavens - not the police I hope!' and they exchanged worried looks. Mr Grenville suddenly emerged, closing the door behind him.

'Thank you both for coming.' His voice was low. 'I'm afraid there's very bad news for Anna Jessop. Mr Maynard, you're her teacher but I know Miss Summers has had some contact with the family and I thought she should also be here when we get Anna. Her brother has come to collect her: their father died about two hours ago.'

Edith gave a gasping cry but stifled it at once, her hand tight against her mouth. Adam Grenville gave her a sharp look. 'He had a coughing fit which brought on a massive haemorrhage.'

She groaned, but had herself under control. It was impossible not to feel guilty about what had happened, but she must think of Bram now and remain as calm as possible so that she could comfort him.

194

'Could Mr Maynard fetch Anna?' she asked. 'I'd like to see Mr Jessop alone for a moment.'

The Headmaster's eyebrows rose slightly but he murmured agreement and she went into the office. Peter was standing by the window, wiping a handkerchief roughly across his eyes. Her confusion was quickly replaced by compassion.

'Oh, Peter - I'm so sorry!'

He gazed at her miserably. 'Father said he was better,' he whispered. 'He even looked better, in spite of everything. It happened so suddenly. I didn't even have time to call Alexei from across the landing!'

Edith gave a sympathetic murmur. 'Was Bram with him... at the end?'

Peter moved back and she had the odd sense that he was trying to get away from her. He spread his hands in a gesture of despair.

'Oh, this is awful! Bram left last night, Miss Summers. Father was going to tell you when you came back with Anna today.'

A cold calmness possessed her. 'What do you mean? Where has Bram gone?' But she thought she knew the answer. He had left home, too angry at his father's opposition to their engagement to stay under the same roof with him. Now he would regret that, dreadfully.

'To Russia.'

She almost laughed out loud. 'Oh, Peter, don't be silly. You're muddled because of what's happened. It's - '

'Bram left last night. He ought to have told you! Father said he should. He's travelling under a different name and he won't contact us until he's settled there.'

'I don't understand: it isn't possible. He can't have gone just like that. What about papers - for travelling?'

'Everything was prepared. He's known for some time that he'd be called back. He left a note for you, Miss Summers. Father said it was the least he could do.'

He held out the crumpled envelope and she took it and opened it quickly, surprised that her hands were so steady. But the words seemed to shift before her eyes.

"My Dearest - I have to go without saying goodbye for if I see you again I know I shall never be able to leave. Father will explain everything to you. I love you, always - Bram."

She crushed the paper savagely in her hand. Behind her the door opened and Mr Grenville came in with Anna. Edith was aware of Peter explaining what had happened to his sister; of the girl's sobs; of her own voice murmuring what comfort she could. And all the while her mind was numb, operating automatically and quite without feeling. She was glad of that.

She didn't want to feel anything. She wanted only to stay forever in this half-alive state that was without pain.

Anna did not cry for long.

'Can I see him? I want to see him.'

Peter murmured something and Edith suddenly found that the office was empty. Her hand hurt and she realised it was clenched into a fist. When the Headmaster returned she was staring at Bram's note.

His voice full of concern, Mr Grenville asked if she was unwell and without thinking she held out the note to him. Puzzled, he took the paper, unfolded it and read the message. She watched his face redden, knowing she had put him in an awkward position, but knowing too that she had to share with someone else the terrible thing that had happened to her.

'He's gone to Russia.' She spoke in sharp, disjointed sentences. 'We were going to announce our engagement. I only saw him last night.' Then her voice began to shake. Mr Grenville led her to a chair and she sank down, feeling as though all her bones were crumbling into nothing.

'I'll find someone to take over your class and then call a cab and get you home,' he said. 'Will you be all right for a moment?'

She nodded and when he had gone reached for Bram's note on the desk and read it again in the sudden, desperate hope that she had misunderstood. But the words were unchanged. She thrust the paper into her pocket and slowly, wearily stood up.

******

Polly leaned forward in her seat, peering out of the car window at the houses as they drove slowly along the street.

'You're sure we haven't passed it?'

Clara's chauffeur turned his head slightly in her direction.

'I have been keeping a careful check, Madam. I believe the house you want is right at the end of this row.'

She sat back against the Daimler's comfortable upholstery and tried to hang on to her patience. All this was taking so much time!

The car halted and she was out of it before the chauffeur had time to open her door. Ignoring his pained look she hurried up the path.

She was admitted by an elderly woman - the housekeeper she supposed - who at once showed her into the parlour. Adam Grenville jumped up from his chair and she could see the hope fade from his face.

'Edith hasn't returned then, Mrs Summers?'

She shook her head. 'Clara - Mrs Riseborough - said she would telephone here if Edith came back while I was on my way to you. I felt sure you wouldn't mind.' She was aware of the housekeeper discreetly leaving the room and now she cried out, fearfully, 'Mr Grenville, please tell me what's happened!'

He drew forward a chair and she was glad to sit down for she was suddenly trembling. For a moment her mind went blank and then she became aware of him putting a glass of something into her hand.

'Forgive my asking, but I know your husband was seeking advice on the state of his health today. I hope he has had good news?'

She sipped a little of the brandy. 'I'm afraid not. He's been admitted to hospital at once and there's talk of an operation.' She jerked her head up, feeling steadier. 'But I'm more worried about my daughter at the moment, Mr Grenville.'

He sat down opposite her, perching inelegantly on the edge of his chair, and now that she could see him clearly she realised he was only a year or two older than herself: a pleasant-looking man with fine, deep-set blue eyes. Eyes that were now very uneasy.

'When you telephoned Clara you said that Edith had been unwell at school but left before you could arrange for her to be taken home.'

'That's right, though not so much unwell as very upset. We heard that the father of one of the girls in the choir had died suddenly. Your daughter knows the family well - the Jessops.'

She remembered the name at once; but since Christmas Edith had not mentioned the family.

'Do you think she's gone to them?'

'No, she hasn't. I went to their home as soon as Mrs Riseborough told me that Edith had not returned. I felt something wasn't right. But the Jessops haven't seen her either.'

Polly clasped her hands together, forcing herself to be calm.

'My daughter is a grown woman, not one of your pupils, Mr Grenville. There's more to this than you're telling me, isn't there?' And when he looked away she knew she was right. 'What else do you know about Edith and this family?'

He shook his head. 'Miss Summers must tell you that herself.'

'For heaven's sake, Mr Grenville - I'm asking for your help, not encouraging classroom tale-telling. You must understand that - as a parent?'

That seemed to bring him up short and he looked at her directly now. 'You're quite right, Mrs Summers. This is no time to keep silent. I believe Miss Summers has formed an attachment with Bram Jessop, the eldest in the family. He left the country yesterday to return to Russia - sadly it was before his father died. I gather that Miss Summers didn't know he was going and discovered the fact at the same time as hearing of Mr Jessop's death.'

Polly stared down at her hands, feeling the heat of an overpowering rage flood through her. Here, at last, was the reason for Edith's strange, unsettled behaviour this Summer. This was why she'd come home so little and why her secret engagement to Matthew had been broken.

Adam Grenville was clearing away the glass and brandy decanter to give Polly time to recover and she was grateful for his tact. Setting her anger aside she stood up, turning to him. 'Will you please tell me where these people live? Perhaps Edith has tried to follow this man. His family will surely know how he planned to leave the country and that may be a way of tracing her.'

He nodded briskly and said he'd go with her. As he had already spoken to the Jessops it would perhaps be helpful if he put the necessary questions to them.

Polly waited for him in the car outside Shrub Mansions, growing increasingly frustrated, wishing she had insisted on going in with him. The gleam and glitter of the machine drew a crowd of inquisitive, grimy urchins and Clara's chauffeur had to descend from the driving seat to chase them away. Polly was aware of having incurred his very great displeasure.

Adam Grenville reappeared, out of breath but with renewed hope in his glance.

'I spoke to the younger brother this time - when I went earlier he was out making funeral arrangements,' he puffed, climbing in beside her. He lowered his voice so that the chauffeur would not hear. 'They've no knowledge of Bram Jessop's movements but apparently he rented a room not too far away. The brother, Peter, thinks that he and Edith used to meet there sometimes.'

'She might be there now?'

'With luck.'

He leaned forward to give directions to the chauffeur and Polly frowned. She disliked the sound of this room - it suggested an involvement that went deeper than courtship. Then she found her hands were shaking. It didn't really matter how foolish Edith had been as long as she had done herself no harm.

This time she refused to wait outside and when they pushed open the front door and Adam Grenville tutted over the smell and the dirt in the entrance hall she turned on him with great annoyance.

'Heavens, man - I once lived in a lodging house far worse than this and thought myself lucky. I'm not going to fall into a faint out of shock!'

There wasn't enough light on the stairs to see his face but she heard him give a dry laugh.

'At least take my arm, Mrs Summers. The stairs are narrow here. You may not fall in a faint but you could easily fall on your nose.'

She had to hold down an answering laugh, amazed that she could find anything funny at such a time.

'Here, I think.' He was whispering now and when she moved to knock on the door he held her back. Then he opened the door himself and stepped into the room. She heard a voice, frenzied and despairing, barely recognisable as her daughter's.

'Mr Grenville? Why are you here? Oh - please - do you have a message from him?'

Polly pushed past Adam Grenville and confronted Edith. The young woman's hair was in wild disarray and her eyes were red and puffy from crying, but otherwise she appeared to have done herself no harm. But Polly could only guess at her mental state and her heart went out to Edith. She said, gently, 'Let's take you home, dear.'

Edith returned her gaze for a moment and then gave a trembling wail. 'Oh, Mother! Why did you have to come here?'

******

When they at last got her down the gloomy staircase and into the car Adam Grenville suggested they rest at his house before returning to Elm Square and Polly agreed gratefully. She wanted more time with Edith to find out what had happened, or as much as her daughter would tell. At Clara's house there would have to be explanations and no doubt Clara would blame herself for everything. Better by far if she and Edith had a chance to calm themselves and concoct - not a lie, exactly, but some story that would save the girl's face.

Polly glanced at her daughter, huddled in the corner of the seat. She thought Edith too possessed by misery to care yet what anyone thought of her. She'd hardly been aware of the mutterings of the small group of residents gathered at the entrance of the tenement as they left. Polly herself had felt more depressed than shamed at what she had heard.

'Her parents come to fetch her away?'

'Husband must have left her - I told you how it'd be.'

'Husband? Don't make me laugh. They didn't live here all the time, you know, just came and went. If you ask me she's no better than she should be.'

The last words rang in Polly's mind still. She remembered her own mother running down the path after her, holding out the few coins which, Polly knew, she had saved in a tin behind the mantelpiece clock.

'It's not for your sake, girl, so don't think it! But I don't see why the child you're carrying should suffer - just because you're no better than you should be!'

She groaned. What would they do if Edith was pregnant?

The housekeeper was waiting for them with the parlour fire lit and some food and a hot drink ready. Adam Grenville went off to attend to the chauffeur, leaving mother and daughter alone.

Polly handed Edith a sandwich and watched with satisfaction as she ate. Then Edith looked at her, calmly. 'You must have been worried, Mother. I didn't realise it was so late. I've been wandering round in a daze for hours, I think. I can't even remember where I went before - before you and Mr Grenville found me.'

She seemed perfectly calm and reasonable and Polly suppressed a sigh. Edith was erecting barriers around herself, retreating into a cold self-possession. But the tears in her eyes were genuine enough and Polly ached in sympathy as Edith told the story of how she had fallen in love with Bram Jessop, her tone clipped and chilly.

'We used to meet - in that place,' she concluded. 'When Clara thought I was holding rehearsals for the school concert.'

Polly waited, but it seemed there was nothing more forthcoming. She went across to the window and absently adjusted one of the heavy maroon curtains. If they were meeting often it followed as night followed day that they were lovers. But if she said anything Edith might shut off from her completely.

'Matthew found out, of course. That's why our engagement was broken.' Edith's face was impassive. Polly went back to her seat and sank into it wearily.

'Why didn't you tell me?'

The thin, colourless voice wavered for a moment. 'I - I wanted to, Mother. I was going to do so today if Bram - ' her hands twitched in her lap, but she recovered quickly. 'I couldn't say anything before while Father was ill.'

Polly looked up, sharply. 'You thought I'd tell him?'

'No - no of course not, Mother.' Then she lowered her eyes. 'The truth is, I thought you'd try to stop me seeing Bram.'

So there was to be some honesty at least. Again Polly kept silent with difficulty. It was tempting to shout out that she would have done just that - and would have been right to do so. What mother would want her daughter meeting secretly with such a man - someone who had apparently taken advantage of Edith's youth and inexperience. But she held her tongue and took her daughter's hands in her own.

'You're sure he won't come back, dear?'

The young woman's chin lifted. 'I'm sure. His commitment to Russia is greater than his love for me.'

Then her anger broke. 'He thought I had a romantic view of politics; that I wasn't really serious about Socialism. That's why he wouldn't tell me he was leaving, because he thought I'd try to stop him. I hate him for distrusting

200

me like that!'

Polly calmed and soothed. Edith had been hurt, almost to madness, by Bram's desertion and was now trying to put back together the shattered pieces of herself. Hatred and bitterness were poor bonding agents but they would do for the moment.

'You must rest for a while dear and then we'll go home. Clara will be wondering what's happened.'

'What have you told Father?'

Polly shook her head. 'I haven't had to tell him anything. He's in hospital, Edie; he'll probably be having an operation very soon.'

Edith looked alarmed and Polly added hastily, 'Don't worry about that now. We'll both go and see him tomorrow - he'll be so pleased. Now, do you want another of these lovely sandwiches?'

Edith was quickly pacified and Polly knew she'd not properly taken in the news about her father. Of course, she had never suspected how ill he was.

She said as much to Adam Grenville a little while later, sitting with him in the dining room after Edith had fallen into an exhausted sleep on the parlour sofa.

'When she realises the truth she'll give you both all her love and support, I'm sure,' he murmured. 'In a way, her father's illness - worrying though it is - may help her recover from her own pain more quickly.'

Then he added, with some hesitation, 'You might care to tell your friend, Mrs Riseborough, that Edith was upset about Mr Jessop's death, went for a walk and forgot the time and so came here to telephone you. She was waiting for you here when you arrived and you both took tea with me.'

Polly stumbled over words of gratitude but he went on, firmly, 'I know you may be tempted to keep Edith with you over the next few days, but I would urge you to get her to return to her school work as soon as possible. She needs to be kept busy, her mind occupied. If she's at all reluctant remind her that she still has a lot to get ready for the concert.'

Polly smiled in agreement. It was sound advice. He went on speaking but was not looking at her now. 'It's so easy for lassitude and depression to take you over completely. That can be deadly and I know what I'm talking about, Mrs Summers. When my wife died suddenly I was persuaded to take time away from work. It was a bad mistake. I came near to suicide.'

She gave a gasp and reddened, feeling a mixture of confusion and concern. Despite her anxiety over Edith she'd not missed the photographs in the parlour of the plump, smiling woman.

His face was as flushed as her own. 'I shouldn't have said that. And please don't worry, Mrs Summers: your daughter isn't the kind of young woman to succumb to despair. But we'll keep her busy, shall we?'

Polly nodded and there was silence for a moment. Then she asked, 'You have a son, I think?' and was rewarded with a broad, proud smile.

'It was having Paul with me that stopped me doing anything foolish after Elizabeth's death. He's been a great comfort to me ever since.'

'Tell me about your son,' she urged, beginning to relax at last. 'I believe I've had more than enough of daughters for one day!'

******

'...so let us thank Miss Summers, the choir and the dancers once again for such a splendid concert.'

Adam Grenville sat down, the assembled audience erupted into loud applause and Edith's performers, all smiling heartily, took yet another bow before the curtains jerked slowly together, shutting off the stage from view.

Behind the curtains the children gathered about the piano chattering delightedly about the concert. 'Everyone was cheering at the end, Miss - wasn't that wonderful!' Edith smiled with a mixture of pleasure and relief and let them talk excitedly for a while before standing up and getting them all to take off and collect together their colourful scarves, made specially for the occasion in needlework class, and gather up the music sheets and the tambourines. Then she said briskly, 'Home time - you splendid singers and dancers.' And off they went - all happy and pleased with themselves.

But once they left the hall her smile faded and she felt the familiar sensation of dragging heaviness that never seemed to leave her for long.

She had returned to school after only two days' absence and concentrated all her attention on preparations for the concert. What had originally been intended as a short performance expanded into a longer show with a rousing conclusion featuring Christmas songs old and new. Children and teachers alike became infected by her apparent enthusiasm and she couldn't understand why no-one noticed the way that vigour drained away in her rare moments of inaction. But perhaps they did and attributed that to worry about her father.

Arnold Summers had been operated on with little delay and a growth removed from his stomach. The doctors spoke of good prospects for his recovery, but Edith thought they were not as completely confident as they seemed.

Adam Grenville had given her much support over the past weeks and she was grateful for that. But she would never forget the night he and her mother had come to find her and the way she had screamed and struggled against their restraining arms.

Edith held down a shuddering sigh. Sometimes she half wished she could experience again that explosion of grief, uncontrollable though it was. Surely it would be better than this awful, dull composure? Only once since that night had her control been shaken, when Anna Jessop came to say goodbye to her. She, Paul and Alexei were moving away from London.

Edith gathered her things together and hurried out of the hall. There would be tea at Clara's and the now familiar drive to the hospital, where she and Polly would sit by her father's bed, listening to him describe in minute detail what had occurred that day, from his breakfast and first wash to the usual visit of the surgeon and the inevitably late arrival of his tea tray. The account would be generously larded with veiled references to his bodily functions. Mr Summers found these fascinating and absorbing.

The day before his operation she had seen at last not only how ill he was but that he was desperately afraid and she realised that all his fussing over his condition at home and the trial of various patent remedies had simply been ways of putting off confronting the truth.

She had held his thin hand and told him she was sorry she'd not visited him very often during the Summer. Her red eyes and pale cheeks seemed to gratify him and he drew himself up on his pillows and tried to reassure her that he'd be well again soon. She listened and nodded but felt anger building within. If only Bram had trusted her, things could have been so different that summer. They could have been like any other engaged couple, visiting each other's families, providing support and comfort for the two sick fathers.

It was only later, after she'd left Mr Summers looking positively cheerful at being the apparent object of her concern that she faced an uncomfortable truth. To announce their engagement would probably have meant sacrificing the secret meetings with Bram and their love-making. She had known that and connived at the deceit. It was then that the anger against Bram faded, leaving behind this killing emptiness.

As she boarded the omnibus for Elm Square she decided she must talk to her sister.

******

'Go down to Sussex this weekend?' Polly was dismayed. 'But I can't really leave your father, dear. You know he's getting most anxious about coming out of hospital soon.'

Edith held back a murmur of annoyance. The thought of seeing Kate again had lifted her spirits enormously. On the journey home from school she had found herself taking an interest in the view from the omnibus as it rattled along, something that hadn't happened for weeks.

Kate had written as soon as she heard about Bram, a letter full of warmth and understanding, but she'd not suggested coming to London to be with her sister and Edith assumed she didn't want to leave home so soon after her reconciliation with Joe.

'I can go on my own, Mother,' she said. 'I do so want to see Kate: to talk to her.'

Polly frowned. 'I don't like the idea of your travelling alone, Edie. I think you should wait until we're all back in Brighton and your father is settled. Then I can come with you.'

Only Clara's presence stopped Edith from asking angrily if her mother expected her to run off and board the next ship for Russia. She and Polly had come to an unspoken agreement that Clara must know nothing of Edith's deception. She had simply been told of the friendship with the Jessops and Edith's great distress on learning of their loss. If Clara suspected more she gave no sign.

Now Clara helped herself to a muffin and looked from mother to daughter.

'I want to go down to Patcham and visit the Grahams this weekend,' she said. 'Why don't I take Edith to Kate's first and then collect her on Sunday afternoon? It won't be far out of my way and I'd like to see them all in any case. It's been so long - dear little William must be quite grown up!'

Polly looked nonplussed and Clara added solicitously, 'You'll have the house to yourself for a couple of days, dear. No need to do anything - apart from visiting Arnold of course. The rest of the time you can put your feet up with a novel and have a good rest. Now when was the last time you did that?'

Edith was deliberately quiet when she and Clara set out early on Saturday morning, driven in the Daimler. She felt a tremendous sense of release as soon as they left Elm Square but she didn't want that to be obvious, but Clara talked enough for the pair of them - mainly about the Suffragettes released from prison under the Cat and Mouse Act. That led on to the progress of the movement, of course, and the most recent speech by Mrs Pankhurst... Edith listened and nodded and made the right noises.

As they got into the countryside Clara too fell silent and Edith felt the older woman's eyes upon her, concerned and compassionate. At last she said, 'Don't be too hard on your mother, Edith. She's possessive of you at the moment because Arnold is still very ill and she fears for him.'

Edith gave her a startled look and Clara went on firmly, 'I know you find that hard to believe because you're quite aware that she doesn't love him - at least not in the way you understand love. But that doesn't mean to say she's not very concerned for him.'

Edith blushed, wondering at the way Clara had mentioned love and whether there was a hint of irony behind her words. Did she suspect...? But Clara's face had not changed

'I know how worried Mother is,' Edith said. 'But somehow we've grown away from each other this year - and I don't know how to put things back the way they were.'

'Perhaps you shouldn't try,' said Clara. 'Perhaps you should start again, from where things are now.'

She smiled encouragingly, then twisted round to look out of the car window before leaning forward and speaking to the chauffeur.

'A clear road, Sims. My turn to take the wheel.'

The car halted smartly and soon Clara was up in front with Sims next to her. Edith saw, with growing delight, that Clara was perfectly at ease driving the car and that Sims was sitting back with the air of one who has absolute confidence in a well-taught pupil.

'Clara! How long have you been driving?'

'Oh, several months now - though not in London. Some of the streets are dreadfully crowded, you know.' And Clara began to increase speed along the open stretch of road.

It wasn't long before Edith was clamouring to try the experience for herself. Clara stopped the car and after some low-voiced conference with Sims she turned round and eyed Edith sternly.

'Very well: but you must let Sims take the wheel if he feels you're in any difficulty,' she said. 'And you're not to go too fast. I'm not like Sir James Gale - mad about speed!'

They changed places and Edith listened patiently to the chauffeur's lecture on handling the car. She laid her hands on the wheel without trepidation and when she drove away from the roadside she felt an excitement she'd not experienced before. She drove slowly and hesitantly at first, but as her confidence grew she increased the speed, glancing occasionally at Sims as she did so. He was leaning slightly towards her, ready to reach for the wheel if she lost control, but after a while he relaxed his position. His face was impassive but she realised that he trusted her.

Relishing her new-found skill she found herself laughing out loud for the first time in two months.

'Oh, Clara - I must have a car of my own!'

Clara was laughing too. 'Yes, isn't it marvellous? Driving gives one a real sense of independence.'

The journey was completed without mishap and when they arrived in the village Edith couldn't resist showing off a little and was sounding the horn long before they reached the shop. Kate, Joe, Sam and a handful of customers came out to see what the noise was and then stood in amazement to watch Edith bring the car to a halt. She half expected them to applaud.

'You're lucky I didn't drive over you all - this is my first time.'

Kate's laugh broke the awed silence and at the same moment William came pushing through the crowd of legs and skirts, eager to see the show. Edith climbed down, pounced on him and lifted him into the driving seat and there was much laughter.

Clara stayed to have some tea, look round the shop and exchange a little gossip. Then she pressed a parcel into William's hands and drove away: Sims at the wheel.

'The people she's going to see - the Grahams - they're the ones who looked after me before Mother married Uncle Arnold,' Kate told Edith, as they stood in the shop doorway, waving after the car. But Edith wasn't particularly interested. Her brief lightening of spirits had given way to sadness once more. She put her arm through Kate's. 'Oh, I'm so glad to be here. Can we talk?'

Joe and Sam went back into the shop, Kate settled William in his room with the toy Clara had given him and then she and Edith shut themselves in the parlour.

'Joe didn't seem pleased to see me,' said Edith, quietly. 'Does he hate me for hurting Matthew?'

'No, of course he doesn't hate you. But he feels you treated Matty badly.'

'So he knows about Bram?'

'I expect Matty told him, but Joe's never spoken to me about what happened and I've not raised the subject.'

Edith sighed. 'I wonder what they talk about when they're together - Joe and Matty.'

'Perhaps I'm wrong, but I can't imagine men being as open and trusting with each other as women are. They often seem so... so closed up.'

'Yes!' Edith took up Kate's words eagerly. 'That's right. They can be so loving and tender with you, apparently keeping nothing back. Then suddenly they shut themselves off again and you feel totally excluded.'

Kate put an arm around Edith and hugged her. 'You must have been so hurt,' she said, gently.

'Yes. It was horrible.' The relief at saying that was so great that Edith felt her eyes fill with tears. 'I was seething with hatred for Bram at first. Now all that's gone and I can't seem to feel anything.' She clenched her hands. 'But I know it wouldn't have been so terrible if he had said goodbye to me. I'd have been hurt, of course, but - ' She broke off with a groan. 'It's like being told someone you love is dead but not being able to see their body.'

Kate shuddered. 'I should have come to London, dear. I just thought you'd turn to Mother for support.'

'How could I tell her the truth about me and Bram?' her sister demanded. Kate flushed and shook her head.

William came in looking anxious and asked Kate if his father was downstairs. He went back to his game once she had reassured him.

'He gets worried if Joe's out of sight for long,' said Kate with a frown. 'When Joe's at the smithy William often asks me if he's really coming home. I think it's going to take some time to learn to trust his parents again. When Joe left I thought William coped with it so well but now I can see it went deeper with him than I guessed.'

It was Edith's turn to provide comfort. 'He'll get over that, especially if he sees that you and Joe are really happy together.' She smiled. 'And you are, aren't you?'

Kate smiled at last. 'We have our disagreements, as we've always done, but I think we're more careful with each other now.'

Edith could sense this when they all sat down to eat at midday and she was able to turn her attention to Sam.

'I hear you and Flo have set a date for your wedding - that's splendid.'

He was cheerful and optimistic as always. He and Flo would be married in March and her mother and sister were already busy at work on the wedding dress. Kate was to bake and decorate the cake.

'We're going to rent one of those houses in Farm Lane,' Sam went on. 'We'll not have much room but there's a bit of garden.' Then he lowered his voice and asked Edith how she thought her father would respond to receiving an invitation.

'For I don't think Flo will consider it a proper wedding if you and Mrs Summers don't attend, Miss Edith,' he added cheerfully.

'Well, I'd be most upset if you didn't invite me, and I'm sure Mother would love to come.' Then she added tactfully, 'As for Father, I know he'd be pleased to have an invitation, though he may not be well enough to fulfil it.'

Sam's brows creased in a frown. 'I'm sorry to hear of his illness. He's always been such an active man - kept us all busy in the shop. I hope he'll be well again soon.'

When the meal was finished Joe sat back in his chair. 'Have you told Edie our good news, love?' he asked Kate.

Edith saw Kate redden as she shook her head.

'Well, no need to keep it secret any longer.' Joe picked William up and settled him on his knee. 'There'll be a little brother or sister for this young man next year.'

Sam beamed his congratulations and Edith added hers. But she felt disappointed that her sister hadn't told her that morning. Kate gave her an apologetic look.

'Do tell Mother, won't you, Edie? And explain that I would have let you all know sooner but we didn't like to say anything while Uncle was so ill.'

'Can't think why,' Joe blustered, full of himself. 'It might have cheered Polly up.'

'I also wanted to make sure everything was all right this time,' said Kate softly and Joe's smile faded. It was Sam who broke the silence.

'I'd best go and open up,' he said briskly. 'And there's several orders still to do.'

After Sam clattered downstairs Joe turned back to Kate.

'I'm sorry, but I thought we could start telling people.' He gave her a hang-dog look. 'Actually, I mentioned it to Matty when I saw him earlier.'

'Well, I wish you'd waited,' Kate replied, with a snap in her voice.

'What little brother?' asked William suddenly. They looked at him, smiling, realising he had been puzzling over his father's words all this time and waiting for the chance to seek clarification. Kate got up and took the boy from Joe.

'I'll tell you all about it,' she said, lovingly.

Joe had gone down to help Sam and Edith was finishing the washing up by the time Kate and William emerged from the parlour. She could see from Kate's relaxed manner that the little boy had happily accepted the idea of a newcomer in the family.

'He thinks it's going to be a special present for him,' said Kate.

She was in the shop weighing out currants when the bell rang and when she saw it was Matthew she spilled some of the fruit on the counter. The place was empty and she thought he must have waited until the last customer left.

'I saw Joe head up the High Street on his bicycle,' he said hurriedly.

'His Mother forgot to order soap so he's taking that up for her. Matty, Edith's here - well she's just taken William out for a walk but she'll be back soon.'

'I just want to see you, Kate. For a moment.'

She frowned but realised it was foolish to try to avoid this meeting so she called Sam in from the storeroom and asked him to keep a lookout in case Edith returned earlier than expected. Then she took Matthew up into the kitchen. Almost automatically she filled the kettle and put it on the stove.

'I had to come,' he burst out. 'Joe told me about the baby. I'm pleased for you both, Kate, honestly I am. But I couldn't help remembering what happened between us.'

She was thinking that this was the first time they had been alone together since that afternoon in the school house. He had come to supper once or twice after Joe returned but with the three of them together in the old way and Matthew seeming perfectly relaxed she had found it easy, deceptively easy, to be with him. But now they were alone it was different.

Alarmed she turned towards the door. 'Matty, please - you must go.'

But he had taken hold of her shoulders, pulling her round to face him.

'There was so much, Kate! And if you'd stayed, this child might be - '

'Don't!' She jerked herself free. 'Don't you dare say that, don't you dare think that, Matty!'

He opened his hands in a vulnerable manner that made her heart jerk and to her horror she saw his eyes fill with tears. If he broke down she didn't know what she would do. She reached to take his face between her hands.

'You must go, Matty. Edith could be back any minute. Please be sensible.'

She wasn't quite sure what she meant by that but there was no time to consider it because he was kissing her, his mouth soft and yearning. And to her horror she found herself responding. Was there no end to her own stupidity?

She pulled herself free from his arms, breathless, trembling but determined not to give way again. And he was calmer now, stepping away from her, turning towards the door. Then she heard Sam's voice calling her and hurried out on the landing in time to see Edith and William coming up the stairs. Below them Sam hovered, his face a comic mask of perplexity.

William launched himself at his mother, chattering about seeing some fish in the village pond. Kate tried to quiet him but he was in full flow. She gave Edith a despairing look.

'Matty's here,' she hissed. 'He didn't know you were visiting us.'

Edith paused a moment, then came on up the stairs pulling off her gloves. Kate said, 'If you'll go into the parlour, Edie - '

'What? Matty can sneak downstairs?' Edith gave a fleeting smile, reached the landing and called out cheerfully, 'I'm here, Matty. Do come out and say hello.'

Kate looked at her with admiration. Edith appeared to be perfectly self-controlled but Kate could see the tension in the twitching of a nerve at the side of her mouth and the way she was winding her gloves between her fingers.

Matthew stepped out of the kitchen. His manner matched Edith's and he, too, was smiling.

'Hello Edie.'

She put out her hand to him and gave an odd kind of sigh. 'Matty, I'm glad you're here.'

William had stopped talking and was busy wrapping himself around Matthew with joyful cries. Kate unwound him.

'Well, let's not stand here,' she said briskly. 'Go and sit in the parlour, you two, and I'll make us all some tea.'

She sat William at the kitchen table with a cake to keep him quiet and propped the door open so that when Joe returned she could keep him out of the parlour. It might be that Edith and Matthew could take up their friendship again and that was worth encouraging. Of course her motives for wanting them friends again were not altruistic. She shivered a little, remembering how easily she had fallen into temptation again today. But she knew she would be better able to resist if Edith was part of Matthew's life once more.

At last Joe appeared and she pulled him into the kitchen with a whispered explanation. He looked surprised, then put out. She slid her arms round his neck.

'You and I are happy; wouldn't it be nice for them to have a little happiness too?'

He grunted. 'Those two - is that possible...?'

She kissed his cheek. Over his shoulder she saw William watching them with a contented smile.

In the parlour Matthew was explaining that he wouldn't have come if he'd known she was staying with Kate and Joe; but Joe had said nothing that morning.

'But I suppose he was too full of his news about the baby.'

Edith nodded. After her initial, confident reaction to Matthew's presence she now felt at a loss, unable to look directly at him. She sat beside the fire and he perched on the piano stool. With the width of the room between them they made careful conversation, mainly about Mr Summers.

'Mother told me you'd written to her,' said Edith. 'That was kind of you.'

He smiled. 'Joe tells me your father is to go home soon. He must be improving quickly.'

'I don't know,' she admitted. 'The doctors say very little, but Mother and I get the impression they've done all they can. Now we have to hope the growth doesn't recur.'

From the corner of her eye she could see his startled look.

'I didn't realise,' he muttered. 'I thought the worst was over.'

He rose and came across to her - an impetuous gesture that ended in his standing aimlessly by her chair.

'You and your mother must be very worried.'

She smiled vaguely in his direction and murmured something about hoping for the best. Then she gestured towards the other fireside chair and Matthew sank down into it gratefully.

He fiddled with the cord trimming on the arm for a moment then asked abruptly, 'How are things at Shrub Grove?'

At once she felt on safer ground and she talked about the most recent happenings - the concert, the progress of pupils he knew, snippets of gossip about some of the teachers. After that it seemed natural for her to enquire about Matthew's work. Now it was his turn to talk while she listened. It was obvious that he had lost none of his enthusiasm for teaching.

'At first I thought the village youngsters rather slow after the ones at Shrub Grove,' he confessed, 'but I soon discovered that many of them are very bright indeed. They just have a different attitude to life from the city youngsters. I think they're less inclined to rebel or question - but they've got the same kind of determination. And the same kinds of problems to deal with, of course.'

He leaned forward, his eyes alive with pleasure. 'You must come and see the school one day, Edith.'

She flushed and saw that he too was embarrassed. To cover her own confusion she murmured, with a shaky laugh, 'So you will be staying here? I thought you might want to go abroad.'

'Oh...' he shrugged, 'I'm here to stay.'

Edith's sense of relief was not entirely unexpected. She had known for a long time that Matthew's presence in her life was important to her. She wanted to ask if they could take up their friendship once again but was afraid to speak out so boldly. She had hurt him and, though she knew he had a forgiving nature, she could appreciate that he might want to keep her at a distance in future.

'I'd love to come and see what you're doing here, Matty. Next time I visit Kate, perhaps? I expect I'll be here much more often when Mother and Father go back to Brighton.'

She thought he drew back a little and wasn't surprised. He must be remembering the Summer, when she had virtually ignored her parents' existence in order to be with Bram. She stared at him miserably and suddenly he reached out and took her hand, clasping it briefly but strongly and releasing it almost at once.

'Then we can meet sometimes,' he said gently. 'I'd like that.'

He had changed, she decided - he wasn't judging her any more. But before she could ponder the reason for this they heard the clatter of cups on a tea tray outside the door. Then Kate and Joe came in, followed by William, who was triumphantly, if somewhat unsteadily, carrying a plate of jam tarts.

******

Edith stepped off the train, knowing from Polly's bleak smile in greeting that things were no better. On her regular visits to Brighton she had seen for herself her father's gradual decline. At first it seemed he had all but

211

recovered and needed only to gather his strength again before resuming a normal life. He even talked hopefully of a holiday abroad to avoid the English winter. But as Christmas drew near, Mr Summer began to complain of stomach pains and holiday plans were forgotten.

'He knows there's no hope this time,' said Polly sadly, as they walked to the car. 'To be honest I think he's too weary to care.'

Edith saw that her mother was blinking in the chilly light and tentatively moving her shoulders as though they were stiff. This was obviously her first time out of doors for some days.

'Is the nurse still here?' she asked and Polly nodded.

'Pamela is a great help, but your father isn't happy being looked after by a stranger, as he puts it. So I do most things for him.'

'Well, now that I'm home you can send her away if you like,' Edith offered. Polly smiled and looked relieved.

'Oh, if you could help that would be marvellous, Edie. I know it will do your father so much good to have you here.'

As they got into the car Polly turned and gave her daughter something approaching a roguish smile.

'Perhaps you'd like to drive instead of Mitcham? Clara tells me you're most accomplished behind a wheel now.'

It was a friendly gesture and Edith felt warmed by it, though she was tactful enough to refuse the offer. She and her mother were growing easier in each other's company but nothing like their old closeness had yet been achieved.

As the chauffeur drove them away from the station Polly's manner continued to grow brighter and she wanted to know what Edith had been doing in London.

'Well, before school finished I was rehearsing carols with the choir, of course. Then Clara and I went to Holloway yesterday with the welcoming party for the Suffragettes who were arrested at the November demonstration...'

'They've been released? Poor souls, they must have had a terrible time.'

'Oh, didn't you hear, Mother? They all received remarkable treatment: allowed to wear their own clothes and exercise together. One of them said it was like a holiday in a rather shabby hotel - though I think she was exaggerating. Anyway they were treated like political prisoners and not common criminals. That's quite a victory.'

Polly seemed eager for any news so Edith chattered on until they reached the house and was glad to see her mother looking happier. In the days that followed they had little time to talk together and when they did Mr

Summers was their sole topic. The nurse was duly dismissed and the two women shared the care of the dying man between them.

Edith's arrival had cheered her father and he seemed to draw new strength from her presence. She sat with him for hours, talking mainly about the school and the choir and she was touched to see the pride in his eyes.

'I'm glad you're doing that, Edith,' he told her.

Gradually his condition worsened and now the doctor prescribed stronger doses to dull the pain, so that Mr Summers slept more and more and when he was awake had difficulty in following what Edith said. He was happy, though, when she was at his bedside.

Despite Polly's weariness she still had time to think about Christmas and Edith was dispatched into Brighton one afternoon to buy presents for William, Kate and Joe. She avoided her father's shops, not wanting to face the questioning, and instead explored the stores along Western Road. She was still looking in windows long after most of her purchases had been made and she realised that she couldn't make up her mind about buying something for her father.

She shivered a little, imagining the scene on Christmas Day. She and Polly would eat their dinners separately, so that her father should not be left alone. There would probably be the pretence of setting aside a portion for him, even though he was taking little but liquids now; and they would open their presents together in his room, unwrapping his for him too and showing him what he had got, even though he wouldn't really understand what was happening.

So, it wouldn't be worth buying anything, she knew that. All the same she went into the smartest department store and chose a discreet but well-styled dressing gown.

There were letters waiting when she got home. Kate had written asking if she could come and help. Adam Grenville had posted all the cards Edith's pupils had been unable to give her in person and had included a brief note of sympathy and good wishes, which seemed to please Polly. And there was a letter from Matthew, which Edith pounced on with delight. He was full of concern for her and her parents and his words heartened her so much that when Polly asked if they should take up Kate's offer she shook her head.

'We can manage, Mother. In any case it would be difficult for Kate to leave William: he'd worry about her.'

Polly agreed. She was anxious, too, that Kate might tire herself and put the new baby at risk.

'You're right, dear. We're coping very efficiently between us,' she said and gave a smile which warmed Edith.

They both sat up late on Christmas Eve, Polly at her husband's

213

bedside, Edith reading by the drawing room fire. Carol singers had been round earlier and when Arnold seemed to rouse himself at the muffled music outside the front door and looked about him with something approaching interest the two women were as pleased as if a child had done something clever. They brought the singers into the hall and Cook and Doris served mulled wine and cakes. It had been, thought Edith, a short but pleasant respite from the almost overpowering sadness that enveloped the household now. She set her book aside, rubbing her eyes sleepily, and turned once more to Matthew's letter.

She had not seen him often since that first strained meeting in the Autumn, but they had fallen into the habit of writing to each other nearly every week. The letters were friendly and they wrote generally about work or political matters and she found she looked forward to hearing from him.

She came to herself with a start. The letter was on the floor and the fire nearly out and she realised she'd been asleep for some time. She heard her mother's voice out in the hall and something in the tone made her jump up and hurry to the door.

Polly took her hand. 'I've just sent Mitcham for the doctor,' she whispered. 'I was coming to fetch you.'

'Father's worse?' She was unable to keep her voice steady.

'Much worse, I'm afraid. You must say goodbye to him, dear.'

Edith began to cry, taken unawares by the strength of her own emotion. Her mother's arms were about her, firm and comforting, and she wished she could stay like that and avoid what was to come.

Gently Polly guided Edith into her father's room and the two of them took up station, seated on either side of the bed. Edith had to force herself to look into his face and was surprised to find no cause for terror. He seemed no different. The shrunken cheeks were perhaps a little greyer and the mouth was slack, but his eyes were open and he seemed aware of his surroundings.

Polly reached to clasp one hand and Edith did the same. Her father looked straight at her and blinked.

'Yes, I'm very glad you help out at the school,' he whispered, as though they were still conducting that same conversation. 'But I hope you'll marry, Edith.'

He shifted his head to look at Polly and appeared to want to say more but the effort of speaking to Edith had exhausted him.

Polly squeezed his hand. 'Of course she'll marry, Arnold. I'll make sure she has a fine wedding.'

His head moved slightly - he might have been attempting to nod - and then he closed his eyes and dozed. Edith looked down at the almost fleshless hand lying in hers and felt a strong surge of pity.

Her mother rose abruptly and bent over her husband's body.

'He's passed away,' she said softly and kissed the lifeless hand she still held, then set it down on the coverlet. Edith stared at her father. He had died without her knowing it. The man who delighted in ostentation, who had fussed and fretted and bustled everyone about had quit life in a most uncharacteristic fashion. Edith leaned forward and kissed his cheek, but cautiously, not really sure that it was true.

Then suddenly there was rush and bustle in plenty as the doctor hurried into the room. Edith went out into the hall where the servants hovered and was surprised to see Cook's woeful face and Doris snuffling into a handkerchief. In a daze she found herself back in the drawing room where Doris, her tears dried, rekindled the fire and brought Edith a glass of brandy.

'You stay here, Miss, until the doctor's finished,' she murmured. 'Cook will help Madam with the laying out.'

Edith blinked at her, muddled, letting Doris arrange cushions in the chair behind her and fetch a rug for her lap as though she was an invalid.

'I'll bring in some tea now, Miss.'

When she had gone Edith put the brandy aside. She looked at the clock on the mantelpiece and saw, with a shock, that less than an hour had passed since she had woken so suddenly. It was after midnight. Christmas Day. She thought, dully, that her father would not, after all, have his presents opened for him. She was wondering what she would do with the dressing gown, wrapped and lying in her room upstairs, when the tears overcame her.

She didn't cry for long and was calm again when Polly came into the room. The doctor had gone and Cook had taken over what final tasks needed to be performed for Arnold Summers. Mother and daughter sipped their tea and stared into the fire.

At last Edith said: 'I keep thinking about when I was a little girl. Was Father happier then? I'm sure I can remember him laughing sometimes - laughing properly, I mean.'

Polly looked at her gratefully. 'Yes, I believe he was happier when he was still making his way, though he'd never have admitted it.' She added tentatively, 'Perhaps you should try to remember him like that...'

But Edith shook her head. 'He behaved so very badly to Kate. I'm not a hypocrite, Mother.'

Polly sighed. 'What he did to Kate - and to me - well I think that was his way of trying to protect you.'

Edith leaned forward, gazing earnestly into her mother's face.

'Please tell me - I just don't understand. Why did you stay with him?'

Polly looked startled and Edith added hurriedly. 'I can understand

215

why you did before the truth about Kate came out. But afterwards - surely there was no reason for it?'

'So you'd have had me leave and cause a scandal to punish him,' Polly murmured. 'Well, I won't deny that I toyed with the idea - but only for a little while. After all, he was your father, Edie, and although I've never loved him in any romantic way we've been companions for a long time.' She hesitated for a moment and then went on, 'I've never experienced love - the love between a man and a woman I mean - and what you don't know you don't miss.'

The two women exchanged cautious glances.

'Mother, I can't believe you've not had - well - admirers,' murmured Edith and Polly looked puzzled.

'Admirers? Well, I suppose so... But I'm a married woman, Edith.'

She looked away, suddenly embarrassed. 'I expect you think that very old-fashioned, but try to understand. After all, I've done my best to understand your - your relationship with Bram Jessop.'

Edith started and went hot and cold all in a moment, but she looked directly at her mother and saw no condemnation in her face. They clasped hands and sat together in silence for some time.

When Polly roused herself the fire was almost out again.

'We mustn't sit too long,' she said. 'There will be a lot to do tomorrow - I mean today - even though it is Christmas. We'll have letters to write and arrangements to make. We'll have the funeral as soon as possible.'

Edith straightened up to ease her back. 'What will happen afterwards? I mean, will we keep this house?'

'I've never been completely comfortable here and nor have you, I think. But we don't have to make decisions like that all at once.'

Suddenly brisk, Polly replaced their cups on the tea tray.

'I want you to go and stay with Kate for a while, after the funeral,' she said. 'You've been cooped up here for too long.'

Edith was startled. 'I don't want to leave you alone, Mother.'

'Don't worry - I'll visit Clara,' Polly smiled.

Edith was tempted to protest. They were re-establishing their friendship now and she felt reluctant at the idea of separation. Then she gave herself a mental shake. Of course her mother must go to Clara: a woman who was herself a widow would be able to give help and support to another in that position. She returned her mother's smile, confident that nothing and nobody would come between them again.

Her thoughts swung back to her father and she gave a shiver.

'What is it, dear?' Polly had seen the sudden tears.

'I was feeling sorry for him, Mother - going into the dark, all alone.'

'I know what you mean, but he didn't believe it would be at all like that. He thought there would be trumpets to welcome him and a good turnout of angels and plenty of light and splendour.'

'Oh, Mother!' Edith found herself laughing softly. 'Yes, that's just what he would have expected.'

'Well, why not?' Polly's tone was practical. 'I definitely prefer your father's version of the hereafter, don't you?'

******

The organist struck two wrong notes in succession and Edith smiled into her gloved hands and gave up trying to pray. She sat back on the pew and glanced around the church, noticing how sparse the congregation was this chilly Sunday morning.

She wondered again why she'd come and had to admit to herself that it was probably connected with her father's death and the recent funeral. Kate and Joe hadn't wanted to attend church this morning and were both surprised when Edith said she would go alone.

Out of the corner of her eye she saw a group of servants from the Hall come up the aisle and settle themselves fussily in their usual seats. That doubtless meant that Sir James and Lady Janette would be here soon. They'd been out of the country for Mr Summers' funeral and had only just returned from France, so Janette would probably pounce on her after church, full of condolences.

Edith brushed a speck of dust off her skirt, feeling dismal. Janette would see what a fright she looked in this terrible black crape. Of course she'd made sure the material was made up in the most flattering style she could find but there was no getting away from the fact that black just made her look pale and drab. Mourning gave her mother an interesting air; slimmed down Kate's fast-expanding figure. To be told that at least one looked "neat and tidy" in black was no consolation.

To add insult to injury Janette appeared at that moment, on her husband's arm, resplendent in a dark green tailored coat and feathered hat, her shoulders weighed down with furs. Edith slumped sulkily and pretended to be busy with her hymn book. When she looked up again James and Janette had taken their seats and she was just in time to catch sight of Matthew slipping into the pew beside them. He glanced round, saw her and smiled and she was so pleased to see him she beamed. Now Janette noticed her and gestured for Edith to join them but the organist increased volume at that moment and the choir came pacing into the body of the church so Edith, grateful for the distraction, stayed where she was.

It was easy to single out Arthur, tallest and broadest of the choristers. He sounded in fine voice this morning, Edith thought, and reflected that he

217

certainly had good reason to sing out so gladly.

The large number of mourners at her father's funeral had not been the only surprise after his death. His will revealed that as well as providing for his wife and daughter and leaving his chiming watch to William he had set aside a substantial sum of money for Kate.

'I knew he was altering his will to include something for you,' Polly had told her daughter. 'He was very anxious that you should go ahead with your plans for the shop.'

Edith thought privately that her father might also have been anxious to make up for the way he had treated Kate in the past, but she did not say so. Once over their initial shock Kate and Joe had started to discuss plans for using the money. It was decided that some of it should go into Arthur's business and the brothers become partners.

'We get all the work from the Hall now,' Joe had explained to Edith. 'Not just the carriages but Sir James's cars too, so we need an extra building. Quite a few county families with money to spare are buying motors now and they'll want somewhere to get their repairs done.'

Edith had agreed, seeing the eager enthusiasm on his face, but later she'd asked Kate anxiously if there was any risk involved.

'I've gone into it all thoroughly, you know,' said her practical sister. 'The smithy is a growing business. And we'll still have enough money for what I want to do.'

This, it transpired, included buying the house next door to the shop and turning the ground floor into a department for ironmongery and using the upstairs rooms for drapery and haberdashery. Meanwhile, Kate and Joe would move to a house on the outskirts of the village - at the end of a terrace with a long garden at the back.

'And Sam and Flo will take over running the store when they're married,' Kate concluded, with satisfaction. 'It'll be high time by then for me to give up, won't it Joe?'

Edith saw the loving look between husband and wife, but when the sisters were alone she grinned at Kate. 'Give up? You'll never do that, will you? Not after the stand you made during the Summer.'

'Of course I won't,' came Kate's hearty response. 'The finances of the shop and the smithy are my responsibility - much to Art's relief I must say - so I'll always be involved in the running of things.'

The service came to an end at last and Edith submitted, with good grace, to being fussed over by Lady Janette. This was quickly followed by an invitation back to the Hall. Edith struggled for an excuse and found Matthew at her side.

'Edith promised a long time ago to come and see the school,' he said.

'You'll have to wait your turn, Janette.'

Sir James gave a grunt. 'Hear you're driving now, Miss Summers.'

'Goodness, Edith - how very dashing,' smiled Janette. 'James is going to take up racing - on a proper track, thank goodness. At the moment I'm on tenterhooks whenever he's out in that wretched car. I'm convinced he'll run into a cow or a sheep or something.'

'Or maybe a wandering peasant,' Matthew grinned. 'They can take the shine off your headlamps.'

Janette frowned at him but Sir James gave an amused snort. Then he nodded at Edith.

'You should buy your own car - daresay you can afford it now. I'd be pleased to advise you if - '

'James!' With a hasty apology for this tactless reference to the recent bereavement Janette hurried her husband away, leaving Edith and Matthew smiling at each other.

'Motors seem to govern his life at the moment,' Matthew sighed as they made their way through the churchyard gate.

She shrugged. 'I suppose there are worse activities. Now, be honest Matty, is it really convenient for me to visit the school or were you just being kind and saving me from hours of gossip at the Hall?'

'Good Lord, Edie, of course it's convenient. We've got a particularly fine display of paintings up on the walls. I've been longing to show them off to someone who'll really appreciate the hard work the children put into them.'

As they walked Edith passed on Kate and Joe's latest news. Matthew shrugged. 'Moving house, expanding their business and going into another venture at the smithy - well, they're certainly making a fresh start.'

She thought his comment rather sharp and wondered if he shared her concerns about Kate's plans.

'I hope they're not over-reaching themselves,' she murmured but his reply was cut short by the cheerful yapping of a dog, scarcely more than a puppy, which came bounding from behind a bush at the side of the path and circled round them. There was a shout and Edith looked up to see Michael Thomas hurrying towards them.

He bawled something at the dog, which promptly rolled over on its back. Edith laughed and bent to tickle the exposed stomach.

'My apologies,' said Michael, taking out a handkerchief and wiping his forehead. 'I keep forgetting he only understands instructions in Welsh. He was trying to round you up. Pretty clever, don't you think?'

'Well, I'm not flattered to be mistaken for a sheep,' said Edith, with a smile. 'But he's a friendly chap. I didn't know you had a dog, Dr Thomas.'

The dark eyes looked from her to Matthew uncertainly.

'He was a Christmas present from my children.'

'Oh.' Edith managed to keep her voice neutral but she could see Matthew's eyebrows shoot up in surprise.

'I've been in Wales recently,' Michael went on. 'I decided it was time I had a holiday.'

'Visiting your family?' put in Matthew with cool politeness and the doctor nodded.

'Silly to have made a secret of it,' he muttered. 'The truth is that my wife and I have been living apart for some time. She didn't want me to see the children again but this Christmas I decided I must.' His voice dropped even further. 'I knew they'd begin to forget me.'

'And did you see them?' Edith asked quietly.

'Yes. In the end my wife didn't refuse or make a fuss as I'd feared. I was able to stay with my parents and the children came to visit me for a while each day.' He gave a triumphant smile. 'We've arranged that they shall come to see me here during their school holidays.'

Edith thought that courageous: gossip in the village would be intense. She glanced at Matthew but his face was impassive. Feeling uncomfortable she asked the doctor how many children he had and his gratitude for her interest was obvious in his lengthy description of his offspring.

Then he broke off suddenly. 'Oh, forgive me, Miss Summers. I've not long returned and heard only recently about your loss. Please accept my - '

'It's getting cold,' said Matthew abruptly. 'You shouldn't be standing about, Edith - you'll take a chill.'

Michael hastened to agree with him and so hurried farewells were said. The dog ran after Edith and Matthew for a few yards but then responded reluctantly to his master's bellowed summons.

'Well, I'm amazed,' Edith found herself whispering, even though the doctor was well out of earshot. 'To think he was married all the time - and with children too! Do you think Joe and Kate know?'

Matthew shrugged, then burst out suddenly, 'What a scoundrel the man is!'

She saw that he was very angry but couldn't let that pass.

'We don't know the whole story, Matty.'

His mood changed abruptly. 'No, you're right; we shouldn't judge anyone out of hand,' he said, in a calmer voice.

Relieved, Edith added with a smile, 'Will he ever train that dog? Welsh indeed!'

Matthew looked down at her and there was a new softness in his eyes that warmed her. Without thinking she slipped her arm through his, the way she had so often done before last Summer. He caught her hand and held it in place and they walked on soberly together.

They spent a long time in the schoolroom, looking at the workbooks and the pictures and models on display. Edith was impressed with what his class had done and he acknowledged her praise with an immodest smirk. To keep the mood between them light and positive she began to talk about the house in Brighton and Polly's plans to move.

'But she'll stay in Brighton, won't she?' he asked sharply. 'I mean she has friends there and Kate and Joe aren't far away - and you'll be coming back from London still?'

Was there anxiety in his voice? Was he afraid she wouldn't be coming to Sussex so often? Edith wished she knew what his feelings were and wished, too, that she could fully understand her own.

'Edie, you're shivering. Have you really taken a chill?'

He took her into the school house and livened up the parlour fire then poured her something from a bottle on the sideboard.

'This is Kate's ginger wine,' he said. 'Guaranteed to warm you.' He handed her the glass. 'You're looking very pale. I hope I've not tired you out.'

'Don't be silly, Matty,' she responded with a touch of asperity. 'I look awful because I'm in black. It never has suited me.'

He gave a wicked grin. 'No, it's not your colour at all. How long do you have to wear it? A year? More?'

She groaned. 'This stuff for six months and then Mother says I can go into half-mourning. Not that grey's much better but - ' she broke off, seeing his eyes. 'Oh, you're a beast, Matty. I'm doing my best to put up with it and not complain, so don't tease!'

The wine was making her increasingly bold and without thinking she gave him one of her old, flirtatious smiles.

'Do you remember that day on the train when we all first met? You said you hoped we could all stay friends. I never thought we would, but you were right.'

His eyes seemed to cloud over and she felt him withdrawing from her. In a panic she put her glass down, leaned forward and clutched his hand.

'I shouldn't have said that - it was foolish! But Matty, please don't shut yourself off from me again, please! We were getting on so well...'

She floundered in the banality of her own words and wasn't surprised when he pulled his hand free and stood up.

'What on earth do you want of me, Edie?' He sounded tired and wretched.

'Want?' She gazed up at him, momentarily confused. Then the answer came clear in her mind. She got to her feet.

'I want you to make love to me, Matty.' And she stepped forward and kissed his mouth.

He gave a gasp of utter astonishment, then caught her by the shoulders and for a moment she thought he would shake her. But he pulled her into his arms and kissed her with a hunger as great as her own.

It was cold and damp in the bedroom and they huddled together, naked beneath the covers, as though seeking shelter rather than satisfaction. They clung to each other, kissing feverishly, and the words she had spoken so often to Bram - in Russian, learnt from him - rose automatically to her lips, but she translated them into English just in time.

'Love me; love me.'

'Oh yes. Always.'

Strange that the response was the same. No, not strange really. She opened her eyes and looked fearfully into his, half expecting to see that familiar fleeting look of loss and desperation. To her relief she saw instead that his desire was mingled with the tenderness that had already touched her so strongly. In the moments before her mind and body dissolved she knew she must not lose him again.

******

Jane Weaver settled herself in the high-backed chair and sipped her glass of port with a satisfied air. Everything had turned out well, after all. She had been anxious about the marriage ceremony, even though Flo and Sam had explained it all so carefully beforehand. Would Flo feel properly married, being as it wasn't in a church and there was no proper vicar? But she needn't have worried. It had been a perfectly suitable service - nothing outlandish - and all the people at the Meeting House were very pleasant. She'd half expected them to be a glum lot, despite Sam's cheerful reassurances.

She had taken to his parents as soon as they were introduced but Sam's young sister presented cause for concern as she was a pretty little thing and Jane was worried she might outshine Flo. Again her fears proved groundless. Kate and Nell had been busy behind the scenes, helping put the finishing touches to Flo's dress and hair and Edith had loaned her a fine necklace which looked just right about Flo's neck. Yet it was her own happiness and contentment that made Flo beautiful on her special day.

Jane put her empty glass aside. Now that the meal was over Joe and Kate had taken the guests upstairs to their big drawing room at the front of the house, leaving two of the Parry girls, hired for the day, to clear the dining room table. It was a stroke of good luck that Kate and Joe had moved into their new home in time for the wedding. Jane had been in agonies over how she would fit all the guests into her own small parlour, but Kate solved the problem by insisting that there was more than enough room at Western House.

That was certainly true Jane thought, with a slight compression of her lips. The size of her son's new home both impressed and concerned her. As well as this dining room there was a small back parlour and a large kitchen and scullery on the ground floor and the drawing room above. Then there were three bedrooms and even a lavatory upstairs as well as the one outside. Of course that was all very fine, but along with the expansion of the village shop and the smithy Jane couldn't help worrying that Kate hadn't bitten off more than she could chew. For all these changes were down to Kate, Jane knew, and while anxious that all would go well she couldn't help but admire the young woman's enthusiasm and energy. She didn't quite approve of the way Kate kept such a close eye on matters - surely it wasn't decent for a pregnant woman to be chivvying up builders and arguing with suppliers who had brought the wrong items - but she could see that a sharp mind was needed to hold everything together. Jane sighed. She was almost afraid to be pleased at Joe and Kate's good fortune in case something should happen to spoil it.

'Are you going upstairs, Mum?' It was Nell, very smart in her best oatmeal linen. 'We're going to have some music.'

Jane eyed her eldest daughter sadly. Good fortune still had not touched Nell and her husband in the form of a child.

'But if you're tired,' said Nell, 'stay down here for a bit. I'll sit with you.'

'No, I just wanted to get my breath back. It's been a busy day, you know.'

Nell smiled. In fact there had been very little for her mother to do but she'd been up since daybreak, bustling about.

'Kate did us proud with the food, didn't she?' Nell murmured, watching as the stiff white linen tablecloths were bundled together for shaking outside the back door. 'What a beautiful cake, too.'

Jane found something new to worry about. 'I hope someone's put the top layer away safely, Nell. Flo will want that for her first christening.'

Nell reassured her mother but quickly changed the subject.

'Mrs Summers looks well, don't you think? Kate says she's very pleased with her new house in Hove. Smaller than they had before but that will suit her better when Miss Edith gets married.'

Jane sniffed. 'It's still very soon for that young lady to be marrying after her father's death.' Then she added sharply, 'Not that I've noticed an engagement ring on her finger.'

Nell frowned. 'Well there must be an understanding between her and Matthew. Everyone thinks so and they're always together - like Art and Irene Johnson.' She saw that her mother was about to launch into a discussion of her eldest son's long courtship and added hastily, 'I'd better go up. Tom will be wondering where I've got to.'

Jane's mood softened and she eyed her daughter fondly. That was true enough - Tom would be on tenterhooks until his wife was back at his side and there was no doubting his devotion to Nell. No silly business about "an understanding" when they were walking out together - Tom had proposed, straight off.

'I'll be up in a moment,' she said. 'We must make sure Art doesn't start on any of those music hall songs. I don't want him upsetting Sam's parents.'

When Jane got to the drawing room Edith was at the piano accompanying herself and Matthew in a lively duet. Waiting quietly by the door for the song to finish Jane witnessed an exchange of looks between the couple and felt her face redden. She hastily revised her earlier opinion. The sooner these two were safely married, the better!

As the guests applauded Kate called to her to take a chair near the fire and she and Joe settled his mother comfortably. Arthur stood up to sing now and while Edith was sorting out his music Polly drew up a chair beside Jane's.

'What a lovely day it's been,' she murmured. 'You must be so pleased everything's gone well for Flo and Sam.'

Jane gazed fondly at the newly-weds then settled herself for a gossip with Polly.

'I expect you've heard about my new house,' said Polly, smiling. 'I can't tell you how much I'm enjoying doing it out to suit myself.'

Jane nodded. 'And Edith's helping with that, I'm sure.'

'She said she would...' Polly frowned a little. 'But whenever she's not at the school in London she seems to be here with Matthew.'

There was an awkward pause which Jane ended by saying, stoutly, 'Well, I suppose that will be the next wedding.'

Polly leaned closer, lowering her voice. 'When I try to talk about it Edith changes the subject. I do hope they won't decide to get married quietly - I promised her father we'd do things properly, but Edith has such a mind of her own.'

Jane pursed her lips. Really, daughters these days had no idea. Not that sons were a great deal better... and she cast a stern glance in Arthur's direction. He beamed cheerfully back at her, reminding her sharply of his father in a mellow mood, then burst into song.

Jane turned back to Polly. 'I expect you miss Mr Summers,' she said softly.

Polly's startled look was quickly replaced by one of gratitude.

'I didn't think I would - not quite so much,' she admitted. 'You can't wipe out all the years together, even if some of those weren't particularly happy.'

'The first year alone is the worst,' said Jane, thoughtfully. 'All the anniversaries come round - birthdays and the like - and you have to see them through on your own. After you've done that it gets easier...'

Polly nodded and Jane looked around at the guests. Dr Thomas was sitting by the window, a little apart from the others. Best place for him, she decided sourly. 'You heard about the doctor, I suppose?' she whispered to Polly. 'Turns out he's got a family, hidden away back in Wales! Joe's still keeping up the acquaintance but I notice Kate doesn't invite the man here so often now. And she's having Dr Warner for the confinement, of course.'

'Well, he delivered William,' Polly smiled. 'I wonder if it will be another boy...'

The song ended and Joe appeared at Polly's side. 'We were wondering if you'd mind us having some dancing, Mother-in-law?' he smiled. She was confused for a moment, then saw Sam's parents looking anxiously at her mourning clothes. Unexpected support came from Jane, however, and it was decided that dancing was quite in order on such an occasion.

Flo and Sam rose solemnly and began to circle round the room, as Edith played the piano. They were followed by Nell and Tom and a stumbling Arthur with the cool-looking Irene Johnson. With some disquiet Jane saw Dr Thomas murmur politely to Sam's parents and receive permission to lead out their daughter.

Joe stood behind Kate's chair, murmuring something about how well the day was going. She felt his hand on her shoulder and leaned back a little so that her head rested against his arm. Softly, he stroked her cheek.

Since their reconciliation they had become more demonstrative towards each other. She thought happily that it was as though they were newly-weds - no, better than that. Back then he was a gamekeeper still, working long hours and getting home tired out. Now he came back happy, in his element at last. And there was no awkwardness about her involvement in the shop. He accepted that as her work - praising her business skills.

She smiled up at him then glanced to where William sat in a corner of the room playing quietly with the model theatre Flo and Sam had given him. He had whispered to her, during the wedding breakfast, that he was making up a play to entertain the new baby when it arrived. They were all happy. She prayed it would stay like that.

Edith came to the end of one waltz and struck up another without pause, smiling up at Matthew who was turning the music for her. They, too, had survived an unhappy time and were re-making their lives on stronger

225

foundations, Kate thought. Yet she wished they would be more circumspect.

Edith had gone back to her work at Shrub Grove but came hurrying down to Sussex every weekend. At first Matthew had occasionally visited Edith and Polly in Brighton but now Edith drove out from town to be with him. Kate lived in constant fear that Polly would discover that Edith never occupied her bed at Western House on these visits.

'They're happy together,' she pointed out to Joe when he tutted over the secrecy involved. 'It's as though Bram Jessop never existed.'

Joe turned that argument on its head. 'But he did exist, love. She put Matty out of her mind smartly enough when that Russian arrived on the scene and now he's been forgotten and Matty's top dog. What's going to happen if someone else catches her eye?'

She'd held her peace with difficulty, hoping Joe would become resigned to the relationship when Edith and Matthew got married. They were taking their time over making an announcement, though, and she wondered why it was so long in coming.

Kate heard Joe humming along with the music, then he bent over her. 'Why don't we dance?' he urged.

'In my condition? And in mourning, too?' But she was already standing up.

'I want to get close to Art,' he murmured. 'Find out what he's saying to Irene.'

'Nothing very exciting, I imagine - unless they're discussing ferrets.'

Joe chuckled and swung her into his arms.

'Oh, Kate and Joe are dancing,' said Flo, happily. 'Isn't that nice?'

Sam nodded, looking away from her only long enough to see the two glide by. Already he had told Flo several times how beautiful she looked and his pride in her made her feel that she would burst with pleasure. It had been a lovely, lovely wedding day: she would remember it always.

Her eye lit upon Sam's sister, still dancing with Dr Thomas. It was lucky her parents hadn't heard the gossip about the doctor. The girl was smiling at him in such a silly, coy way but the doctor was behaving properly enough: in fact he looked rather bored.

Sam drew her closer. 'What are you looking at? You should have eyes only for your husband, Mrs Bundy.'

She gave a shiver of delight at his words. 'Perhaps it's time I got changed,' she said. 'We'll have to leave for the station before too long.'

'The sooner the better,' he returned and Flo felt her heart begin to thump. She knew she wasn't really beautiful, any more than Sam was tall and handsome, but there was no mistaking the excitement in his eyes and the knowledge that she alone was responsible for that made her feel light with happiness.

She turned away quickly to ask her mother to come and help her. Jane and Mrs Summers sat side by side and Flo was touched by the sight. How sad that they should be on their own. She could scarcely remember her father, had little to do with Mr Summers, and knew that neither man had been without faults. Yet she was sure her mother and Mrs Summers would infinitely rather have their husbands with them than be alone on this happy occasion. She felt a rush of pity for the two women.

At that moment they laughed at something Mrs Summers had said and then looked up at Flo, their faces still alive with laughter. She reflected, with a puzzled frown, that they didn't really look as if they needed her pity.

1915–1919

'Mrs Summers?'

The voice was vaguely familiar and Polly looked round quickly to find herself face to face with Adam Grenville. She couldn't think what he was doing in Brighton but was pleased to see him and stretched out her hand with a warm smile. Then she realised he was in uniform and her smile froze in confusion.

Enjoying the unexpected December sunshine she had paused to look out over the slate-coloured sea. She wondered how long he had been standing nearby, watching her, before deciding to speak.

His hair and moustache were more generously touched with grey now and his face very thin. Knowing what he had been through she felt an overwhelming pity for him. She had written to him at the time, of course, but she would have to say something now they were face to face. It was difficult to find the right words.

'How nice to see you,' she said. 'I'm just on my way to the station. I'm living with Kate and Joe now - while the war's on.'

He nodded. His silence unnerved her and she was about to launch into an account of how she was renting out her house in Hove and had needed to see her solicitor about various arrangements, but she stopped herself in time. He wouldn't be interested in such trivial matters.

'I was looking at the sea,' he said. 'It's calm today. Hard to believe there's a war raging on the other side.'

This was her opportunity. 'We were all so sorry to hear about your son,' she murmured. 'Such a terrible loss.'

He hunched the greatcoat around him. 'I was glad to get your letter, Mrs Summers. It gave me a great deal of comfort.'

'How is your sister?' asked Polly, after a long pause.

'Oh, still kindly taking care of me, but more importantly very busy with fundraising and that sort of thing: keeping herself occupied with war work.'

'You too, I see,' said Polly, indicating his uniform. He looked blank for a moment, then shrugged.

'Yes, I suppose so.' His eyes darkened. 'I joined the army in August, because I wanted the chance of revenge. And all I've been given is an office job in London! The only time I get out from behind a desk is on an occasion like this when I visit a nursing home to make sure the servicemen are being looked after properly.'

'It must be frustrating,' she said. 'Sir James Gale joined up quite early on, hoping to be given a command, but he's still working in Whitehall and getting more and more disgruntled.'

Adam nodded. 'I bump into him sometimes,' he said, then added harshly, 'Both of us keep pestering and pestering to be sent to the front. They'll have to give in eventually.'

Polly suppressed a shudder. She sensed that all he really wanted was to die in battle and recalled that he had once confided how close to suicide he had come after his wife's death.

He asked about her train but she smiled at him and said she had at least an hour to spare and they began to walk together along the front. She asked for news of Shrub Grove and he looked surprised at first, then refocused his attention with difficulty and slowly began to recall the changes and problems experienced at the school because of the war. Both his male teachers had joined up immediately and he found himself with an all-female staff.

'It wasn't easy for them keeping discipline over the older boys,' he said. 'I found it difficult myself. Most of the lads were fired up with the idea of getting into the army and into the war as soon as possible.' He gave a weary sigh. 'But at least we escaped the bombing.'

Then he turned to her and said, with an effort, 'Talking of school reminds me how long it's been since I last heard from Matthew. I saw him at Paul's funeral, of course, and he's written to me occasionally but he says little of what's been happening to you all.'

'Well, I expect you heard that Kate and Joe had a second child, Grace?'

'Yes, I think... How old is she?'

'Three, and very beautiful. She takes after Kate - lovely dark hair. And now they have a third child, born at the beginning of this year. They've called him Benjamin - Ben for short. So I have three grandchildren to spoil.'

He murmured absently, 'You don't look old enough to have any,' and then was acutely embarrassed at what he'd said. Polly just laughed: the compliment pleased her.

Somehow things were easier between them now. He listened carefully as she told him about Weaver Stores and Weaver Garage and he seemed pleased to hear that both businesses were thriving. Seeing she had his full attention, Polly cast around for other news.

'Joe's eldest sister, Nell, has had to move in with Mrs Weaver. Her husband joined up this year and they lost their farm cottage.'

She saw his surprise and continued with some heat: 'We were all disgusted. Poor Tom was tempted to enlist because he thought the pay would be better and his master urged him to go ahead - be patriotic. Then the old devil promptly reclaimed their cottage saying he'd need it for another worker. And he pays the new man less than he paid Tom!'

'But that's outrageous,' Adam muttered and she was glad to see his concern. He was not, then, entirely self-absorbed.

'Joe's on the Parish Council now,' she added, 'but unfortunately he couldn't do anything to help them - or others like them.'

There was silence and she racked her brains for another topic.

'Did Matthew mention Sam and Flo Bundy? Flo is Joe's younger sister. Well, they manage the Stores. They have a little girl, Dorothy - Dolly for short. She's nearly two.'

He nodded. 'And what of Edith and Matthew?'

'Well, I wish I could tell you they're happy, but - ' the words were out before she could stop herself and she wasn't surprised when he asked anxiously what was wrong. His concern seemed genuine enough and Polly found herself tentatively confiding part of her anxiety.

'Edith is so unsettled,' she sighed. 'She's totally opposed to the war - she says that every Socialist should be. Naturally, she's turned against Mrs Pankhurst and Christabel and now she supports the work of the Women's International League.'

She glanced at him and added, quickly, 'Don't think I disapprove of Edith's attitude. I believe we have to fight this war but I can understand her views and I admire her for sticking to them.'

She waited apprehensively for his response, thinking he might take issue with her, forcing her to defend her position, but he only nodded gravely.

Heartened, Polly said: 'And I was very, very proud of her this April when she tried to get to the Hague for the International Congress of Women. She was terribly frustrated at not being allowed to go, but so many of them were refused permission, as I'm sure you know. I suppose the government felt that a group of women gathering to explore ways of achieving conciliation was too much of a threat! In the end I think only three delegates from this country got through.'

They both started as some children came running past them, calling to each other, and Polly paused, her attention caught by their high-pitched, delighted laughter. Then she gave a troubled sigh.

'When my husband died he left his controlling shares in the business to Edith,' she said. 'Earlier this year she sold up and divided her money between several causes, mostly those involved in peacemaking activities.'

Adam looked shocked. 'Good heavens! She gave all her money away? Couldn't Matthew stop her?'

Polly said hurriedly, 'He doesn't interfere with what Edith does. As

230

far as he's concerned she's her own woman.'

The well-shaped eyebrows rose and she turned her gaze towards the sea, wishing she'd not said so much. Still, she had his full attention now. He obviously felt that his earlier involvement in Edith's affairs gave him some right to take an interest and that pleased her.

'I was surprised they got married so quietly,' he observed and though his tone was soft she sensed the unspoken question. 'When she left Shrub Grove so suddenly we all guessed a wedding was in the offing.'

Polly walked on silently, still not looking at him. His next words shook her.

'I believe they have no children yet?'

She realised he thought the couple had married in a hurry because Edith was pregnant and that something had gone wrong. Her eyes stung and she blinked furiously, shaking her head. Adam seemed to sense that he had probed too deeply.

'I suppose Edith is able to teach music at Matthew's school?'

Polly flushed. 'No - they felt... Well, no.'

He stared. 'But she has a natural gift. Polly, what a waste!' Then he checked himself. 'I'm sorry. I have no right to say such things.'

She smiled to let him know she was not upset. The conversation had taken an uncomfortable turn but despite that she was glad to see his own worries were momentarily forgotten. Glad, too, that he had used her name so easily.

They walked on more briskly now, Polly's long stride matching his. She was glad she'd decided against following the fashion for narrow skirts. Edith liked them, of course, for they suited her. Still, even she refused to wear those foolish hobble skirts which had been all the rage not so long ago.

She asked about the nursing home he was visiting and how many servicemen were there. He said nothing for a moment, and then burst out: 'My God, how I dread going to these places!'

The words came pouring out in an angry rush. 'It's so horrible to see all the young men, in their beds or their wheeled chairs, or hobbling about on crutches... Each time I feel I'll explode with rage at what's happened to them.'

He began shaking and Polly gripped his arm tightly, making him slow his step.

'Do you want to find somewhere to sit down?' she asked softly. 'I can catch the next train.'

He shook his head and now that he had started to talk it seemed he could not stop. One cause of his own deep sense of frustration was the fact that the young men in the nursing homes didn't appear to share it.

'They put up with it all so patiently! Some have lost limbs, others will

231

never walk again, but they're all so cheerful and uncomplaining!'

Polly gave a soothing murmur. She thought it unlikely that the patients were as resigned as he seemed to think but decided this was not the time to say so. He had himself under control again and she eased her grasp on his arm. She hunted for a topic of conversation to fill the awkward silence that had fallen.

'I suppose it's only a matter of time before Asquith introduces conscription?'

He shrugged. 'It can't be avoided now.' His voice became angry again. 'This war is being conducted by a group of old soldiers who can't accept that times have changed - and I'm not just saying that because they won't let me fight. It's an absolute disgrace, the mess they're making.'

'Surely the Coalition Government will improve the situation?'

'Not with Asquith still in charge and Kitchener as War Secretary.' Adam's hands clenched into fists. 'We can be grateful to Northcliffe for exposing that business of the shortage of shells when he did. There's no doubt Kitchener has to go: I think Lloyd George is the one to get us through this war.'

Polly nodded, smiling at him. 'How refreshing to hear you say that. You've no idea how tired I get sometimes of being the only Liberal in a family of Socialists!' He gave a sudden laugh and from the surprised look on his face she guessed that didn't happen often.

'Well, I'm being a bit unfair,' she added. 'Joe and Matty would like to see Asquith replaced and they've revised their opinion of Lloyd George. But as far as Edie and Kate are concerned he's aligned with those who betrayed women over the vote and they'll never trust him.'

Adam didn't respond and she feared his thoughts had wandered away again.

'Why don't you come down in the New Year and see us all?' she said quickly. 'I know Matthew would love to show you his school - all the pictures and things the children are doing for Christmas will still be on display, I'm sure.'

She thought he was on the verge of making some excuse but then he gave her a thoughtful look. 'You're being very kind,' he said in a softer tone.

Polly shook her head. 'You helped me once when I was in some distress,' she said. 'I'd be a poor creature if I didn't try to return that kindness now.'

They entered the station as she spoke and she didn't catch his reply in all the noise about them, but their eyes met and she knew her words had pleased him. Then, strangely, it seemed they could not look away from each other. She wanted to speak, to cut across the sudden tension between them,

232

but there were no words.

A porter whisked close to them with a trolley and they stepped back instinctively and then smiled at their own caution before making for the platform.

He saw her on to the train and said a brisk farewell. She was glad he didn't linger and she leaned back against the seat and drew several deep breaths to calm herself. It had been rather silly to stand, for what seemed like an age, gazing into his blue eyes and feeling her heart thump with frightening speed. That was the sort of behaviour for young girls, not middle-aged widows!

She straightened her hat and delved into her handbag for her copy of *Nicholas Nickleby*, an old favourite. It was disconcerting to discover, half-an-hour later, that she hadn't turned a single page and that instead of reading was wondering if Adam had noticed that her eyes were not really brown at all but an attractive shade of hazel.

Joe was waiting at Hassocks station with the horse and trap and as he helped her in Polly saw his face was grim. She anticipated trouble at home but knew him well enough not to press him. As soon as they were out of the station yard and on to the road he burst out - 'Well, we've had a tedious bad day of it and no mistake! Arthur's gone and enlisted, with not a word of warning to any of us!'

Polly stared at him, surprised and concerned. It was amazing that Arthur should do anything without first consulting Joe and his mother.

'I didn't realise he felt so strongly,' she murmured.

'Of course he doesn't. Apparently he and Irene were out in Brighton a while back and some damn fool gave Art a white feather and told him he ought to be fighting in the trenches and not enjoying himself with his young lady. Seems it's been preying on his mind ever since.' Joe shook out the reins in exasperation. 'As if these people know anything about what it's like in the trenches. I wish they could hear some of the things Tom told me when he came back on leave, then they'd not be so busy with their precious white feathers!'

The vehicle rocked as they took a corner at speed and Polly clutched his arm anxiously. Joe suddenly relaxed, giving her a rueful smile, and slowed the horse's pace.

'I'm sorry, Polly, but it's all made me very angry.' Then he added with brusque honesty, 'Of course Art would have been called up anyway when conscription comes in. He'd not have wanted exemption. But this has all happened so suddenly - and Mother's in a right old taking.'

They stopped at a gate from which an empty farm wagon was slowly emerging. Riding up beside the driver was Michael Thomas. His dog, known locally as Daffy, sat in the empty wagon, head dangling over the side. The doctor waved cheerfully at Joe then recognised Polly and pulled off his hat with a friendly smile.

He had lived down the gossip about his family and after Dr Warner's sudden death two years ago the villagers had accepted Michael as their senior GP. He had found a respectable, elderly widow of unimpeachable reputation to be his housekeeper and he had his children to stay with him whenever possible. They could often be found at Western House playing with William and Grace.

These two were watching for the trap from the top of the front door steps and when Joe pulled up they scrambled down, William first with the news.

'Grandma - Briar's had her litter! And none of them looks like the Daffy dog, so he's not the father. I said he wasn't! Anyway, Mother says I can keep one as long as I share it with Grace. Come and see the puppies - you must!'

Joe rolled his eyes as he helped Polly down and she laughed. 'When I get my breath, William. What I want first, as you know, is - '

'A nice cup of tea,' whispered Grace and her father lifted her up in his arms.

They went down the passageway into the kitchen where Kate, with a pink-faced and smiling Ben on her hip, was setting out teacups on the big table by the window. Kate kissed Polly who immediately took charge of the baby while tea was poured.

'I'll need to get on with the cooking in a minute,' Kate said. 'We've had company, as Joe probably told you. His mother was here - absolutely furious about Arthur.'

'She must be so worried,' Polly murmured and Kate nodded.

'Oh yes. All her anger was to cover up her fears. I asked her to stay and see you, but she said she was too upset, but that you'd understand.'

'Yes, of course. Are Edith and Matthew still coming later? Then let me help you get the meal ready, dear.'

That would be taken in the front parlour of course, Polly knew. She smiled to herself, comparing this spacious house to the gamekeeper's cottage with its low ceilings and small rooms. Kate and Joe had come a long way since then. The thought made her superstitiously anxious and she asked Joe if Arthur's leaving would affect the business.

'Well, I'll have to replace him I reckon,' he said. 'Since Sir James gave up his racing we've lost that custom, of course, but there's still enough regular work to keep us going.'

'I'll be looking for a new assistant, too,' Kate put in. 'Miss Castle reckons she can get much better pay doing war work.'

'In munitions, I suppose?' And Kate nodded.

Joe sniffed. 'Well, at least when she goes we won't have Michael Thomas hanging round the grocery department all the time!'

Kate gave a gasp. 'Mother, all this business made me forget why you went to Brighton today. Did you get things sorted out with the solicitor?'

'Yes, it was much more straightforward than I feared. The Heaths will move in at Hove before Christmas and they'll keep on Cook and Doris which is a great relief. I've been so worried about those two being on their own down there. Of course, I promised Mitcham his job back when the war is over but we can sort that out when he returns.'

'Grandma, Ben's dribbling.' Grace slipped off her father's knee, and mopped her brother's chin with the edge of her pinafore. The boy gurgled, hiccupped and dribbled some more. Joe took him off to settle him for a nap.

As they peeled potatoes in the scullery Kate watched William and Grace playing at the kitchen table and gave her mother a wry smile. 'He absolutely dotes on her, of course. But I'm a bit worried that he's not so fond of his little brother. I caught him putting a spider in Ben's pram yesterday.'

'Oh, they all do naughty things at times.' Polly would hear nothing against any of her grandchildren. 'By the way, we must remember to ask Edith about giving William piano lessons. I'm sure he's got a lot of talent, Kate, and that she'd love to teach him.'

By the time Edith and Matthew arrived everything was ready. The blue and white china dishes of vegetables were keeping warm in the range and the joint was out of the oven and ready to be carved.

Joe waited until the gravy had been passed round the table before breaking the news about Arthur. As Polly had expected, Edith took it like a personal insult and treated them to a scathing lecture on the iniquities of war.

Polly ate steadily, scrutinising her younger daughter across the table. She had not misrepresented matters to Adam: there was definitely an air of dissatisfaction about Edith these days. She looked as pretty as ever, with her hair drawn back over her ears and coiled loosely on her neck, in the new, softer style. But her voice was too sharp and her mouth seemed often drawn down in disapproving lines. Polly laid down her knife and fork, suddenly losing her appetite.

Matthew was sitting quietly beside Edith, but paying more attention to Grace, perched next to him on several cushions to bring her up to table level. As Polly watched he mashed the child's potatoes into some gravy. Dark and fair heads bent together over the plate and Polly smiled sadly as Matthew's long hand guided Grace's tiny fist.

Joe had naturally taken up cudgels in defence of his brother.

'It's not fair to call Art foolish, Edie. No man likes to be thought a coward and you can't deny there's a lot of pressure on single men to enlist.'

'Coward is a stupid word,' snapped Edith. 'A man decides he doesn't want to slaughter his fellow human beings but because we're at war he's called a coward for it! Even good Christian souls forget that God said 'Thou shalt not kill' and pack their menfolk off to destroy or be destroyed.' She leaned across the table towards Joe. 'I suppose you know that hundreds of soldiers at the front who get tired of fighting are also called cowards and are shot as traitors?'

'We don't know how many are court-martialled and shot,' said Matthew sharply. 'You may be exaggerating, Edie.'

She turned on him. 'Even one would be too many! But this government's not going to tell the truth about it in any case, otherwise they'd find themselves with no more volunteers.' Her voice rose in angry despair. 'If the Labour Party had followed Keir Hardie and urged the workers to strike rather than support the war we'd not have had all this unnecessary carnage.' Suddenly her lip quivered and Polly thought that for a moment she looked like a hurt child. 'But now he's dead and the Labour Party's lost its conscience.'

'Oh, Edie!' Kate turned her attention from pressing William to eat more cabbage to defending the ILP. Polly sat back and listened wearily as the sisters argued about politics, wishing there could be a break from war talk for a while.

But after the meal, when they sent the children upstairs to see if Ben was awake, it was Polly who raised the subject again as she recounted her meeting with Adam. They were all concerned about the man's unhappiness.

'It's hard to believe his son's dead,' murmured Edith, turning to Matthew. 'Do you remember he came into school once, Matty: such a polite, friendly boy...'

She broke off and Matthew reached for her hand, holding it tight until she had recovered. There was great tenderness in his manner and Edith obviously drew strength from that. Polly thought, with relief, that whatever the problems of their relationship their affection for each other was still strong.

'I'm really glad you asked Mr Grenville here, Mother,' said Kate. 'I hope he'll come.'

'Well, I knew you wouldn't mind dear, and I feel it would do him good to get away from London and his work, if only for a while.'

'But how ridiculous of him to have enlisted!' Edith was angry again.

The parlour door opened and William sidled into the room, looking guilty.

'Ben's crying,' he told his mother. 'I tried rocking the cot, but he won't stop.'

Kate rose with a sigh. 'You're sure you didn't bounce him?'

William cast a hurt gaze after her as she went out and Polly, catching Matthew's eye, gave a wry chuckle.

'I didn't bounce him,' the boy said defensively, aware of Matthew's disbelieving grimace. William was not quite so easy with him, now that he was one of Matthew's pupils at the school.

'At least,' William added, reluctantly, 'not very much.'

******

Edith glanced out of the parlour window and saw Matthew hurrying across the school playground and into the cottage.

'Sorry - I was putting out those pictures I want Adam to see,' he called out, sharply. 'I've just time to change my jacket.'

'Plenty of time, I'm sure,' she said cheerfully. 'They'll all have had one of Kate's splendid lunches, so they won't be in a hurry!'

There was only a grunted response. He hurried upstairs and Edith turned her attention back to laying the table, spreading out the white crocheted cloth and noting with satisfaction the way the polished surface showed through the lacy stitching. She began to set out her best plates and cutlery, listening as she did so to the sounds from the bedroom above. The slamming of a cupboard door indicated that he was still very annoyed with her.

She looked over to where Dilys Thomas stood, disconsolate in the doorway, winding one long, untidy plait around her fingers.

'I'm sorry, Dilys, but I haven't got time to play the piano with you now. We've got visitors for tea.'

'I know,' the girl sniffed. 'I went to see if William could play but Mrs Weaver was washing his face, ready to go out.'

Edith guessed the child was angling for an invitation and sighed to herself.

'Where's your brother, dear?'

'I don't know. Out with the dog I expect. Da was going to take us for a walk but he's been called over to the Hall because Lady Janette hurt her ankle dancing last night.'

'Entertaining some of those mindless military men Sir James is forever bringing down here, I expect,' Edith muttered with a measure of satisfaction. 'I'll tell you what, Dilys: there's a plate of little cakes on the kitchen table. You can take a couple home with you for your tea.'

When the girl had gone Edith pushed the chairs into position. Joe wouldn't be with them this afternoon for, with Arthur away now, his work at the garage had doubled, even though he had taken on another apprentice. She decided she would put her mother and Matthew on either side of Adam at the table. She guessed she'd have to bite her tongue to avoid saying anything about the war that might offend him, so the further away from him she sat the better.

'But he knows your views,' Polly had assured her. 'He accepts that many people are pacifists.'

Matthew came clumping downstairs, one shoe on and the other in his hand, waving a broken shoelace at Edith and demanding a replacement.

'Trust you to do that now,' she grumbled. 'I need to butter the scones and I can't remember where the laces are.'

'Well if we're not ready it's your fault,' he muttered. 'Why couldn't you have told me about this new scheme of yours when you got back from London, instead of waiting until just now?'

'You're so busy with school work I've hardly seen you to tell you anything,' she retorted, then snatched the shoe from him and hurried into the kitchen, delving into cupboards and searching the dresser shelves. He came to find her.

'I've just seen them coming up the lane,' he hissed. 'I'll go and put on my other shoes.'

'It's all right - I've found some laces.'

They glared at each other for a second or two and then Edith softened.

'I'm sorry, Matty. We'll talk about London later, shall we?'

He kissed her cheek. 'Yes, of course. And I'm sorry too. Don't look so worried, love.'

'Oh, I just want this afternoon to go well. From everything Mother's said, Adam is in a bad way.'

'In need of friends,' Matthew murmured. 'Look, I'll just do my shoes - ' he broke off, puzzled. 'Have we only got these few cakes for tea?'

It was Adam who arrived first at the cottage door, with Grace and William clutching either hand. He was not in uniform and Edith thought at first that her mother had exaggerated the situation. There seemed to be nothing abnormal in his manner and he greeted Edith cheerfully. But when he was off-guard she saw that his features settled into worn, sad lines and his mind often seemed to wander elsewhere. She guessed he had deliberately chosen to come ahead with the children whose chatter required little concentration.

Polly and Kate came up the path, Kate pushing Ben in his pram and Edith was glad of the excuse to hurry to the door and take her young nephew in her arms. Matthew had come down to the parlour now - he could take on the task of making conversation.

Thanks to Matthew's determined efforts tea was a cheerful meal and as soon as it was finished he took Adam away to look over the school. Polly settled into an armchair to read a story to William and Grace, and Edith went upstairs with her sister to put Ben down for a nap.

After praising the new rugs on the bedroom floor and the deep-fringed scarlet silk shawl, thrown almost casually across the bed, Kate asked her sister what had happened that week in London.

Edith was bubbling with excitement. 'Clara and I went down to Sylvia Pankhurst's centre. Honestly, Kate, there's so much happening there. She's doing such a lot for the women who live in the East End - she's a marvellous person. Anyway, I'm going up again next week to stay overnight with Clara. She's having a dinner party and Catherine Marshall has been invited - she's working like a Trojan for the No-Conscription Fellowship, you know. And we're hoping she'll persuade Bertrand Russell to come!'

She flung open the wardrobe door.

'I must show you the dress I've bought,' she said, eagerly. 'You'll love the skirt.'

She held the dress against her, posing in a languid attitude, while Kate admired the champagne-coloured satin with its bead trimming.

'I'm sure that will impress Mr Russell,' she murmured dryly, and they both burst into giggles.

Then Kate gave a sigh. 'I'm going to have to close our haberdashery and linen departments - well, not close exactly but cut down on stock and not bother to have an assistant upstairs. The eldest Parry girl has also decided to leave.'

'To earn more in munitions?' Edith's mouth was a thin, censorious line. 'Does she realise she's letting you down?'

'Oh, you can't blame her,' said Kate, quickly. 'And people are buying fewer fancy items and household goods so it makes sense to draw our horns in. The grocery department is still doing well.'

'I heard that food prices are going up.'

Kate shrugged. 'Oh, I daresay some people will want to cut down on their orders. But Joe's keeping busy. Not so much work with cars now, of course, but horses need shoeing and cartwheels mending, war or no war.'

Sensing that her sister did not want to pursue the topic Edith enquired after Arthur. She knew there had been no letter from him for some weeks and Kate's worried grimace was not encouraging.

'Joe had a postcard yesterday, but that was sent before Art last wrote to his mother, so we don't know what's going on.'

'He couldn't tell you anyway,' said Edith sharply. 'They have their letters home censored you know. Not the officers, of course - that's one of their privileges.'

Kate sighed. 'Let's not talk about the war,' she said firmly and Edith bit back a protest. If conscription could not be prevented then Joe might be called up. Matthew would have automatic exemption because of his job, but for Joe it might not be so easy, so she could understand that Kate was worried. So she smiled and told her sister about Dilys Thomas and the cakes.

'Luckily I'd baked a batch of them and could replace the half-dozen she took!'

Kate laughed. 'Poor girl - she has such a huge appetite but she never seems to get any fatter. Just taller and taller.'

She yawned and stretched then glanced thoughtfully at her sister. 'Edie, do you think that Mother is slightly smitten with Adam Grenville?'

Edith was startled for a moment then said, repressively, 'Just sorry for him, I expect. She'd never marry again, surely?'

'Why not? You don't expect her to stay a widow for the rest of her life, do you? She deserves some happiness.'

'She seems happy enough as she is.' Edith frowned. 'I'm sure she enjoys doing as she pleases at last. Not everyone sees marriage as a woman's only means of fulfilment.'

She felt Kate's sharp gaze upon her and hoped the old argument would not be re-opened. But Kate only said, 'I don't think you like Adam, do you?'

'Oh, but I do!' Edith was anxious to be fair. 'At least, I like the man he used to be. Adam Grenville the soldier is almost a different being.'

'He's full of grief and bitterness, certainly,' Kate agreed.

Edith pursed her lips, then said reluctantly, 'I can't forget that he was there, with Mother, when I was half out of my mind about Bram leaving. Now, whenever he looks at me I remember that time and think I can still see the pity in his face.'

'I'm sure that's not the case, Edie. I don't think he can see or feel anything much beyond his own misery. It's clear he doesn't have courtship in mind just now, but I think he enjoys Mother's company.'

They went downstairs to find Polly sitting upright on one of the parlour chairs, her hat on the wrong way round, an old tablecloth about her shoulders and the fire tongs clutched in one hand. William and Grace strutted before her.

'How dare you defy me!' she intoned, menacingly. 'Any more of this and I shall turn you into toads!'

William shook his fist, heroically, but Grace just giggled. Polly eyed their mother with relief.

240

'I think we'd better stop playing now,' she murmured. 'I keep forgetting whether I'm the wicked queen or the wicked witch.'

Kate laughed and the children were quickly settled in front of the parlour fire with their books while Polly shed her costume and smoothed her hair.

'I'm so glad you're staying with us, Mother,' Kate murmured. 'And not just because you're so good at playing games with these two.'

'Well, you know how much I enjoy being here. But as soon as the war is over I'll want to go back to my own home, dear. You do know that?'

'Of course. Well, if Lloyd George makes sure the army is better equipped perhaps things will be over sooner rather than later.'

Edith's self-control gave way. 'So our soldiers are now in a better position to kill German soldiers, egged on by their rulers who stay well away from any battlefield. Most satisfactory!'

'There's no need to rant at me, Edith!' Polly's voice shook. 'You know I don't rejoice in any form of killing.'

'No sane person would.' Adam's voice startled them and they all turned towards the door. He stood there, looking uncomfortable but determined, Matthew hovering anxiously behind him.

'But most people want this war over as soon as possible,' Adam went on. 'Increasing our production of effective weapons is bound to help achieve that end.'

Edith glared at him. 'The war could be over tomorrow without another shot fired, if both sides would talk peace.'

He blinked, shaken by her ferocity and Polly gave Edith a reproachful look.

'I notice that a lot of women are only too happy to go and work in the new munitions factories, Edie,' she said.

'Is it any wonder, when they've been kept down for so long?' Edith gave a snort of exasperation. 'I don't approve of what they do and the work is really dangerous, but those jobs often give them the chance of having some financial independence. Any woman would jump at the opportunity.'

'Independence!' Polly's voice was suddenly bitter and Edith flinched. There was an empty silence, then Kate let out a slow breath.

'Shall we have some more tea?' she said, quietly.

Edith set the tray on a small side table and handed round the cups without a word. She didn't regret her outburst and knew that her mother's angry response had nothing to do with her views about the war. But she wished Adam had not been involved and resolved to keep herself under better control for the rest of his visit.

Adam was praising the school, the work Matthew had done, and the

241

standard his pupils had achieved.

'You've only to look back over past work to see the tremendous improvement there has been,' he said and his enthusiasm was clear. 'Writing and spelling are particularly good: a real success, Matthew.'

He sounded so much like his old self that Edith relaxed for a moment, smiling with the others as Matthew flushed, looking both embarrassed and gratified. But Adam's next words came as a surprise.

'I'm sorry, though, that you're not teaching music here, Edith. It seems such a terrible waste of your talents.'

She thought there was some reproach in his tone and she responded defensively, without thinking: 'Oh, I've not given up teaching, Adam. I'm going to be working with a new choir at the end of January.'

She avoided Matthew's eyes, but could sense the annoyance in the sudden hunching of his shoulders.

'I met someone from the Women's Co-operative Guild when I was in London this week,' Edith went on defiantly. 'When she heard I'd taught music she asked me to organise a choir for some of their group.'

'Well, that sounds an interesting project,' said Adam and Edith cast a challenging look at Matthew, who gave a reluctant nod.

'It's perfect for Edith, of course,' he said. 'My only worry is that she'll be in London quite often and I'm always afraid there'll be another Zeppelin raid.'

Edith held her tongue with difficulty. He had made no mention of these fears when they wrangled over this earlier. Instead he had been sulky, saying he wished she didn't have to keep rushing off to find good causes and she had flown into a temper, reminding him that he should be glad she was so circumspect.

'I keep my "causes", as you call them, in London so as not to embarrass the village headmaster on his own ground!' she snapped. 'You should be grateful I don't parade around the village with a No-Conscription banner!'

Now it seemed they could all sense Matthew's silent disapproval, for both Kate and Adam tried to change the subject, speaking over each other in their hurry to do so.

William jumped up suddenly and ran to the window.

'It's Father - on his bicycle,' he announced. 'He's early!'

Kate joined him at the window in time to glimpse the expression on her husband's face. 'Oh - something's happened!'

Joe came in and went straight to Kate. 'Nell's just had a telegram,' he said. 'Tom's been wounded, shipped home and in some hospital in London.' Then he glanced round at the others. 'No details as to how bad he is. Nell's determined to go up there at once, of course so, Matty - er, Edie - could I borrow the motor to take her? Quicker than her getting the train.'

'Yes, of course,' said Edith quickly. From the corner of her eye she saw Adam slowly straightening his cup and saucer. His hands were trembling and she guessed, with a sudden rush of pity, that he was remembering how his own terrible news had come. But when he spoke his voice was firm and authoritative.

'Perhaps it will help if I come with you and your sister, Joe. I have contacts in the hospitals - that might speed your enquiries?'

The arrangements were quickly made. Jane Weaver was more upset by the news than her son had expected so Polly offered to go with Joe and Adam to provide what support she could. William and Grace had been listening intently and were clearly anxious so farewells were said cheerfully enough and Kate settled the children by the parlour fire to read them a story. Edith went upstairs and found Ben wide awake and happily chewing the fringe of the scarlet shawl. She took him down to the kitchen to give him some milk and after a while Matthew came in with the tea tray and cups.

'Tom's a tough sort of fellow, isn't he?' he muttered. 'He'll be all right.'

Their eyes met and Edith sighed.

'I'm sorry I brought up the subject of the choir work,' she said. 'I wouldn't have spoken out if Adam hadn't said what he did.'

'Oh...' He shrugged dismissively, but then reached out for her hand, his voice troubled.

'He's right, though - you should really be working with the children here. Why don't we take the risk, Edie?'

She pulled her hand free. 'No, it wouldn't be worth all the worry. You love this job, Matty.'

He gave her a wry smile then bent his head and they kissed. There was a measure of sadness in their embrace, she thought. Then Matthew straightened up saying briskly, 'Let's hope Tom's doing well and that we get news of him soon.'

******

At first things seemed hopeful. Joe telephoned Flo at the shop to say that Adam had found where Tom was being treated, arranged for them to visit as soon as possible and had also organised lodgings for them near the hospital. Then several days passed with no news. Kate and Polly took turns to spend time with Jane Weaver. 'Though I don't know if we're being of much help,' Kate confessed when she and her mother found some time to talk together at Western House. 'All I seem to do is make pots of tea!'

Polly gave a sympathetic murmur. 'I've been on tea-making duty

243

here too,' she smiled. 'So many people call in asking after Tom - I hadn't realised he was so popular. Edie called him a dark horse!'

'I suppose she's gone up to London today,' said Kate with a frown. 'Will she be staying with the Wilsons so that she can start her choir work?'

'Not yet - I think that begins later this month.' Polly glanced at her daughter. 'Don't you approve of what she's doing?'

Kate sighed. 'Oh, of course I do - it's just that things seem difficult between her and Matty just now and I don't see how spending more time away is going to help that.' She shrugged, then smiled. 'But that's their business of course. And mine is our next meal, so I must get the potatoes on! Let's hope we have some news tomorrow.'

But as time passed with no word from London they began to grow fearful. Edith and Matthew came for tea at the end of the week and then stayed on into the evening, sitting with Polly and Kate in the kitchen and talking quietly. Just as they were making ready to leave they heard footsteps on the path outside the kitchen window and the next moment Joe was in the room, blinking his eyes against the light. He had Adam with him and both men looked exhausted.

'We've brought Tom home,' said Joe and when the exclamations of amazement died down he added, 'He's up at Mum's now and she and Nell are making him comfortable in bed.' He turned towards the door again. 'I must get hold of Michael Thomas.'

'I'll go,' said Matthew quickly, pulling on his coat.

'Tell him it's urgent,' said Joe. 'They had to amputate Tom's arm and he was doing well at first but some infection set in.'

Polly gave a groan, hurriedly suppressed, and busied herself pouring brandy for Joe and Adam. Adam seemed half-asleep on his feet and she had to take him by the arm and make him sit down near the kitchen range.

'We were so worried when we didn't hear anything,' said Kate and Joe sat down too, with a weak smile.

'I should have telephoned again but you know how I hate those machines,' he muttered and Polly snorted in agreement.

They had arrived at the hospital to find the doctors pleased with Tom's progress. His arm had been amputated at a field hospital in France but he was making a good recovery and Nell was able to see her husband straight away.

'But the next day he was worse,' Joe went on. 'Needed constant attention but the staff were all run off their feet because more and more wounded poured in off the troop trains. Nell told me straight that Tom wouldn't survive if we left him there. My gums, she's just like Mum sometimes! Luckily Adam came over to see how things were going and he got hold of the doctor in charge. Said we must get Tom somewhere he could be properly looked after and that he'd take responsibility for our actions.'

'Thank goodness you were there, Adam,' said Kate.

Joe chuckled. 'And then he managed to find a van big enough to bring Tom home in while I drove Nell in the car.'

Adam grimaced. 'I'll have to get it back to the owner first thing tomorrow.'

Both Polly and Kate demurred, saying it was more important that both men have a good long sleep.

'We could certainly do with it,' said Joe. 'We've none of us slept for the last two nights.' He gave a sudden shudder. 'That hospital was a terrible place: sights to turn your stomach...'

Kate laid a comforting hand on his arm. Adam looked down into his empty glass, his face bleak, and Polly wished it was right for her to make some gesture of comfort.

Edith, who had been sitting a little way from them and listening intently, now came forward.

'Don't worry about the van, Adam. Matty and I can return it tomorrow. He'll drive it and I'll follow in the car.' Her voice was soft and full of warmth. 'Your first action of the war has been to save a life rather than to take one. You should be proud of that.'

Adam gave her a cautious look then his face lightened in a smile. 'Thank you, Edith. Yes, I'm glad I was able to help.'

Edith nodded briskly, then turned to Joe.

'I'll walk down to Flo and Sam's and let them know what's happened,' she said. 'She and I can go to your Mother's together. I daresay Nell's tired out too and Mrs Weaver might like some help looking after Tom.'

It was with a glow of satisfaction that Polly watched Edith put her coat on, grateful for her daughter's words to Adam and her thoughtfulness in respect of Jane Weaver and Nell. A difficult girl, Edith, but pure gold for all that.

Both Adam and Joe slept late and there was little time the following day before Adam had to get the London train. Kate and Joe urged him to stay on for a while, but he had already taken extra leave to go to the hospital so had to be back at his desk at once.

Polly could see that his disappointment was genuine and in the short while they had alone together before Joe took him to the station she also saw that there was a new vigour in Adam's manner.

'I believe all this has done you good,' she said frankly, and he gave a reluctant nod.

'It felt right to be active at last. The thought of going back to my

245

office now positively sickens me.' Then he smiled. 'It was good of Edith and Matthew to take the van back today. I know you worry about those two, Polly, but they seem content together. I think your anxiety is unnecessary.'

She turned her head away in annoyance, speaking sharply and without thinking.

'It is not unnecessary! If they were married I'd be less anxious - but they're not.'

He gaped at her and she wished she could call back the hasty words. Adam's face had reddened.

'Not married? But we heard at school...'

'All pretence.' Polly's tone was flat and miserable. 'When Edith moved into the school house with Matthew everyone assumed there had been a quiet wedding, with no fuss, because Arnold had died fairly recently. It upset me to hear Edith telling people who enquired that they'd got married by special licence when they were on holiday - though you may be sure I said nothing to contradict that! They're content to call themselves Mr and Mrs Hersey, to protect Matthew's job and my feelings - '

She broke off, her voice shaking and he gave a sympathetic murmur.

'My dear, you don't need to say any more. It obviously distresses you a great deal.'

His gentleness was soothing.

'No, I'd like to talk about it, Adam. I've not been able to confide in anyone, not even Clara. She has modern ideas, I know, but I think this would shock even her.'

They shared a wry smile and Polly went on, 'They say their feelings for each other are as strong as if they were legally married but that they don't hold any true religious beliefs so a wedding is irrelevant.'

'No wonder Edith can't teach at the school: it would be an end to Matthew's career if she did and then they were found out,' he murmured sadly. 'But they've been together - what - three years? Perhaps as they get older they'll see how foolish they're being and put things right.'

'Well, I hope that too - but my real fear is that without realising it they're deliberately leaving each other free. Which means that deep down there isn't the trust needed to hold them together.'

She looked anxiously into his face and he smiled again.

'Because of that business with Bram Jessop? Well, that may be so, but trust grows when people share their lives. Time will change things for them, I'm sure.'

Polly nodded slowly, saying she hoped he was right and feeling her spirits lighten a little as she did so.

'I presume Joe and Kate know,' he said.

246

'Yes. Kate shares my feelings, though I don't understand why for she's a modern thinker as well. But I know she'd be happier if they were married. Joe's just the opposite. He believes Matthew would be better off without my daughter!' She added, with a shudder, 'Kate and Joe will keep it all secret, of course, but I live in fear of someone else finding out. You can imagine what the gossip would be like in the village.' Tears pricked her eyes.

'Well, for all that you're very tolerant,' he said admiringly. 'Some mothers would have broken with a daughter who behaved as Edith has done.'

Polly felt herself go hot and cold.

'I love her, Adam. Besides, I'm hardly in a position to sit in judgement upon her.'

She ignored his puzzled gaze and moved away, hearing with some relief the sound of footsteps in the hall. William came rushing in to say that the horse and trap were ready to leave.

Adam shook her hand, pressing it warmly. 'Please write to me Polly: I'd like to have news of Tom. And the next time you're up in London perhaps you'd allow me to return your hospitality and take you out to dinner?'

She was confused but found herself murmuring agreement. William, hovering in the doorway, insisted briskly that they hurry up.

Polly stood with Kate and the children at the front door, waving as the trap drove away. Kate slipped an arm round her mother's waist.

'Joe and I have invited Adam to stay when he next gets some leave so you'll see him again before too long, Mother.'

Polly gave her a sharp glance. 'Don't you be so artful, Kate. It doesn't suit you.'

******

Kate patted Grace's hand, lying so still on the counterpane, and reassured the little girl that she would be back soon. Then she followed Michael Thomas out of the bedroom.

'As you guessed, it is measles,' he said as they went downstairs. It gave Kate no comfort to have her anxious diagnosis confirmed. It seemed that troubles came upon the family in quick succession these days.

'William recovered very quickly when he caught it; do you remember?' she murmured hopefully.

'Of course. I said at the time that I hardly liked to charge you for doing so little.' He glanced back at Kate as they went downstairs and added heartily, 'At least you know all the rules this time. Important to keep the bedroom curtains drawn, remember?'

She nodded, her worry abating somewhat in the face of his brisk confidence.

'By the way, has Grace been playing with her cousin recently?' he

247

asked.

'Yes, they had a tea party for their toys here last weekend. Oh - should I warn Flo?'

He shrugged saying it was probably too late as his next call was on the Bundys. Dolly had woken that morning feeling ill.

'No rash yet, according to Sam, but I daresay that'll appear soon enough.'

Kate's concern focused momentarily on Flo and Sam. This would be the first real illness Dolly had suffered and she knew they would be frantic with worry. There had been a lot of sickness in the area lately, much of it in families who'd received news of the death of a husband or son in the war, and she knew that Michael and his new partner had been fully stretched. At the moment, though, he seemed cheerful enough and lingered by the door, saying, 'I was round at Mrs Weaver's yesterday to see how Tom's doing. Bright as a button!'

Everyone, including the doctor, attributed Tom's swift and full recovery to the nursing he had received from his mother-in-law. Jane had announced her absolute determination that her daughter would not be left a widow and by the time the primroses were blossoming Tom was on his feet again.

'We can use his help, once he's completely well,' said Kate. 'Joe reckons he'll be able to supervise the lads in the garage and I need an extra assistant at the shop quite often. But we don't want Tom to think we're offering charity.'

'Get Jane Weaver to persuade him,' the doctor smiled. Then he added, 'I gather you've heard from Arthur after a long silence?'

'Yes, thank goodness. Several letters came at once so they must have been held up along the line. He sounds terribly bored; sitting in a dug-out all day, mending his socks and killing lice.'

Michael gave a mirthless laugh. 'Say no more, please. I'm thinking of joining up myself.'

'Are you serious?' Kate was startled. 'I thought you shared Edith's views about the war.'

'So I do, but they need good doctors out there to patch up the wounds and cut off the gangrened limbs and try to put shattered bodies back together again. So I'm not sure it's right for me to linger here in this safe country practice.'

His words made her shiver. 'What about your children?' she asked and he gave a tight smile.

'What about all the children left without their fathers?'

They heard Grace calling from upstairs and the doctor opened the

248

front door, adding, 'Oh, I've just remembered - you should warn Joe that old Miss Baker is kicking up a fuss about the noise the draymen make when they're delivering to the Golden Lion. She told me today she wants the council to do something about it, which probably means she'll come down here and moan at Joe.'

'As if we don't have enough to contend with!'

'Well, her nephew was killed a week or so back; the apple of her eye, I gather, so she's probably not feeling herself.'

Kate swallowed her annoyance. 'I'll warn Joe. I know he'll do whatever he can to help her.'

Grace was fractious that morning and needed almost constant attention, but whenever she could leave the sick room and get on with some housework Kate found her thoughts turning, with sympathy, to Miss Baker and others like her. It seemed the war had come closer and closer over the past few months and she felt helpless against it - as helpless as she had been to prevent Grace catching the measles. What was Joe going to do if and when his turn came? They should have discussed it, she knew, but instead had deliberately, foolishly, put the subject aside.

A breathless Sam Bundy appeared at midday.

'I just popped round while the shop's quiet to let you know Dolly does have the measles. Dr Thomas said Grace is down with it too.'

Cautiously they compared symptoms.

'Flo's worried, as you can imagine,' said Sam, his forehead creased in a woeful frown.

'Then why don't you get her mother to come over and lend a hand?' Kate suggested. 'She's seen all her children through this sort of thing - as well as setting Tom to rights.'

His round face cleared and lightened, as if by magic. 'That would be just the thing!' he declared.

He was all for rushing off straight away but Kate made him sit down and have tea and some bread and cheese, to save Flo having to make him a meal. While he ate she checked that Grace was sleeping, then sat down herself to give Ben his food.

'Hope he doesn't catch it, poor little chap,' said Sam, but Kate responded calmly that she didn't see how that could be avoided. She was deliberately trying to appear unruffled for Sam's benefit, but deep down she was frightened for her youngest.

'What will you do, Sam, if they call you up?' she asked and he grunted, swallowing the last of his cheese.

'I imagine it's a case of when, not if,' he murmured. 'Now they've introduced conscription for single men it's only a matter of time before they extend that to married men too. Flo and I have discussed it. I can't fight, as you know: the Quakers issued their declaration opposing war long ago. But we believe I should apply to do medical work of some kind: driving an ambulance or helping in a hospital.'

'But you might be sent out on the battlefield if you do that,' cried Kate, in agitation. 'You don't need to put yourself at risk. Conscientious objectors don't have to do any work connected with the war if it's against their beliefs.'

His eyes were sad. 'I know. Some brave souls have gone to prison rather than compromise on that. But there's so much suffering at the front amongst the soldiers - we've seen what happened to Tom - so I feel I've got to do what I can to help.'

She didn't know what to say and so changed the subject, asking if he'd been busy at the shop that morning. Sam pulled a long face.

'Not really. I reckon that if Tom can help out on Saturdays with the grocery orders we won't need to hire other help. And I was wanting to talk to you about the quantities we have from the wholesalers.'

'Yes. We'll need to make some more changes,' said Kate reluctantly. 'But let's wait until the girls are over the measles, shall we?'

He jumped up at that, eager to be off to fetch his mother-in-law and Kate asked if he would call in at the garage and let Joe know about Grace.

'We were both fairly certain before he went this morning, but perhaps you'll tell him anyway, Sam - and say he doesn't need to worry: she's doing well.'

But by the time Joe got home that evening Grace's condition had worsened. Without even bothering to wash he hurried upstairs to sit by the little girl's bed. William, who had been keeping constant watch over his sister since he got back from school, came downstairs looking mutinous.

'Father says I was fussing her,' he grumbled to Kate. 'I was only trying to wipe her forehead, the way you showed me. She's got so hot and sticky.'

Kate put the custard she was making on the back of the stove to keep warm and gave William a hug.

'Now, can you lay the table for supper, while I get Ben to bed?'

William nodded and said, thoughtfully, 'I suppose he might get the measles too?'

Kate responded crossly, 'We must hope he doesn't. He's much smaller and weaker than Grace - just think how ill he would be.'

She and Joe agreed to take it in turns to stay up with Grace that night, but as she tossed and turned feverishly in her bed, often vomiting and crying out in her distress, neither of them could sleep and so they sat up together.

'Should we fetch Michael again?' asked Joe in desperation, wiping the tangled dark hair away from the fragile little face.

'He won't be able to do any more than we can,' said Kate. 'Look, take away her pillow, Joe; it's only making her hotter.' She added, soothingly, 'William was just like this, remember?'

If he did he wouldn't acknowledge it. He loved all his children but Grace was his special treasure and he took on her suffering as if it was his own. Kate watched as he laid his head down beside the little girl's as if that would encourage her to rest and be still.

Towards morning Grace grew calmer. Between them they changed the sweat-soaked sheets and washed her. Kate went to fetch a clean nightdress and when she got back Grace was holding her father's hand and asking weakly for something to drink.

'She'll sleep now,' Kate told him, when they had settled the child. 'Why don't you go to bed and get what rest you can? I'll stay with her.'

He stood up and stretched, but was reluctant to leave. 'Let's hope Flo and Sam haven't had such a bad night with Dolly,' he murmured.

'Your mother's there in any case.'

Kate suddenly remembered what Sam had said earlier that day. 'When he's called up Sam's going to refuse to fight because of his religion,' she told Joe, keeping her voice low so as not to disturb Grace. 'He's prepared to drive an ambulance though, or do some kind of non-combatant work.'

Joe gave a grunt. 'I'll not do even that for them.'

'You'll refuse to fight?' She felt a rush of pride, mingled with fear for him. 'What will they do to you?'

'I suppose I'll have to go before one of these tribunals.' He gave her a straight look. 'Daresay they might send me to prison.'

She knew this was a possibility, but hearing him say it made her heart sink. He went to her quickly. 'Don't look so scared,' he whispered, drawing her into his arms. 'It may not come to that.'

She was shivering. 'They could send you out to France whether you agree or not. Edith says - '

'Now hush, love. There's no use worrying ourselves yet: let's wait and see what happens.' He gestured towards the bed. 'We've enough here to fret about at the moment.'

She gave him a wan smile. 'How long have you felt like this, Joe?'

'Since it began, I think, though I've only made my mind up since conscription came in. Seeing that hospital where they took Tom - all those men dying or terribly wounded - their suffering made no sense to me. I can't feel like Adam does, that I want to get revenge for them. I'm not going to fight for my country because I don't reckon my country should ever have got into this war.'

She knew that tone of stubborn finality but when he looked into her eyes she also knew that, although he was determined and that nothing would sway him, he wanted her approval. She tightened her arms about his waist, holding him close.

'Good,' she said softly. 'If I was a man I'd do the same as you.'

She felt his body relax against hers. 'Now, go to bed, Joe or you'll be fit for nothing in the morning.'

He was at the door when she remembered Michael's message, with a sinking heart.

'Oh, Joe - we may have Miss Baker calling tomorrow...'

******

Edith took off her hat and dropped it into one of the fireside chairs. At the table Matthew looked up from the work he was marking and asked anxiously for news.

'Well, Grace seems to be over the worst of it,' she told him. 'They've had a bad time with her the last two nights but she was much better this morning and ate some breakfast. Oh - and Flo had sent word that Dolly's on the mend, too.'

Matthew smiled cheerfully but Edith shook her head.

'The trouble is that Ben's running a temperature now. I said we'd have William to stay here, if that would help, so Joe will be bringing him over when he's had his supper.'

She took off her coat and went to the mirror, glancing quickly at her reflection and smoothing back her hair. The gesture reminded her of her father and she pulled a long face.

'I wish I'd been here to help,' she said, thoughtfully. In the mirror she saw Matthew's eyebrows rise but he said nothing. He was still unhappy about her working in London and the fact that he maintained a polite silence on the subject annoyed Edith intensely. She knew there was more she could do to help her cause, but felt unable to broach the subject with Matthew.

She paced over to the table and stood beside him, staring absently at the composition he was marking.

'Why didn't you tell me Joe's news when I first got home?'

Matthew laid down his pen. 'Well, you were talking about the choir and the latest actions of the No-Conscription members... Then, when I mentioned Grace's measles, you rushed off to Western House. So I didn't have much chance.'

She wished he would look her in the eye. 'It's marvellous though - don't you think? I didn't realise the depth of Joe's commitment to Socialism:

252

how brave of him to make a stand like this.'

'Is it because of his commitment to Socialism?' Matthew sounded dubious. 'Well, maybe so. I just assumed he'd come to the decision because he's sick of the whole idea of war.'

Edith ignored this. 'You can imagine how I felt when Kate told me - especially as I'd just heard today about Sir James getting his posting to France.'

'He and Janette are very pleased,' he said firmly and when she shot him an enquiring glance he added, 'They called in here yesterday before setting out for London.' There was an uncomfortable pause and then he added sharply, 'Oh don't look at me like that, Edie! They know your views and were being tactful in coming when you weren't here.'

'Good of them to think of others' feelings,' she snapped. 'A pity they didn't consider the effect of closing up the Hall and moving to the London house.'

He looked puzzled and she explained resentfully, 'Kate will lose the regular order from the Hall and she doesn't need that - trade's been poor lately.'

She expected some concerned response from him but he only shrugged wearily and picked up an exercise book. 'Jenny Bartley's compositions are really very good. I think I'll award her the improvement prize this year.'

Edith was about to brush his words angrily aside when he added in a harsh tone, 'She wasn't in school today. Her parents got a telegram saying Ernie's been killed.'

She groaned, putting a hand on Matthew's shoulder. All three Bartley boys had gone to war and now all three were dead. The number of losses in the village was growing.

'Sam's also going to refuse to fight, but on religious grounds,' she said. 'Kate says he's going to do non-combatant work though, which is a pity.'

'Why on earth do you say that?' Matthew slewed round impatiently. 'Sam's sticking to his beliefs - he's just as brave as Joe.'

She didn't want the tension between them to get any worse but couldn't let this go unchallenged. 'Even if he's not going to fight he'll be helping the war effort,' she said, trying to keep her voice calm. 'I think that what Joe's doing is the only possible action for a man of conscience. I've never admired him so much.'

Matthew gave a sharp laugh. 'Did you tell him that?'

'He wasn't there,' she admitted. 'I will do when I see him.'

'He'll not thank you for it.'

She looked at Matthew carefully now, aware of his heightened colour,

253

and grew uneasy.

'Don't you approve of Joe's decision?'

His obvious surprise offered some reassurance.

'Approve? Well, I don't think that's the word I'd choose, but I shall certainly support Joe and defend him against criticism - and there'll be quite a lot of that, I imagine.'

She still couldn't relax. 'I'm glad your exemption was automatic, Matty.'

He sighed and put the exercise books to one side.

'Look, Edie, I've got to tell you this and there's no easy way to do it. I've decided to ignore the exemption. At first I thought it would be right to stay here - after all, educating children is important whether we're at war or not. But now I've changed my mind. I have to go and fight, along with the rest.'

She was horrified. 'But it's wrong! You know it's wrong!'

'I don't know that, Edie.'

She clutched his shoulder. 'I don't understand. The only struggle we recognise is that of the mass of people against their oppressors. Don't you believe in that any more? Or are you afraid of what people will think if you don't enlist? That they'll compare you to James. Is that it?'

'How can you say that?' It was an explosive cry. 'My God, Edie, if I was truly convinced that staying out of the fighting was right then not all the cries of "coward" would send me scuttling into uniform. If you don't know that then you don't know me!'

'What then? What is it? Make me understand!'

His anger had died. He spoke slowly, choosing his words with care.

'It's easier, I think, to be a Socialist in peacetime - but things have changed so quickly. We're still at war with the ruling class, but that's been superseded by this war with Germany.'

She tried to interrupt but he would not let her. 'Yes, it has, Edie! The more I've thought about it the more I believe that we must first defend basic freedom so that Socialism will have a chance to grow. That means defeating Germany.'

'Which means killing German soldiers!' she shouted. 'Men and boys like the Bartleys - ordinary men sent out to fight by rulers as corrupt as our own. You can't involve yourself in such wickedness.'

His face twisted hopelessly. 'Oh, you have no doubts, I know that. You're so strong. Sometimes I hate your strength, Edie, because it makes my uncertainties seem like the worst kind of weakness!'

She wanted to cry out that she wasn't really strong. Couldn't he see how difficult it was to stand by her political beliefs, especially now when anyone who spoke against the war was considered a traitor? She struggled to find the right words but she had never needed to explain herself to him before and she stumbled over empty political phrases and stared at him hopelessly, seeing him draw away from her.

'There's no point in arguing,' he said. 'Better if we agree to differ.'

'Oh, listen to yourself!' Her anger flared up again. 'Agree to differ? This isn't an argument over whether we need new curtains, Matty! You're betraying everything I believe in and everything I thought you believed in too.'

His face went pale but he shook his head. 'I've made up my mind.'

'You've closed your mind! Well don't think I'll sit quietly by and let you do this. I'll do everything I can to stop you.'

'What will you do? Leave me?'

She thought there was sarcasm in his voice and she laughed sharply. 'You'd like that, I daresay. But I've no intention of leaving you. I'll stay here and I'll make you understand what you're doing. Of course you can put me out - if you dare!'

They were silent, staring at each other, the resentment between them so powerful that at first they were not aware of the tapping at the parlour door. Then Matthew's gaze shifted and he cleared his throat.

'Come in!'

It was Joe, red-faced with embarrassment, and William clutching his father's hand, his eyes wide and a little fearful. They had obviously overheard the shouting.

'I'm sorry we've come so soon,' said Joe, 'but Michael has been to see Ben and he says it is the measles - well we knew as much. Anyway, if you could have William...'

'We'd be delighted,' said Matthew heartily. 'Come on, William - got your case, I see. So let's take your things up to your room and then I expect you'd like something to eat, wouldn't you?'

The three of them went out and Edith picked up her hat and slumped in the armchair, frantically trying to make sense of what had happened in the last few moments. Without her realising it Matthew's beliefs had undergone an alarming change. The knowledge that he had not been able to speak out and share his doubts with her shook her deeply.

The door swung open again and she looked up accusingly but it was Joe who came in.

'Unpacking his case. If he can stay until Ben's over the worst of it we'd be very grateful.'

She nodded absently then burst out, 'Matty's decided to join up! Did you know he was going to do that, Joe?'

He looked uncomfortable. 'Well, I guessed that was how he felt. We've talked about the war and conscription and I told him my views.'

Edith felt sick. Matthew had come to his decision in spite of going against that of his closest friend. It must be the first time he and Joe had taken opposing political positions and if Matthew had gone that far how would she be able to change his mind?

She said, dully, 'I thought he believed in the stand we've been taking against conscription - against the war.'

Joe shuffled his feet. 'A lot of Socialists feel the war has to be fought, Edie. It doesn't mean they've abandoned - '

'Aren't you angry with him?' she cut in, but the answer was apparent in his face.

'Lord no. Matty's doing what he believes is right.'

Edith threw up her hands. 'You know that much of the mess our society is in now has been caused by people doing what they believed was right, while the rest of the fools stood round and let them do it!'

Before he could answer she hurried out. Matthew was at the bottom of the stairs with a glass of milk in one hand and a slice of cake on a plate in the other.

'William wanted some supper - ' he began, but she took the food from him, saying sharply that she would put the boy to bed.

'Yes, good.' Matthew was calm again. 'He's very worried about his brother, you know. He's always been a bit jealous of Ben and now he feels guilty that the little fellow has fallen ill. He could do with a bit of comforting.'

'Don't worry,' she snapped. 'I can look after William.'

The boy was in the guest room placing a row of toys on the bed. When Edith entered he looked at her as though expecting a reproof.

'I've only brought a few,' he said and she smiled at him.

'So I see. Will they be enough?'

He relaxed. 'Oh yes, thank you. They like to sleep with me.'

He held up a shapeless woollen creature that Edith thought might be a rabbit.

'This is the one Ben likes to play with, but Mother said he wouldn't need it tonight and that it should come with me for company.' His eyes darkened. 'I'll only have to stay here tonight, won't I, Aunty Edie? Ben will be better by tomorrow?'

She put down the plate and the milk, sat on the bed and put her arms around him. He scrambled on to her lap and they hugged each other.

'It may take a little longer than that before he's properly well again so you can go home. Maybe a few days.'

When William was in bed and asleep she and Matthew ate their supper in the kitchen as usual. They talked a little and always about unimportant matters, village gossip. Edith knew she should take up the argument again but she felt too low in spirits to do so tonight.

In bed she turned to him in silent desperation, kissing him fiercely as though the power of desire might shake his firm resolve. But only their bodies were shaken and afterwards, when she lay spent in his arms listening to his wild breathing gradually slow down and soften, Edith felt a greater sense of misery than if they had not been able to satisfy each other. She waited until she was sure he was asleep, then turned her head into the pillow and found some release in tears.

******

Kate looked up as Joe came into the kitchen.

'I don't suppose they're asleep yet?'

He grinned, shaking his head. 'Still, they're quiet enough. Grace should drop off soon.'

She set plates on the table and began to dish up their meal. 'Did you have a look at Ben's eyes?' she asked.

'Well, yes, but I can't tell if there's anything wrong. They're not watery.'

'I hope I'm fussing over nothing,' Kate murmured as they sat down to eat. 'We thought he'd come through the measles without any problems.'

'Better be on the safe side, though. Get Michael to give him a proper examination and see what he thinks.'

She nodded, then suddenly found tears pouring down her cheeks. Joe pushed his plate aside and leaned over the table to clasp her hand.

'Don't give way,' he said unsteadily. 'You've been so strong up till now. I can't bear to see you cry.'

Even before he had finished speaking she was wiping her face roughly, angry at displaying weakness. She gazed miserably at Joe, trying to regain her self-control.

'Don't let that bacon get cold,' she ordered huskily. 'I boiled it just the way you like.'

He seemed reassured and tucked into his meal with something of his old vigour, which pleased her. Over the past few days his appetite had all but deserted him. That wasn't surprising of course. The tribunal had been a dreadful experience, even though they were prepared to have Joe's plea for exemption from conscription on moral grounds rejected out of hand.

'Some of the men who sit on these tribunals are out and out hypocrites,' Edith had warned them, angrily. 'The No-Conscription Fellowship has evidence of tribunals granting exemption to men employed by local aristos while refusing to listen to conscientious objectors, so don't

257

expect fair treatment.'

And she was right. The members of the local tribunal seemed to take Joe's calmly expressed objections as an insult directed to each of them personally and took it upon themselves to castigate him publicly as a coward. Joe defended himself and the hearing ended in uproar, with the chairman thumping the table and screaming abuse at "traitors and shirkers".

'Such closed minds - and the hate in their eyes,' he told Kate. 'But it strengthened me. I'd rather be struck down on the spot than go out and fight for that bunch of scoundrels.'

Kate had half expected he would be taken away at once, and made sure everything was ready but Joe explained it would not be as quick as that.

'Now my exemption plea has been rejected it's assumed I'm called up. When I fail to report to camp I'm marked down as a deserter and only then will the police come and arrest me and haul me up before the magistrates for failing to report for military service. So I'll be here for a while yet, love.'

They tried to make the most of what time was left, for after a court appearance and fine he would be packed off to prison for the standard period of hard labour and allowed no letters or visits during the first two months. They dreaded explaining matters to the children and were surprised to find that, although fearful for their father, both William and Grace seemed to understand what he was doing. Joe was relieved but on reflection Kate felt the children wouldn't really grasp the gravity of the situation until he had actually gone. At the moment it was too much like a new game and they were excited, wildly so sometimes. Their high spirits affected Ben too, even though he was too young to understand what was going on. Kate dreaded their reaction when the game became reality but did not share her fears with Joe.

'Flo had a letter from Sam today, did she tell you?' she asked when he had finished his meal and pushed the plate to one side. 'Seems he's going to be a stretcher bearer.'

Joe nodded, frowning. 'That's a dangerous occupation - though I didn't say as much to Flo.' He glanced at Kate. 'Will she and Dolly manage on their own, do you think?'

Kate smiled at that. 'On their own?'

Flo had sent Sam off with a cheerful smile to hide her fears and the very next day a trap had made the journey from Smithy's Cottage to the Bundy's house, bearing Jane Weaver and enough luggage to indicate a long stay. Flo might be without male support now but she was certainly not alone.

Joe gave a wry smile. 'Yes, she'll be all right.'

Then the smile broadened into a teasing grin. 'No need to worry about you, of course. You've managed before without a husband about the place. Still, it's good Polly's here to help out with the children.' Now the smile faded. 'She thinks they'll come for me tomorrow, doesn't she?'

Kate nodded. 'That's why she's staying with Edie tonight. And to help with their packing, of course.'

She couldn't be still, so set about clearing the table and washing up. When she went back into the kitchen Joe had poured the tea and was sitting with his feet propped on the fender, smoking his pipe.

'I was hoping to see Matty,' he said gruffly, 'but I don't suppose he'll be back from his training before I get carted off. Tell him, all the best from me, won't you?'

Kate nodded, sitting down opposite him. Matthew had written to Joe from camp as soon as he had heard the date of the tribunal and she knew Joe had been greatly cheered by his friend's support. But she had felt angry and did not want to read the letter, although Joe passed it to her automatically. She could understand Edith's sense of betrayal at Matthew's actions. She felt it herself, on Joe's behalf.

She said as much now as she sipped her tea. Joe eyed her thoughtfully. 'Don't be too hard on poor old Matty - he's doing his best to follow his own conscience.'

Kate gave a snort of annoyance. 'Do you think Matty and Edith - their relationship - will survive all this?'

'Ours did.'

'That's the second time you've mentioned that this evening, Joe. Is it on your mind so much?

He smiled. 'In a way I'm glad it happened - proved we can manage apart from each other if we have to.'

'Of course we can,' she responded, forcing an answering smile.

'Though you're the one who's going to have to put up with Edith's rantings,' Joe grinned. 'Do you really think it's a good idea for her to move in here?'

'Well, the new headmaster will need the school cottage and our top floor room's big enough for her - and Matthew when he's home on leave.'

He drew hard on his pipe but it had gone out.

'I think we're right, putting Tom in charge at the garage,' he muttered as he searched his pockets for his tobacco pouch.

'Oh yes: he'll keep the lads in order and make sure the work's done. I'll keep an eye on things too, of course, and when Art's home on leave he'll do his bit.'

Joe knocked out the pipe into the grate and began refilling it.

'And you, Nell and Flo can cope at the shop?'

Kate nodded. 'I'm pretty sure we'll lose the youngest Parry girl soon.

Didn't you see her sister back from London last Sunday, going off to church in that fancy get-up?'

Joe laughed. 'And their dad spending her munitions money in the pub!'

He lit his pipe again and puffed strongly for a moment to get it going. Then he said deliberately: 'Now we've fixed it up with the solicitor you're properly in charge of the whole business, Kate. I'll back you whatever you decide has to be done.'

'But if it comes down to it you'd rather we lose the shop than the garage.'

He blinked at her. 'Will it come to that?'

'I - I don't suppose so. But Uncle's money has all gone of course, so there's nothing to fall back on if we do get into difficulties.'

He gave her an encouraging smile. 'You'll manage, love; you always have done.'

They sat together a little while longer but Joe was having no luck keeping the pipe alight and after a while he suggested that they go to bed. He went up first, to look in on the children, leaving her to put out the lamps and make sure all was safe downstairs. As she opened the scullery door to let the cat out Kate thought the darkness unusually oppressive around the house. For a moment she stood in the doorway as though defying whatever hurtful force lurked outside in the shadows. Then she shut the door quickly and for the first time she bolted it.

Joe was already in bed. 'Yes,' he said briskly, 'we'll get Michael round tomorrow to look at Ben. No point in waiting.'

Kate nodded and began to undress.

'In a way I hope Michael doesn't join up,' Joe went on, clasping his hands behind his head. 'You might need a friend like him while I'm - well - away. There's bound to be some unpleasantness.'

Kate pulled her petticoat up over her head, concealing an annoyed grimace.

'I shan't need his cynical tongue to defend me and the children,' she said firmly. 'I've my own family and yours about me.'

She slipped into bed and he took her into his arms at once. They were quiet for a moment, holding each other, and then he gave a groan.

'Kate, I'm afraid.'

She was shaken to hear him admit it, even though she had been aware of his fear.

'Because of being locked up?' she ventured, but he shook his head.

'Afraid of giving up. The first two months - that'll be the worst time. If I let them break me...'

'They'll never be able to do that,' she said and tightened her arms about him. She wanted to talk about his strength and how he must think of them all supporting him but then realised this was not enough. So she kissed him fiercely until she felt his body respond. This at least was a way of holding back fear.

*****

Kate saw that he was in uniform and stepped forward angrily. Uniforms had come to symbolise for her all that was destructive. Then she became aware that Matthew's face was pale and anxious, and anger was replaced by surprise.

'What's happened - why are you dressed like that?' she demanded and he sighed.

'Surely you heard us arguing?'

Kate shook her head. 'I've been down here in the kitchen all afternoon. Mother's taken the children out for a walk and I'm afraid I was dozing at the table.'

'But you can't have missed Edie slamming the front door behind her? She said she'd get the car and have a drive somewhere.' He pulled a wry face. 'So I've changed my plans and I'm taking the train this afternoon instead of tomorrow. I'm sorry I'll miss saying goodbye to everyone but it's for the best. You know how awkward things have been these past few days.'

His manner was brisk now, almost cheerful, but she guessed how upset he must be. He had come back on a short leave and on Monday was due to take ship for France. But the days here had been difficult to say the least.

'Will you go back to your barracks, or camp, or whatever it is?' she asked.

He shrugged. 'I'll telephone Adam when I get to London and see if I can stay with him. At least he won't rant at me all hours.'

'But Edie will go with you to the station?'

'I don't suppose so. As I said, she's gone off elsewhere.'

There was a miserable silence. Kate thought of him going away alone and was at once reliving events of less than a fortnight ago when the police had come for Joe. They had arrived early, before the children were awake, before anyone was about in the village. Kate had been in despair, wanting to run and fetch Jane Weaver and knowing there was no time.

'Mother and I have said our goodbyes,' Joe told her as he dressed hurriedly.

'But why have they come at this hour?'

'Out of kindness, love, so the neighbours won't see.'

Afterwards she had acknowledged herself grateful for that, but at the

261

time the sense of rush and secrecy only increased her frustration.

'One good thing,' Joe muttered as they went downstairs together, 'Edie's not here. I was afraid she'd want to send me off with drums and trumpets.'

Kate had laughed in spite of herself and the two uniformed men waiting in the hall looked up in surprise.

'You've no news of Joe, I suppose?' Matthew asked and she shook her head wearily. There would be silence now until Joe had served his first two months, but whenever she saw Jane Weaver the question was there in her unhappy eyes and at the shop Flo asked outright each day, catching herself up at once with a blush at her own foolishness. The children demanded information regularly, of course, but their needs were more easily satisfied. When she tucked them up in bed at night they would all picture their father settling down in his prison cell for sleep, happy that one more day of his sentence had passed.

Matthew was asking about Ben, and Kate tried to drag her attention back to reality.

'Ben?' she murmured vaguely.

'Edie said you've been worried about his eyes.'

'Oh, yes.' Her brow creased into a frown. 'Dr Thomas prescribed some lotion to bathe them with and they don't seem to be irritating him any more. But there's possibly been some infection and Ben will have to have his eyesight tested regularly.' Her own eyes swam for a moment. 'I wish there was some way of letting Joe know that.'

Matthew nodded and changed the subject.

'I went up to the school yesterday.'

'Oh, yes. Edie said you might. Are you pleased with the new headmaster?'

'Yes, of course,' he said hastily. 'But he told me what had happened to William. I'm surprised none of you said anything to me about it.'

Kate bit her lip. She could do her best to stop the children worrying about what was happening to Joe in prison, but she was unable to defend them against all the consequences of his imprisonment. William had returned from school one day that week with bruises on his face and dirt in his hair, having been bullied and knocked over by some of his fellow pupils.

'They say Father's a conchie and that all conchies are cowards,' he had told Kate and Polly in a trembling voice as they cleaned him up. They might have overdone the fuss they made of him, Kate thought, for a little while later, when he had recovered, she heard him boasting to Grace about how much damage he had done to his attackers, by way of kicks and bites. The whole incident had made her anxious for William in more ways than one and she was glad to hear that the headmaster had dealt firmly with all the boys concerned.

She explained this to Matthew adding, 'Edie was furious about it at the time, of course, but she realises it's better we all let the matter drop.'

'She's angry about everything these days,' said Matthew, then looked embarrassed at having spoken.

Kate knew she should keep silent but couldn't help herself. 'Surely you can see why, Matty? You're not really so insensitive that you can't appreciate how your enlisting is just tearing her apart?'

He began pacing up and down. She was aware of his anger and self-pity and watched quietly, and after a while he seemed to relax. He took out a cigarette and searched his pockets for matches. Kate got up and fetched a box from the cupboard. He stood looking at them.

'Can I write to you?' he asked suddenly and she was startled.

'To me? But Edie will pass on all your news.'

'I don't think she'll want my letters, Kate, but I'd like to have someone to write to and perhaps you'd write back in turn. Let me know how she is?'

'Matty, don't say things like that. Of course Edie will want your letters and she'll write to you.' She heard her own voice rise in agitation as she tried to reassure him. 'Don't talk as though everything is lost between you!'

'Dear Kate... But I'm afraid it is you know.'

Before she could stop him he took hold of her and kissed her mouth. His lips were soft and trembled against hers and for a moment she was overwhelmed. Then she wrenched herself free and stepped away from him.

'How can you be so selfish, Matty?' she said, in a low voice and he stared at her for a moment before her meaning hit home. Then he flushed.

'Oh, Kate, I'm sorry. I - '

'And you're wrong about my sister,' she interrupted. 'Edie loves you dearly still; that's why she's so hurt.'

He turned away and seemed preoccupied with lighting his cigarette so she could not tell if he believed her. When he looked at her again she saw that he had his emotions under control. They could behave as if nothing had happened, she thought, with an inward sigh of relief.

'There's a train around three, I think,' he said. 'I'll have to go soon.'

And now she felt sure they would not fall into temptation again she could afford to be kind.

'Then I'll come to the station with you,' she said. 'That's if you'd like to have a friend to see you off.'

'A friend.' He gave her an inquiring look and smiled at last. 'Yes. I should like that.'

She left a note for Polly, explaining where she had gone and then they set out. There were quite a few people waiting on the platform at Hassocks and one or two who knew Matthew came up and shook his hand and wished him well. The same people bestowed either frosty or acutely embarrassed greetings upon Kate and she found it hard to keep the polite smile fixed upon her face. She realised this was the first time she'd been out properly since Joe's arrest, apart from going to the shop and the garage.

'I suppose I'll have to get used to being treated like this,' she murmured to Matthew. 'They probably wouldn't acknowledge my presence at all if I wasn't with you.'

He looked at her helplessly. 'I wish there was something - '

'Oh, don't worry, Matty. I shan't mind if they cut me off: I've got Mother and Edie.'

A sharp whistle heralded the approach of the train. Matthew picked up his case with a determined air and Kate sensed that he had taken hold of himself. There would be no more self-pity. He was eager to be away.

Then she saw his face change and he stared beyond her with growing astonishment. She turned to see Edith running along the platform towards them and her heart gave a jump of delight.

'I was afraid I'd missed you!' Edith gasped out and before Matthew could reply she had flung her arms around him. His amazement changed to wary joy.

'You're wrong to do this and you know it!' Edith cried out, tears beginning to stream down her cheeks. But still she clung to him, her hands clutching at the rough khaki as though she would never let him go. Not exactly a kind farewell, Kate thought wryly, but Matthew seemed to understand. Near to tears himself he made no attempt to soothe Edith but silenced her with a fierce kiss.

Kate left them and hurried out of the station. Edith's car was in the middle of the yard, the driver's door hanging open. Kate closed it and got in on the passenger side. She wondered whether Matthew would delay his departure now and then the thought struck her that Edith might take it into her head to go up to London with him. She knew she couldn't just leave the car here and wondered if it would be difficult to drive...

She heard the train pulling slowly out of the station and a few moments later was relieved to see Edith appear. Her sister had her hat pulled well forward to shield her face and when she got into the driving seat Kate caught a glimpse of red and puffy eyes and automatically reached out a hand. Edith lowered her head.

'It's lucky you left that note for Mother,' she whispered. 'I'd driven all the way to Ansty in a furious temper before it occurred to me that Matty

264

might really leave as he'd threatened. I don't know why but I couldn't bear the thought of him going without my saying goodbye. So I rushed back - oh, I was nearly too late!'

There was a long silence, then Edith fished a handkerchief out of her pocket, wiped her face and blew her nose and then settled her hat at a more defiant angle.

'But you both decided it was still best for him to leave today,' Kate prompted and Edith gave a resigned shrug.

'Oh yes - I'd only make his life a misery again if he stayed. But I've promised to behave better when he comes home on leave.'

She turned to her sister. 'Kate - what if anything happens to him...?'

'No, don't think like that,' said Kate sharply. 'You've work to do - get on with that and don't let yourself give way to fear for him.'

Edith at once grew calmer. 'It's just as bad for you, isn't it? Joe may not be at the front but you're still afraid for him.'

'Of course. You know what they have to put up with in prison and Joe's never been shut away before. I worry so that it will affect his mind...'

It was Edith's turn to offer comfort but her soothing words were interrupted by an angry shout somewhere behind them. The sisters turned to see a red-faced farmer trying, without success, to manoeuvre a horse-drawn wagon into the station yard. He gesticulated at the car and shouted again that it was blocking his way. Kate was embarrassed but the situation seemed to cheer Edith greatly and she leaned out and waved merrily at the farmer. His answering wave was much less pleasant and he bellowed at her to move her vehicle. With a wicked smile Edith started the engine. Behind them the horse shied nervously at the explosive noise and the farmer's furious gestures were cut short as he struggled to control the animal. With a roar and a scattering of grit and dust the car sped out of the yard, leaving confusion behind.

'That'll teach him,' said Edith crisply, though she didn't enlarge on what the unfortunate farmer's lesson might be. Kate gave a reluctant laugh.

As they drove into the village she asked Edith to put her down at the shop.

'I'll just check they don't need any help with the orders,' she said. 'You go back and let Mother know that Matthew's gone.'

There seemed to be more customers than usual in the shop but as she closed the door behind her Kate looked about with considerable dissatisfaction. Out of necessity all the goods were now displayed in this one area again and she was reminded uncomfortably of the way the shop had been in Betty Halfpenny's day and of how her own plans had gone awry.

But her dismal reflections were banished by the wretched look on Flo's red face as she looked up and saw her sister-in-law. Kate realised something was wrong - even Nell was looking worried. And the half-dozen or so women at the counter sounded argumentative. Kate moved forward and the voices fell silent and all eyes turned to her, some shifty, some hostile. She recognised the same response she had experienced at the station.

'Is there a problem, Flo?' she asked as she lifted the counter flap.

Flo gave her a miserable look. 'These ladies have come to cancel their orders,' she muttered and her tone was guilty, as though she was somehow to blame. Kate smiled at her encouragingly.

'Well, they're perfectly entitled to take their custom elsewhere,' she said, deliberately keeping her voice light and cheerful. Then she turned her smile upon the women at the counter.

'That's just what I said,' put in Nell, calm now. 'Flo thought they might have some complaints about our goods, or our service perhaps, so she was just trying to find out what's wrong.'

Kate was grateful for Nell's stolid presence. All the customers were regulars and as she quickly calculated the loss of their usual purchases and regular orders she felt her heart sink. Flo had obviously hoped to persuade them to change their minds, but Kate thought it a pointless task.

'We've no complaints about the shop,' said one of the women abruptly and Kate was not surprised that the articulate Mrs Johns seemed to be the ringleader. Behind her Gertie Bartley's grey face hovered, eyes glinting with a hard light.

'But we object to mixing with conchies when we come shopping,' Mrs Johns went on and there was a murmur of agreement.

Nell gave a snort and Gertie put in hastily, 'Oh, we don't mean you, Mrs Green. Your husband's done his bit for his country; he's no coward.'

'Well, neither is my husband,' snapped Flo, no longer defensive and the women eyed her with some confusion.

'He's not fighting though,' said an uncertain voice and Flo's eyes narrowed.

'That he isn't! You know perfectly well, Mrs Burke, that we're Quakers. We condemn violence - neither the kingdom of Christ nor the kingdoms of this world can be defended by killing!'

There was an uncomfortable silence, then Mrs Johns mumbled that whatever Flo might say it wouldn't change their minds.

'No indeed,' said Kate quietly, 'because your quarrel is really with me, isn't it? When you talk about conchies and cowards you're referring to my Joe.'

Mrs Johns looked almost grateful that they'd come to the point at last.

'That's right, Mrs Weaver. I know it's not your fault - '

266

'But you'll punish me all the same? Set your mind at rest, Mrs Johns. I agree completely with everything my husband has done and if there was conscription for women I'd go to prison too rather than fight in this wicked war.'

A low hiss seemed to run through the group and Kate was momentarily shaken by the strength of their antagonism. She gripped her hands together below the counter to stop them trembling.

'Well said, Mrs Weaver!' The voice came from near the door and Kate was amazed to see Miss Baker smiling at her.

Gertie Bartley spun round furiously, identified the speaker and cried out, 'I don't know how you can bring yourself to say such a thing, Miss Baker, with your Gerald hardly cold in his grave.'

The older woman, thin and frail-looking in her plain black clothes, came slowly forward.

'Gerald shouldn't have died,' she said evenly. 'Just as this war shouldn't have happened. If enough men took the stand that Mr Weaver has taken then the war would have to end and there'd be no more killings.'

'You're wicked to say so!' Gertie screamed. 'All our brave soldiers are fighting and dying to keep us safe - ' she broke off, overcome by sobs and the other women gathered round to comfort her.

'You take no notice of what she says, Gertie,' grunted Mrs Johns. 'We all know she's got a soft spot for Joe Weaver.' Then she added sneeringly, 'Typical old maid!'

Miss Baker's colour did not change but her bearing seemed to become even more dignified.

'I have always admired Mr Weaver, if that's what you mean,' she responded. 'I think he's done a splendid job on the parish council. I believe you thought so too, Mrs Johns, for you've sought his help often enough.'

Faces grew red and angry and Kate saw one woman rolling back her sleeves. It was time to bring matters to a close.

'I have a business to run,' she said sharply. 'Perhaps those of you who no longer want to shop here would be good enough to leave. As soon as you've settled all outstanding accounts.'

There was another silence and furtive glances were exchanged.

'Settle up?' Mrs Burke was dismayed and her eyes widened as Kate reached along the counter for the credit book.

'Certainly. I know that most of you pay promptly in any case, but some have been glad enough to take credit - even from a conchie. Anyone who can't clear accounts today will have to come to some arrangement with me so that the money is eventually paid.'

She saw Nell and Flo exchange a satisfied glance but felt only distaste

267

for what she was doing.

The crowd at last dispersed and only Miss Baker was left.

'It was kind of you to speak up for Joe,' Kate told her, but Miss Baker shook her head.

'He has always been prepared to listen to people like me and try to help, even if our problems seem trivial. That means a great deal, you know.' She stepped forward to the counter. 'I certainly don't intend withdrawing my custom and I'm sure my immediate neighbours will go on shopping here. For one thing,' she added dryly, 'they won't want to traipse into Hurst for their groceries!'

Kate left Miss Baker placing her order and went out into the storeroom to check on the number of bags of flour in stock. Then she wandered upstairs, her mind buzzing with figures as she tried to work out more accurately how far profits would drop each week with this sudden loss of custom.

The sight of the haberdashery department, bare of stock, the walnut counter and smart wood and glass display shelves and fittings all gathering dust, added to her sense of defeat. She couldn't bear to look into the room beyond where bolts of fashionable materials for clothes and furnishing had once filled the now empty shelves.

The goods had all been packed away, ready for the time when business would improve but now she faced the fact that she must not wait for that any longer. She should sell all useless stock and use the money to pay the outstanding wholesalers' bills.

But what if that wasn't enough? Suppose the shop could not survive on the grocery sales alone? Suppose more people withdrew their custom? She clenched her fists and stared around the bare room. Her uncle had said the business would prosper and he had been right. Maybe it would be the same after the war, if only she could hang on until then.

Slowly she moved towards the stairs. From below came the sound of an angry voice and she wondered, with a sigh, if there was going to be another unpleasant scene with aggressive customers. But when she hurried into the shop only Jane Weaver was at the counter, brandishing her umbrella at her trembling daughters.

She turned on Kate, red-faced with fury. 'They've just told me what happened here today,' she snapped, 'and I want the names of those women! They're going to get a piece of my mind!'

※※※※※※

'Oh, Grandma! Look what I've done!'

Polly raised her head quickly at this mournful cry to see Grace staring helplessly as a pool of water spread across the table in front of her. She tutted as she hurriedly mopped up the mess, relieved that she had thought to lay some newspaper in front of the children before they began painting. Grace was near to tears because the Christmas card she was making for her father had been spoilt, but when William pointed out that now she could make a bigger one she was mollified.

'I've finished my card,' William added. 'I'd better leave it to dry before I write inside.' He glanced at Polly. 'Do you like it, Grandma?'

'It's very beautiful.'

'And what about the one I did for Uncle Matthew? Do you think he'll be pleased I drew a Christmas pudding on it? Do the soldiers have a pudding on Christmas Day?'

She could see he was in an inquisitive mood.

'I don't know, dear. Would you like to draw another picture for Ben? He can have that when Aunty Edie brings him back from his walk.'

'Oh, yes! I'll do a picture of an elephant. He likes them best.'

The children settled, Polly resumed her seat and read through the letter she had been writing.

"Dear Adam... I can hardly believe that it will be Christmas in only three weeks. This year seems to have gone in a flash. The children are already making their cards (the one Grace has painted for you has a cat on the front, though you may not recognise it as such) and getting excited about the presents they hope to have. Poor little things - we'll do our best to make it as happy a time as possible, but it won't be the same without their father.

"We have learned that when Joe's initial term of imprisonment is up we should not expect him home. Absolutists are usually called up again straight away, which means they're handed over to the military at once and then back to a civil prison to begin a new sentence. All this is done under the Cat and Mouse Act the government used to torment hunger-striking Suffragettes!

"Kate is now able to visit Joe once a month. She says he is bearing up well, though he's frustrated at being allowed so few books to read. For that first month he worked alone in his cell, as you know, and though he can now do work with other prisoners no talking or communication is allowed. However, they manage to get round this harsh regulation in a variety of ingenious ways: you can never quite crush the human spirit. Their food is poor, of course, and they have little exercise. There is much ill health but the prison authorities pay scant attention.

"Here, Kate has additional worries about the business. The only people using the shop now are relatives, friends like Dr Thomas and dear Miss Baker, and customers who either owe money in any case or who can't get things delivered from elsewhere. Luckily the garage-cum-smithy is still doing good business, so Tom and the apprentices are being paid. As there is no other smithy for miles around the local farmers have obviously chosen to 'forget' that Joe is a partner!"

Polly frowned. There was much more she could say but Adam knew of her worries about the business. As discreetly as possible she had tried to offer money from her own savings to keep things going. Kate had refused but Polly was determined to find some way of helping.

Grace smiled at her grandmother. 'This is a much better picture,' she said. 'Will Mother be home soon?'

Polly glanced at her watch. 'In a little while. As soon as I've finished my letter we'll start getting the tea ready.'

She knew that Kate would come home tired. She had gone to the garage first thing to sort out some problem over an outstanding bill and was then going to the shop to help Flo clear the storeroom, ready for the usual delivery of goods. Despite her money worries Kate had decided to stock up as usual rather than keep stale goods.

Polly turned back to her letter.

"You mustn't think that we're all gloomy here. With a house full we manage to keep each other cheerful and Nell and Flo are regular visitors, along with Jane Weaver and Miss Baker. Edith still goes up to London regularly, staying with Miss Wilson and going to various meetings, but she also helps look after the children here and is giving both William and Grace regular piano lessons.

"Dr Thomas called in today - his regular visit to check Ben's eyes. He says they're no worse, which is a blessing, but he thinks the poor little fellow will have to have spectacles before too long. It seems such a shame that a child should have to put up with a handicap usually suffered only much later on in life."

Here Polly adjusted her own glasses and her sigh was for herself as well as Ben. At least she could make sure that Adam would never see her wearing them! She dipped her pen in the ink once more.

"I'm so glad you'll be able to come and stay with us for the New Year. We're all looking forward to seeing you and hearing the news from London.

"I understand your increasing despair at still being tied to your desk as you put it, especially when we have suffered such heavy losses at the Front. However, you cannot expect me, as a friend, to share your hope that you will, even yet, be sent out to France."

She hesitated before signing her name, wondering if her final words gave too much of her feelings away. During the past year she had grown increasingly fond of Adam and she felt sure he was happy in her company.

Kate liked him, as did the children, though Polly knew that Edith was still somewhat uncomfortable with him. Polly had been surprised and touched to learn that Adam wrote regularly to Sam and Matthew, and would have done the same with Joe if prison regulations allowed more than one letter a month.

Jane Weaver said such concern from Adam was only to be expected. 'He'd be bound to take an interest - a man like that,' she told Polly during one of their afternoon gossips. 'Well, you saw for yourself the way he put himself out to help our Tom.' Then she had added, thoughtfully, 'He's a decent, upright gentleman, Polly Summers, and there aren't many of those about.'

Clara had said much the same when they last met and her letters to Polly included regular enquiries about the progress of the relationship. But although Adam's grief at the loss of his son seemed to have eased there was still a measure of reserve in his manner that prevented Polly from behaving as more than a friend towards him.

'Time for tea!' she announced and they tidied up quickly, putting the cards safely out of harm's way. The kettle was on and coming to the boil as Edith arrived, with Ben.

'I've just seen Michael Thomas,' she said, unwrapping Ben's two layers of scarves. 'His wife's very ill, so the children are coming here to stay with him until she's better. He's going to put them into the school to keep them occupied up to Christmas.'

'Well, Owen and Dilys won't say nasty things about Father,' said Grace quietly and Edith and her mother exchanged anxious looks.

'Let's put out some of the cake I made today,' Polly said quickly. Then she remembered there had been a letter for Edith from Matthew that morning and asked gently how he was.

'Tired out, of course,' her daughter sighed. 'And he thinks our losses are appallingly high.'

'Yes - Adam says it must be like a madhouse out there,' Polly agreed. 'He thinks as I do - that we'll see no improvement until Lloyd George takes over.'

'Oh, if guile and cunning can win the war for us then Lloyd George is certainly our man,' Edith sneered. 'Look at the way he's been grovelling to the Tories: he'll do anything to step into the Prime Minister's shoes.'

Wearily Polly started to assemble her arguments in support of the War Secretary. 'You can't deny that his drive to win the war has drawn the nation behind him,' she began and was interrupted by a furious lecture. She wished Edith would not be so strident in expressing her political views and found herself wondering how Matthew had put up with being harangued day and night.

'Here's Mother!' Grace, perched up at the kitchen window gave a

271

cheerful cry which broke into her Aunt's diatribe.

'And she's got Dolly and Aunty Flo with her,' crowed William.

Glad of the distraction Polly set out two more plates.

Kate came in with a broad smile on her face. Both she and Flo were in a state of high excitement about something Polly could see and she felt her own spirits lift.

'You'll never guess who's been to the shop this afternoon!' declared Kate and when they looked at her expectantly she went on with a laugh, 'It was Lady Janette, come in person to see if we could manage an order for the Hall.'

'Oh, perhaps they're moving back - become regular customers again!' Polly's voice was high and hopeful and Kate nodded.

'It's even better than that,' put in Flo. 'Her Ladyship is turning the Hall into a nursing home for wounded servicemen, so she'll have to cater for nurses and patients as well as her own staff. They need things straight away because people are already there, getting the place ready.'

Kate beamed at her mother. 'Thank heavens I decided to re-stock in spite of everything. We've got just enough to meet Lady Janette's first order, haven't we Flo? And I'll get on to the wholesalers first thing tomorrow.'

Flo smiled at her. 'I nearly died when you said that about Sam and Joe.'

'What did you say, Kate?' asked Edith and her sister shrugged.

'Well, I wanted to be sure she knew about them straight away - not find out later and perhaps take her custom elsewhere.'

'She looked straight at Lady Janette,' said Flo, 'and said "I think you should know that my husband and Mr Bundy are conscientious objectors, my lady. My husband is in prison because he refuses any involvement whatsoever in the war and Mr Bundy is a non-combatant - a stretcher bearer at the front." I was ready to drop but all Lady Gale said was, "Yes, I know and I respect their beliefs." Something like that, wasn't it Kate? And all the while her motor car was outside the shop, for everyone in the High Street to see!' And Flo clapped her hands together like a delighted child.

'So the whole village will soon know,' said Polly, with great satisfaction. 'That will bring some of your other customers back, Kate, you may be sure.'

They all laughed - all save Edith, whose voice cut coolly across the laughter.

'You'll benefit from the suffering of men injured in a war that shouldn't be happening. Can you really do that, Kate?'

Polly wanted to snap out a furious retort. Edith must surely guess how close the business had come to disaster? But she saw the look on her younger daughter's face and realised Edith was hating herself for speaking in that way to Kate yet felt she had to do it. It was what she truly believed. And Polly's anger dissolved into admiration.

Kate went to her sister and put an arm round Edith's shoulders.

'I know that, dear. But if you're really saying I should refuse to supply the Hall - well, I can't. I have the family to think of - everyone who relies on the business. Without this I'd likely have to close the shop - sell up.'

Polly gasped and Edith stared unhappily at her sister. Kate hugged her and kissed her cheek.

'But you're right to remind me and you mustn't stop doing that, Edie. You're my good conscience.'

Their high spirits ensured that they had a merry tea party, though Polly was too taken aback by what Kate had revealed to relax completely. She watched William happily cutting bread into slices and popping them into his brother's ever-open mouth. He showed great affection for Ben nowadays, Polly noted with approval.

When Flo and Dolly had gone Kate took her two youngest off to get them ready for bed and Edith went up to the drawing room to give William his piano lesson. Polly tidied up then settled herself at the kitchen table to finish her letter to Adam. He was bound to be interested in hearing about Kate's change of fortune.

But when Kate returned she quickly set the letter aside.

'Things were really that bad?' she asked sharply and when Kate nodded she sighed. 'But I would have loaned you whatever you needed to stay open, Kate. You must know that? So why keep all this to yourself?'

Kate sat down next to her. 'I've been too ambitious, Mother. I didn't leave us with enough to fall back on when trade slackened and the bills kept coming in.'

'I understand that, but I still can't see why you didn't want my help.'

'Oh, Mother, it's not that I didn't want it but that I felt I didn't deserve it. I'm not a little girl who's got into a scrape: I'm a woman running a business who has been too reckless and has to find her own way out of the problems that's caused.' She leaned towards Polly anxiously. 'I'm learning from my mistakes and paying for them too - I could hardly ask you to do the paying for me.'

They looked at each other for a moment, then Polly took off her glasses and rubbed her eyes.

'Yes, I understand what you mean, Kate. Just remember, though, that it's not always an admirable thing to take too much on yourself - to be too independent.'

Kate looked startled and Polly went on gently: 'You've tried to keep all this worry to yourself, on top of your fears about Joe and the children. Suppose your health had broken down under the strain? How would that have helped your family?'

She saw that her soft reproach had touched Kate deeply and she said no more on the subject but offered to make them some more tea.

'I think I'd prefer a glass of sloe gin,' said Kate, shakily and Polly nodded enthusiastically.

They raised their glasses in an unspoken toast and Kate's eyes grew brighter. 'Adam has to inspect nursing homes, doesn't he, Mother? Perhaps they'll send him down here to oversee Lady Janette's new venture.'

******

Polly thought it would be foolish to pin any hope on Adam being sent to Sussex and only a few days later she was proved right, when the early morning post brought a letter from him. It was brief but she had to read it through several times to herself before she was able to take in the unwelcome news.

'Adam has been given a command in France,' she told her daughters, her voice bleak.

'Oh Mother - how awful!' Kate gave Polly a sympathetic hug. 'Does he say when he has to leave?'

Polly looked at the letter again, her heart beating uncomfortably fast. 'Before Christmas: they embark early next week,' she said flatly.

'Is he coming here to say goodbye?' asked Edith. 'If he does I'll go up to London and stay longer with Margaret. You'll all get on much better if I'm out of the way.'

'No need, dear.' Polly felt calmer now. 'He has a lot to do and won't be able to come down, but he's asked if I can go up to London to meet him this Saturday.'

Edith's eyebrows rose but Kate prevented any thoughtless comment from her sister by saying cheerfully, 'That's good. At least you'll have some time together.'

Polly gave her a rueful smile. 'He just says he wants to give me the Christmas presents he's bought for the children,' she murmured but Kate did not look disappointed.

'Well, he needs some excuse, Mother.'

It was only Kate's determination that finally got Polly on to the train at Hassocks on Saturday morning. She had spent the first part of a sleepless night coming to terms with the knowledge that the pain of seeing Adam again only to say goodbye would be made worse if he continued to treat her just as a friend. The rest of the night was passed in heated embarrassment over what she would say and do if, on the other hand, he suddenly became a wooer. She

274

got up certain that it would be better to stay at home.

'Have you considered how Adam will feel if you don't go?' Kate demanded. 'Imagine him waiting for train after train, getting more and more worried...'

Polly thought sourly of her daughter's words when she arrived at Victoria, for Adam was nowhere to be seen. She waited near the barrier for 15 minutes then decided miserably that he was not coming. She would have to take a cab to Clara's and face explaining what had happened.

She was walking to the entrance when he came hurrying in. She brushed his apologies happily aside. For she had seen the look on his face before he spotted her and knew he had been fearful that she might have gone.

'I've been seeing my sister off at Liverpool Street,' he explained. 'She's gone to stay with friends for a while, though she'll come back to fuss over me when I get leave. She sends you her very best wishes, of course.' Then he seemed to relax. 'So, I've booked myself into a rather splendid hotel for tonight and I'm going to take you there now for tea. And I thought that this evening we'd go out to dinner and perhaps to the film theatre. I remember how much you enjoyed seeing *A Woman's Revenge* in the Summer.'

She found herself laughing and all her fears about this meeting with Adam fled. It would be happy not miserable. They were two good friends with mutual interests sharing a little time together and she need not think beyond that.

The only time her new-found confidence was shaken came when they danced that evening. They had decided against the film theatre and chose to eat at a restaurant where a small orchestra was playing. They watched other couples take to the floor and after a while Adam asked if she would like to dance.

When he put his arm about her and clasped her hand she had a great deal of trouble getting her breath. She was sure she would stumble or, worse still, tread on his feet, but to her profound relief she managed the first few steps without trouble and after that they moved together in easy harmony.

'Oh, that was marvellous!' she exclaimed when the music finished and they went back to their table. 'I've not danced in years.'

'Really? I'd never have guessed. It's been a long time since I've done that myself.'

They beamed at each other and after that danced again and again.

It was late when they left the restaurant and Adam was worried about getting her back to Elm Square, but Polly reassured him.

'Clara is out tonight at some party that's likely to go on until the early hours. I'm afraid she's leading rather a racy life just lately.'

He did not smile. 'I think a lot of people are doing that. Young men come back from the fighting and want to forget the dreadful things they've been through, so it's all dancing and drinking and devil take tomorrow - for those who can afford it, anyway.' Then he pulled a droll face. 'Listen to the hypocrisy of the man. I was about to ask you back to the hotel for a farewell glass of champagne.'

She agreed absently. 'You leave tomorrow then?'

'I'm afraid so. I have to get down to Dover and we sail in the early hours of Monday.'

Back at the hotel they decided against champagne and ordered mulled wine which they drank seated comfortably on a sofa in front of the fire in Adam's room.

'My sister treated me to quite a dressing-down before she set off,' he said suddenly and with a shamefaced smile. 'Instead of the hero's send-off I'd expected she told me she thought I was going out to France wanting to die.'

Polly nodded and he gave her a searching look. 'Do you think that too, my dear?'

She waited a moment, relishing the endearment, before answering.

'When we first met again, in Brighton, and you told me you were pestering anyone with influence to get sent to the front line then, yes, I did think that, Adam. Lately though I feel that might have changed.'

There was a long silence. He was staring at the leaping flames in the grate.

'You're right,' he admitted. 'It's not the same. You and your family have made me so welcome in your lives and that's made such a difference.' His voice grew softer and she had to bend her head towards him to catch his words.

'No-one can replace Paul, of course, and I'll never be able to think of his life being cut short without terrible pain. But my sister is wrong - I no longer want to follow him.'

She told him she was glad, keeping her voice steady, though relief had brought her close to tears. Then she finished her wine thinking sadly that soon he would notice the time and suggest calling a cab to take her to Elm Square. Then they would say a rather awkward goodnight and separate; and that would be the last time she would see him before he left tomorrow - perhaps the last time she would see him at all.

'You're shivering, Polly.' His voice was full of concern. 'Move nearer the fire, do.'

She shook her head. 'I'm not cold,' she said and before she could stop herself added, 'I'm frightened, Adam, that something will happen to you.'

She was glad they had not turned up the lamps. If she kept her face towards the fire he would not see her confusion.

'It's good of you to worry about me,' he said, but his response annoyed her.

'Well, of course I worry,' she snapped. 'I've grown to love you dearly, Adam. Everyone else seems to realise that - I'm amazed you don't!'

He gaped at her in astonishment then gave a splutter of laughter. 'But you sound so cross about it, Polly!'

She turned on him, thinking for a moment that he was mocking her, but he grasped her hand and hurriedly put down his glass.

'Forgive me, my dear. I've been hoping against hope you felt like that, but when you spoke out it took me completely by surprise. Oh, it's an awkward business falling in love at our age, isn't it?'

He gave her no chance to reply but drew her into his arms and kissed her with soothing tenderness.

Now they sat side by side in the firelight, holding each other and talking in whispers. Adam said his obsession with getting into the war had got in the way of realising how he felt about her, though he was always aware of only being content in her company, of looking forward to his visits to Sussex.

'It all became startlingly clear when I was told about this posting,' he said. 'I was excited at the thought of doing something at long last, but underneath I was badly shaken. I couldn't work out why until I found myself thinking more and more of you and gradually realising that I just didn't want to leave you.' He gave a gusty sigh. 'Even so I'd probably have been too unsure of myself to put my feelings into words if you hadn't said what you did.'

It was a long time before they spoke again. She found that his kisses were becoming more demanding and her own uninhibited response alarmed her. It would be so easy to get carried away...

She sat upright, drawing herself out of his grasp. He sighed.

'I wish I'd faced up to how I feel about you before now,' he muttered. 'We could have got married by special licence - '

She interrupted him. 'I wouldn't want to marry you like that - all in a rush,' she said. 'We've both been married and then lived alone. We need time to think very seriously about marrying again.'

'You'd rather we followed Edith and Matthew's example and lived together out of wedlock?' His eyes were teasing and she gave a shaky laugh.

'Adam, I'm trying to be sensible about this!'

He was contrite at once. 'Forgive me and kiss me again to keep me from saying foolish things.'

Polly shook her head. 'Please listen to me - there's something you don't know, but you must if you're thinking of marriage. Kate was born out of wedlock.'

277

She waited fearfully, not for what he might say - for she knew he would not be hard or hurtful - but for the look, the movement that would betray his dismay. As she held her breath Adam took her face between his hands.

'The first time we met I felt there had been a great sadness in your life,' he whispered. 'I wanted so much to comfort you.'

She laughed then, out of sheer relief. He did not kiss her but drew her back into the circle of his arm and they leaned against each other, as if this had been their shared hearth and home for many years and they were talking companionably together at the end of the day.

She told him the circumstances of Kate's birth and he remembered her unguarded words the night they went searching the seedy tenements for Edith.

'Yes, that's right,' Polly recalled. 'I told you I'd lived in far worse. That was when I lost my position and was turned away by my father. I rented a horrible little room at the top of a lodging house and tried to get work skivvying, but by then my condition showed and no decent family would employ me. The landlady knew of work, though. I don't need to tell you what she had in mind. That was when I decided to give up trying to cope on my own and I turned to Clara for help.' She gave a sigh. 'I was so lucky, Adam. Not many girls in that situation have such a friend to go to.'

He nodded gravely. 'And that's why you told me you're in no position to judge what Edith is doing. But it's different, Polly. She and Matthew are unmarried out of choice.'

She went on quickly to tell him about her marriage to Arnold - that it had been difficult at first but not unhappy and how it had changed under the strain of her husband's growing prosperity. She was glad she could tell him that, at the end, she had once again been a good companion to Arnold, easing his last days.

'It was not all bad, our marriage.'

He looked at her earnestly. 'None of this makes a scrap of difference to my feelings for you. I love you and want us to be married as soon as possible.'

'When you come home for good,' she said, with a decisiveness she didn't really feel. 'Then we can take up our lives properly again.'

'But if anything happens to me I'd want - ' he broke off, uncertain, and she clasped his hand tightly.

'Knowing I was your widow wouldn't lessen my grief.'

This time when they kissed she wanted desperately to lead him into the bedroom and take him into bed. Only Clara would know if she didn't return to Elm Square that night and she could rely on her friend to keep silent. Why shouldn't they satisfy the desire that flamed up between them? Surely they both deserved this?

But, at heart, she knew neither of them would think it right and was not surprised when he stood up, straightened his uniform jacket and went to the window, drawing the curtain aside.

'Good heavens!' His voice was low, wondering. 'There are millions of stars. Come and look, dear.'

She hurried to his side. The sky seemed smothered with points of light.

'How lovely,' she whispered, then added prosaically, 'Very cold out, I imagine.'

'Shall we go and find out? I don't want to say goodnight to you yet.'

His enthusiasm delighted her and she was bubbling with happiness as they got their coats on, each making sure the other was well wrapped up. Outside it was icy in patches under foot but they clung together and managed to set a good pace. She was glad they had chosen this. They would have that other time of happiness, she was sure of it.

They passed near a street lamp and she could make out the contours of his face, hard in the unflattering light. Suddenly it was easy to imagine him in charge of soldiers, giving orders, leading men out into battle. She shuddered, anxious to put such thoughts from her for a while. She was nearly as tall as he was and did not have to reach up far to touch his cold cheek with her lips. He gave a murmur of pleasure and held her closer as they kissed. Then they walked on in the direction of Elm Square, talking about nothing more important than their favourite music-hall songs.

******

'Polly, you can't stay here, you know.'

Polly looked up, aghast at having being discovered, and found Clara hovering at her side. She realised she must have been sitting in the waiting room for some time, too deep in her own unhappiness to notice what was going on around her.

'I've brought the car,' said Clara, sitting on the bench beside her.

Polly pulled herself together and wiped her eyes, then drew down her veil and turned to her friend.

'I was seeing Adam off.'

'Yes, I know,' said Clara patiently. 'Alice told me where you'd gone.'

'Oh, she didn't wake you, did she?' Polly was remorseful. 'I made a point of slipping out quietly so you wouldn't be disturbed. I guessed you were in late last night.'

'Early this morning, in fact,' smiled Clara, 'but not long after you, dear. I spent the evening flirting with a perfectly charming Major, so that

279

wasn't particularly tiring, even if he was young enough to be my son.'

Polly smiled in spite of herself. 'And you a member of the No-Conscription Fellowship! Whatever would Edith say if she knew?'

'Ah, well... Edith tends to see things very much in black and white, doesn't she? I'm old enough to know life can't always be like that.' Clara straightened up. 'Now, dear, tell me what happened - has Adam proposed?'

Polly frowned. 'Well... yes... in a way. Oh, don't look so exasperated, Clara! We're going to be married as soon as the war is over.'

She was enveloped in a warm, sweet-scented hug and heard Clara's murmur of delight. Then she was hustled out of the chilly station to where the chauffeur was sitting, bored, behind the wheel of Clara's car.

'It will be nice to drive,' said Polly absently as they climbed in. 'My feet are still hurting after last night.'

Clara's brows drew together in a startled frown and Polly pretended to search in her bag for a handkerchief to hide her amusement. She was in a strange state, between laughter and tears, but hoped she would soon grow calmer.

Alice had woken her, as arranged, in time to get to the station and Adam was waiting. She was used to seeing him in uniform now and yet he looked different somehow and she thought he was already distanced from her and wondered if she'd been wise to come. He smiled though and drew her arm through his and they walked slowly up and down the platform, saying little but glad to be together.

All at once it was time to part and they held each other close, gabbling now - words of love, instructions about writing letters and taking care - and then he was gone in a blur of smoke and tears.

She looked down at the drops splashing on her gloves as though unsure where they had come from. Clara laid a comforting hand on her arm and thrust a large, sensible handkerchief at her.

Her tears had all been shed by the time she travelled back to Sussex and she spent much of the journey wondering how to break the news to her daughters. Kate would be delighted, that went without saying, but Edith...? Polly knew quite well that although Edith respected Adam she would not want him as a stepfather. She'd get used to the idea, of course, but initially she might be upset. Polly rather dreaded having to face her younger daughter.

So she was taken aback when she stepped out on the platform at Hassocks to find Edith waiting for her.

'I've brought the car, Mother - in case you were loaded down with Adam's Christmas gifts.'

Polly lifted her bag and responded in the same wry manner. 'Some lovely story books - nothing too heavy.'

Edith kissed her mother then stepped back. 'And are you going to marry him?' she asked bluntly and Polly, relieved it was out in the open, nodded her head firmly. There was a moment's hesitation then Edith gave her mother a hug.

'You're happy,' she said. 'That's all that matters.'

As they drove away from the station Edith said, in a cheerful tone, 'Well, we can have a double celebration - your engagement and your hero's triumph.' And when Polly looked blank her daughter laughed out loud. 'Don't say you haven't heard, Mother? Lloyd George is our new Prime Minister.'

'Oh, that's marvellous!' Polly felt a glow of delight. She was convinced that with a strong man as leader the war would soon be over now and Adam home again.

When they arrived at Western House Polly thought she would go up to her room and lie down for a while but as they walked past the kitchen window she saw that Kate had visitors. She and Edith sighed in unison, then exchanged guilty smiles.

Arthur and Irene Johnson were sitting at the table, side by side, drinking tea and wearing slightly dazed expressions. Jane Weaver was comfortably settled, close to the range, with Ben on her lap. She allowed Polly and Edith to greet the returned soldier and then rushed in with her news.

'He's back on a week's leave and he and Irene here have got engaged!'

Polly looked from Jane's triumphant face to Arthur's ruddy countenance and saw that the poor man was totally bemused. His engagement had obviously come as a complete surprise to him. Irene caught Polly's eye and spread her hands in a small gesture of resignation.

Behind her Polly heard noises suggesting that Edith and Kate were struggling not to laugh. Holding her own amusement under control with almost desperate ferocity Polly crossed over to Jane and kissed a plump, shining cheek.

'My dear - congratulations!'

******

The hubbub of excited talk continued as the hall began to clear and Edith sat back in her chair, realising that for the past hour or so she had been perched forward on the edge of the seat, listening intently to the speaker. She willed herself to relax and glanced at Margaret Wilson, sitting beside her. Margaret's eyes were gleaming.

'That was so inspiring, Edith,' she whispered. 'Just think - the Russian people taking power at last.'

'Yes, and if it can happen there it can happen in this country too!'

'I'm really glad we came,' Margaret went on. 'There are so many contradictory reports in the newspapers about the situation in Russia, so it's

281

good to hear an accurate account - and such a strong speaker.'

Edith agreed. 'Though he didn't say much about the position of Russian women in the future. I'd like to go and ask him, if you don't mind waiting a little, Margaret?'

They stood up and stepped into the aisle.

'Miss Summers?'

She did not recognise the voice behind her, but when she turned the dark-haired young woman with the thin, oval face, looked vaguely familiar. Now she was smiling broadly.

'Do you remember me? Anna Jessop.'

Edith felt the blood rush into her face and was glad of Margaret's presence and friendly greeting.

'Anna Jessop - I recall the name. You sang in Edith's choir at school. Perhaps you've not heard - Miss Summers is now Mrs Hersey.'

Anna gave a happy smile and began to congratulate Edith but was interrupted sharply.

'I thought you and your family had moved away from London.'

'Yes. Yes, we did, Mrs Hersey. But I'm a nurse now and working at the East London Hospital. I've been living here for some months.'

Now there was only one question Edith wanted to ask, so urgently that her throat tightened painfully and she could not speak.

'And you have brothers, of course. Are they back in London too?' asked Margaret.

'Peter's studying music here,' said Anna. 'He was so surprised when he won his scholarship but we just knew he'd do well.' Her eyes grew troubled. 'Alexei is still rather unsettled. He doesn't stay in one job for very long, I'm afraid, but then his health isn't good. That's why he didn't have to go into the army.'

'What did you think of the speaker?' put in Edith brusquely. Anna murmured politely but without apparent enthusiasm that the talk had been very interesting.

'Of course, you were all born there,' said Margaret cheerfully. 'Are you excited about what's happening in Russia?'

'This is my country now.'

The clipped response seemed to put an end to their conversation and Edith looked around to see that the hall was empty. Anna started to edge towards the door.

'I have to go. It's been so nice seeing you again...'

They murmured their farewells and Anna seemed about to hurry off. Then she glanced back at Edith.

'Are you staying in London, Mrs Hersey?

282

Edith was surprised. 'Just for tonight. I go back to Sussex tomorrow evening.'

'Well, I wonder if you'd have time to come round to my lodgings tomorrow morning? I never did return the story book you lent me, but I've kept it safe all these years.'

The lie made Edith draw a tight breath. Anna must have news of Bram and she wanted to pass it on in private. Had she guessed, then, or been told about the relationship between her teacher and her eldest brother?

Edith hesitated in an agony of uncertainty. Whatever Anna might have to say to her she wasn't sure she wanted to hear it. Wouldn't it just stir up old memories best left undisturbed?

Margaret touched her arm. 'I'm sure you'll have time, Edie. It's not every day you meet a former pupil who has turned out so well. I'm sure you'll have lots to talk about.'

Edith scribbled down Anna's address and they arranged a time to meet.

After that she dared not allow herself to think about what she had done or what Anna might say. On the way back to the Wilsons and all through supper she talked endlessly, giving every scrap of news she could lay thought to.

'Kate? Yes, she's well and looking so much better now that business at the shop has picked up again. The children are fine. Little Ben's nearly three now. A lovely boy but very stubborn at times! No, his eyes are no better - it's a shame.

'Kate's worried about Joe, of course. He's got very thin and he's been ill several times this past year. Once when she went in on visiting day he had such a bad cough that she came home really frightened. But he got over that, thank goodness. Michael Thomas says it's probably the frustration at being shut away that's undermining Joe's health as much as anything.

'Yes, the doctor's still in the village. He was thinking of joining up but his young partner enlisted and Michael couldn't really leave the practice. Besides, he also works at the nursing home now so I suppose that salves his conscience.

'Oh, Lady Janette devotes all her time to the nursing home - I've heard she runs the place with positively Prussian discipline. The nurses are more afraid of her than their own Matron...

'Sam is well, thank goodness, in spite of being in the thick of it. Poor Flo worries herself terribly about him, of course...

'Isn't the Women's Peace Crusade campaign going well? I'd have given anything to get to the first demonstration in Glasgow, but it just wasn't possible. Over 12,000 people there - isn't that splendid? The newspapers hate it all though - the way they report our activities you'd think we wanted anarchism and bloodshed instead of peace...'

At last Margaret got a word in. 'How is Matthew, Edith? Is he due home on leave soon?'

'No - he came back only a month ago.'

And a difficult time they'd had of it, for she had been elated by the initial success of the Women's Peace Crusade and so her anger with Matthew once more boiled over, despite all her efforts. She could tell from the terrible weariness that possessed him, both physically and mentally, that he had lived through gruelling experiences and part of her wanted him to confide in her. But there was the other part, still raw from his betrayal, that would not let her play the tender confidante. Their only closeness had come in bed and they made love every night of his leave - though with a desperation that unnerved her. When he left she had wept for a long time.

'And you've not mentioned Mr Grenville,' said Margaret, hesitantly. 'I hope he's well?'

'He writes regularly - Mother heard from him yesterday in fact,' said Edith carelessly. But after a moment she added in a serious tone. 'His main concern is for his men: his letters are full of anger about the conditions they have to live and fight in. I - I suppose Matty must feel the same. I wish...' she broke off then added furiously, 'Dear God - when will this country come to its senses and start questioning the morality of sacrificing so many lives to acquire a few yards of French mud!'

******

The long climb up to Anna's door left Edith feeling depressed. The lodgings were different yet the treacherous stairs, the gloom and the smell were all so familiar. And she felt so tired, having spent much of the night anticipating all the ways in which Anna might tell her that Bram had died a hero's death.

Anna greeted her with an air of suppressed excitement and drew her quickly into the room. It was small and plainly furnished but Edith recognised a few of the ornaments from the Jessops' rooms in Shrub Mansions and her depression deepened. She cursed her own stupidity for coming.

On the floor under the window was a mattress made up into a bed.

'I've a - a friend staying here at the moment,' said Anna and there was a coyness in her manner that made Edith wonder if the young woman had a lover. Her hopes began to rise. Perhaps she had not been invited here to receive news of Bram but to be introduced to Anna's future husband.

The girl darted to the door on the far side of the room and tapped on it.

'You can come out now!' she called joyfully and Edith composed her

284

features into what she hoped was a serious yet friendly look, ready to greet Anna's young man.

It was Bram who came into the room.

Her insides jerked sickeningly as though she had fallen from a great height and she stared at him in disbelief. His face went a dull red and then drained of colour altogether. Anna laughed.

'Oh Bram, you don't mind, do you? I know you're here in secret but I wanted you both to meet again! When you asked me about the meeting last night I was just longing to tell you who I'd met - but I wanted it to be a surprise for you!'

He had found his voice now. It sounded different and Edith realised his accent was heavier.

'It has certainly been that, Anna. Won't you get Miss Summers a chair?'

'Not Miss Summers, Bram - she's married now. To Mr Hersey - you remember him, at the school?' And Anna chattered on as Edith sank into the chair.

She was gazing at him, drinking in his presence, but not uncritically. She saw that he had shaved off his beard and that without it he seemed older. His hairline was receding so his pale brow looked larger than ever and the hair itself was flecked with grey. He had on a suit, old and rather worn, but neat enough and she wondered, with sudden anger, who had been responsible for the tidy job of some patching on one sleeve.

'How are you, Bram?'

'I'm well, as you see. And you - and Mr Hersey?'

She nodded gripping her hands together in her lap.

Anna gazed at her brother proudly.

'Bram's the leader of his Soviet - a very important man,' she said.

Edith raised her eyebrows and said wryly that she was not surprised. She was congratulating herself on so quickly regaining her self-control when he shot her an ironic look and her senses seemed to dissolve.

Anna gave a gasp. 'I shall be late at the hospital! Mrs Hersey I'm sorry I can't stay but Bram will give you some tea and tell you all our plans. I know you'll be happy for us.'

They watched her as she hurried into the bedroom.

'She never did know about us then,' Edith murmured, almost to herself and Bram shook his head.

'No. Anna has organised this little reunion for us in good faith, I'm sure, thinking us merely old acquaintances. Edith, I'm sorry this has happened.'

She shrugged, wishing her mind would return to normal. It seemed to be working so slowly, as though she was half asleep.

'I think I would like some tea,' she said vaguely and he busied himself with the kettle, clearly glad to have something to do.

Anna returned, buttoning a heavy grey coat over her uniform. She kissed her brother and gave him instructions about a stew to be heated for his dinner.

He gripped her hand. 'Surely you don't have to go to work today,' he muttered. 'Stay with us and talk.'

'No, I must. If I stay here they may send someone round to find out if I'm ill and I don't want to risk you being caught.'

She went to Edith and held out her hand. 'We're not likely to meet again, Mrs Hersey, so I want you to know that I'll never forget how happy you made me - made all of us - with our singing and dancing.'

Edith took the girl's hand in her own. 'I wish you every happiness for the future, Anna,' she said softly. The young woman smiled cheerfully and then was gone.

Gradually Edith felt her mind clearing and when Bram brought her the tea she was able to say in a reasonably steady voice: 'I suppose that what Anna just said means you're going to take her away?'

'Take her home, Edith. Her country needs her now and many like her: young people who can use their skills and strengths in the service of the new Russia.' He sat down near her adding thoughtfully, 'Peter and Alexei will come also, of course.'

'But Anna said Peter is studying music here.'

'The revolution needs musicians too.'

She swallowed some tea. It was hot and scalded her mouth but somehow this eased her tension.

'So it's really happened - all that you were hoping and working for, Bram. Were you in Petrograd when they tried to quell the crowds and instead the garrison mutinied?'

He nodded, his face impassive. She hoped he might tell her what it had felt like when they learned that the Tsar had abdicated but he did not speak and so after waiting for a moment or two she went on.

'To have overthrown the monarchy with so little loss of life - that's a fine achievement: and now the power is where it belongs, in the hands of the people!'

'It's not finished yet,' he responded gravely. And when he saw her puzzled frown he leaned forward and began to speak in a low, earnest tone.

'From what Anna told me of the meeting last night the speaker had limited knowledge of what's really happening in my country. Comrade Lenin is in command and we've defeated the counter-revolution. But do you suppose the rulers of Europe will sit back and happily watch a Bolshevik government free the peasants and give them land and release the factory workers from exploitation?'

Slowly Edith shook her head. She had imagined him taking his family home to a country where Socialism had been achieved and all was well. Now she saw there was still everything to fight for.

'You'll still be in danger,' she said, her voice trembling a little.

Their eyes met at last and she felt her body soften in the warmth of his gaze. For a moment she relished that feeling and then it became unbearable. She stood up hurriedly, spilling some of her tea on the floor.

'This is stupid! I should go.'

'No. Please...' His voice wavered too and although she had turned away from him, put down her cup and was pulling on her gloves she knew she could not manage the distance to the door.

'Don't go yet, Edith.'

He was beside her and with a helpless sigh she made a vague movement towards him and found herself in his arms. They clung together and she burst into tears of defeat.

'Don't cry, my darling: please don't cry. I can't bear to see you unhappy.'

His voice was raw with longing but the trite words helped restore some self-possession. She pushed him away.

'What on earth do you care about my happiness, Bram? You left me with nothing but a pathetic note in explanation.' Her tone sharpened as the memory of her actions after receiving that note rose fresh and shaming in her mind.

'My father had promised to explain everything to you,' he protested. 'I couldn't see you again because I knew that if I did I'd never be able to leave!'

'What could your father have said that would have made it any better?' she asked dully.

Bram spread his hands in a helpless gesture then moved away from her and said abruptly, 'Is your husband still teaching?'

'No - he enlisted. He's in France.'

'Poor devil,' Bram muttered.

'Kate's husband is in prison - a conscientious objector,' snapped Edith, her anger growing. 'I was sure Matthew felt the same as Joe about the war, but I was wrong.'

He looked at her as though trying to probe behind her words and she said bitterly, 'And you and I know Matthew's wrong, don't we? You didn't join the army to fight against Germany - you were involved in the real war to free your people!'

'The circumstances are different, Edith - ' he broke off in exasperation. 'Oh, don't look at me like that - the way you always used to, with worship in your eyes. I don't deserve it!' He thrust out his hands towards her, palms upward. 'Do you want to know how many people I've killed?'

She stepped back, suddenly sickened by his words, staring at the hands that had so often caressed her. She wanted to shriek aloud in sheer frustration. He came to her quickly, snatching her into his arms and holding her tight against him, muttering hoarsely in Russian. She couldn't understand the words but she understood the hunger in his voice and in his body as he wrapped himself about her and she was lost.

He locked the door and drew Anna's pretty curtains and they undressed and collapsed into each other's arms on the mattress. She thought she had never felt such urgent desire - it was as though she had not made love for years.

When her sanity returned she found her cheeks were wet with tears and that some of them were his.

Bram wiped his eyes and rolled onto his back, pulling her with him so that her head lay on his chest. He told her he loved her and she sighed, dreamily, content for the moment to believe him.

'Tell me about your life in Russia now,' she demanded suddenly.

He groaned. 'I don't want to talk about any of that. I've another name and identity there - I'm another man. Don't ask me about what he does. Just let me be Bram Jessop again for a while.'

Edith gave a sharp laugh. 'How useful to have two lives. What if Edith Hersey could become Edith Summers again as easily as you take on your fresh identity? How would that be?'

He held her close. 'Is Edith Hersey so very unhappy?'

'There's no such person, Bram. Matthew and I live together but we're not married.'

He pulled back, staring at her, disbelief dissolving into misery. Edith began to cry.

'Don't Edith, please. I can't make sense of anything with you in tears.'

But he took her in his arms again and she grew calmer. She had not intended to say any more about Matthew but now she wanted to explain, though whether out of honesty or a desire to hurt Bram she did not know. She found herself telling him everything - how she and Matthew had been sure that retaining their freedom would only help the relationship; how hopeful she had been when they first set up home together and how, until so very recently, she felt they had done the right thing because they were making each other happy.

'Now I feel I don't know him any more.'

He murmured vague words of understanding which gave her little comfort. They lay quietly for a while and then he started to kiss her neck and breasts, eager for her again, but she held him away.

'When do you go back?'

The pain in his eyes told her that it was soon. 'At the end of this week. We're sailing from - but no, you don't need to know that.'

'Yes I do. I'll come with you.'

'What?' He struggled to sit up. 'It's impossible, Edith.'

'Why? You're taking Anna and your brothers out, so one more won't make a lot of difference.'

'But you'll need papers - '

'You can get those, surely.' She gazed at him eagerly. 'It doesn't matter how much it all costs - I can let you have the money.'

He drew a deep breath. 'Edith, think what you're saying. Do you really want to give up your life here and your marriage - ' He silenced her protest. 'Oh, I know what you've just told me, but Matthew is a husband to you, whatever you might say.'

She gave him a hard look. 'My life is in a mess, Bram. What I had with Matthew has failed. All the work I do here for Socialism and for peace and the vote seems only to end in frustration: we achieve so little. This is my chance to be happy with you and to be involved in building the New Jerusalem I've dreamed about for so long.'

He gave an irritated snort.

'You dream too much, Edith. You're so busy dreaming you might not recognise your New Jerusalem.'

She scarcely heard his muttered words. 'It's fate, Bram. I didn't marry Matty because this was meant to happen.'

'But what about your family - your mother and your sister?'

Her heart seemed to lurch. 'I - oh, I'll miss them so much!' The words were torn out of her and she had to hold down a sob. 'But I'll see them again - won't I?'

He made no response and she knew, in truth, that if she went with him she might never be able to return. But she put the knowledge away and sat up, wanting to take some action that would confirm her decision.

'I'll go home now and pack my things and say goodbye to Mother and Kate,' she said hurriedly. 'I shall have to write to Matty and explain. But I can leave the letter with Mother - ' Now images of Matthew reading such a letter tumbled unwanted into her mind and she pushed them away. She dared not think of him at the moment.

'I'll be back here by tomorrow - the next day at the latest,' she said

289

anxiously. 'I'll need to get some money together, of course. Will I be able to stay here do you think?'

He was caught up in her intensity. 'Yes - yes. I'll explain to Anna. Don't bring much; just a change of clothes. I'll make arrangements about your documents.' Then he put his arms around her again. 'It will be a long and uncomfortable journey, my darling.'

Edith forced out a laugh. 'Oh, how will your pampered darling bear it?' Then she was serious again. 'We've a lot to do. We should make a start.'

But she did not protest when he laid her down against the pillow murmuring the well-remembered words, 'Once more; just once more...'

She dressed with as much haste as she had undressed, her mind preoccupied with the thought that she must not miss the next train. It would be infuriating if she had to waste valuable time waiting at the station. She looked round for her hat and saw that Bram had finished tidying the bed and was standing quietly, watching her. She gave him a distracted smile.

'Oh, Bram, I wish I could just stay here with you until it's time for us to leave!'

'No, you must go and put everything in order. Don't say any more, Edith - just let me kiss you.'

******

As the train pulled out of Victoria she leaned back in the carriage and wondered how they would be travelling in a few days' time. By ship, eventually, but would they go straight to the docks or across country to some other port? Perhaps they would have to stay in seclusion for most of the journey, somewhere cramped and stuffy below decks. She would put one or two books in her bag in case she needed something to occupy tedious hours of inactivity.

Edith frowned, wishing she had asked Bram what sort of clothes she would need. Something plain and simple, of course, but would her winter coat be warm enough to keep out the Russian cold? Oh, but that didn't matter. She could get something more suitable as soon as they arrived.

She began to conjure up pictures of what their life would be like in Russia. She didn't even know if Bram had a home to take her to. Wherever they lived Peter, Alexei and Anna would have to stay with them at first; though if Anna was nursing...

She woke up with a jump and looked about her, dazed and muddled. They would be at Hassocks before long. She stared out of the window but saw nothing of the passing scenery, for now her mind was contemplating, fearfully, the letter she must write to Matthew.

"I have gone to Russia to be with Bram and work for Socialism." Yes, that seemed right. She must try to be honest and clear.

"Don't think that I don't love you, Matty - it's just that - " But she did not love him any more, did she? That's what she had told Bram.

"I know you'll be the first to admit that we haven't been happy together for some time now. We seem to have drifted apart without realising it; only when you told me you were quite prepared to fight in this awful war did I see how separate we have become..."

She chewed absently at her thumbnail. It all had such a hard, no-nonsense tone, which she knew would hurt him. But whatever she said would be hurtful. Edith sighed and the words and phrases spun round in her mind as she dozed once more.

Polly looked up and pulled a saucepan from the stove as Edith went into the kitchen.

'Oh, you're here - thank goodness!' she cried. 'We've had such dreadful news. Arthur's been killed.'

Edith gaped at her mother. 'No... no. That can't...' Then she slumped in a chair staring at her twitching hands.

'The telegram came this morning. I don't know any details - perhaps there aren't any. Kate's closed the shop and the garage of course and Nell and Flo are with their mother. Jane was beside herself. They had to send for Dr Thomas to give her something to help calm her.'

In her mind's eye Edith saw Arthur dancing at his sister's wedding celebration and she burst into tears.

Polly hugged her, but only briefly. 'Now we must be strong, dear, to help the family. Kate's staying at Smithy's Cottage and I've just made some soup to take up there. I don't suppose they'll want to eat anything but...' She clasped Edith's shoulders firmly. 'The children are in the parlour - Dolly too: she's sleeping here tonight - and William has got them drawing pictures. Will you look after them till we come back, Edie?'

She stood up, taking off her hat and gloves. 'Yes, of course, Mother. What have you told them?'

'Well, Dolly guessed what had happened when she saw her mother in tears so they know the truth.' Polly gave a wry smile. 'That's why they're being so good - they're upset but they really haven't taken it in properly. You may have some problems with them later, but I know you can manage.'

Edith nodded. Her own plans could go ahead once Kate and her Mother returned - there was still plenty of time to explain everything to them and to leave them her letter for Matthew and get back to London in two days' time. But now she must concentrate on keeping the children as calm as possible.

It was late and the children were in bed when Kate and Polly returned. Jane Weaver had slept a little that afternoon but then woke in great

291

distress and had to be given more of the medicine Dr Thomas had left for her. She had seemed calmer when Polly was sitting with her and so Kate had been able to cook properly for the others and sort out essential matters concerning the garage with Tom.

'He's a good man - completely reliable and able to take charge,' she said. 'I don't think I realised that until now.'

And then they all settled in front of the kitchen fire and talked about Arthur and wept for him.

Edith woke early the next day and took out the bag she normally used for her visits to London. All that she needed could be easily packed in there. Once the older children were off to school she could talk quietly and sensibly to her mother and Kate, explaining her decision, then write her letter to Matthew and set off on the afternoon train. It would be difficult - even more so because of the news about Arthur - but perhaps that loss would help them to bear her own departure.

She had reckoned without the children. Of course there was no question of them going to school and before she could arrange some time to be alone with either her mother or sister she was drawn into organising reading and quiet games to keep the youngsters occupied. Polly went off to Smithy's Cottage soon after breakfast and Kate set out for the shop, explaining that there were orders to be made up and sent out even though the store was closed. But she planned to use Tom and the apprentices to help out and promised Edith she would be back round midday.

'Yes, you must,' said Edith anxiously. 'I need to talk to you and Mother before I go back to London this afternoon.'

'Another meeting? Oh, Edie, I'm sure Clara and Margaret can manage without you.' And with that Kate was gone.

The children were quiet to start with but as the morning wore on they became more difficult to control and Grace and Dolly demanded dressing up clothes and paraded round the parlour in shawls and old scarves, while William bounced Ben until the little boy was roaring with over-excited laughter. When the parlour door opened an exasperated Edith looked round in relief. It was Matthew.

The children shouted a happy welcome and gathered around him, Ben clutching at his knees and gurgling with delight. Matthew looked at Edith and she was taken aback by the change in his face. His skin was grey and drawn and his eyes almost lifeless.

'I saw Tom and Kate at the shop on the way here,' he muttered. 'They told me about Arthur. Kate's coming home very soon to see to the children.'

She went to him then and let him hold her. He kissed her cheek but his arms slackened almost at once and she drew away again quickly, praying her sister would not be long. Kate would see they had some time together undisturbed and then she could tell Matthew to his face that their relationship was over.

Matthew seemed to draw his thoughts back from far away.

'I have to go back tomorrow,' he said. 'One of my fellow officers was killed. His father is an MP and he wanted to know how it happened - parents often do... I was detailed to come home with - with the body. I saw the father early today and then came straight here.'

'A privileged parent,' said Edith sharply. 'Mrs Weaver hasn't had a visit from Arthur's commander.'

'No. I know. But he seemed a decent sort of person.'

There was such unhappiness in his voice that she wished she had not spoken. Matthew sat down and let the children look at his uniform, playing with the jacket buttons and trying on his cap. William expressed deep disappointment that Matthew did not have a gun with him.

Then Kate rushed in, whisked the children off to the kitchen, and left them together.

'Let's go up to our room,' said Edith, quietly. 'We need to talk without being disturbed.'

But once there he began to pace about and she found it hard to find the right words.

'Matty, I've something to tell you - '

But he did not hear her. 'I have to go back tomorrow morning, Edie.' And he came close to her, putting an arm round her shoulders. Once again she tried to speak, but he silenced her with a hard, demanding kiss.

'Let's go to bed, Edie.'

He pulled her against him, nuzzling at her face and neck as she struggled.

'Ah no, Matty, no...'

But she wavered. Perhaps it would be an easy way out. Let him make love to her - at least he would have that happiness to remember. Yet there was something desperate in his manner that alarmed her. He was all but dragging her onto the bed, breathing harshly and she felt a swift-growing sense of revulsion.

'No Matty, stop it. Don't be like this!'

He looked down at her then tightened his hold. 'Come to bed, Edie. What else is there?'

The cold despair in his voice shook her. There would be no happiness, just the mechanical satisfaction of desire. Let it be this way, then - a hurried, animal coupling that would leave them both ashamed. After that their parting would surely seem right.

He undressed hurriedly, not looking at her - not looking at anything. She felt she was in the room with a complete stranger and anger and fear made her fumble over buttons and hooks. She had only taken off her dress when he pulled her onto the bed but it was obvious that didn't matter. He had no interest in kissing and touching her to excite her feelings. As he pushed her petticoat up over her knees, fumbling to find his way, she closed her eyes against the darkness in his. Surely it must be over soon. She listened for the final gasping cry that would release her.

But it did not come. Instead he suddenly stopped moving. She felt him raise himself and when she opened her eyes he was looking down at her in horror. Then he gabbled something incoherent and shifted away from her. She knew she ought to get out of bed, without a word, but instead she found herself stroking the fair head, half-buried in the pillows, and murmuring his name.

'Oh, Edie, I didn't mean to do that!' he sobbed and she went on smoothing his hair until he was calm. Then she took him in her arms and he clung to her as though for protection.

'You were right,' he said at last. 'I shouldn't have gone into this war.'

His tone was full of guilt and a terrible sorrow but she didn't feel triumphant or vindicated, only full of pity for him. She tightened her hold and pulled the covers up around them, for he had begun to tremble.

'I've been so afraid,' he went on, his voice high and thin. 'All the time, every single day, I was afraid of death and afraid of dying in such a terrible place for no good cause; and that's the kind of fear that eats at you and leaves you something less than human.'

Edith kissed his face softly. It was cold.

'I could see it happening to the men around me,' said Matthew. 'Especially the officers. We were losing so many men, you see, and we felt it was our fault somehow. Then we heard there was to be another push. The men were quite cheerful about it - to be doing something perhaps - and I was afraid, as usual.'

This time Matthew had waited in vain for the numbness that generally came upon him before battle, enabling him to lead his men over the top of their trench.

'Oh, I managed to get out with them when the signal came, but all the time, as we advanced, I wanted to shout out for them to stop and go back. I was completely convinced that none of us should be there.'

He had stumbled on, aware of his men advancing in straight lines at a steady pace, as though taking part in a drill, and being mown down in the mud as they did so. Looking ahead he had seen others, strung out on the barbed wire like bundles of rags. Then he had fallen into a shell hole, a deep one partly filled with water. Floundering in the glutinous mud which threatened to suck him under he had felt a hand grasp at his shoulder, hauling him upwards. He scrambled into a dip at the side of the shell hole, just above the water line, and found himself crouching next to a white-faced fellow officer.

'He had been trying to regroup his men when he was hit and tumbled down into the hole. His knee was injured and bleeding, but I patched him up and it didn't look too bad. I even told him he was lucky to get a Blighty one.' Matthew paused. 'That means - '

'Yes, I know what it means,' she said gently. 'He would have been sent home.'

Matthew groaned. 'We joked about it, sitting there in the middle of that hellish place, smoking my cigarettes. Then we both must have dozed off for a bit - amazing as that sounds. It seemed dark when we woke up and his knee was hurting unbearably so I said we must get back to our lines.' His voice thickened and shook. 'We got out of the hole, but it wasn't darkness - just a great cloud of smoke which suddenly drifted away. We had no cover and the shooting started almost at once. He was killed. Such a stupid, pointless death. I brought him home to his father today.'

Matthew began to weep, almost without noise but as though he would never stop. Her throat grew tight and her heart beat fiercely as she strained him against her. It was by pure chance that the other officer had been hit and that Matthew had escaped unhurt. Knowing that it could so easily have been the other way round shook her to the core.

He slept at last and she dressed and went downstairs. With luck he would sleep until the morning: she hoped so for he was completely tired out. But she wanted to prepare him something to eat in case he woke and felt hungry. The kitchen was empty and she stoked up the fire and filled the kettle.

And while she was at the sink she began to shudder uncontrollably. A picture flickered across her mind of Bram waiting for her in Anna's lodgings and that opened the way for the host of thoughts she had been desperate to keep at bay and although she fought hard for self-control it was a losing battle. She bent over the sink and sobbed.

Kate's arms were tight about her, drawing her into the fireside chair, finding a handkerchief so that she could wipe her face.

'He's in a bad way?' she murmured and Edith nodded, scrubbing fiercely at her eyes. Then she sat upright.

'Kate, you've closed the shop? Then can I have the key, please? I need to telephone Clara and give her a message to pass on.'

'To your group? Oh, let me do that, Edie. You stay here in case Matthew wakes.'

'No. It won't take long and I need to get out for a moment - clear my head.' She looked up. 'He's been through so much Kate. I never truly realised...'

Clara was in a lively mood, until Edith explained what had happened, and then she was fearful for Matthew and offered to do anything she could to help. So Edith's request was agreed at once and she was soon back at the house where Kate had prepared a light meal for Matthew.

He was just waking when Edith took the tray upstairs to their room. She knew she was too confused to work out any logical reason for staying with him, but stay she would. Had she been swayed by his realisation that he had been in the wrong all the time? Certainly she was desperately afraid for him and when he had eaten she begged him to stay in England.

'Desert? No, I can't do that, Edie. I have to see it through, now. Do you understand?'

Yes, she understood about seeing things through but she didn't know if it was brave to do so.

'Kate will be giving the children their tea soon, Matty. Do you have the energy to come down and see them?'

He smiled for the first time since his arrival. 'Just you try to stop me!'

******

"Dear Edith,

"I went to see your former pupil, Anna Jessop, as you asked, and explained why you would not be able to visit her as arranged. She seemed very disturbed at first and I realised she thought it was Matthew who had been killed so I quickly explained about Arthur and she was reassured. I should have remembered that she was one of Matthew's pupils too.

"I said that you knew she was going away and would very much like to have an address for her once she was settled. She said she would try to arrange that, but seemed rather worried. Perhaps you should consider, dear, that as a nurse she may be sent to the front and could find it difficult maintaining correspondence.

"You're right, I think, about there possibly being an admirer on the scene. She invited me in readily enough but I sensed she was not alone in her rooms and so I didn't linger. She's an attractive girl: I hope her young man appreciates his good fortune!

"I have written separately to Mrs Weaver, of course, with my condolences. It is such a dreadful loss for her and the family, and I can't imagine how Joe will feel when he hears about his brother. It's shameful that Kate must wait until her visit next month before telling him the sad news.

296

"I suppose you won't have heard from Matthew yet. It's a pity he had to return to France so soon but you were lucky to have that brief time together.

"Under the circumstances I expect it will be a while before you come up to London again but I look forward to seeing you then. My fondest love to you all..."

Edith folded the letter and tucked it away in her pocket. At the piano William was thundering his way through a ballad, investing it with a passion it did not, in truth, possess. She was about to correct him when the drawing room door opened and Irene Johnson came in. William stopped playing immediately and stared at her, his face reddening. Ben, who had been sitting quietly on a chair near him, listening to the music, now leaned forward and peered with open curiosity.

From the sofa Edith ordered the pianist to continue and beckoned Irene to come and sit beside her. The woman was calm and dry-eyed and when she sat down gave every appearance of being interested in the music. William eased his pace a little, perhaps in deference to Irene's sensibilities, and the resulting performance was more pleasing. Ben watched him owlishly and with total admiration.

'He's very good,' whispered Irene. 'Arthur told me William would be the musician of the family.'

Edith touched her hand. 'I'm so sorry - ' she began, but Irene shook her head.

'Don't say anything like that, please. I've been with Mrs Weaver but I had to come away because she kept saying how much worse it was for me.'

Edith looked at the pale but resolute face. Irene Johnson was not a beauty but there was a strength in her features that Edith liked.

'And it isn't?' she prompted.

'I'm very fond of Arthur - was very fond - and we were good friends but neither of us intended marrying.' She saw Edith's startled look and added in explanation, 'Arthur just wasn't the type... and I've always planned on having my own post office one day if I can. We enjoyed each other's company and if we were together no-one else bothered us and there was no gossip. Do you see what I mean?'

Slowly Edith said that she did, a new respect growing in her for Irene and for Arthur.

'But your engagement?'

There was a laugh, guiltily quelled.

'Mrs Weaver managed all that on her own, you know - even now I'm not quite sure how she did it. Arthur got in a panic about it, of course, but I reassured him that I'd not hold him to it after the war. I pointed out that if he

297

was cast as the jilted lover he could pretend to be too broken-hearted to even look at another woman again. Poor dear, he was so grateful.'

Edith, imagining the scene, had to struggle with her own laughter.

William came to the end of the piece and the two women clapped enthusiastically and Ben cheered. William swung round on the piano stool and looked directly at Irene. With a wisdom beyond his years he said gently, 'Would you like me to play one of Uncle Arthur's favourites, Miss Johnson?'

His hands moved sensitively over the keys and Edith felt the tears rise as she listened. Irene's eyes glinted but she kept them fixed on the boy as he played. Her next words came to Edith in a sigh.

'I'll miss Arthur, though. He was a good friend.'

Edith thought suddenly that Matthew had long been her good friend, while she and Bram had so much between them but had perhaps never managed to build friendship.

William concluded with a flourish and there was more applause. He slid off the stool and eyed his aunt speculatively.

'I've just thought: I shall be able to wear a black armband, like the other boys at school!'

******

As soon as Edith heard the front door shut she put the saucepan of milk back on the stove to re-heat. The footsteps came slowly down the passage and when Kate opened the kitchen door the weariness of the day showed on her face. She gave Edith a vague smile and sat down at the table, taking off her hat and unbuttoning her jacket.

'I missed the earlier train.'

'Well, we guessed as much. Mother put the children to bed and she went up not long ago. Have you eaten, love?'

Kate nodded. 'I wasn't allowed to leave that cake for Joe - I don't know why I bother taking one in each month, really, but I suppose if I didn't they'd change the rules just to spite us. Anyway, I had some of that on the train coming home.'

Edith urged her sister to have something more substantial now, but Kate said she had no appetite.

'I'd like some hot milk, though.'

'I've just put it on.'

'And if we've any brandy left I'll have a drop in my cup.'

Edith prepared the drink then asked hesitantly, 'Well... how did Joe take the news?'

Kate's unhappy face gave her the answer.

'It was horrible,' she said slowly. 'He didn't seem to understand me at first and he made me tell him over and over again how Arthur had been

298

killed. When it finally sank in I could see that he wanted to weep - I wish he'd been able to relieve his feelings like that - but there are always warders watching and he wouldn't give them the satisfaction of seeing him break down. I wanted so much to put my arms round him and comfort him, but that's impossible too.'

Edith clenched her fists. 'To be treated like a criminal - it's disgusting!'

'He said he just wished he could be at home to help his mother and sisters,' Kate went on, her voice unsteady. 'All the way back I've been imagining him alone in his cell, longing to be free.' She gave her sister a bleak look. 'More than one man in that prison has gone mad. I'm so scared it will happen to Joe - that something like this will turn his mind.'

'Not Joe,' Edith responded, staunchly. 'As you just said, he wouldn't give them the satisfaction.'

Kate managed a smile. 'I've been telling myself that, too.'

She helped herself to more milk and Edith lit a cigarette and leaned back in her chair. She had taken to smoking during Matthew's brief visit but had earned her mother's immediate disapproval so only indulged herself when Polly was not about. She waited for Kate to say more about her visit to Joe but she only asked about the children. Edith reassured her. She guessed that any moment now Kate would go off to bed and the chance to confide in her sister would be lost, so she spoke in a hurried and unintentionally aggressive tone.

'I've had a letter from Bram.'

'What? After all this time? Oh, Edie, how distressing for you.' Kate leaned forward to touch her sister's hand. 'He's in Russia still?'

'No - well he's on the way back there. He came to London to fetch his family home. Oh, Kate - I met him there, just before we had the news about Arthur. I was planning to go with them - I would have done if Matty hadn't come back.'

Kate shook her head, bewildered. 'Go to Russia? Oh, Edie...'

Edith took a folded paper from her pocket and pushed it into her sister's hand.

'This is the letter - please read it, Kate. There's nothing shameful in it.'

Kate stared blearily at the page. She was desperately tired and longing for her bed. Even without the lengthy train journeys visiting Joe was always a draining experience, for their time together was so short and yet so charged with emotion. Today had been worse, of course, for their talk had all been of Arthur. When the allotted time was up she remembered she had not passed on the children's messages to their father and she was still calling out to him as he was hustled off by one of the warders. She had felt raw, as though part of her had been physically torn away.

Now she had little energy left - yet here was Edith in need of sympathy. She tried to focus properly on the letter.

"My dearest, It's clear from your message that you have decided not to come with us. Please do not think too harshly of me when I say that, at heart, I am relieved. I feel we could not have found real happiness together, for, in spite of what you say, I am sure there are still strong bonds between you and Matthew which could not be broken without pain. In the end I think the guilt would have destroyed us.

"I hope we will both find a measure of peace and happiness in our lives, even though we are apart. But if ever you have need of me, write to the address I have given here. They will know how to contact me, though you will appreciate that may take some time.

"I am enclosing the documents I had made for you. I have no need of them. I love you always, Bram."

Kate held out the letter. 'This must have hurt you very much,' she said and wasn't surprised when Edith snatched the paper and crumpled it between her hands.

'It did. I don't need soothing words from him or reassurances that he'll always love me.' Her mouth tightened angrily. 'Nor do I need to know that I can contact him and that I have the papers I'd need to go to him so easily to hand. If we're not to be together then I want distance and silence between us. That's the only way I can bear it!'

Her voice rose and shook and she leaned forward as though about to throw the letter on the fire. Kate held her breath, willing Edith to do so. But her sister changed her mind, smoothed out the paper and, folding it carefully, put it back into her pocket. Then she stood up and began to pace up and down.

'I was coping - coping well, I thought,' Edith muttered. 'What happened in London was beginning to seem like a dream.' She turned to her sister. 'And I've had a letter from Matty, totally different from anything he's written before. It was as though he was talking to me and confiding all his fears. It made me feel close to him again, the way we used to be. And he wrote about the future and how we can work together to make it better: not just for ourselves but for everyone.'

She sat down again, and lit another cigarette, her hands shaking. 'Then I read this from Bram and I've not been able to stop thinking of him all day. I want to write and say that I'll go to him.' She leaned back, staring at her sister, and gave a wild laugh. Kate deliberately sharpened her tone.

'You've made your choice, Edie: you can't go back on it now.'

'I know, but I want them both. I want to be safe and quiet at home with Matty and fighting for Socialism through terrible dangers at Bram's side. Oh, sometimes I wish I'd never met either of them!'

'There'd only have been someone else,' Kate pointed out, then yawned mightily before she could stop herself. Edith gave a sharp laugh.

'You're nearly asleep, Kate. Go on to bed, do. I'll lock up.'

At the door Kate hesitated, unsure of how to put what must be said.

'Edie... why don't you destroy that letter, and the papers he sent? It would surely make things easier for you.'

Her sister shrugged. 'Not really. As long as we're both alive he'll always be a temptation to me.'

******

Kate thought that if she had come on her own she would have been pacing along the platform by now, peering to see as far as she could down the track for the first sign of the train. As it was she must sit patiently beside her mother-in-law in the waiting room.

She looked at the crochet work Jane was busy with then muttered, 'The train's so late.'

Jane shook her head. 'Only a few minutes. Don't worry Kate; it will get here. It's not fallen off the tracks.'

Kate felt a surge of panic. Suppose that was just what had happened? How terrible if, on the very day of his release from prison, Joe was killed in a railway disaster! She stifled a groan and chewed at her glove.

Jane worked steadily on, looking almost untouched by troubles and anxieties. Of course that wasn't true. It had taken Jane a long time to recover from the shock of Arthur's death. Her hair was white now, her face marked with deep lines of grief and she always wore black. Suddenly she sat up and gave a little grunt of annoyance then lifted the piece of crochet and Kate saw that it was a mess of dropped stitches. 'And here's me telling you not to worry,' she said wryly. 'Come on, let's go and wait on the platform.'

He climbed slowly down from the carriage and walked towards them, carrying a small suitcase. He was thin - the suit that had once fitted so well hung off his bony frame and he was hunched up like an old man. The gold of his hair had faded and his eyes seemed to have lost their colour altogether. This was no new sight for Kate, yet she felt a rush of protective anger and wanted to hold him and hide him away. She was aware of Jane struggling with tears. Quickly Kate pushed her forward so that she could be the first to greet her son. Joe set down the case and wrapped his arms round his mother's stout little frame, pressing her head against his shoulder as she wept. Over her head his eyes met Kate's and they smiled at each other in relief.

Kate came up now and Jane freed herself at once, turning away to dab at her eyes with a black-bordered handkerchief while Joe kissed his wife. There was no passion in his embrace and Kate did not expect it. There would be time enough later.

'Where are the children?' he whispered.

'At home. They were just too excited to bring to the station.' She stared at him. 'This feels like a dream, Joe - you're here!'

'No, I want the rest of it to be the dream - all that time in prison. I want to forget it and get on with living my life just as before.'

It was Jane who spoke first. 'But it can't be like that, Joe, and well you know it!'

He thought she was referring to Arthur and he drew her close again, hugging her to his side.

'Poor old Art,' he muttered. 'I don't know what I'll do without him.'

Jane's eyes were full of tears again but she went on in a firm voice: 'I don't just mean Arthur. Nothing can be the same as it was before. You're not to try and forget what's happened to you, otherwise there'd be no point in what you've done. You're to remember everything and make sure other people do too. Art would have wanted that. He was proud of you, Joe Weaver!'

They all hugged each other again then walked slowly, arm-in-arm, along the platform. Jane snapped out angrily that she had been sent Arthur's medals.

'Awarded because he died so bravely!' she snapped. 'And they thought it would comfort me to have them! As if a few bits of ribbon could be of any comfort. I felt like sending them back with a piece of my mind, but then I thought Irene should have them. I had such a job persuading her.'

Kate caught her husband's eye and saw his quizzical look. So he had been party to Arthur and Irene's secret!

Then Joe sighed, 'Do you think it will frighten the children, seeing me all skin and bone?'

'We've told them you haven't been fed very well,' said Kate carefully. 'I think they understand.'

'Miss Baker called in this morning,' said Jane. 'Left some patent medicine for you that's supposed to stimulate the appetite. She's been a good friend to us.'

Joe looked surprised. He was remembering that his mother used to have little time for Miss Baker, Kate thought. She had not told him about the difficulties at the shop during his absence so she hurried to change the subject before he started asking awkward questions.

'All the family's at home - there's quite a crowd, I'm afraid.'

'Matty too? He's up and about again?'

She hesitated. When they left Western House to come to the station Matthew had been recovering from a bout of coughing which seemed fierce enough to break his thin frame in two. She had seen the blood on his handkerchief and noticed the skill with which her sister whisked the soiled cloth out of sight, while cheerfully reassuring everyone that Matthew was all right.

Jane glanced at her son. 'We've got him back on his feet,' she said briskly. 'Those army doctors were a pessimistic lot - just like they were with Tom. But Matthew tires easily and you must remember that, Joe. He uses one of those chairs with wheels to get about in, so as not to use up too much of his strength walking.'

Joe pulled a face and Kate squeezed his arm. 'He's writing a book,' she said. 'It's about his experiences at the front - but he'll tell you about that when you see him.'

They went out into the station yard and Kate gestured towards the dark brown motor car, near the entrance.

'Your transport home, sir!'

Joe gave a surprised laugh which turned to a cry of pleasure as Adam got out of the driver's seat and came hurrying up to them. The two men shook hands with furious fervour and then turned to the car.

'I'm travelling up and down from London quite a lot now,' said Adam by way of explanation. 'This makes life easier.'

'I should think it does. Good engine?'

The next moment they were burrowing under the bonnet.

'I don't believe this!' cried Jane. 'You've your children waiting at home to see you Joe Weaver - come out of there this minute!'

They were soon speeding towards the village, Joe sitting next to Adam and obviously relishing the experience. He asked archly when Adam was planning on becoming his father-in-law.

'That depends entirely on you,' Adam replied. 'I'm all set with Matthew as my best man but Polly won't agree the date until you've promised to give her away.'

Kate leaned back in the seat smiling, but could not relax completely yet. Joe still had to see the children.

Grace and William stood on the front doorstep with Ben between them. Kate watched the two eldest carefully as they looked at their father. William's lower lip was trembling and his face reddened and she knew he was angry at what had been done to Joe. Grace's eyes were full of an unhappy concern that suddenly made her seem years older. Ben merely stared with mild curiosity, blinking his weak eyes.

William stepped forward and, trying to be grown up, held out a hand for his father to shake. But Joe ignored that and swept the boy into a hug which made William squeal with delight in a most un-grown up way. Next Grace was swung into Joe's arms and Kate saw the tears brimming in his eyes as he gazed at the little girl.

'We've got a big tea for you, Father,' Grace murmured soothingly and patted his head.

Ben trotted up now, craning to peer into Joe's face. For a moment Kate thought the boy was going to turn away, disappointed. She had tried to keep Joe alive in Ben's mind, every day showing him the picture she kept beside her bed, but this skeletal figure with the close-cropped hair looked nothing like the handsome, muscular fellow that Ben knew. Kate started forward, hoping to cover the awkwardness. So many men were coming home after the war to find that their youngest children did not recognise them.

Then Ben gave a beaming smile and pushed his head against Joe's knees.

'Tickle!' he bellowed.

Jane and Kate stared at each other, not understanding. But Joe did. With a choking laugh he hoisted Ben up.

'I've only got a few bristles,' he said, but he rubbed his face against the child's and Ben was helpless with mirth. Kate, remembering now how Joe had tickled his son each night with his once luxuriant moustache before settling him down to sleep, laughed and wept with relief.

Joe was looking with some concern at Ben's eyes.

'He's going to see a special doctor and get some spectacles,' William informed his father.

Ben smiled angelically. 'No I'm not,' he said in a tone which brooked no argument. Kate and Joe glanced at each other and laughed, uncertainly.

They swept indoors and Joe was pounced on by his sisters, waiting in the front hall, all smiles and tears, and then passed on to Sam and Tom to have his hand pumped up and down. Polly came hurrying out of the kitchen, tugging off her apron, and received a loving embrace and strict instructions to make her wedding plans as soon as possible.

The parlour door was flung open and Matthew stood there, an anxious Edith at his elbow. If the friends were shocked by each other's gaunt appearance they made no sign. Joe grasped Matthew by the shoulders and pulled him into his arms - a quick, fierce hug.

*****

Kate sat at one end of the parlour table and looked down its length to where Joe was munching his way through a slab of cake, arguing some point with Matthew, seated beside him. She thought Matthew looked nothing like an invalid - his face was animated and his eyes alight. He ate little, though, and Kate saw that Edith had transferred most of the cake on his plate to her own.

She found herself thinking that perhaps Matthew's health would improve now that Joe was at home - then pulled herself up with an effort. Hard, on a day like this, to face the truth which Michael Thomas had set out so clearly when Matthew was invalided out of the army not long before the war ground to a halt.

'The gas got to his lungs,' the doctor told Edith, Kate and Polly, standing here in the parlour while Matthew lay upstairs in a fever. 'With careful nursing he'll get over this present sickness but he's never going to return to full health.'

Kate and Polly were stunned but Edith faced the news with cold anger.

'You say he won't get better, Michael. Will he get worse?' she demanded.

'Yes. It will take him eventually. He already knows that.'

'Well, I don't!'

And when Matthew at last left his bed he was so much improved that it was impossible not to hope that Michael was wrong. Kate knew her sister clutched at every sign of improvement, encouraging Matthew to live as normal a life as possible. But there was no denying that walking the least distance or climbing stairs tired him out. Lady Janette had the running of the estate now, for Sir James was in a clinic being treated for shell shock, and she insisted the couple move to a small cottage on the edge of the estate where Matthew could have a bedroom downstairs. Edith pushed him everywhere in the chair, announcing that it was important for him to conserve his energy and that he would soon be able to get about on his own again. It was clear that Matthew drew strength from Edith's determination and before long he had begun on his book.

Kate poured hot water into the teapot and after letting it stand for a moment began to refill cups passed up the table. She had to ask twice if Sam and Flo wanted more tea, for they were whispering and giggling together like a couple of children rather than a long-married couple. And she wondered, with sudden apprehension, what it would be like when she and Joe were at last left alone together.

She caught Adam's eye and he smiled happily. Kate knew he loved family gatherings like this and she watched with satisfaction as he passed plates and cups, talking to Polly on one side and Nell on the other, making sure Jane had everything she wanted and sparing time for a consultation with William about the contents of a particular fruit pie. Kate was glad he got on so well with them all, for this meant that he and Polly would be regular visitors to Sussex after their marriage. Adam had not been given his old job back, but instead was offered the chance to train new teachers at one of the London colleges. So he and Polly would live in Stepney.

At the end of the table Joe was talking about the general election, asking Matthew and Edith about the Labour candidates. He gave a broad grin.

'And this time women will vote as well - that'll be a proud moment for you, Edie.'

Kate groaned inwardly. Though Edith had given up all her activities in London to look after Matthew she had lost none of her strong political views.

'Well, I will be proud, Joe,' said Edith firmly, 'even though I can't vote myself this time. The Suffrage Bill they pushed through only gives the vote to women over 30, you know, and I'll still be 29 on polling day.'

Joe's face was a picture of comic distress and Edith laughed out loud.

'The battle's not over yet then?' said Joe, and Edith shook her head.

'I don't think it ever will be, Joe. It's more than the vote we're after now.'

Kate could see that the delicate truce between her husband and sister might not last if Joe decided to follow up Edith's last remark. So she enquired loudly if anyone wanted more cake. But her tactics proved unnecessary, for Tom was getting to his feet.

Clearing his throat he called for silence and everyone turned to look at him. Kate had long since ceased to feel sorry for Tom with his empty sleeve tucked into his jacket pocket. He had proved himself a reliable and capable organiser and she felt Joe would need little urging to take him into partnership in Arthur's place.

Tom was making a halting but heartfelt speech welcoming Joe home and they all clapped and cheered when he had finished. He didn't sit down, though, but waited patiently for silence. Then he turned a deep red.

'And Nell and I have a home-coming present for you, Joe. In about six months you're going to be an Uncle again.'

Nell, blushing as deeply as her husband, tugged at his jacket in embarrassment. With a shout of delight Joe jumped out of his chair and rushed round to shake Tom's hand and kiss his sister. A babble of excited chatter broke out, with everyone wanting to congratulate the couple.

Kate watched her mother-in-law. Jane was, for once, speechless; staring at her eldest daughter with her mouth wide open in surprise. In the end it was Nell who had to go to her, hugging her mother and smiling and reassuring her that it was true. The black-bordered handkerchief came out again and for a while Jane wept happily, but her tears didn't last long. She was soon bustling about, getting Nell to a sofa where she was ordered to remain, with her feet up, for the rest of the day.

As she poured out glasses of sherry for the party, so that they could toast the expectant parents, Kate glanced surreptitiously at Jane's beaming face and wondered if, after all, her mother-in-law would leave off wearing black.

******

Joe had got into his nightshirt while Kate was calming the over-excited William and when she came into the bedroom he was sitting on the bed winding up his watch.

'Grace and Ben are asleep - tired out,' she reported, 'but William's still full of energy.'

Joe pulled a wry face. 'He's growing up fast - they all are. I've missed - ' But he did not complete his sentence, only shook his head as though putting away unpleasant thoughts.

He pressed his watch against his ear. Kate was delighted: this was what he had always done, night after night.

'It's as though you've never been away,' she told him and he smiled at her.

But as he swung his legs under the covers she saw how thin they were. His wrists looked almost too fragile to support the big hands and his nightshirt fell away from his neck, even though all the buttons were done up. She turned away quickly to hide her emotion and began to unpin her hair.

'That's some surprise Tom and Nell gave us,' laughed Joe. 'After all this time, too!'

She nodded. 'And I want to talk to you about Tom. He's done wonders for us. I'd have been lost without him.'

Now she turned to face him. 'I didn't tell you, Joe, but things got very difficult before Lady Janette set up the nursing home. We could have lost everything.'

He looked startled and she said quickly, 'But we came through - in part because Tom organised everything so well at the garage. He knows so many local people who need that sort of work done and I could leave him to run the place while I was at the stores.'

Joe was reassured. 'Then he must be a proper partner. And as soon as I get back to work we'll see about building up the motor car side of things again. We'll still need your help with the accounts, though - I'm sure of that.'

'And the shop?'

'It stays in your name, of course. Now, for goodness sake let's leave all this till tomorrow, woman!'

Her delight at this demonstration of his faith in her held her for a moment. But she saw the yearning in his face and began to quickly brush out her hair, suddenly nervous.

'Did I tell you about Sir James?' she asked hurriedly and he nodded.

'Poor devil - has there been any improvement?'

'Not that we've heard. Lady Janette's living in London now, to be near him, though she still comes to the Hall every so often. They're going to carry on using it as a nursing home.'

She saw his face darken and knew where his thoughts had led him.

'Matty looks bad,' he muttered. 'Is there really nothing to be done for him?'

'He's seeing other doctors,' she said. 'Adam drove him and Edie up to London only last week.'

'Yes, he told me.' Joe's voice shook. 'I don't know what I'll do if he dies, Kate. It was bad enough losing Art - but Matty... I couldn't - '

She put her arms about him until he was calm again.

'Did he tell you about his book, Joe? Edie says he works at it every day.'

Joe nodded. 'It sounds good. I'm going over to the cottage tomorrow to read some of the early chapters and I offered to help him - writing to his dictation if he gets tired.'

He gave a weak smile. 'He wants to put in what happened to me in prison - but I don't know...'

'It mustn't be forgotten, Joe. Remember what your mother said. What you've done and your reasons for doing it are of such importance.'

'And Matty wants to be involved in helping raise funds for conchies coming out of prison with no job to go back to - no families, some of them. Money's needed for medical care and to help get them back on their feet. I think it would do Matty good to be part of all that.'

'Edie will be pleased,' said Kate and he gave a reluctant laugh.

'When I first saw her today I thought she was much more subdued,' he said. 'But she's not really changed - and thank God for that. Matty needs all that spirit and determination of hers - better for him than being fussed and moped over.'

'You're right, of course, but it's so difficult for her; she worries desperately about him but tries not to show it.'

'We'll help her all we can,' he said firmly.

He stroked Kate's hair, lifting it in his hands, then drew her into his arms.

But as she slid down into bed beside him he looked away and seemed unsure of himself. Then he gave a deep sigh.

'Oh well - better let you see the worst, I suppose,' he muttered and undoing the buttons at his neck pulled his nightshirt up and over his head.

She managed to hold down a gasp of horror at the sight of his pale, wasted body. His arms would never again be rounded and muscular, his chest broad. Michael Thomas had said he would grow strong again but it would be a skinny, wiry strength. The golden good looks had gone for ever.

She swallowed hard, knowing sympathy would only make him feel worse.

'We'll have to keep you in the hallstand,' she said briskly, 'with the rest of the walking sticks.'

His shoulders began to shake and she wondered in panic if she had gone too far, but then realised he was laughing. She pulled him down into the pillows and kissed his face, running her mouth tenderly over the sunken cheeks as he lay back, relaxed at last.

'I've been dead without you, Kate,' he whispered. 'Make me come alive again.'

******

Matthew drew a long, rasping sigh. 'That was so lovely,' he murmured. Edith gazed down into the haggard face which seemed even more drawn in the lamplight and murmured agreement, trying not to let her concern for him too quickly replace the tenderness between them.

When they first started making love again she had been desperately frightened, sure that his lungs could not withstand the coughing which often racked him afterwards. But when she begged him not to touch her he had wept with a violence that frightened her even more.

'I might as well be dead, Edie, if I have to lie beside you night after night and not love you. We're so close again.'

She had relented at once. It was true that in spite of the moods of depression which sometimes gripped him and her own sense of helpless frustration they were sharing greater closeness and warmth than ever before. So they had learned how to make love carefully and still bring each other pleasure.

'I'm glad the party didn't tire you,' she said and he laughed.

'Of course not. It's so good to have Joe back with us. And what about Tom and Nell - who would have guessed after all this time! I wonder how Nell managed it?'

Edith raised her head and stared at him. 'Matthew Hersey, what are you suggesting?' And they smirked mischievously at each other.

Matthew took hold of her hand.

'I couldn't help feeling envious of them, though,' he said, more soberly.

'Of Tom and Nell?'

'Of them having a child. And I can't help wishing... It wouldn't be right, though.'

'Not right for us to have a child, you mean?' she breathed. 'But why shouldn't we, Matty?'

He did not answer straight away, but pulled himself up and, leaning over, adjusted the lamp beside the bed so that the flame burned bright again.

'Yes - it would be... well, a commitment to the future - to life. Does that sound foolish, Edie?'

'No, no! You're right. We'd be showing our faith in the future.'

But she had chosen the wrong words. His eyes clouded over.

'Oh... it would be irresponsible. A child should have two parents.'

'It would have two - why are you so pessimistic, Matty? When you were brought home the army doctors said you were dying, but you proved them wrong - '

'Ah, that was all Jane Weaver's doing - and yours of course,' he put in with a wry smile.

'Well, whoever it was you didn't die. And the last time he examined you Michael Thomas was surprised at how much better you are now, so you've proved him wrong too. Are you planning to lie around playing the invalid for the rest of your days and probably outlive us all?'

She watched him from the corner of her eye, trying to gauge the effect of her words. He rubbed his chin, thoughtfully.

'Do you want a child, Edie?'

He was wavering: she knew it.

'Of course I do.'

Once again she feared she had overdone her enthusiasm, for it seemed to raise new doubts.

'You don't think it would be so very reckless of us?'

'I think it would be perfectly splendid of us!' And she laughed, knowing that she had won him over.

'We must get married, then,' he said and added with a chuckle, 'We could make it a double wedding with Adam and Polly. You and your mother could give each other away. Oh no, I forgot, we're already Mr and Mrs Hersey as far as the locals are concerned. A quiet visit to London, then? Will tomorrow suit you?'

Edith smiled but a shiver of superstition caught her out. 'Let's wait until I'm pregnant,' she murmured.

He was tired all of a sudden and so they put out the lamp and settled down for sleep. As usual she stayed alert until his ragged breathing grew softer and only when she was sure that he slept did she allow herself to relax. She was just dozing off when Matthew rolled over in his sleep and caught his breath and coughed. Edith, wide awake at once, turned towards him, willing him to fall silent again. But another cough followed and another and in seconds he was struggling to sit up, hands clawing at his throat as he gasped and choked.

She was out of bed immediately, lighting the lamp, pulling him upright, undoing pyjama buttons, adjusting his pillows so that he was properly supported. After so many times, the routine had become efficient, almost automatic. But as she sat with one arm around him, holding a basin, she felt desolate and defeated.

The coughing fit left him drained and they spoke little as she sponged his face and chest and made him comfortable again. Leaving a low light burning she went through into the kitchen to wash out the bowl and refill his water jug, in case there should be another attack tonight.

Thinking of the hopelessness in his eyes as he fell back against the pillows she began, almost frantically, to calculate how soon she would be likely to conceive. Matthew must not be allowed to give up the fight for his own survival.

******

Polly heard the tapping at the door and lifted her head from the pillow to look at the clock by her bed. She saw that it was gone eight and sat up guiltily.

'Come in,' she called and Grace tiptoed into the room, smiling excitedly.

'Grandma, it's your wedding day!'

'So it is. And you are my bridesmaid come to tell me to haste to the wedding!'

Grace giggled and took a flying leap onto the bed. She was still in her nightdress but had lost her slippers somewhere and her feet were icy. Polly made her tuck down deep under the blankets.

'Mother is making your breakfast and you're to stay here until she brings it on a tray,' said Grace importantly. 'Then she's going to get me dressed and I'm to wait in the drawing room until it's time to go to church.'

'Poor Grace,' murmured Polly. 'I'll come and wait with you if you like.'

'Oh, you mustn't, Grandma. You have to do your hair and put on your dress and make yourself beautiful. That will take a long time.'

Polly held down a laugh. Making herself beautiful certainly would take a long time, she thought - longer than the few hours left before she must go to church. Luckily Adam didn't seem to mind, or even notice, that his bride-to-be was on the plain side.

She shut her eyes again, listening vaguely to Grace chattering about

311

the dresses that she and Dolly would wear as bridesmaids. She wished all the fuss and bother was over, but she had been wishing that for months. She and Adam had hoped for a small, quiet wedding, but the minute they went to see the vicar to arrange for their marriage in the village church they knew it would turn out otherwise.

Instead of a simple exchange of vows in the presence of a handful of people they found themselves agreeing to hymns and the choir and the organist playing and the church bells being rung. After that it seemed churlish not to ask Grace and Dolly to be bridesmaids. In fact Adam was charmed by the idea.

'I draw the line there, though,' he said to Polly with a grin. 'If you let them dress Ben up in a satin suit to carry your train he'll completely steal our thunder.'

'I'm not wearing a train,' Polly had snapped and he was immediately contrite.

'Is all the fuss getting you down, dear? We can run off to Gretna if you like.'

Kate came in with Polly's breakfast tray and ordered Grace out of the bed.

'You need to get washed and brush your hair,' she said briskly and Polly thought, with amusement, that she could have been addressing either of them. Kate bent and kissed her mother's cheek.

'Take your time getting ready, dear. I'll come up and help you with the dress if you like.'

Polly thought suddenly how much she would miss life at Western House. It was much busier after Joe's return and she had found herself thinking regretfully of the times she had spent with her daughters when all the menfolk were absent. The last occasion they had been together in such a close yet easy way was before Christmas. Kate and Polly had gone to register their votes and even though Edith was not yet eligible she had accompanied them. They dressed in their best to mark the occasion and when they got back Kate had cooked them a splendid meal and served it in the parlour with her best crockery and silverware. Edith had produced a bottle of champagne and they all toasted the Suffragettes and Mrs Garrett Fawcett and got pleasantly tipsy and were still sitting over the remains of the meal when Joe brought the children home from his mother's.

Now Polly looked at Kate anxiously. 'Oh please, yes - do come and help me dress.'

Kate smiled gently. 'Everything's under control, Mother - don't worry. Joe is polishing his shoes for the umpteenth time. William is instructing Ben at great length on the kind of behaviour expected of a grandson at a wedding. Oh yes, and Edie's here and says that she left Adam at the cottage in a state of complete panic.'

This last piece of news had a wonderfully calming effect.

'Oh, men...' Polly sniffed. Then she added quickly. 'What about Matthew?'

'Nothing to worry about there. Edie says he's looking better today than he has done for months and has Adam well in hand.'

Polly surprised herself by eating all the breakfast Kate had brought her. As she spread marmalade on her toast she thought of Adam and hoped that he wouldn't be too nervous to eat anything. Since the war he had suffered from poor digestion and it was best that he didn't miss the first meal of the day.

She pushed the tray aside, remembering their brief, hurried discussion last night, wishing she had not spoken out so bluntly. She could still see the pained look on Adam's face as he said anxiously, 'Do you really think you might need somewhere to run away to when we're married?'

She had reassured him and they parted on happy terms. All the same she knew they would have to talk about her house again and she wished they had got the matter sorted out before the wedding.

William appeared with a jug of hot water for his grandmother. Ben followed his brother into the room like a shadow and watched carefully as William poured the water into the china hand basin.

'Grandma...' William murmured and she could tell it was going to be one of his more awkward questions. 'When you die and when Uncle Adam dies and you both go to heaven, won't it feel strange having two husbands, because Grandfather will be there too, won't he?'

She got Ben to fetch her wrap and fussed over putting it on to give herself time to compose a suitable answer, but in the end found herself responding cravenly, 'I don't think it's very nice to talk about people dying when they're just getting married, do you?'

He considered this seriously, while hopping about the room on one leg, with Ben following.

'I suppose not,' said William, 'but don't you have to be prepared for these things?'

Ben fell over and William hurried to pick him up.

'Mother isn't going to dress him in his best clothes until the very last,' he told Polly. 'She says he'll only get filthy.'

He and Polly exchanged grave looks. Ben did, indeed, have the extraordinary ability to locate dirt in the cleanest-seeming places and transfer it, at speed, to his own person.

'I don't like best clothes,' said Ben firmly. Polly gazed down at her youngest grandson's mop of fair, almost white curls, his round pink face and the blue eyes staring myopically at her. She felt her heart melt. He was the most stubborn of the three and had quite a temper sometimes, but with his angelic looks and warm smiles he ruled the house and all loved him. William was more sensitive and Polly felt he would grow into a most interesting man. But Ben would be the heartbreaker.

'We went up to the smithy yesterday, Grandma,' said William eagerly. 'Uncle Tom let us work the bellows. Ben wants to be a blacksmith when he grows up.'

'And you,' Ben urged his brother.

'No, I'm going to be a concert pianist,' said William casually, inspecting a scab on his knee. 'Miss Baker thinks I have genius.'

'And me!' said Ben forcefully.

'He wants to learn the piano,' William confided in Polly. 'But he couldn't be a concert pianist and a blacksmith, could he Grandma?'

Ben's face took on the determined look Polly knew only too well. To prevent any possible outburst she pushed back the covers and got out of bed.

'Away with you both so that I can get washed and dressed, or we'll all be late.'

William's face creased into a frown. 'Oh yes - we can't start the wedding without you!'

The idea amused him hugely and he chuckled. Ben joined in and they rushed out of the room hand in hand, yelling loudly.

Polly was wondering whether a careful application of face powder might not come amiss when she heard the sound of a motor car horn outside and went to the window. Clara was descending from her vehicle, a vision in strawberry silk with a matching hat. Polly eyed her wedding dress hanging on the wardrobe door and immediately felt that it looked drab and insipid. And it was too late to find anything else!

When Kate came in a short while later she found her mother desperately trying to re-arrange her hair style. 'I look as old as Mrs Methuselah!'

'Don't be silly, dear.' Kate took the brush and comb from her mother's trembling hands and proceeded to brush the offending hair with long, calming strokes.

'Clara's here,' she murmured. 'All tricked out in some sort of pink. She's going to drive me and Edie and the children to church, which will make William's day for him. Now, I think you should keep your hair the way you always have it. It suits you like that and if you try a different style you'll only worry about it coming down during the service.'

Edith came in, exquisite in a pale blue suit, totally unselfconscious about her newly bobbed hair. Polly had been rather shocked at the severity of the cut, though she had to agree with Kate that it suited Edith. Matthew approved, of course, and Edith didn't seem to care for any other opinion.

'Clara is annoying,' Edith grumbled, sitting herself on the bed. 'I've been trying to talk to her about the plans for combining the relief coming in for COs from different organisations. Ramsay MacDonald's agreed to be one of the chairmen of a Joint Board - it's a big step forward. But she's too busy playing with Ben.' Then Edith's mood changed. 'Are you ready for the dress, Mother? I can't wait to see what it looks like on!'

For the next few minutes they concentrated on the intricate process of getting Polly into the dress and adjusting skirt and bodice, sleeves and cuffs. At last Kate and Edith stood back and Polly was left alone before the full-length mirror. She was pleased with what she saw. The dress, in soft, champagne-coloured silk trimmed with matching lace, flattered her figure with its simple cut.

She looked at her daughters who were beaming with pride and suddenly felt herself grow cold.

'Do you think I'm doing the right thing?'

She saw them look at each other, startled and concerned. Edith asked gently what she meant and Polly confessed that she wasn't sure.

'Adam isn't at all like Father,' said Edith, reassuringly and Polly pulled crossly at one of her cuffs.

'When I married your father he wasn't like that either!' she snapped out, muddled, and wasn't surprised to see Edith trying to suppress a smile.

Kate said: 'If you have any doubts, Mother, you must call the wedding off - even if it just means postponing it.'

Edith added her support. 'Kate's right, Mother. We can send everyone away, if that's what you want. It would be ridiculous to go on with this just because everyone's expecting a wedding.'

Polly laughed and felt her panic ebbing away. 'Oh, you are dear girls. How many daughters would be so understanding when their mother behaves so foolishly?'

She sat down at the dressing table. 'I don't really want to call it off, you know, but there's just something bothering me.'

Kate and Edith settled themselves side by side on the bed, as though there was all the time in the world, and with this encouragement Polly told them what was worrying her.

'You see, Adam has been expecting me to sell the house in Hove.'

Edith opened her mouth to protest but Kate nudged her and she kept silent.

Polly explained that she had agreed with Adam at first - it seemed the practical thing to do. But over the past week or so her thoughts on the matter had changed. She had gone down to the house to see that repairs had been done after Mrs Heath moved out and had found herself getting more and more upset as she walked from room to room.

'I know I didn't live there for long but buying it, turning it into a home, that was the first thing I've ever done for myself. It means more to me than I guessed.'

'So you want to keep it,' said Kate.

'I tried to explain why to Adam last night, but I think he believes I want it as somewhere to run back to if - well - if there are any differences between us in future.'

'You must keep it, Mother,' said Edith firmly. 'Why shouldn't you have a measure of independence? Look what having the shop has meant to Kate. If more married women - '

'Yes dear,' Polly interrupted gently, 'but Adam doesn't quite see it like that and I can understand his feelings, especially as I'm not really sure why I feel the need to hold on to the place.'

Edith shrugged. 'I advise you to stick to your decision, Mother. Adam will come round.'

Polly looked at Kate, who smiled. 'I think that in a few months' time you'll have sold the house without a second thought, wondering why on earth you were so bothered about it.'

She saw her mother's puzzled look and her smile broadened. 'I mean that you'll be so happy, dear, that you won't need what the house represents any more.' She slid off the bed. 'In the meantime tell Adam you want to keep it so you'll both be able to have a holiday by the sea whenever you get tired of London.'

Polly drew a deep breath, shedding her remaining fears as she did so. Really she had been very silly to make such a fuss. As her daughters arranged her hat and veil she knew that Kate was right.

'Why did you say that to Mother?' Edith demanded in a low voice as she and Kate made their way downstairs. 'You've given her a nice cosy way out.'

'And you'd have her make a stand against convention?' Kate stopped on the landing outside the bathroom door. The cat had made herself comfortable on a discarded pair of Ben's trousers but Kate shooed her away. She picked up the trousers, examining them carefully.

'Mother's no fool, Edie,' she murmured. 'She understands what the house symbolises. But I don't think she's really ready to make the sort of stand you have in mind - certainly not an hour before her wedding!'

Edith gave a reluctant shrug. 'Well, I hope she doesn't sell. She may never need to run away to it but she'll always know the house is there.' She laughed suddenly. 'I think you were just afraid she'd cry off and leave us eating your wedding breakfast for the next six weeks!'

Kate smiled absently. 'I'm sure Ben put these trousers on this morning and I haven't changed him yet. He must be running around in his drawers!'

They looked at each other and laughed. Then Edith murmured tentatively, 'Have you ever found yourself thinking back to when it was just you and me and Mother here, and wishing we could have that time over again?'

'Oh, yes. You too?' Kate's voice was eager with relief. 'After Joe had only been back a week or so I was having to hold down my temper because he seemed to be forever contradicting what I was telling the children to do, or questioning the way I run the house. Even now I sometimes wish I was on my own again. That's awful.'

Edith nodded vehemently. 'I suppose it takes time to get used to - to being a couple - like before.'

They hovered for a moment on the landing then moved down together just as Joe's voice from the kitchen was raised in a bewildered bellow - 'Ben, you scallywag, what are you doing without any trousers on?'

******

By the time Polly went downstairs the main party had left for church in Clara's car. Joe appeared in the parlour carrying two small glasses of sherry and although Polly felt in no need of stimulation she kept her patently nervous son-in-law company. She thought he cut a good-looking figure in his black suit and told him so.

'Well, that's a relief,' Joe smiled. 'It's one of Matty's you know - I'd not have been able to get into it a few years back but it fits me perfectly now.'

'You're gradually putting on weight,' said Polly in an encouraging tone. She did not add that Matthew was gradually losing his but the thought hung between them for Joe said carefully, 'He'll be all right today. Edith's had his chair taken up to the church and tucked out of sight in the Lady Chapel. If Matty looks at all tired Sam will bring it in so he can sit down.'

Polly was glad. There was no reason why Adam's best man shouldn't do his part from a wheeled chair but Matthew had been quite determined to stand by his former headmaster's side throughout the service.

She saw the sadness in Joe's eyes and pressed his hand.

'I was thinking of dear old Art, too,' he told her. 'He loved singing for weddings: he'd have given you such an anthem.'

'He had a fine voice,' she agreed. 'Oh, I've just remembered that Jane tells me there's talk of having a memorial for the village, with the names of all

317

those we lost inscribed on it.'

'Yes - all round the country I've heard,' said Joe sharply. 'Easy to do that and then forget why it's there. Look at the so-called peace conference in France - more like a division of spoils of war if you ask me. We need proper, active commitment to a peaceful future - backing up the League of Nations.'

'I agree with you, Joe. But you surely don't think anyone is ever going to forget this war?'

There was a small crowd waiting outside the church to see her arrival and Polly saw one or two heads laid together and comments passed but she felt no embarrassment. Besides, some of the chatter would be about Joe. Local people had begun to realise what he had been through in prison and though few talked to him directly about the stand he had taken it was rare these days for anyone to pass him in the street without a greeting and a genuinely solicitous enquiry after his health.

Grace and Dolly, demure in their pink dresses, took their places behind Polly and Joe and they all paced slowly down the aisle. Polly had to strain to see the two waiting at the altar - she had determined she would not wear her glasses today of all days - but as she got nearer she recognised Adam's familiar figure and Matthew, rather pale but standing squarely at his side and smiling with no touch of strain upon his face.

She wondered if Adam was still nervous. He turned towards her as she came up and their eyes met warmly. It was rather like coming across an old friend in somewhat unusual circumstances, she thought, and she took her place beside him, feeling happy and at ease as the organ music faded.

'You look lovely,' he whispered. 'I'm relieved you don't favour strawberry.'

Polly, who had seen Clara all aglow among the congregation even without her spectacles, smothered a laugh and as the vicar moved forward he eyed bride and groom repressively.

The wedding breakfast was thoroughly enjoyed by the guests and the cake greeted with gasps of delight, and Polly was very pleased on Kate's behalf. There was some delay over the cutting of the cake, for Flo had recently given Sam a box camera and he insisted on taking a photograph. But at last the ceremony was over and Polly and Adam were able to relax and chat with their guests. They were not going on a honeymoon but spending a few days at Elm Square while Clara visited the Grahams, so there was no need for the newly-weds to leave until late afternoon. So they joined in the dancing and helped entertain the children, for all the world as though it was just another family party with a few extra guests.

'I wish we were staying,' murmured Polly as they drove away and she leaned out of the window, waving until the cheerful crowd at the front door was lost to view.

Adam smiled and she realised she might have been tactless.

'I mean - '

'I know exactly what you mean, my dear.' And he took her hand and raised it briefly to his lips.

She remembered the gesture and his words some hours later when she was sitting before the bedroom mirror at Elm Square, letting Alice unbutton her dress. Would he be so understanding now if she told him, when he came upstairs, that she was really very tired and would just like to go to sleep? She stared blankly at her reflection. And in any case was that true?

Though they arrived in London quite late they had sat in the drawing room for a while, talking over the events of the day. They shared some anxiety about Matthew. He had begun coughing towards the end of the service and although he overcame the spasm quickly he made no protest when Edith insisted he be wheeled out of church instead of walking.

'He was cheerful enough at Western House, though,' said Adam, optimistically.

'I just wish he'd eat more.' Then Polly smiled. 'Perhaps Jane should supervise his meals.'

'Good Lord, yes.' They recalled the way Jane had fussed over Nell, vying with Tom to force tit-bits on the blooming mother-to-be.

'That child, when it's born, will be spoilt beyond anything,' Adam warned.

'Unlike my grandchildren, of course! Oh, Adam, I must tell you what William came out with this morning. He's very concerned about what happens when we die...'

They talked for a while longer then Polly rose, saying she would go up.

'I'll be with you soon,' he murmured and at the door he drew her into his arms and kissed her lovingly.

She realised now that she was afraid, and the thought was so bizarre that she laughed out loud and Alice gave her an odd look. Polly sent her away, saying she could manage by herself now, and when she was alone undressed in a hurry and picked up the new nightdress which had been laid out for her on the bed. It looked flimsy and foolish, quite unlike her normal night attire and when she put it on her heart sank. She felt like an old woman pretending to be young. Twice as ridiculous as Clara in her strawberry silk.

She heard Adam go into the dressing room next door and she scrambled into bed, pulling the covers up to her neck. It was horrible, after such a lovely, happy day, to suddenly feel so wrong and uncertain and out of place. She loved him and wanted them to be lovers. So why was she afraid?

319

But she knew the answer. Her only sexual experiences had been that first degrading and painful assault by Kate's father and then Arnold's hurried and unsatisfying embraces.

She sat up straight, aware that there was not a little self-pity mingled with her fear. Working herself into a state would not help in the least. She got up, found her handbag, extracted her spectacles and a book and then settled herself once more against the pillows.

'*Our Mutual Friend* - that's one of my favourites.'

She had been too engrossed to hear him come in and now she looked up, blushing fiercely. Adam stood beside the bed, wrapped up comfortably in a dressing gown that had seen better days. She snatched off the glasses and tossed the book on to the floor. He watched her uncertainly, as though waiting for some sign. Polly suddenly felt desperate, wishing she was a hundred miles away.

'I like your dressing gown,' she blurted out. 'I wish I'd been sensible and brought something comfortable with me, instead of this.' And she tweaked sullenly at the lacy frills cascading down her bosom.

'Oh, I was just thinking how very attractive that looks,' he murmured. 'Besides, I haven't been able to resist cutting a dash myself.' And he undid the dressing gown to reveal a pair of crisp, new pyjamas. 'Sam tells me these are all the rage.'

They were smiling at each other now and the smiles soon turned to laughter. Adam climbed into bed, put an arm about her and she leaned contentedly against his shoulder.

'About the house in Hove,' she said suddenly. 'I will sell it, but - '

He pressed a finger against her lips.

'I've been unreasonable about that and I'm sorry,' he said firmly. 'You must do with it as you wish.'

'Well, I was thinking that when Edie is left on her own she may want it. If not I'll sell it and make some of the money over to her.'

'That's an excellent plan - but would she take up either offer?'

Polly gave a wry smile. 'How well you know her! Perhaps she won't but at least the money will be there.'

Adam said thoughtfully, 'I wondered whether - with Matthew ill - well, I thought they might marry at last.'

'I hoped so too and I've spoken to Edie about it but she got quite angry with me. She simply won't accept that he's going to die, Adam.'

Then she thought of the way Edith and Kate had supported her that day and her heart lifted again, warmed by the memory and she turned to Adam and felt his arms tighten about her. She wondered how she could ever have felt afraid. They loved each other and would show each other how best to express that love with their bodies. He bent to kiss her and the frills got in the way, but only for a moment.

******

Edith wandered into the kitchen glancing quickly through the letters in her hand. They were all for Matthew and she put them down on the table and turned her attention to making herself some breakfast.

She knew he wouldn't wake for another hour or so. He had worked late last night, finishing the final chapter of his book, the chapter which had taken so much trouble and required so much rewriting. Edith had been taking down his dictation and after what seemed an unusually long pause she looked up questioningly to find Matthew smiling at her, decidedly smug.

'That's all,' he exclaimed, 'save for writing END at the bottom.'

She read over the last paragraph and realised it was true. With a flourish she finished off the work then jumped up and went to kiss him.

'Matty, that's wonderful! I'm so proud of you.'

He was proud, too, she could see that, even though he said he wished he had time to write it all over again. She dismissed this as nonsense and poured them a small glass of brandy each to celebrate the completion of his work.

The drink had proved a mistake for it set off a fit of coughing which left him so weak that she had difficulty getting him out of the chair and into bed. He seemed feverish and she wanted to fetch Michael Thomas but after a while Matthew's temperature dropped a little and he grew calmer.

'It's the excitement and the drink,' he croaked. 'I don't need the doctor to tell me that.'

She had sat beside him until he was asleep and then went back to the table where she had been working and gathered up the sheets of paper. She pinned them together and put them with all the others piled, chapter by chapter, on the dresser; each pile held down by a large book.

The handwriting varied throughout the manuscript, sometimes from page to page. Matthew had soon found it too tiring to write and so she and Joe had taken turns, with Kate occasionally putting in an hour or so, Polly and Adam helping when they came to visit and even William laboriously copying out corrections.

It had started as an autobiography, but Matthew soon abandoned that and turned it into a novel which, he said, gave him greater scope.

'Then you must write a preface saying it's based on your own experiences,' Edith had urged him. 'It will carry so much more weight as an anti-war novel if people know it was written by a serving officer.'

And now it was finished and they would look for a publisher. Her mind turning over suitable phrases for a letter of introduction Edith sat down

321

at the table to tea and toast.

When Matthew woke and she set his breakfast tray on his lap she announced that there was still much to be done to get the book published.

'Mind you, opinions about the war are changing,' she said, perching on the side of the bed. 'Look at the way the War Office is trying to exonerate itself from blame over the treatment of COs. They're saying they never wanted those men called up in the first place, let alone punished. Next thing you know they'll be blaming the conchies for putting themselves in prison.'

Matthew pulled a wry face. 'Even so I think it may be difficult finding a publisher. And it doesn't really matter. The people I love can read it, now that it's all down on paper. Having it published before I die would be a bonus, but I'll not be disappointed if it doesn't happen.'

Edith gritted her teeth. She had been afraid that once this task was completed he might start letting go.

'There are lots of letters for you, as usual,' she said eagerly and brought them to him. 'You read them through while I wash up and then I'll help you to dress.'

'No... sit down a moment, Edith. I want to talk to you. We must get a solicitor out here - it's time I made a proper will. That thing I scribbled out before I went to France probably isn't even legal.' He sighed. 'God knows, there won't be a lot to leave you, though: we've gone through all our savings.'

She sensed he was on the verge of a depression and got ready to ward it off, saying in a deliberately glib tone: 'Good heavens, we're not poverty-stricken yet!'

'Oh, don't treat me like an idiot, Edie. Do you think I don't know we're living on your family's charity - money from your mother and Adam?'

She flinched at his bitter tone, but anger was better than self-pity.

'And your aristocratic relatives' largesse,' she snapped back. 'Janette sends us something regularly, in James's name. Poor soul, he'll never be able to handle his own affairs again.'

'Well, at least I can still do that - so I want to see a solicitor as soon as possible!'

She bowed her head, overwhelmed by unhappiness and he softened at once.

'It's only sensible to do it now,' he murmured. 'I worry so much about how you're going to manage - especially if there's a child to care for.'

His voice was hopeful and she hated herself for having to dash that. As she shook her head miserably he reached for her hand.

'But there will be,' she said hurriedly and moved away, tidying the room briskly, aware that his eyes were upon her. The tension between them was unpleasant and when they heard knocking on the front door she felt relieved.

Michael Thomas was on the doorstep. 'I'm on my way home from Smithy's - Mrs Weaver insisted I call in and tell you that Nell has had her baby. A boy - they're calling him Arthur. He and Nell are fine. The only problem with the labour was keeping Mrs Weaver from taking over the whole affair.'

They laughed, then Edith called out the news to Matthew, at the same time drawing the doctor indoors.

'He had a bad turn last night,' she whispered. 'Could you just have a look at him - please?'

When Michael came out of the bedroom he closed the door firmly behind him.

'Let your husband make his will, Edith,' he said crisply and she drew a sharp breath.

'His health is deteriorating,' the doctor added more gently. 'It will put his mind at rest if he can do this.'

'It seems so... final. As though he's giving up.'

He watched her with appraising eyes and she felt disconcerted. 'You'd not give up, would you?' he murmured. 'You'd defy death to the very end.'

'I might have done once. Now I think perhaps I'd try to bargain.'

Michael Thomas smiled. 'Well, let Matthew put things in order. He's feeling low now the book is finished but he'll come round again. He's involved in helping the COs, so make sure he keeps that up. And I hear Joe is standing for the parish council again - perhaps that will give Matthew a new interest. There may be objections because Joe's been in prison and we need to fight those.'

She agreed and the doctor made ready to leave.

'Michael - I need your help. The name of a specialist.'

His good humour vanished. 'Not again, Edith. I won't have you dragging your husband round to see doctors who simply can't do anything more for him!'

'It's not for Matty: it's for me.'

After the doctor had gone she went back into the bedroom and found Matthew getting up.

'Good news about the new baby,' he said. 'We must buy a little gift, Edie. What do you think would be suitable?'

'I'll look for something when I'm in Brighton today.'

'Brighton? Surely you could get something at Weavers?'

She kept her voice even. 'There are some other things I need - and I thought I'd call in on Father's solicitor. You won't mind him handling the

323

will?'

'No, of course not.' He shot her a grateful glance. 'Well, I'd better get on. You said there were some letters?'

She found those for him first then fetched his clothes. He was poring over a page of spidery writing as she laid out his shirt and trousers.

'My God, Edie, this fellow here has been trying for months to get a job and still no-one will employ him because he was jailed as a conchie. On top of that his wife and children are sick. We must get this to the NCF at once.'

'Let Joe deal with that,' she objected. 'You ought to work on the manuscript first - '

'Don't fuss so,' he snapped. 'I'm not yet too feeble to organise my work.' And he stared belligerently at her, obviously wondering why she was laughing.

******

In the sharp Winter morning Wolstonbury stood out clearly. The vivid light played tricks on the eyes so that Kate felt that if she reached out a hand she could rest it on the hilltop.

She would not have lowered her eyes, all the time the vicar was intoning the sad, familiar words, but William began to cry again and she held him against her, bending down to give him her handkerchief. Joe took the boy's hand, his own head bent, weeping quietly.

It seemed to Kate that her vision was filled now with the coffin resting beside that dark hole. A great shudder passed through her and she tried to comfort herself with the thought that Matthew would be glad to be buried here, behind the village church, with Wolstonbury in the distance. It was a crowded graveyard now: the war had seen to that, and the parish council would have to buy another piece of land for future use. But Matthew would not mind being close to Arthur and the Bartley boys and so many others. She shook herself angrily, crushing down such maudlin thoughts. Matthew was not here.

On the other side of the grave Kate caught her mother's glance, bleak but dry-eyed as she grasped Adam's arm, then her gaze travelled reluctantly round to where Edith stood. No tears there, either. Edith had an arm around a sobbing Flo.

Indeed Edith seemed not to have wept at all. She had been sorrowful but perfectly calm ever since she stepped into the kitchen at Western House a week ago, while Kate was yawning and preparing breakfast.

'Matty died in the night,' she said. 'I've just been down to the doctor's and he's going back to the cottage. He said he'd sort out what needs to be done.'

Kate's legs buckled and she sat down quickly. She gazed at Edith in horror.

'He died in the night? But why have you left it until now - '

'There was nothing to be done for him,' said Edith gently, as though explaining to a child. 'I sat by him until it was light. Just thinking... remembering...'

'I wish you'd come to me,' whispered Kate.

Edith knelt by her chair. 'I have now.'

They held each other tight, but only for a moment. The children could be heard on the stairs, clattering down for their breakfast.

'What shall I say to them?' gasped Kate, her mind numb with misery.

'I'll talk to them, if you like. You go up and tell Joe.'

Once again Kate looked anxiously at her husband. He had checked his tears now and was gazing out across the Downs as she had done. His initial response to Matthew's death had frightened her dreadfully - she thought he would sink completely into a black despair and she had not known how to prevent that. It was Polly who had brought him back to his senses.

'Joe, everything's at sixes and sevens,' she groaned. 'We need to make arrangements for Matty's funeral but there's so much to do. Please, you must help us.'

He had taken charge at once, seeing the undertaker and consulting with the vicar and Kate's fears for him diminished.

'Keep him busy,' her mother advised. 'I'm trying to do the same with Adam.'

In the end Joe and Adam had shared responsibility for the funeral arrangements and as a result everything went smoothly. Although the village church was crowded no-one was uncomfortable; all the floral tributes were displayed to advantage; the hymns were suitable, not too long or depressing; the vicar's address was brief and uplifting. And when Sir James Gale, sitting vacant-eyed in his pew throughout the service, set up a loud whimpering as the coffin was carried out there was someone on hand to help Lady Janette get her husband away through the vestry.

The vicar's voice ceased and Kate realised the coffin was about to be lowered into the grave. Her son gave her an agonised look and with a nod to Joe Kate led the boy away, out of the churchyard. Perhaps it had been a mistake to let him come but he stubbornly refused to go to Smithy's Cottage with Grace, Ben and Dolly.

As they walked up the High Street towards Western House William wiped his eyes. 'There were lots of people in the church,' he said at last. 'Everyone liked Uncle Matty, didn't they?'

'Oh yes.'

She had felt only relief these past few nights when Joe left their bed to pace out his grief in the living room. It had meant she could lie alone in the dark, letting memories of Matthew tear at her. She had thought that time long forgotten. The pain told a different story.

'Why are people coming to eat with us?' William asked truculently. 'It's like a wedding!'

'Only family are coming and Aunty Clara: it's traditional, William. Besides, it's a cold day so they'll want something warm inside them after being in the churchyard.'

'Why has Aunty Clara got all those big black feathers on her hat?' asked William, momentarily diverted. Kate answered absently and William returned to his original complaint.

'Aunty Nell and Grandma Weaver haven't been in the churchyard and they're coming to dinner.'

'Do you want me to shut them in the coal shed while we're eating?'

He gave a giggle and mother and son smiled at each other lovingly.

'I wouldn't mind you shutting Arthur in the coal shed,' said William, saucily. 'Grandma Weaver makes such a fuss of him and he's so fat and he dribbles.'

'You used to say nasty things like that about Ben. Do you remember?'

But he denied that flatly and when he was reunited with his brother a little while later he made a great fuss of him.

All the younger children were brought back from Jane's so that they could join in what was, after all, a family meal. They were subdued, of course, even a little frightened at seeing all their elders in black. But after a while their unquenchable spirits set them chattering and laughing and somehow this gave a lead to the grown-ups who began to talk more easily, even to smile. Kate was glad, knowing Matthew would have been pleased. But she noticed that William wore a disapproving look and when the talk turned to Christmas, not far away, he hurriedly excused himself from the table.

'I expect he's going to cry about Uncle Matty,' Ben whispered to his mother, then added reassuringly: 'It's all right. I've had my cry.'

******

Kate went into the kitchen. Edith was at the scullery sink, one of Kate's big aprons tied over her black dress and her sleeves rolled up, energetically making a great deal of froth as she tackled the washing up. Biting back an exclamation of annoyance at such extravagant use of good soap Kate said evenly, 'Don't bother with that, Edie - we can do it later.'

Edith gave her sister a wry smile. 'I need something to keep me occupied. If you can trust me with your best china we may as well get it done

326

now.'

With a nod Kate reached for a drying-up cloth and for a moment or two the sisters worked in silence. Then Edith said, slowly, 'You know, the worst thing about today is that I keep thinking 'Oh, I must tell Matty that', or, 'He'll be so amused when I tell him about Clara's hat'; and then I suddenly realise that he's not here to tell any more. It's horrible.'

'Joe said something like that yesterday,' Kate sighed, carefully wiping suds off the only plate Ben would use and laying it tenderly on the scullery table. The pattern of mice around the rim danced merrily as her eyes filled.

'Where is Joe?' Edith asked briskly and Kate blinked the tears away.

'He's gone for a walk with Adam. I hope it will do him good - Adam seems to be the only person who can draw Joe out of himself at the moment. I've not been able to offer him any comfort.'

'You knew it would hit Joe hard,' Edith reminded her. 'But he'll need you after today, when life has to get back to normal - whatever that might be.'

'We thought it would hit you worst of all,' said Kate frankly. 'You didn't even seem to believe that Matty was dying.' She looked more closely at her sister and made a discovery. 'But it wasn't like that at all - was it?'

Edith's shoulders jerked upwards in a defensive gesture but she made no denial and Kate felt a great admiration for her sister. Knowing and accepting the truth about Matthew, Edith had still struggled fiercely for him until the last possible moment.

Outside, the cat leapt onto the scullery window sill and stared at them curiously through the glass. Edith searched round for dirty crockery, found none and so emptied the washing-up bowl.

'I wish I hadn't had to lie to him though, Kate. Matthew wanted a child and I let him believe it was possible, even when I knew it wasn't.'

'Not possible?'

'I went to see a doctor in Brighton - a specialist. There's something wrong with me. I can never have children.' Her mouth twisted in a mocking grimace. 'All those years of being so careful - quite unnecessary!'

'Oh, Edie - you could have told him, surely? Matty would have understood.'

'I know he wouldn't have reproached me! But I thought that the hope of having a child would keep him alive.' Edith began to tremble. 'And perhaps I had to lie to myself too. I thought I'd only wanted a baby for Matty's sake, but that wasn't true.'

The sobs began, wild and fierce, and Kate put her arms around her sister, whispering helplessly, knowing the soothing words would have no effect. After a while she felt Edith stiffen and wondered if she was about to faint. But the sounds her sister was making had altered and Kate realised that

327

she was laughing. She wondered, fearfully, if Edith was having hysterics.

But Edith was leaning away from her, looking out of the scullery window and Kate turned her head just in time to see a strange conveyance rattle past. William was pushing Ben's old pram - he had obviously taken it from the shed - which had a wooden plank placed across it. Grace sat on one end of the plank and Ben the other. William turned the pram sharply, ready to take a run down the garden path and the plank wobbled precariously. Grace and Ben clung on, squealing, but with delight rather than fear and William gave a great cheer. Kate's heart lurched.

'Oh, those children!' She sprang to the door. 'When did they get into the garden?'

'They followed Mother and Clara out.' Edith, spluttering with laughter, leaned against the kitchen door jamb while Kate sprinted out after the children. She stopped the pram just at the point where the path began to slope downwards.

'William, what are you doing!' she cried. 'Hold Ben while I get Grace down and don't let him fall when the plank tips.'

'It's an aeroplane, Mother,' Grace explained. 'William said girls can't - '

'That's enough! You could have hurt yourselves!'

Polly and Clara came toiling up the garden path, the feathers on Clara's hat waving in agitation. They had seen the aeroplane and thought themselves too far away to prevent disaster. Kate, calming the two horrified women and countering William's furious protests, felt like screaming. She cast a helpless glance at Edith but her sister was still leaning in the doorway, laughing aloud. Kate thrust Ben at her mother.

'They're to go up to the living room and play quietly.' And her tone forbade all argument. Polly and Clara took the children away and Edith wiped her eyes and gave Kate a mischievous look. 'Are you going to send me to my room for being naughty?'

Kate gave a reluctant laugh. 'Aeroplane indeed! Oh, come on, Edie - let's go and sit in the parlour for a while and have another sherry.'

They sipped their drinks and Edith eased off her shoes. 'I want to go back to the cottage, this evening,' she said. 'There's a lot to be sorted through.'

'Leave it a day or two,' Kate advised. 'It's bound to be upsetting for you.'

'Then I'd better get it out of the way as soon as possible. Besides, I want to go up to London before Christmas. I need to get Matty's book published - among other things.'

Kate swallowed the contents of her glass quickly and poured herself another. It had come to her that Edith was free now to do as she wished and, although she would obviously mourn for Matthew for a long time, she was entitled to begin making a new life for herself. She watched, uneasily, as her sister lit a cigarette.

'Do you think you'll go to join Bram?' she asked softly.

'I don't know - not yet anyway. It would be too easy, Kate.' Edith looked at her through the cigarette smoke. 'I need to be on my own for a while.'

She paused for a moment, then went on firmly. 'I've always had someone - a man - to be responsible for me. First there was Father, fussing over me, wanting me to be his little princess for ever and ever. When I went against his wishes I turned to Matty and we got engaged. Then there was Bram and when he left it was Matty once more. Now Matty has left me, but lo and behold thanks to Bram's forethought I can turn back to him and let him take control of my life.'

'It sounds strange put like that,' said Kate, slowly.

'That's because I've missed out words like love and caring. I don't reject the love they've all given me; I know I've been lucky to have that. But at the same time I've never been completely in control of my own life. I have to find out if I can do that.'

She was very calm and Kate realised how much Edith had changed over the past year. Whatever her plans might be they would be carefully considered. The old, abandoned enthusiasm had gone, leaving in its place a thoughtful maturity.

Polly came in, looking harassed and Edith greeted her with a smile. 'Have the children flown away, Mother?'

'I wish Clara would. She's behaving so childishly herself that it's just making them more excited. I've left her to it.'

Edith laughed. 'I hope she's taken her hat off. Ben will have those feathers out of it before she can blink.'

Kate put some more coal on the parlour fire and drew up an armchair for Polly.

'Edie's thinking over plans for the future,' she said and Polly frowned.

'You don't have to decide anything yet awhile, dear, surely?'

'Well I need to earn a living, Mother.' Edith put out her cigarette and added hastily, 'You and Adam have been wonderful - helping us while Matty was alive. But now I must fend for myself.'

Polly lowered her head and a sigh escaped her. 'I suppose you'll go to Russia.'

Edith gasped then gave a wry smile. 'I'm not ready yet. When I last saw Bram he said I was too busy dreaming to see the real New Jerusalem but

329

I didn't know what he meant at the time. Now I do. I've been involved with ideals and not reality. I've had a vision of Socialism that has never taken real people into account. I'm a political innocent and I want to change that, to learn. Partly for Matty, because he was always so patient with me, and partly for Bram because if I go to him it must be as his equal in understanding. But mostly for myself.'

'How will you learn whatever it is you need to know?' asked her mother, anxiously.

'Well, you remember the MP whose son was killed - Matty brought his body home? He kept in touch with us and said he'd like to help get Matty's book published. And when he wrote to me with condolences he mentioned that he's retiring very soon. We need women in Parliament.'

Kate was thrilled. 'You'll stand yourself?'

'Perhaps. But if I can be more helpful campaigning for a woman candidate then I'll do that. I just want to be involved. Two women have already won seats, so it can be done!'

Polly gave a snort of amusement. 'Now, Edie, do you really think there will be room for you and Lady Astor in the House?'

She rose and went to the sideboard. Kate thought her mother was going to pour herself a sherry but saw Polly take the back off a framed photograph of the children.

'I put this here a long time ago for safe keeping,' she murmured, drawing out a piece of paper. 'It's time you had it, Edie.'

Edith found herself staring at the sketch of her Bram had made during the week they lived together: a younger version of herself, softer featured, smiling, tender.

'I thought it was lost,' she faltered. 'Why are you giving it to me now?'

'It's a good likeness - you should have it by you,' said Polly. Then her face changed, lit by sudden warmth. 'Edie, I'm proud of what you're planning to do. All the same, I want you to - well, to remember that you deserve some happiness. I know from my own experience that it can come late in life and be all the more joyful for that and I don't want you to leave it too late before finding yours.'

Edith flushed and she gave her mother a grateful look. 'Thank you. I won't forget that.'

The door swung open and Grace slipped into the room. 'They're being very silly upstairs, Mother,' she said. 'Ben pulled some feathers out of Aunty's hat and William stuck them in his hair and started doing a war dance round the living room.'

'Is Aunty Clara cross?' Kate asked, anxiously, getting ready to go to the rescue.

'No - she's laughing a lot.'

Polly placed a stool so that the girl could sit by the fire. 'You'd better stay here with us,' she said. 'We're being sensible.'

Edith smiled wryly and put the sketch on the table beside her. Thoughtfully she lit another cigarette.

Grace was watching the flames flickering in the grate. 'Mother,' she murmured, 'William said girls can't fly aeroplanes. Is that true?'

'Well, there's no reason why a girl shouldn't fly,' said Kate firmly, 'so you can tell him he's wrong.'

Edith puffed out some smoke and touched her niece's shoulder. 'Should you like to fly an aeroplane one day, Grace?'

The girl rested her chin on the side of Polly's chair, giving the matter full consideration. Then she yawned.

'I don't know; but I'm glad I can if I want to.'

END

Printed in Great Britain
by Amazon

63781509R00190